The Healer

The Healer
Copyright © 2020 by John Thomas Tuft.

All rights reserved. No part of this book may be reproduced in any form or by any electronic or mechanical means, including information storage and retrieval systems, without permission in writing from the publisher and author, except by reviewers, who may quote brief passages in a review.

This publication contains the opinions and ideas of its author. It is intended to provide helpful and informative material on the subjects addressed in the publication. The author and publisher specifically disclaim all responsibility for any liability, loss, or risk, personal or otherwise, which is incurred as a consequence, directly or indirectly, of the use and application of any of the contents of this book.

978-1-952405-48-8   [Paperback Edition]
978-1-952405-47-1   [eBook Edition]

Printed and bound in The United States of America.

Published by
The Mulberry Books, LLC.
8330 E Quincy Avenue,
Denver CO 80237
themulberrybooks.com

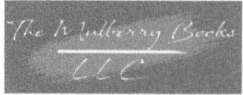

The Healer

JOHN THOMAS TUFT

Chapter 1

"Dr. Redstone. Dr. Redstone. Code zero. Repeat, code zero!"

Gideon Waters paused halfway through the doorway to the room of his next duty station to listen. A *Dr. Redstone* page alerted all assigned personnel to multiple severe traumas coming into the emergency room soon. Code zero meant it was not a drill but the real thing, so they should drop everything and come *now*.

Gideon stepped back into the hallway, catching himself holding his breath as he waited to see if the page would be repeated. Jarring static momentarily filled the corridor as the hospital operator keyed open the channel but didn't speak right away.

"On-call patient aide, ER. On-call patient aide, answer Dr. Redstone. Code zero." Her voice sounded slightly incredulous, as though she too wondered why a PA, a glorified orderly, was being summoned on the call.

Gideon looked up at the speaker in surprise. The urgent page was meant for him. In his first six months on the job at the Riverside County Medical Center of Western Pennsylvania, he had never been paged on a code zero Redstone alert. He dreaded what he would find in the ER. They were desperate if they wanted him there.

He hurried through the labyrinth of hallways. The three-story hospital, perched on the top of Round Knob above the city of Bridetown, spread its sterile hallways in three long wings over acres of old cornfields. Gideon was working full-time and saving his money to pursue a degree in physical therapy. That is, he had been saving money until one night eight months ago when his wife, Christine, announced that she was pregnant. Dreams of college and being part of a profession would have to wait. He sighed. *One thing at a time,* he reminded himself. *JP would tell me that one thing at a time is all a sane man can handle.*

At thirty-three, he sometimes worried that it was getting too late to start a real career. But it couldn't be helped. He had been excited about the opportunity when Christine got the job at the Riverside County school. They bought their first house in the older section of the county seat. They'd laughed at the quaint name—Bridetown. It seemed that 123 years ago when the town was incorporated, the local sign painter imbibed a little too heavily one night, and while coping with a ferocious hangover the next morning, he'd left out the *g* for what was to be the town of Bridgetown. Not wanting to pay for a new sign, the name was adopted.

The *swoosh* of the pneumatic doors into the ER summoned him from his daydreaming. The controlled chaos of the trauma teams quickly drove away all remnants of homey sentiment.

"PA! Get started! Move it!"

A nurse with close-cropped silver hair, the weathered face of a lifelong smoker, and a voice to match motioned impatiently for Gideon to hurry it up.

Then he smelled it. Blood. The green scrubs of the doctors, nurses, and techs hurrying in and out of the rooms were brown with it. He knew its odor would stick to the inside of his nostrils for the next couple of days.

"In here," the charge nurse commanded. "They're slipping and sliding in all the blood."

"What happened?" Gideon asked quietly as he stepped into the trauma room. He'd never seen so much blood before. It covered the floor, splattered the walls, and dripped continuously from the stretcher. The doctors' gloves were bright crimson.

"MVA." Her businesslike tone softened a touch. "Fog on the boulevard. They hit head-on. The police say it looks like neither one had time to react. Probably lost control on the wet road. This lady didn't have her seat belt on. Pretty far along too. On impact, she got thrown around and impaled on the stick shift. They're trying to keep her alive while they get the baby out."

"My God!" Gideon gasped.

"Clean it up without getting in the way." The nurse's tone was back to impersonal, professional sternness.

Gideon retrieved a damp mop from the closet and made quick swipes around the trail of blood leading into the room. The murmuring of the staff suddenly stopped.

"Damn! Lost them both." A doctor not much older than he was pronounced the time of death and walked past Gideon without seeing him.

Gideon stole a quick glance at the hideous violation of the woman's body. Tubes ran out of every opening of her naked, shattered form, a horrible gaping wound showing where her womb so recently cradled new life. A sterile drape covered her face. He couldn't stomach the sight and looked away. The nurses looked stunned as they undid the life-support apparatus and finished the job by rote.

Gideon hesitated. "How's the other victim?" he asked an EMT, whose young face showed fear.

She looked at him as if he were from another planet. "The doctors think he's going to make it. It's going to be tough when he learns what happened. You never forget something like this. Nobody does."

Gideon backed out of the room, intending to fill a bucket with disinfectant. He heard his shoes squeaking as he walked and looked down. They were stained red. Streaks of blood crept halfway up the pant legs of his white uniform.

A cry of shocked recognition came from the next trauma room. "It's Elijah Marks!"

Gideon spun around. A trauma nurse hurried by as he stepped to the opening in the cubicle.

"It's the hospital chaplain," she said. "He was on his way in to make some late presurgical rounds. Broken back, fractured legs, possible internal bleeding, and a concussion. Looks like he'll make it, thank God. Did you clean up that bloody mess?"

"I'm taking care of it, Nurse." Gideon glanced in the room. The man's face was gray and drawn, bearing witness to the terrible pain. He made no sound.

"Gideon."

The gruff voice of Chuck Baker, his supervisor, sounding gravelly and strained, called to him from the nearby nurse's station. The barrel-chested man looked down at the floor, shifting his weight from foot to foot.

Gideon frowned. "What's wrong, Chuck?"

The older man took a deep breath and met Gideon's gaze. "I'm real sorry, Gideon. Whenever you're ready, I'll drive you home."

"Home? Why would I go home, Chuck? I just started my shift! Christine's probably just getting settled in front of the television after dropping me …" His voice trailed off.

Chuck ran thick fingers through his thinning gray hair. "I'm real sorry, Gideon."

Gideon felt like his heart was going to explode and burst through his ribs. His voice rising, he cried, "What are you talking about? Chuck, tell me! What happened?"

By now he was shouting, cold panic flooding his senses. The lights in the room were too bright; the floor spun, and the noises of the emergency room blended into a dull roar.

Chagrin blanketed Chuck's features. "I'm sorry. I thought somebody had told you when I heard that page. When I saw that you were already here, I figured …" Chuck's head swiveled side to side, looking for a way to finish.

"Here? She's here?" Gideon felt like someone was strangling him. The baby was due in just over six weeks. A heavy weight pressed on his chest, making it difficult to breathe.

He pushed past the apologetic figure in front of him and ran to the adjacent room. He stopped at the side of the body, covered now with a clean sheet. His trembling fingers finally reached out to lift the corner. It was her hair, her lips, her beautiful cheeks.

With an anguished scream, his eyes wild with disbelief and shock, Gideon dashed to the room next door. Two doctors grabbed him, desperately trying to fight off the enraged man as he struggled with superhuman strength to get at the now unconscious figure.

"Murderer! I'll kill you!" He screamed and screamed until he ran out of voice. The doctors let go, and he collapsed into a corner, sobbing and alone.

Chapter 2

He hung by his fingertips, face pressed against the cliff, fighting the panic hammering at his chest. At first, he tried concentrating on the rock face, a miniature moonscape pitted and worn by centuries of wind and rain. He stared at it until his eyes crossed.

Then he screamed. Hanging one hundred feet above the waiting rocks, the sheer terror combined with the grating anger and aching loneliness that had gnawed at him relentlessly ever since Christine and the baby were killed a year ago coalesced into a childlike plea of desperation.

"Daddy! Daddy, come for me!" Gideon screamed over and over, his face contorted, sweat dripping from curly brown hair, stinging the corners of striking gray-blue eyes.

His voice trailed off, ending in a choked sob. The rock reflected his cry, and he thought he felt a faint vibration against his cheekbone where it pressed against the unyielding stone. He hadn't called out for his father since awaking as a little boy from a nightmare. But this was one nightmare he could not escape, and Daddy would not be answering.

Gideon tried gripping tighter. His fingers ached terribly, sharp pains shooting through his wrists, down both arms, and into his shoulders. He bent his head back, trying to see over the lip of the ledge, but it only served to further strain his already palsied arms. Looking down, he saw the toes of his boots swinging sickeningly in the empty space above the river valley below.

His breathing coming in gasps, he could only whimper once more, "Daddy."

His feet scrabbled frantically against the rock in a desperate search for a toehold. He had to get some weight off his arms and soon. The tips of his boots pawed relentlessly, loosing small pebbles that made clicking sounds as they careened off the wall on their dizzying plunge to the bottom.

Forcing his thoughts to slow down, he inhaled deeply, concentrating on the sound of his own breathing. Maybe he should simply let go. Maybe it was time.

He began to shake his head violently back and forth. No, that would be betrayal. Not on the same day that he'd buried JP. He'd driven back to the little western Virginia town to bury his grandfather in the small plot beside his grandmother and mother. JP left him the farm as well as their tradition of coming to the mountain for a slow, mind-clearing climb.

Except today he had hurried. After the funeral, he put on his jeans and his boots and headed to the mountain. He wanted to get to the top, get back down, and leave. In his haste, he'd been careless; he stumbled and slid over the edge. Only the tips of his fingers saved him. Now he clung precariously to the mountain.

His left leg started to cramp. Just when he thought his arms could not bear it any longer, thunder rumbled from the far side of the ridge. Within seconds, the first drops of rain struck his forehead. He realized that soon the rock would be too slippery for the bone-white grip of his fingers.

Lightning split the air so close he could instantly smell the ozone. He felt the rock tremble under the onslaught. His body began to shake with a violent chill. He was going to die.

Feeling the last ounces of strength slipping away, his feet resumed their frenzied search for a toehold. A brilliant flash lit the scene, followed by a tremendous blast.

Impossibly, miraculously, Gideon spotted a narrow ledge to the left some twenty feet below him. He didn't want to stop to think about it. There was no other way. He had to let go. He needed to persuade his clawed fingers to release and slide over wet rock at a death-defying angle. Once he released, there would be no control. Hopefully, the mountain would catch him.

At the next blinding strobe of lightning, he pushed off. Sharp outcroppings of rock tore the skin on his cheek as he fell. He hit the ledge with enough force to buckle his legs. Out of control, he toppled sideways. His head smacked a small boulder. For an instant, he felt as if he was floating serenely on a comforter of soft wind. For a split second, he heard his mother's voice calling to him through the tempest. How could that be? Then everything went black.

The darkness stretched into forever. Would he be allowed to stay there? he wondered from some primal corner of his mind. Away from the pain and sadness, the frustration, the loneliness.

The thoughts were interrupted by a painful jolt. Something was tightening around his waist, then around his chest and under his arms. He was being dragged unceremoniously across the rocks. He tried to shout, to tell whoever it was to let him be, but no words came.

A roaring sound started close by, hurting his ears, like the fierce howl of a chain saw. He laughed at the absurdity of someone cutting timber in this awful storm. The roar died abruptly.

"He's coming around," a woman's voice said.

"What kind of idiot goes rock climbing alone in the middle of a downpour?" It was a man's distant voice.

He felt a cold flask on his lips. Hot brandy burned his throat, making him gag and sputter. He tried to sit up before whoever it was drowned him.

"Whoa, easy," said the woman. "Jonathan, he's bleeding pretty bad. We need to get him to the hospital."

A strange click-clank sound grew nearer and then stopped. "Can you walk?" asked the man.

He opened his eyes. The world spun dizzily. He closed them tight and nodded his head. The motion sent waves of pain and nausea through him.

"Who are you?" asked the girl.

"Gideon," he managed to gasp. "Gideon Waters." He tried opening his eyes again.

A young woman in her early twenties, thick blonde hair streaming out from under a Pittsburgh Steelers cap, leaned over him, her startling green eyes filled with concern. He couldn't help noticing the soft, tanned skin underneath the rain trickling down her cheeks.

"I'm Laurel. Laurel Rayn. No puns please." Her laughter melted into the sound of water running across rock. "And this is Jonathan."

Gideon followed her gaze to a man with dark skin, an untrimmed beard, wire-rimmed glasses that fogged in the humidity, and black hair pulled back into an unruly ponytail held together by a rubber band. The man nodded solemnly.

"What the hell are you doing out on the mountain in this weather? Lucky for you, Laurel and I were out on the ATV and spotted you trying to pull that flying Wallendas act."

Gideon waved one hand feebly. "It's a long story. Thanks for getting me," he said to Jonathan.

"Don't thank me," the man said with a knowing smile. "She did all the work."

Gideon looked at Laurel with surprise. "You pulled me off that ledge?"

"Sure, no problem." Her eyes showed pleasant satisfaction at the surprise in his eyes.

"How?" Gideon pressed.

"We can talk about that later," she replied. "Right now we need to get that nasty cut sewn up. Come on, try and get up nice and easy. I checked your arms and legs but didn't feel any obvious fractures."

Gideon wiggled his arms and hands, legs and toes. Everything appeared intact. When he sat up, a sharp pain stabbed near his breastbone, making him cringe.

"You might have a broken rib," Jonathan casually observed.

Gideon extended a hand toward him for help. Jonathan only laughed. "Sorry, that's between you and Laurel."

Only then did Gideon see the metal crutches with the arm guides supporting Jonathan. Below the khaki shorts, metal braces encased Jonathan's legs. Gideon didn't know what to say and tried to get up on his own to cover his embarrassment. Before he got to one knee, the dizziness struck with a vengeance, and he wobbled drunkenly.

"Hold on, cowboy," Laurel said firmly. "Lean on me."

Gideon relented and flung one arm over her shoulders, allowing her to pull him upright, where he rocked unsteadily.

"Stubborn, isn't he!" Jonathan teased.

"Well, I just fell …" Gideon started to protest indignantly, but Jonathan waved him off.

"Defend your honor later. This downpour is going to flood the crossing if we don't get out of here now." He shook his head, looking for all the world like a St. Bernard as the water flew from his shaggy beard and ponytail.

They struggled along the path, Gideon leaning heavily on Laurel for support. Jonathan brought up the rear, his crutches and braces making the slap-squeak Gideon recognized from his delirium.

"Are you two married?" he asked Laurel stupidly, trying to take his mind off the sword thrusts of searing pain every time he dared to breathe.

She chuckled. "No, we're good friends." She dug a handkerchief from the pocket of her jeans, then dabbed at the blood flowing from Gideon's cheek as they walked.

They soon reached a clearing where a large, three-wheeled Suzuki all-terrain vehicle with monster tires waited. Jonathan climbed on first. Then Laurel helped Gideon get situated behind him.

"You're going to have to hang on tight. Jonathan's a terrible driver."

Jonathan grinned wickedly. "You're all heart, Lars."

"What about you?" Gideon asked her.

"I'll start down on foot. Jonathan will come back for me."

She stopped his protestations with a firm "Get going!"

With a lurch that almost threw him from his perch, Jonathan gunned the motor and headed down the steep mountain road.

The driving rain made visibility near zero. Jonathan hunched over the steering bar, straining to stay on the road. His crutches were tied on behind Gideon and clanged noisily at every bump. Suddenly the ATV went into a violent skid as Jonathan jerked to one side to avoid a tree that had come crashing down, smoldering from a lightning strike. Then it was a quick jerk in the other direction as he fought to maintain control. Gideon hung on for dear life, too frightened to ask any more questions.

They bounced over the log bridge. Rusty Creek, swollen by the downpour, lapped at the roadway in small, angry waves. Finally they hit pavement and made good time into town.

"Can you make it in?" Jonathan asked as they pulled into the driveway outside the emergency room of Coalwater County Medical Center.

"Yeah, I think I can make it. Go back for Laurel." Gideon shakily dismounted and patted Jonathan on the shoulder. "Thank you." He wanted to say more, but Jonathan was already roaring back toward the mountain.

In the emergency room, Gideon gave his name to the triage nurse and took a seat. He dabbed at his cheek with the gauze she had given him while the events of the last—how long? Hours? Minutes? He couldn't remember. He didn't know how long he'd been out. His head throbbed where it had struck the rock. Standing on stiffening limbs, he began to pace awkwardly around the waiting room, wondering about the odd Good Samaritans responsible for his rescue.

He watched as ambulances pulled up with victims of the storm. The trauma rooms filled, and an elderly man was wheeled to one side to make room for those in more serious condition.

"Sonny. Come here."

Gideon turned around. From the hallway, the old man beckoned with liver-spotted hands. Gideon hesitated, not wanting to get sidetracked.

"I said, come here!" The intensity of the old man's voice surprised him. What was the urgency?

Reluctantly, Gideon stepped over to the gurney. "Do you need something?" he asked solicitously.

"You're the one. I know!" The man's voice was filled with conviction, and a fierce fire burned in his eyes.

"Excuse me? Sir, what do you want?" Gideon asked, a bit annoyed.

The man grabbed Gideon's hand and held on tightly. Gideon tried to pull away but could not. "I know who you are," the man insisted. "We've been waiting for you."

Bewildered, Gideon shook his head and looked around for a nurse to help.

"It's in the blood!"

Irritated, Gideon backed away from the abandoned stretcher.

"Hey, you can't wander around all over the place!" a voice shouted. "Sir, you're bleeding."

A nurse with copper-colored hair and a no-nonsense look yelled at him from across the trauma area. "You'll have to find someplace else to wait. You're not supposed to be back here."

Gideon looked around. Spying an unmarked door, he stepped through, gasping at the hot pain stabbing his ribs. The blood flowed from his cut, dripping continuously off his chin. He took in his surroundings with dismay.

In the center of the dimly lit room lay a small girl in a jungle of tubes and wires. Gideon tried not to react to her grotesquely swollen face and the smell of decay in the air when she opened her eyes at the sound of his footsteps.

"Are you going to help me?" she asked in a plaintive voice.

"I—I, well, I came into the, uh, wrong room," Gideon stammered.

He started for the door on the far side of the room, but as he passed her bed, the little girl said, "I'm scared."

Gideon stopped. What should he do?

"It will be okay. Are your parents here?"

"My mom's on her way, I think." Tears spilled across her cheeks. "Mister, you're bleeding." She held out a hand with an IV needle inserted in it to reach his cheek. Her touch was so soft Gideon barely felt it. When she let it drop, Gideon noticed that her fingers were coated with his blood. It ran across the tape holding the needle in place.

"I'm sorry. Let me clean your hand," he said gently, sensing the hopelessness of the little girl's condition.

She shook her head. "Thanks for coming to visit me." She closed her eyes again, and Gideon started to tiptoe out.

As he opened the door, she whispered, "Here, this is for you."

Gideon looked back. She held out a small necklace with some sort of trinket on it.

"I can't take that, honey," he said. "You need to rest now."

"No, you're supposed to have it," she insisted. "You need it."

Reluctantly, Gideon took the proffered gift. A lump rose in his throat at the sight of the small, ragged edge of the half of a heart friendship charm dangling from a tiny chain.

"Thank you," he said in a choked voice.

The girl smiled and closed her eyes again.

Back in the waiting room, a great weariness settled over him. Finally his name was called. The doctor sent him for x-rays, then sewed up the gash in his cheek. As he clipped the last stitch, the nurse with the copper hair burst into the cubicle with an odd look on her face.

"Doctor, come quickly," she said in a bewildered voice.

"What is it, Nurse?" he asked.

"The Thompson girl …" She hesitated.

"Well, what about her? I'm almost finished here, and there's not much more I can do for her," he said with some resignation.

"You have to come see." The nurse was insistent.

"See what?" The doctor pulled off his gloves and crossed his arms over his chest.

The nurse glanced at Gideon and back to the doctor. "It's … well, Doctor, we really don't know … but it's just …"

The doctor glared.

The explanation came in a rush. "Doctor, she's sitting up and asking for pizza!" The nurse's voice filled with wonder. "She was in end-stage renal failure. Her liver was hopeless. But now she's pink, and"—her surprise could not be restrained—"she's wanting pizza. I've never seen anything like it!"

The doctor sighed. "I think we've both been on too long today, Sandy. That girl will not last the night."

"I know, I know," said the nurse. Another nurse burst in, followed by a resident, both looking extremely confused.

"Fred, you're the attending. Come see this!" exclaimed the other doctor. "You won't believe it. I mean, I wouldn't if I hadn't seen it with my own eyes."

"Is there a full moon tonight?" asked the doctor as he snipped the last stitch in Gideon's cheek.

"Come and see," said the nurse. She fairly danced out of the cubicle. The others followed, leaving Gideon alone.

Curiosity got the better of him as he pulled his shirt over his tightly bandaged chest. Easing off the exam table, he peeked around the curtain. People in hospital scrubs scurried like ants to the little room where he'd met the girl.

Halfway down the hall, the door opened, and the little girl's gurney appeared, followed by doctors yelling orders for new labs and every scan known to medicine. Some in the noisy knot of people smiled broadly, while others frowned skeptically.

"There he is!" the girl called out when she spied Gideon. "That's the man who made me better."

Everyone stopped talking to stare at Gideon. He backed away, an eerie tingling creeping up his arms.

"I don't know what she means," he protested. "I only went in there by mistake."

The child continued to fix her eyes on him as they wheeled her away.

"It's him!" he heard the girl insist one last time as he stepped into the evening. The rain had stopped, and the air was cooler.

"Not the way I planned on spending my day," Gideon muttered to himself as he considered what to do next.

He heard soft footsteps behind him. At first he didn't want to turn around. The footsteps receded as Gideon walked faster. *Just get me out of here*, he thought. Then he remembered that his car was back at the mountain, ten miles distant. But JP's farm was only three. Might as well head there for the night and worry about the car in the morning, he figured.

"Wait!" a faint voice called. "I know who you are."

Hesitating, Jonathan turned around. The elderly man from the emergency room hobbled toward him as fast as his creaky legs would allow. Gideon hesitated beside some overgrown spirea bushes lining the street. A chill ran up and down his spine. His eyes darted from side to side. The old man kept coming, calling to him across the vast parking lot.

Out of the night shadows, a car suddenly careered around the far side of the building. Tires squealed as it accelerated around the rows of parked cars. The old man heard it, although, without its lights on, Gideon wasn't sure if the man could see it. Without breaking stride, he suddenly turned away from where Gideon watched, half-hidden by the bushes.

"What's he doing, crazy fool?" Gideon said aloud. "He's headed right into the path of that idiot."

Gideon started back along the line of shrubbery, his eyes still trained on the old man. He watched unbelieving as the bent figure walked into the middle of the aisle and stopped, never moving.

Gideon thought he heard a shout right before the awful impact. The frail body flew over the hood, bounced off the windshield, and landed with a sickening slap of flesh on pavement. The car did a spin turn and headed back toward the body.

"No!" screamed Gideon as he started running. Pain shot through his chest where the cracked ribs violently protested this excess. Gideon stopped and bent double between two parked cars, retching in pain. The screech of stressed tires echoed off the walls. Before he could react, the car roared past Gideon huddled in agony, disappearing into the night. An eerie silence descended.

Groaning against the white-hot poker in his side, Gideon stumbled over to the crumpled form. Blood ran from his ears and nose. His eyes flitted open at Gideon's approach.

Gideon gingerly knelt beside him. "Don't try and talk. You'll be okay."

The old man coughed up a stream of pink bubbles. "I knew … get away … I yelled …" His breathing grew more and more labored. Gideon saw the sallow cast to his skin as the man fought against horrible pain.

"I'll get help," he told the battered form. "Don't worry. I'll go get someone."

The man rolled his head feebly from side to side. "Go," he gasped. "It's you … you're the Healer."

Gideon's voice trembled. "You're hurt. Don't try and talk now."

From somewhere, the man summoned one last bit of fire. "Get away!" His eyes flashed with fierce intensity. "You have the broken heart, don't you?"

Before Gideon could reply, an unearthly rattle came from the man's throat. Blood spurted from his mouth, running onto the pavement around Gideon's boots. The eyes lost their fire, their spark of life, staring without seeing the bright stars of the new evening.

Gideon whispered, "Go in peace," and gently closed the old man's eyes. His brain screamed at him to heed the dead man's warning.

"What am I running from?" he asked the night sky as he reluctantly set off along the empty road, leaving the slain prophet alone.

Chapter 3

The mock Victorian streetlamps cast pools of light that glistened on the wet streets of Frenchville. The town appeared deserted as Gideon hastened away from the center of the county seat, heading for the farm. It didn't seem possible that ten hours ago he had stood over the slash in the earth of an open grave, watching with empty dread as JP's body was lowered into it. How could he be gone?

The hike up the mountain had nearly cost him his life. Then the strange events in the hospital and the savage hit-and-run murder of the old man. He fingered the small necklace that the young girl insisted he take, wondering what to make of it. He should call the police, he told himself. But what if he'd just witnessed some sort of hit? Getting away, fast and clean, seemed perfectly reasonable. Don't get involved in other people's messes—that was his motto. After all, no one had helped him out with his own, had they?

Gideon sighed. Years ago, he would be hurrying home to the safety of JP's warm home, anticipating the savory smell of the ever-present wood shavings nesting around the wizened leather boots of the man who'd been a father for Gideon. The breeze teasing the leaves overhead reminded him of the soft whisper of the whittling knife following the natural curves and blemishes as JP shaped the branch into a graceful bird or scampering grinny.

These sensate memories brought tears to Gideon's eyes, and for a time, the ache of grief vanquished the nettles of his physical pain.

At the age of thirteen, after the death of his mother, Gideon decided that he didn't want to love anyone anymore. It was JP who waited him out, letting the boy hate him all he needed to since he was the only one around to hate. He seemed to understand how much hurt a thirteen-year-old could feel without getting too anxious himself.

The steady drip of the last of the rain accompanied the steady beat of his boots on the berm of old State Route 8 as he approached the intersection with Ridge Road on the town's outskirts. If he stayed on the state road, he would walk through the heart of the small valley to reach the farm. He hesitated, remembering something he hadn't thought about in a long time. Mind made up, he chose Ridge Road instead.

Clouds scuttled across the moon, but he didn't need extra light. Gideon knew the way by heart. After a mile, when the road began to ascend the ridge line, he turned off onto a small dirt track that followed the contour of the foothills, the woods he'd explored as a boy off to this right. The pain in his ribs kept up a dull throb, but it didn't deter him from his search.

Finally, he recognized the spot. Slipping and sliding on the wet grass, he skidded down to Waters Creek. It took gritted teeth and one hand hugging his ribs, but he managed to jump the small, gurgling stream. A quarter of a mile away, at the edge of the far pasture of JP's land stood the old weeping willow.

Gideon approached it with a mixture of nostalgia and grief. And, always, the awe welling up from the heart of a boy, out for an evening's walk with his mother all those many years before. Whatever the season, at every opportunity, Gideon begged his mother for one of their walks. She always answered with a smile. But this one particular evening, it had been a sad, weary smile …

They kept to the routine of circling the barn and meandering through the apple orchard, before making their way across the green expanse to their tree.

"Why does my dad hate me?" Gideon invariably asked. He needed an answer, and it was always the same. It didn't satisfy his hurt, but it did let her know as he grew older that he still harbored hatred for the man who left them both with a gaping hole in their lives.

"Your father doesn't hate you." His mother sounded like she was choosing the words carefully, as though answering him for the first time instead of the hundredth. "As a matter of fact, he loved you so much that it broke his heart to leave." Then, quietly, that long-ago summer's eve, she added, "And mine."

"Then why did he go?" Gideon demanded, noticing her sadness but more caught up in his own desperate craving for an explanation for the empty place at the table, the birthdays with no cards, no calls, the serpent that crawled around inside of him, trapped and seething.

She bent low to enter the quiet sanctuary under the umbrellalike branches. "He had to go. He didn't want us to be hurt. It was something he couldn't help, but he knew what was best and stood by his conviction."

"I don't understand," Gideon insisted grimly. "If he loved us, he would have stayed. I hope he never comes back."

She stared at him for a moment, and he saw in her eyes the deep loneliness. "He won't."

The words struck at the very soul of his world. She sounded like she knew—knew for sure to let go of all hope. Had she talked to him?

"He won't?" It was not a wish he had believed would really come true. No, this was all wrong.

"The day he left, I knew it might be the last time I saw him." Her voice sounded strange, scaring Gideon.

"But why?"

"I hope you get to learn the reason for that, Gideon. I hope with all my heart." With that, she stopped talking for the longest time.

They sat under the tree, hearing the low murmur of the brook in the distance, lost in its endless song. After the night had deepened so that he could barely make out her face, she said, "Did I ever tell you about the tap root?"

"Sure," he answered. "A million times. It's the root that goes from here, underground, all the way to Waters Creek out there."

"That's right. It finds a way through all the obstacles, everything that stands in its way, to get to what it needs in order to survive, to live." His mother touched his face with work-worn hands. "Did I ever tell you the old Indian legend about why the willow weeps?"

He shook his head, hoping that she would forget and tell him again. She smiled and continued: "Once there was a young brave who was in love with the prettiest of all the maidens in the tribe, who also happened to be the daughter of the chief. One day, the young brave came to his maiden to tell her that her father, the chief, was sending him on a daring and dangerous mission.

"Their enemies had stolen the prize horses, the ones they depended on in battle, for hunting, and for helping the tribe when they moved to the mountains for the summers. They embodied the spirit of the tribe. The maiden begged the warrior not to go, to let her intervene with her father.

"'No,' insisted the brave. 'I must do my duty. It is a great honor to defend the tribe and to avenge the insult to the spirits of our ancestors. My blood is a gift to my people. It would be as terrible as not speaking the truth or deceiving you, my love, for me not to go.'"

Gideon was spellbound by his mother's words under the cool umbrella of the tree.

"'Then I will wait for you in this spot where I can see both the mountains and the stream, until you return,' promised the girl.

"The brave put on his war paint and crossed the stream, heading for the enemy lands. Every day, the girl went to this spot and waited. A week passed, and still her love did not return. She began to spend the nights here as well, singing beautifully of her lover's strength and his skill. And that is the song of the water.

"The summer passed, and the chill winds of fall began to blow. The young warrior never returned, and his maiden died tragically of a broken heart. Her father, the chief, buried her at the same place where she had kept her faithful watch. Overnight, a willow tree grew on the very spot. To this day, if you stand underneath the branches, you can feel her tears at the loss of her one true love."

Gideon stood there in the silence, feeling anew the sense of wonder he'd experienced that long-ago night, as again he felt the gentle drops of moisture caressing his face and arms. His tears mingled with those of the tree as he thought about his mother, wondering what she would think of him now.

"I have my father's blood, but JP gave me back my life," he said aloud, letting the tears flow unimpeded. He thought of the man with the hand-carved walking stick, cussing out the birds in his strawberry patch beside the old barn. Or sitting on the porch in the evenings, adding his benediction to the majesty of the sunset with two fingers of scotch, lustily booming out some old song over the gently rolling fields. On the occasion of each equinox, it was three fingers of scotch. As well as on birthdays, holidays, weddings, funerals, his anniversary. On the anniversary of his beloved Lydia's death each year, however, he didn't touch a drop.

"I miss him. I miss my mother. And, God, I miss Christine. She was my light. And my child, I miss my child who never had a chance to see these mountains. It wasn't right." He was alone now. No more family. He settled back against the trunk of the tree, catching an occasional glimpse of the stars through the leaves overhead.

"Be honest with yourself, even if it breaks your own heart," JP always preached to him. "Fight for what's right. Don't count on winning, but don't quit either." Words, Gideon knew, he'd abandoned after the accident.

He closed his eyes, and, as always, an image of Christine awaited him. The faux rabbit fur of her jacket collar brushed against her cheeks, red from the cold of a winter day. Her jet-black hair hung to her waist, the way he liked it best. Her eyes teared in the frigid wind shrieking through the rusting girders of the bridge in Bridetown.

"Love a woman in small, confident steps," JP passed on to him. "Let her know where your love begins—with her. But confide to her the awe of knowing you will search for a lifetime and still not find its end."

In his dream, Gideon took her in his arms, whispering in her ear so the wind would not snatch away the words. He drank in her smell as his fingers crept beneath her jacket and under her sweater, making small circles on her back.

"The sweet spot" JP called it. "That little hollow of pleasure where the curve of her spine meets the swell of her promise. Touch a woman there. Touch her so softly that only one bit of the tip of one finger caresses her skin. When you can do that, she will teach you to be her lover."

Christine sighed contentedly, snuggling into him. Gideon's thoughts were finally stilled, and he slept.

The pain in his ribs nudged him to consciousness. The effort was like swimming in sludge, the wearying ache cloying to the frayed edges of his awareness. He groaned as he pulled himself to his feet. His damp jeans and the sour smell of his fear combined with the stench of dried blood urged him toward the tonic of a long, hot shower at the farmhouse.

Stepping out from under the weeping willow, he basked in the first warm rays of sunrise and rain-cleansed air. Limping slightly from his bruises, Gideon headed for the house a half mile distant.

The apple orchard needed some attention, he idly observed. Good trees came from good pruning, and the neglect showed. *It must have torn JP's heart out to see it like this*, Gideon realized. "I wasn't here. And for what?" He picked one of the puny green apples and flung it back along the path his footprints had left in the dew-laden grass.

In the yard behind the white clapboard farmhouse, the clothespoles stood as lonely sentinels. How often he had felt reassured at the sight of his mother hanging sheets across the taut lines, now rotted away. The flowers she'd planted around the old pump were long ago choked out by weeds.

"JP, I let you down." His words echoed as one more forlorn signpost of the past.

He tried the screen door, but the latch held it tight. Trudging around to the front, Gideon noticed that the twin pines on either side of the steps had grown taller than the old house and so wide that they nearly hid the entire first floor. He started across the porch, then stopped. Something was odd. The front door stood partly ajar. Why would the rest of the house be locked up tight but not the front door? he wondered.

He slowly approached and gingerly pushed on it. The familiar creak of the hinges echoed eerily. A soft humming came from the living room, off the foyer to the right. He glanced up the stairs, foolishly wondering if his room still looked the same.

"JP wasn't one for shrines," he reminded himself.

When he stepped through to the living room, the humming suddenly grew louder. With the shades drawn, he couldn't see in the dim light. The house faced west, so the sun rose at the back. He automatically leaned over to flick on a lamp.

The wild thought flitted through his mind that he had entered the wrong house. There were people sleeping on the floor. No one stirred at the sudden light. Looking closer, Gideon abruptly leaned against the door post, gasping for breath, choking on the bile filling his throat.

This was impossible, insane! The humming rose from the hundreds of flies flitting around dark puddles of blood covering the floor.

"Oh, God! No! No!"

Gideon forced himself to step closer and roll over the closest form, disturbing a swarm of insects in the process. The eyes of the doctor who stitched up his cheek the night before stared back at him, frozen in terror. Flies instantly found the new feast of caked blood on his chest.

Gideon cautiously checked the others. The nurse with the copper hair and the one who excitedly announced the healing of the small girl lay together, their fingers tightly intertwined in death.

He recognized the other doctor, his body awkwardly huddled over a small form.

"No!" Gideon's agonized cry filled the old house. He tugged at the stiff corpse, panting with the frantic exertion. The body finally flopped over.

The little girl. Her face was peacefully composed, her eyes closed, the long lashes resting against the chalk-white curve of her cheeks. She could have been praying. Except, like the others, for the slashing wound that gaped darkly from ear to ear.

Chapter 4

Two days earlier and nearly one hundred and fifty miles away from that grisly scene of carnage, Elijah Marks and his wife, Jennifer, descended through the canopy of leaves above the banks of Slippery Rock Creek, enjoying their annual pilgrimage to McConnell's Mill State Park. The fair-sized creek wound through a gorge with steep, tree-covered slopes on either side. A narrow road led down the opposite side past huge rocks and ancient trees, crossed the water over a covered bridge, then followed the creek upstream, where it passed a rustic grain mill.

After parking their car at the top of the gorge, they descended the zigzag path to the bottom. The couple giggled like two teens, letting gravity pull them faster and faster down the slippery path, carefully skidding to a stop at each sharp turn, holding hands to keep each other from plunging headlong into the scattered boulders near the trail.

"Is your back all right, Eli? Are your legs okay, honey?" Jenn asked in a discreet whisper.

Eli scowled. He didn't like the fact that she could read his face so well. After the accident a year ago, doctors had implanted a morphine pump in his abdomen with a catheter that ran to his spinal cord.

His back and legs ached terribly. They always ached terribly, but he brushed her question aside. "I'm okay."

They heard it, the thunder of water crashing over the dam. The sound drew them with its power, deeper and deeper into the ravine of cool shade.

"Let's walk over the bridge first," Jenn said, tugging Eli up the road. "I like to imagine the old wagons and horse-drawn buggies rumbling over it, the farmers taking their grain to be ground into flour and meal, and the young lovers coming at night for some privacy and romance."

She raised her eyebrows at him at that last picture.

"You mean I might get lucky on the bridge?" he joked, letting himself be drawn into the magic of the place and the moment.

As they stepped onto the rough planks, a car approached from the other side. The boards shook till their teeth rattled, the engine noise echoing in the small space, drowning out all other sound. When it passed, Eli looked at her with a bemused expression.

"Not quite the same effect as a horse and a buggy, wouldn't you say?"

They walked to the middle of the bridge and stopped.

"May I have this dance, kind sir?"

Her lover bowed low, then took her in his arms. The two of them swayed to their own private orchestra, oblivious to all else.

"Do you remember the first time we came here, Eli?" she asked.

"Sure. It was that day you surprised me with a picnic to celebrate graduating from seminary. You invited all of my friends, got them busy talking to each other, then snuck me down here for some extracurricular activity."

Jenn punched him on the arm. "I don't remember hearing any complaints!"

"Nope, none at all."

Her arms encircled his neck, her lips seeking his for a deep, slow, lingering kiss.

"It's hard to believe that was six years ago, Elijah Jon Marks." Her eyes held a mischievous gleam.

"What are you up to?"

She giggled and headed back toward the mill.

"Let's go see the dam and then walk along the stream, away from all the other people so we can talk." She waggled her eyebrows suggestively.

"What is this all about?"

"Oh, nothing. I only wanted to let you in on a secret."

"What kind of secret?"

"Uh, uh, uh! No prying. Let's go."

Eli lagged behind momentarily, admiring her figure. Her blonde hair cascaded over slender shoulders. She always complained about her hips being too big, but they looked just right, perfectly desirable to his decidedly prejudiced eye.

They passed the mill but didn't go in. They were already familiar with the inner workings, with all of its turbines and gears and the broad belts running through the floor from two stories down. A ranger handed out literature in front, while adventure-seeking kayakers hoisted fiberglass shells above their heads in preparation for a run down through giant rocks in the fast-running stream below the dam.

"You folks be careful," the ranger warned the whitewater enthusiasts. "The water is higher and faster than usual from all that rain the past week. They've been talking about closing it to boats for a while, but no word's come down yet."

Jenn and Eli walked onto the observation deck built over the sluiceway next to the dam. The water spilled over the closed sluicegate, rushing against the stone foundation of the mill.

"They're going to have to open the gate into the mill and let this water run through," he told her. "I've never seen it running this fast and high."

Jenn shivered, gazing at the brown water thundering over the dam in front of them.

"All that power," she said in awe.

They watched in silence, noting the large tree trunks and other debris being swept downstream like children's toys.

"We'd better stay off the rocks while we walk upstream," Eli advised cautiously. "With the water this high, they'll be wet and slippery."

"That's why they call it Slippery Rock, genius," she playfully teased.

They continued upstream, holding hands, trying to imagine what it might have been like to be alive in the days when the mill was in service. No cars, no paved road, no tourists. The contented couple considered themselves guests in the still wild canyon, not tourists.

"Look at those children out on the rocks," Jenny said anxiously. "I can't believe their parents are letting them play there. My kids won't be allowed, that's for sure."

She gave her husband a sideways look of barely constrained joy.

"They'll be okay," Eli reassured her. "Now, what is this secret?" He finally noticed the look on her face. "What? You're kidding! Jenn, is this for real?"

They both stopped walking. Jenn nodded gleefully. Eli wrapped her into his embrace, giddy with the prospect.

When they could speak again, Jenn said, "Come up here in the trees and let's find a dry spot to sit down." She gestured up the bank.

She smiled. The smile etched itself into Eli's mind, the way her eyes crinkled at the edges, the tilt of her head, her one dimple.

As they were settling onto a smooth rock, the screaming started. Frantic cries of terror. Panicky calls for help. People began running to the water's edge, waving and pointing, gesturing toward the mill a hundred yards downstream. The ranger was running toward them, barking out orders.

"Eli, something's happened!" Jenn whispered fearfully, clutching his arm.

"Let's go see," he urged, and they headed back toward the rocks.

At first, nothing untoward was visible. Then, suddenly, a bundle of bright rags bobbed to the surface, caught in the swift current, hurtling toward the dam.

"My baby!" cried a distraught woman. "My baby!"

In a terrible flash, Eli realized what had happened. One of the children Jenn fretted over had slipped. Before he could react, Jenn let go of his hand and in a blur was running alongside the river. Eli watched, unbelieving, as his wife veered onto the rocks and arced into the water.

"Jennifer!"

He limped as fast as battered legs would allow toward the spot where Jenn dove. She came up sputtering and began swimming toward the little girl.

"Jen, stop!" he shouted. She was a good swimmer, but nobody could defy this torrent.

A rope snaked out over the water and hit her on the head. She grabbed it and continued struggling toward the limp body of the girl. Twenty-five yards from the dam, Jenn reached her, quickly looped the rope through the girl's belt, and frantically fashioned a knot.

"Hang on!" yelled the ranger. "You hang on to the rope, too, lady!"

But Jenn was spent, exhausted. The current picked up speed and force as it neared the dam. Others grabbed the rope and pulled. Jenn tried to follow to shore, but the water took control.

As the rescuers plucked the girl from the stream, Eli heard his wife scream. Her frightened cries reached him above the roar of the water. People around him covered their mouths with their hands, watching in horror. In a flash, the raging deluge flung her over the dam.

Chapter 5

Eli wandered alone through the second floor of the well-weathered brick and frame house, muttering darkly to himself. He stopped meandering long enough to look out a bedroom window at the moon rising over the tree-covered bluffs across the Ohio River.

"Jenn, are you ever coming back?" he whispered to the sable sky. The brightness of the moon mocked the darkness that crowded his thoughts, seeping ever deeper, blotting out the sweetness of the memory of Jenn at the old mill, asking him to dance, the smell of warm sunlight in her hair.

He felt weary and afraid, wondering if he might be going mad or if he was only becoming insanely desperate from the overwhelming tension and dread of the past two days. Not much of a choice. Not much of a difference.

"Why is this happening?" he asked, the familiar rush of bleak hopelessness sweeping through his heart.

Eli's fingers traced the grain of the wood in the hand-planed windowsill. He and Jenn poured everything they had into making it their home. It stood in the historic section of town where the houses huddled close together, none of them younger than eighty years old.

How could anyone put a price on such a labor of love—and sweat, tears, bruised thumbs, and frustratingly unplumbed walls and bowed floors?

"It adds charm," Jenn insisted when none of the moldings or chair rails or floor tile came out flush or square.

Eli knew every nail, every board in the house. The two of them were like old, comfortable friends who realized on first sight that they'd been looking for each other all of their lives. Jenn accused him of having an affair with the house, but she was smitten as well.

Originally, the house came with no basement. So, for four wearying months, every night after getting off work at the medical center, Eli climbed into the crawl space to attack the hard earth and rock, carving out a cellar, strengthening the foundation. Jenn referred to that period as his mining days.

After the last shovelful of dirt had been carefully handed out to Jenn, she crawled in. There was no door or stairway yet. In her hand was a bottle of cheap champagne and homemade chocolate chip cookies. By the light of the single bare bulb, they reveled in the earthy smell of the cave shelter, their cherished sanctuary now complete.

"I would trade it all," Eli said aloud to the quiet bedroom. "I'd trade all the hours of working together, all the squabbles over those damn cabinets, the wallpaper, carpeting, paint-splattered faces—everything, just to have you back, Jenn."

He hated being in the house without her. Only silence accompanied him on his halting journey through the vault of yet-to-be-fulfilled dreams. Eli tried to suppress the haunting feeling that it was no longer home, no longer a refuge, no longer his place of comfort. He refused to give up.

He descended the stairs slowly, his back aching with each jolt of a foot touching the next tread. His hand slid easily along the smooth bannister. Jenn had labored for days stripping the multicolored layers of paint, finally exposing the natural beauty of the wood. Hour after hour, she'd worked the chemical stripper into the intricate carvings.

"Our kids will love sliding down that monstrosity," Eli had teased her.

"It's not a monstrosity, Eli. And if anyone slides down it, you'll be the ringleader, I'm sure," came her retort of mock severity. "Injured back or no injured back, you're an incurable adolescent at heart!"

Now Jenn lay in the ICU of the Three Rivers Metropolitan Hospital in Pittsburgh, in a coma, unable to respond to him, barely alive. And the tiny life inside of her …

Eli tried not to think about it. In the living room, his glance fell upon a small picture on the mantel, his favorite one of Jenn. She was smiling, her blue eyes looking to the left, one eye hidden by luxurious flowing hair. The satiny folds of her wedding gown provided a soft background for her bouquet of daisies and baby's breath.

Eli picked it up, running his fingers over the edges of the gold-plated frame. A silent sob clutched his throat, but he was empty of tears. He kissed the glass and tucked the picture into the waistband of his jeans, then protectively pulled his jacket over it. He wanted her close.

He closed his eyes for a moment. When he opened them again, his eyes wandered to the shelves that Jenn called his hall of fame. The simple wooden planks held a collection of baseball caps from different eras of the Pittsburgh Pirates and the remains of his childhood collection of baseball cards.

A 1900 brown and tan beanie cap with a short bill sat next to a 1922 black one with a white P on the front. Beside it was a 1925 model with a red P and one from the old Negro league, the Crawfords. Eli felt a particular affection for the 1979 version with the gold stripes encircling the crown. That was a World Series year when, hopelessly behind by two games, the Pirates battled back to beat the Baltimore Orioles in three straight games to take the championship. Eli cherished the boyhood memory of watching the final game with his father, the two of them screaming and yelling, jumping up to hug each other when the last out put the series into the history books.

The hat also served as a secret hiding place. He lifted the cap and removed the small jewelry box nestled underneath. Cradling it in his hands, he looked around the room where he and Jenn had laughed at each other's silly jokes, wrestled playfully on the floor, trying to out-tickle the other; where in the winter they sat mesmerized by the crackling logs in the fireplace, without needing to say a word as they dared the chill winds blowing off the river to reach them.

Eli opened the lid. Even in the dim light, the diamond sparkled as though trying to drive away the darkness that blanketed the house. Selling off most of his baseball card collection bit by bit, including his beloved autographed Roberto Clemente 1971 edition, without getting caught by Jenn only added to the excitement and anticipation of presenting her at last with this long-delayed sign of his love.

"I wish it was a diamond, one as beautiful as your eyes," he'd said as they walked along the dirt lane near her parents' house that Valentine's evening under the stars. "Instead, this is all I have."

He'd taken her hand and slipped a sixty-dollar ring with a cheap sapphire over her finger. She'd held it to her lips, then to his.

"Hold me, Eli," she whispered. "Hold me. Love me."

Eli remembered her body trembling as he buried his face in her hair. "Are you cold?"

She'd stepped back, her eyes shimmering with tears, laughing. "No, silly. I love you, and I want to be with you. I want to be with you now, right here. I don't care if it's not a diamond. I want to love you, make my life with yours, make love to you right here in the fields with only the moon as our witness."

Eli replayed the memory one more time, shutting his eyes tight to hold it in, keep it from fleeing his desolate heart. Finally he closed the lid on the ring and put it back under the hat. He collapsed onto the couch, surrounded by gray silence.

He roused himself enough to punch the button on the stereo remote. The old Jimmy Webb song "If These Old Walls Could Speak" filled the room, the tones of the piano solo rousing the shadows in the far corners of the house. Amy Grant's voice surrounded Eli, beseeching in her clear voice, "If these hallowed halls could talk/ These would have a tale to tell/ Of sun goin' down and dinner bell/ And children playing at hide and seek/ From floor to rafter/ If these walls could speak."

The song ended. Eli was reluctant to let it go. Only forty-eight hours ago, it had all been so clear: Jenn's teasing smile looking up at him, watching as the news sank into his thick skull. In that moment of realization, pain had been forgotten and hope reborn in him. But there was no one to blame, no one to make pay for the two lives hanging in the balance, so still, so quiet.

Eli stood up, bloodshot eyes studying his watch until he realized that it was time to get to the hospital for the evening visiting hours. The hospital allowed only three fifteen-minute visits a day, and he wasn't about to miss any opportunity to be with Jenn. He had reluctantly let himself be convinced by one of the nurses to come home for a shower and a shave and some rest.

A movement at the far end of the dining room startled him, sending a chill shooting down his spine. He didn't know whether to laugh or scream when he realized that he'd been frightened by his own reflection in the mirror above the buffet.

He moved across the room toward it, barely recognizing the haunted face floating before him. Streaks of gray appeared overnight after the trauma of the accident that had broken his spine. Black bags under his eyes were enough to spook any phantom.

"What do you think, Jenn? Some stud, wouldn't you say?" His voice was that of a stranger. He turned away from the mirror, feeling as though he was staring into a grave.

He made his way to the kitchen, the pain in his back growing in intensity, an incessant cry like a two-year-old throwing a tantrum. The morphine pump appeased it but never shut it up. Eli rummaged through a small cabinet over the sink. Jenn bought it at a yard sale, painted it, put in flowery shelf paper, and proudly called him in one day to admire her handiwork.

"You can put your pills and medicines into it, Eli. That will save you from going up and down the steps so much." She'd smiled, awaiting his approval.

He recalled how he struggled to suppress the sigh that sprang immediately to his lips. He hated being reminded of his hobbling gait and the tired dread of stairs. He had good days when the weather cooperated, but otherwise the pain hovered, mocking the remains of his strength, both physical and emotional. The injuries ended his career, forcing Jenn to quit her college classes and work to supplement his small disability pension.

Jenn stood there by the sink, waiting. Part of Eli recognized the thought and effort she'd made for his benefit, so he rewarded her with a kiss on the cheek. But she saw the fleeting grimace in his eyes.

"I can use it too, honey," she hurriedly added. "I'll put my potpourri and Tylenol in it." Her eyes held love and concern. Perhaps even fear that she'd hurt his feelings by rearranging the house around his disability.

The last thing he ever wanted to see in those beautiful eyes was fear. He knew how tender was the love that enveloped him through those eyes, those arms, those lips …

His fist smashed into the exquisite shelves, sending them crashing to the floor in pieces. "Do you know that I'm with you, Jenn?" he screamed in impotent rage.

He searched the rubble for the Percodan he wasn't supposed to have, swallowed three, and stuffed the bottle into the pocket of his jeans.

"Come back to me," he wailed. "I can't take it without you!" His faith had been draining away over the last year. It terrified him to contemplate letting it go. He didn't know if there was any faith now except for his belief in Jenn and her love.

"Don't worry," she'd say whenever she caught him sitting at his desk, staring at nothing. "It will work out. The pain came for a reason."

Eli always protested, and she always replied, "Eli Marks! Dream a little! This is your chance to be what you've always wanted to be."

"So, what is it I've always dreamed of being?"

She'd smile and melt his heart. "That's for you to figure out. And you will, Cookie Man."

They always ended up laughing together. He could hear it still, filling the room with warmth and hope.

He looked at the clock and sighed. Time to go. He traipsed past the carved railing and out the door. The '76 Toyota wagon sputtered to life, filling the interior with noxious fumes as he pulled away from the curb. Corrosion and deterioration had eaten away the original color long ago. Their first new car, still smelling of showroom seduction, sat in the junkyard, a twisted heap of metal and shattered dreams.

Driving toward the city along the Ohio River Boulevard, Eli tightened his grip on the wheel as a train roared past, heading for the railyard in Conway. The faltering car shuddered as the engines rumbled by, their headlights blinding him momentarily. It was like that night, seeing the car heading straight for him out of the mist as he fumbled around, searching under the seat. It was too quick to scream, no time to react. The police attributed it to the mist and road conditions. He hadn't told them otherwise.

He remembered the shock of finding out that the woman in the other car had died, along with her eight-month-old fetus. Her husband never approached him during the long days in the hospital or afterward. Eli didn't know what he would have said anyway, and he never bothered to look the man up after he was mobile again. Something held him back. He hated himself for his cowardice.

Eli reached the hospital in good time and still had fifteen minutes to wait. The Percodan was starting to smooth away the jagged edges of pain. Eli wanted to avoid the waiting room, so he headed down one of the hallways, forcing himself to not limp.

"I have a joke for you."

The voice came from the last room on the right. Welcoming the interruption, Eli stopped to eavesdrop. Through the open door, he saw a white-haired man seated beside a bed. A frail-looking woman lay unmoving, staring vacantly at the ceiling. Eli caught a trace of a twinkle in the old man's eye. One corner of the woman's mouth twitched uncontrollably.

"A man gets a call from his doctor," he continued. "The doctor says, 'I have bad news for you.'"

"'What's the news?' asks the man.

"'Well, you have twenty-four hours to live.'

"'That is bad news,' the man says.

"'I have even worse news,' the doctor adds.

"'What could be worse than that?'

"'I tried to call you yesterday.'"

The man by the bed laughed nervously, all the while searching the woman's face with the eagerness of a child.

"Did you like that, honey?" he asked, the laugh dying away into a sigh.

A glint of a tear shone in her eye. The man looked up and spotted him in the doorway. Eli started to back away, an embarrassed apology on his lips.

"No, wait!" he called out. "Don't go, young man."

"I'm sorry, I didn't mean to …"

He waved away the protest. "Do you have someone here?"

"My wife. She's down the hall in intensive care. I needed to take a walk."

He nodded. "Martha started out down there when she first had the stroke." He ran thick, calloused fingers through his hair before reaching over to pat her on the shoulder. "It's like a big monster that's moved into our lives—The Stroke.'"

He looked at Eli. "What's your name?"

"Elijah Marks from Bridetown. Call me Eli. My wife is Jennifer."

"I'm Joe. Joe Martinson. Can I buy you a cup of coffee, Eli? I could use a break too."

Eli hesitated.

"I could use the company," Joe added softly.

At the canteen, Joe eagerly began to talk.

"I'm a retired steelworker," he said as he set two paper cups of steaming coffee on the table. "Of course, who around here isn't! In fact, I worked at the big mill up your way when I first started."

The cups had playing cards pictured on them. Eli idly wondered how many cups it would take before the machine dealt him a full house.

Joe settled into the chair and took a big gulp of the ferociously hot black liquid. After smacking his lips, he commented, "The coffee stinks, but I used to drink it this hot all the time. I was a crane operator in the mill. It was too far to climb down for breaks, so Martha always fixed me a big thermos of black coffee, summer and winter. It kept me going, in more ways than one." He chuckled. "Thank God for milk cartons."

He stared into the cup when Eli didn't respond. "So, your wife is pretty bad off?"

"Yeah," the younger man answered without offering any explanation. *It's impossible to not think about her*, he thought to himself. Eli pictured her hanging curtains in the bedroom the day before the fateful trip to McConnell's Mill. Her blonde hair shining in the morning sun, her tight jeans revealing all his favorite curves and mysteries. A flood of guilt threatened to overwhelm him. They'd spent the rest of that morning in bed, laughing, touching, making plans.

Joe wasn't offended by Eli's cryptic answer and faraway thoughts. He only nodded and offered a sympathetic look.

"I guess you heard me telling that stupid joke," he said after a while, draining his cup.

Eli shrugged, not wanting to add to the man's embarrassment.

"It's always been mine and Martha's ..."—he paused, waving one of those beefy hands in front of him—"our way of getting past awkward moments."

He chuckled at himself and rubbed his face. "Even after forty years of being married, I'm still shy around her. I always have been, never knew how to tell her ... how to ask ... well ..." He threw up his hands.

"Listen to me," he said, amused. "At the movies, I always hesitated about reaching for her hand. If we were walking down the sidewalk, I didn't know if she wanted me to put my arm around her or not."

Eli smiled, deciding that he liked this big, shy bear of a man.

"I loved touching her." His startling frankness stirred images in Eli's mind, as well as unbidden longings.

"Martha knows how to take charge. She never let my being shy get in the way. She'd reach for my hand first to let me know that it was okay to hold her. She would tell me a joke, so then I would tell her one. We laughed ourselves silly, making me comfortable and warm like a shot of whiskey. Sometimes she would put on a record and prance around like a model, waving a silk scarf at me and singing along to some old love song."

With a faraway look in his eyes, Joe continued. "I always knew then that it was okay. I didn't have to be afraid that she would say no. I'm the luckiest guy in the world, Eli."

He shook his head. "I don't know why I didn't tell her that more often." He shrugged, his face crumbling. "So, today, I try the old routine of jokes. But she can't respond. I want it to be all right. I want her to be all right. I want to hold her. I want her to hold me …"

The black hole that had been opening in Eli' heart the past days threatened to swallow him. He tried to avoid looking at the tears gathering in the corners of Joe's eyes.

"She's a lucky lady, Joe."

He didn't answer. In the ensuing silence, Eli found his thoughts drifting back to that awful day at the old mill. Thank God for those guys in their kayaks. Cursing his unforgiving backbone, he'd hobbled like a three-legged dog to the deck over the sluicegate, screaming wildly.

There was no sign of her in the angry foam and spray. People had to grab Eli to keep him from jumping over the railing into that roiling mass. Struggling mightily to avoid the demonic hydraulics of the water crashing around the rocks, the kayakers maneuvered as near as they possibly dared below the dam. They paddled back and forth in a desperate search pattern, poking around the rocks, pushing branches and limbs out of the way.

Fifty yards downstream, a cry went up as one of them spotted Jennifer surface briefly, only to strike her head against a boulder. Somehow they caught her. The ranger obligingly told Eli in a matter-of-fact voice that otherwise it would have taken a couple of weeks to recover the body.

The ranger spoke into a radio, and shortly thereafter came a flurry of activity with ambulances arriving, a medevac helicopter hovering overhead, looking for a place to land in the fields near the upper parking lot. Eli walked with the stretcher back up the same zigzag trail, begging Jenny to hang on. The paramedics restored her breathing, but her eyes never opened.

"Jenny, I said I love you a thousand times in those horrible moments. Did you hear me?"

"What?" Joe looked at him with a puzzled expression.

"Sorry. I didn't realize I was thinking out loud."

"That's okay."

"The doctors keep going on and on about pressure on the brain, not knowing how much brain damage, and always the same answer to my questioning if she would awaken: 'We just don't know, Mr. Marks.'"

But I've got a diamond ring waiting for her at home, he wanted to scream at them. *She has to wake up. She has to see it, watch me put it on her finger while bathed in moonlight. Don't you understand? She has to wake up! Our baby needs her!*

For a short while longer, the two grieving men sat in the snack bar with its sticky tables and harsh lighting, cradling their vending machine coffee cups as though they held the mystery of a sacrament.

Joe stood up. "I'd better get back to Martha. She worries when I'm gone. Thanks for the company. Good luck, Eli."

"You too, Joe. Thanks for the coffee."

At the door to the hall, a woman with bushy red hair, and arms and legs that bent at awkward angles, stopped Joe and patted him on the arm. She wore the stiffly starched uniform of a private nurse.

Eli turned to stare out the windows at the rivers that came together at the Point in downtown. The muddy Mon eased its way into the clearer Allegheny. At the moment, he could only see the sparkle of lights dancing across the water. Tows of laden barges slid past and on into the Ohio.

"Mr. Marks?"

He looked up into the face of the unit clerk. He started from the chair, fear instantly knotting his stomach.

"No, no, she's the same," the woman reassured him. "Someone left this at the desk while I was on break. It has your wife's room number on it but nothing else."

Eli took the package from her, and she headed back to her station. He warily unwrapped an old shoebox from a brown paper bag. He lifted the lid and froze. It had to be a joke, a sick, ghastly joke. Surely …

Inside, nestled in old burlap, lay a small baby doll, dressed in flannel pajamas. His heart raced. The doll's blonde hair had been hacked off, leaving a few tufts poking out from the dirty piece of gauze wound around its head.

He leaned closer, bile rising like venom in his craw. The disconnected hollow barrel of a pen pierced the doll's throat. Eli instantly recognized the meaning. Someone had fashioned a crude tracheotomy in a repulsive replica of the respirator tube in Jenn.

Except for one thing. A necklace of frayed yarn lay around the doll's neck. From it dangled a child's friendship charm—the jagged edge of a broken heart.

Chapter 6

"Help her! Somebody help her!" Gideon managed to choke out between dry sobs in the stifling farmhouse. Who would do such a thing? Why the senseless, brutal murders? What had any of them done to deserve this? His mind tried futilely to comprehend the scene before him.

He stumbled blindly toward the kitchen to get a wet rag. Maybe if he washed her ... His hands trembled uncontrollably while he struggled to turn the spigot. They were drenched in blood from the bodies. A strangled cry rose in his throat as he began to splash water on his palms. This was insanity. It must be. What else could it be?

He turned off the water, watching the swirl of pink circling the drain. Dry heaves wracked his body again and again until he hyperventilated. He didn't want to turn around and go back to that scene of slaughter.

The sound of an engine interrupted the wretched silence. Gideon held his breath, his eyes darting toward the hallway leading to the front door, then back to his own beleaguered reflection in the kitchen window. Everything grew still, even the sound of the flies. The hair on the back of his neck stood on end. He waited, his breathing shallow and sounding too loud. When he couldn't stand the tension any longer, Gideon took a step toward the hall. He stopped in midstride.

A stealthy footstep came from the front porch. Sweat trickled down his cheek and across the stitches, making them burn. He didn't dare move. He heard the doorknob slowly turn, then stop.

Gideon began to ease his way over to the back door. Just as he reached it, the front door squeaked, followed by a click that sounded like a gun being cocked. As quickly and as quietly as he could, Gideon drew the latch and bolted into the light.

Gideon ran across the yard without looking back. The barn door's rusted hinges groaned as he tugged and pulled. Panic overwhelmed him.

"I've got to get one of the horses," Gideon said, panting. At last the door opened enough for him to squeeze through. Then reality hit: there were no horses any longer. He was thinking like an eleven-year-old boy. This was real life. JP died in the county nursing home. The farm had been left to fallow long ago.

Pushing the door shut behind him, Gideon took a quick survey of the musty barn. Old tack pegs and rusting tools lined the walls. He peeked back at the house through a crack in the weather-beaten boards. Whoever was in there, it wouldn't take long for them to search the house. If it was the police, he had no believable explanation for the scene of horror. If it was the same people who had brought the victims to the house and butchered them, he could think of no reason for them to come back other than to get him.

Gideon's mind reeled from the savagery he'd witnessed in the past twenty-four hours. To hell with explanations. Right now he wanted to get away; questions could wait. He flinched at the sound of a gunshot. He peeked again.

One shadow passed by the kitchen window, and another flitted through the upstairs bedrooms. "They're shooting first and asking questions later," Gideon muttered to the empty barn. "I sure wish you were here, Brownie."

Brownie was the horse JP gave him on his tenth birthday. By the time Gideon left the farm at age eighteen, he and Brownie had roamed nearly every trail in the mountains and valleys of Coalwater County.

A long burst of gunfire, punctuated by the shattering of glass, filled the air. "Whoever they are, they're not real patient and not real happy," Gideon told himself grimly. After one more brief glimpse, he headed for the back of the barn.

A hurried scan of the orchard beyond the paddock revealed no sign of anyone else lying in ambush. He flung open the door and ran for the trees. As he reached the first row, someone let out a shout behind him. Too terrified to look, Gideon kept on in a straight line through the trees, making toward the distant field and the old willow tree.

Before he traveled another stride, a green apple suddenly exploded directly over his head, sending bits of fruit spraying everywhere. He chanced a look around and saw a short man with a beard aiming a telescope sighted rifle at him from the corner of the barn. Another apple disintegrated at the same time as he saw the muzzle flash, followed by the sharp crack.

His heart pumping wildly, Gideon maintained enough presence of mind to start bobbing and weaving his way through the trees. Bullets thudded into the tree trunks on both sides of him. Another quick look behind revealed the short man pausing to climb into the back of a camouflage-painted pickup. The oversized tires flung mud wildly as the driver sped toward the orchard.

Gideon's breath came in painful gasps as he forced himself on. The fearsome roar of the truck's engine filled the air, surrounding him on all sides.

With his legs giving out, Gideon searched desperately for some protective shelter. Then a higher-pitched sound, vaguely familiar, came through the wall of noise created by the monster truck. He couldn't be sure, but it seemed to be coming from his left.

Gideon stared in amazement at the sight of the familiar ATV careering down the slope from the dirt track beyond Rusty Creek. A black ponytail sailed out behind the shining black face of Jonathan. He whooped with glee as he sped past the willow tree, heading straight for Gideon.

The unconventional tactic worked. The sound of the truck engine changed pitch as it slowed, uncertainty in the mind of his pursuers. Gideon hurried to the edge of the orchard, waving his arms to make sure Jonathan saw him. Without any sign of acknowledgment, Jonathan raced past him, making a looping turn to face the truck head-on.

The driver got over his surprise, gunned his engine, and bore down on the ATV. The sudden start threw the trigger man standing in the back onto the truck bed. The two vehicles headed directly for each other in a deadly game of chicken. Jonathan took one hand off the handlebars and began to fish around in his jacket pocket.

"Look out!" Gideon yelled, rooted to the spot.

The man being jolted around in the truck bed must have yelled something, too, because the driver turned his head to look at him through the rear window, and the truck abruptly veered toward a gnarled old apple tree. The impact sent the gunman flying over the cab, while a shower of crab apples rained on the windshield.

Jonathan let out another shrill war cry and circled back to Gideon.

"C'mon, get on. We don't have all day!"

Gideon needed no urging. He vaulted onto the ATV and held on for dear life as the three wheeler bounced over the terrain and splashed through Rusty Creek.

At the rise of the dirt track, Gideon spied his '69 fire-engine-red LeMans with Laurel behind the wheel. She motioned to him to get in.

"Go with her," Jonathan shouted. "I'll give them a run for their money through the back country."

"But what if you …" Gideon tried to question him, but Jonathan waved him off.

"There isn't any time. Go with Laurel. I'll catch up with you later."

Gideon barely had time to pull his left leg over the rear fender before Jonathan gunned the engine and disappeared in a spray of gravel and dust.

"Let's go!" yelled Laurel, one eye on the farm below them.

The driver of the pickup was helping his buddy off the ground. Gideon hustled over to the car and slammed the door. Laurel threw it into reverse and floored the accelerator. Working the wheel with one hand, she spun the car around, making it rock wildly. They rocketed around corners and bottomed out on ruts as she sped away from the surreal scene.

When he'd caught his breath, Gideon looked over at Laurel. She was grinning back at him.

"Wild enough for you?" She laughed. Her hair danced around her face as air streamed in through the window. "Yeah!" she whooped in sheer delight.

"I was nearly killed back there!" Gideon yelled back in disbelief. "And five other people were killed, one of them a little girl. Their throats were slit like animals! They died in their own blood."

Laurel did a double take, saw that he was serious, and stood on the brakes. The rear end of the car fishtailed, but she expertly kept it under control and slowed down to a more reasonable speed.

"What?" she exclaimed, her eyes wide. "Who's dead? I thought this was another training mission."

Gideon shook his head. "What are you talking about? What training? Some old man's run over in the parking lot, and then I find all those bodies in the house …"

"What parking lot? Where?"

"At the hospital last night. He followed me out of the emergency room."

"Who was he? Did he say anything to you or give you anything?"

"How should I know? I never saw him before!" Gideon exclaimed. "Ever since you two pulled me off the mountain yesterday, it's been one bloody nightmare after another." He stopped, his eyes burning into Laurel's. "I don't even know who you are."

She returned his look, her lips pursed as she considered something. "I think we need to talk to Jonathan," she said finally. "He needs to know what's going on."

She turned her attention back to the road and stomped on the gas. "Nice wheels," she told him appreciatively. When she reached Ridge Road, she headed west, away from Frenchville.

Gideon had the distinct impression that she could tell him a lot more. He started to ask a question but stopped himself. How did she and Jonathan know where to find him? Between the two rescues, six people had been killed. Why should he trust them? Maybe it would be better to proceed with caution.

"Thanks. My grandfather bought it for me when I turned eighteen."

"You look like hell, Gideon." She laughed nervously. "I'm sorry, I just meant that with that nasty-looking cut, all those bumps and bruises and tired eyes, you look like you could use some hot food."

"And twenty-four hours of sleep," added Gideon. He looked down at his clothes. His jeans were caked with dried blood, mud, and grass stains. His shirt was no better. "And some clean clothes."

"We'll do what we can," Laurel said.

Before long, she turned onto what appeared to be an old logging road. Gideon looked around as they climbed higher and higher.

"Dovetail Mountain," he said. "What's up here?"

"Base camp."

Gideon considered her terse answer for a moment. "Are you two in the military?"

Laurel laughed heartily. "That's a good one. Wait till I tell Jonathan." She concentrated on avoiding the steep drop-off to their right.

Gideon tried not to look, yesterday's fall all too fresh in his mind. "If you're not military, then what are you?"

"I don't know if I'm supposed to tell you, but"—she paused, chewing on her lower lip—"why not? After all that's happened, it's the least I can do. We're Guardians."

Gideon watched her, waiting for the laugh that would signal the punchline. None came.

"You're what?"

"Guardians, just like I said."

"What's a guardian? Some kind of paramilitary group?"

She shook her head. "It's the job we're assigned."

"Well, that's real clear," Gideon said sarcastically. "Next, you'll tell me you're guardian angels like those people that wear the red berets on the subways."

"No." Laurel sounded defiant. "Why are you acting so superior or stuck up or whatever?"

Gideon could feel his face getting red as his anger rose. "Superior! All I'm trying to do is ask who the hell you are! I've seen more blood in the last twenty-four hours than in my whole life, nearly been shot, and you tell me I'm acting *superior* or *stuck up* or whatever," he said, mimicking her voice. "Besides, this is my car, and I'll ask the questions."

Laurel's knuckles turned white on the steering wheel. She forced herself to take three deep breaths, slowly exhaling after each one.

Gideon laughed derisively. "Don't tell me you're guardian angels with wings and haloes and all that garbage!"

Laurel turned on him, her eyes flashing. "Forgive me for even opening my mouth," she managed through gritted teeth. She started to say more but stopped.

Halfway up the mountain, she turned off the track and parked the car under tall pine trees with the front end nosed under some scrub brush. "We have to walk the rest of the way. Help me cover up the car."

Gideon suppressed the urge to bombard her with more questions and began to pile branches over the rear of the vintage LeMans until it was concealed. Satisfied, Laurel led him over some rocks and into the darkness beneath the canopy of leaves high overhead. They climbed upward for a while. Gideon's ribs ached, and he longed to stop and rest but didn't want to give Laurel the satisfaction of hearing him ask.

Finally, gasping for air, covered with dust and grime, and still longing for that nice hot shower to wash away the stink, Gideon emerged into a small clearing at the base of a rockface. Laurel was already pulling away the branches concealing the entrance to a cave.

"Over here," she called to him. She bent low and entered the cool gloom within the rock.

Gideon hesitantly followed. Laurel stood in the center surveying their environs. "This is base camp. Get some food and water there toward the back. You look like you haven't eaten for days. And over here are some bedrolls, and at the back of the cave, on the other side of that overhang, there is a pool in the rocks. It's freezing, but it's clean."

Gideon wondered why she rattled on so. Was she nervous about something?

"Thanks," he said. "I'm going to wash some of this crud off and then get something to eat."

He started to pull his shirt over his head, then grimaced and stopped, his body at its limit. Laurel noticed and put her hand to her brow.

"I'm sorry. I forgot to look after your injuries. We're fully equipped, even have some painkillers if you need them."

Gideon managed to get his shirt off and sat down on a pile of blankets, sweat dotting his forehead. He could feel blood trickling from the wound on his cheek. All the rattling around in the car, not to mention the race for his life, must have loosened the stitches.

Laurel rummaged around in a metal box before coming to him with cotton and a bottle of liquid. "Here, let me put this on the stitches so you won't get an infection."

It stung like hell, and he winced and gasped at the burning. Her fingers felt cool and gentle as she steadied herself with one hand on his bare shoulder while working.

"Let's take off that binding, okay?" she asked.

Gingerly, she began to unwind the elastic bandage. Gideon held his breath against the pain as the muscles relaxed and expanded.

"Maybe I'd better take something for this pain after all," he said in surrender.

"It will help you to rest too," assured Laurel. "You're safe here. They don't know about this place. Jonathan should be back in a while, and we can talk then about what's happening."

Gideon took the two proffered Vicodin and tried to get comfortable. His mind kept replaying the scenes of the car bearing down on the old man and the horror in JP's living room. Every time he shut his eyes, he saw blood. He rolled over awkwardly and caught Laurel watching him.

"I don't think I remembered to say thank you," he said. "I was brought up better than that."

"You're welcome," Laurel said softly. "I'm sorry about in the car and … you know …" She stopped and shrugged her shoulders, looking embarrassed.

"Yeah, I know," Gideon replied, noticing how the light from the hurricane lamps streaked her hair with golden highlights. "How long have you been … what did you call it? A guardian?"

"A year. I'm in my final training. Jonathan's my mentor. He's the best. He's taught me so much. I can't wait."

Gideon look puzzled. "Wait for what?"

"I probably said too much again," Laurel said with a sigh.

"No, please, tell me. Nothing else these past few hours has made much sense, so I'm willing to believe most anything."

"You're just teasing me," Laurel said, sparks flashing in her emerald eyes.

"No. I meant it. I'm serious," Gideon tried to convince her. "I feel like I've been thrown into the middle of a hurricane or a tornado. First JP's death and then all these other bizarre things have happened. I really want to know more about you."

Laurel hesitated, studying his face. "All right. I guess it's okay. Jonathan's been training me to be a guardian. They're the people who look after the Healer."

Gideon sat up straight, his eyes wide. "What did you say?"

"I said I've been in training—"

Gideon interrupted. "The other part. Something about looking out for someone."

"Yeah, the Healer. Jonathan said the signs all pointed to his arrival soon. He's been studying the signs for a long time. I didn't expect it would mean all this kind of trouble, though. The bloodtrackers must be on the move, trying to stop him."

She smiled, clasping her hands together like a little girl seeing her first pony. "I hope it's true."

Gideon stared at her blankly, his head spinning.

Laurel thought he didn't understand. "You know. The Healer. The one whose blood can cure any disease."

Gideon shook his head dumbly, hoping against all hopes that he was back under the willow tree, lost in a bad dream.

Chapter 7

The painkiller worked. Soon Gideon closed his eyes against the confusing images bouncing around his brain like a pinball. His shoulders relaxed as the drug bit into the pain. A smile played across his lips as Christine came to him in his dreams ...

He was in the music room, working as a custodian in the same Quaker prep school where he'd graduated four years earlier. The students were gone for the weekend, off to their jobs or keg parties, full of nonchalant disdain for those adults who tried preaching the gospel of a future ripe for the conquering. JP had granted Gideon his wish, expressed in anger over many months, to leave the crowding confines of French Valley and pursue his academic career at a prep school that could accommodate his ever-expanding dreams. He never went home, too ashamed of his failures and too proud to ask for forgiveness. Before he knew it, half a decade had passed, and his dreams were like the cigarette butts that skittered in front of his dust mop, across wooden floors, and into the forgotten corners.

Beyond the faculty parking lot, the mountains of Centre County, Pennsylvania, huddled for warmth under a slate sky. They reminded him of home, JP's farm cradled in the narrow valley, a time that seemed too long ago to be real. Still watching the mountains, he picked up a guitar leaning against a chair and began to play, easily moving into one of his favorite songs:

There's a warm wind tonight
And the moon turns the tide.
When I call in the cat,
She'll go walking.
Where she goes, I don't know,
She won't tell me what it is
That makes her act like this
But I got a funny feeling that it's me,
It's worth believin' ...

"Gideon?"

Gideon spun away from the tableau to the visual feast of Christine Raven, her hip against a desk, fashionable shoes dangling from one hand, a short denim skirt showing off long, shapely legs, accentuated by black tights and sheer body shirt. Shiny black hair framed inviting eyes and full lips.

"That was beautiful," she murmured, pushing her hair behind her ears and cocking her head to the side. "I love your music."

Christine was doing her student teaching in theater arts. She'd enlisted Gideon's help in building scenery for the school's fall productions. Her hair smelled of strawberries, and Gideon constantly fantasized about running his fingers through it as she leaned over him, her hair cascading around his face, her breasts brushing against his chest.

"That was a Gordon Lightfoot song."

"Play some more. I feel like dancing," she softly commanded.

Gideon began performing one of his own compositions, written while valley gazing with JP. It spoke of soaring hawks, playful breezes, wandering streams, and deep longing for refuge. Christine began to move with the music, back and forth, her fingers lightly caressing first one thigh, then the other. She caught his eye and smiled.

He couldn't smile back. She always told him he was too serious, to lighten up. He tried to keep his attention on the mystery and longing of the music. Christine put her head back and let her hair swing back and forth, skimming the inviting curves below. She spun slowly, lost in the yearning of the melody.

Gideon couldn't take his eyes from her, playing on as desire rose, a fiery river adding a fierce passion to the music. He stopped playing, and she slowly ended her dance. The room was still.

She opened her eyes and touched a hand to her cheek, tinged with a flush of pink. "I'm sorry," she said in a husky voice. "I got carried away. What was that?"

"'Dance in a Hidden Meadow.'" He stared, mesmerized, as her chest rose and fell in quick rhythm.

She began to climb the tiered rows toward him. He could hear his own blood surging through every vein. Nearer she came, mouth open, inviting. He stood to take her into his arms, pulling her close, pressing his lips into the taste of hers. He closed his eyes and drank deeply of her, reveling in the incredible joy of her arms around him.

He opened his eyes when he felt her lashes brushing against his cheek. He brought his hands up to cup her face … and gagged. He was embracing the lifeless body of the small girl from the hospital. The wound in her throat gaped hideously, and blood gushed over his hands.

"No! Christine!"

"Gideon, what is it? Wake up."

His eyes snapped open. Laurel knelt over him, using a cool cloth to wipe his brow. He was drenched in sweat.

"Gideon, what is it? Were you dreaming?"

He shook his head, trying to focus, bewildered by the flickering shadows dancing across damp rock overhead.

"It's okay. You're safe." Her hair brushed against his shoulder as she helped him to sit up.

Gideon took in deep breaths, gripped by profound fear. "What's happening?" he asked in a plaintive voice. "Why am I here?"

Laurel made soothing sounds, much as a mother to a restless infant. "You're with us. Jonathan's here."

"But, what is …"

"Are you feeling up to talking?" Jonathan's strong voice filled the cavern, encouraging yet brooking no nonsense.

Gideon slowly rocked back and forth, hugging himself. "I honestly don't know. I don't know what to say, what to think, or what to feel anymore."

"Whatever the reasons for what you did, it's obvious they want you to know that *they* know who you are." Jonathan stood over him.

Gideon shrank from the powerful gaze of Jonathan's coal-black eyes. He shakily pulled himself to his feet, stretching his cramped legs.

"I don't know what you're talking about. Who am I supposed to be?" His voice came out in a bewildered squeak. "Who are *they*?"

"You are the Healer, of course," Jonathan stated. "We have waited for years, watching the signs as foretold by the ancient Aleudar fire guides, the stories of the Chronicles." He paused, then pressed ahead. "I don't want to offend you, but you have made many mistakes, and time is short."

Gideon stepped back. "I'm not this Healer or whatever it is people keep trying to pin on me."

"Then what happened to the child?" Jonathan's voice grew dangerously quiet.

"What child?" Gideon feigned innocence. He looked to Laurel for support, or sympathy, or whatever she could give him. She looked wide-eyed from one to the other without acknowledging either.

Jonathan ran calloused fingers over his weary face, one metal crutch dangling from the forearm. A long sigh escaped through his pursed lips. The silence stretched on.

"Maybe he really doesn't know," Laurel ventured.

Jonathan's eyes smoldered fiercely at that suggestion, his anger making the West Indies accent more pronounced. "Of course he knows," he spat out derisively. "How could he not know? He appeared on the mountain to begin the awaited Redemption, didn't he? His life is spared, when all around others fall. We've been waiting and watching in obedience, have we not?"

The singular passion in Jonathan's voice gripped them as he whispered, "Did his blood not heal where all else failed?"

Gideon shook his head. "That's what I'm trying to tell you. I don't know what's been going on. I came here for my grandfather's funeral, that's all," he insisted. "After I fell and you dropped me off at the hospital, things began to happen too fast. But believe me, I had no control over them. I don't know anything about being a Healer, those Chronicles, or any of it."

"Where did you come from?" Jonathan asked. "You have the blood gift. I know that you do. Why are you testing us?"

"I don't have a blood gift, and I came from wherever the hell I came from," Gideon uttered defiantly. "I haven't exactly been keeping a permanent address lately. Look, I appreciate you two rescuing me, I really do. But I did not cause any of this. You have to believe me! I am not testing you."

He switched tactics, taking the offensive. "Tell me what the two of you are doing hiding in this cave and how you just happened to be on the mountain and then just happened to show up at the farm. That's way too many coincidences, if you ask me."

"We are doing our job. We arrived a week ago after being summoned. Now, you tell me something. I went back to that farmhouse," Jonathan said, his quiet voice betraying the slightest hint of the tremor of rage. "Who warned you not to sleep there last night?"

Gideon thrust out his hand, his index finger inches from Jonathan's chest.

"Nobody warned me," Gideon said through gritted teeth. "I fell asleep under the willow in the back pasture. Right after dawn, I finally made it back to the house, where I found the girl …" His voice stopped, the images of horror rushing back.

"You're asking me to believe a great deal without any proof whatsoever," Jonathan said.

"You're asking me to do the same thing!" declared Gideon.

All three fell silent again, their unanswered questions left hanging in the underground chill. The steady drip of water echoed deep within the bowels of the cave.

"What are we going to do?" Laurel broke in. "I didn't know there would be the killing of children, Jonathan. Do Guardians have to get blood on their hands?"

"I'm not sure why they murdered those people," Jonathan said. "I've known all along the trackers are ruthless, but we've been so careful." He looked at Gideon again, without answering Laurel's question. "You're sure these people knew about your gift?"

"It's not a gift; it was a coincidence!" exploded Gideon. "Listen—how do I know you didn't kill them? None of this is making any sense."

"I always thought the arrival of the Healer would be a moment full of great promise and hope," Jonathan said with a frown. Then, wistfully, he added, "The FireGuide said it would be so. He said to watch for the sign on the mountain."

Gideon noted the sadness in Jonathan's eyes. "I'm sorry I'm not what you expected. Not that I know what you're talking about!" he added in exasperation. "Does this mean that anyone who comes into contact with me or thinks that I'm this 'Healer' is going to be slaughtered? Because if it does, I want no part of it. I resign or whatever I have to do. Besides, if I'm really some kind of healer, why are my ribs and head still killing me?"

"This is not at all how I imagined it would be," Jonathan stated grimly. "And you, of all people, don't have the option of resigning. There is no resigning, no going back. The Sacrament child could already be on the way as we speak. The truth of the summons cannot be doubted. It is all happening as Adam said that it would. Maybe you cannot heal yourself because you do not believe!"

Laurel brushed her hair out of her face and placed a hand on Jonathan's arm. The gesture irritated Gideon for some reason he could not readily identify.

"Maybe we should back up and start at the beginning," she told Jonathan. "He's got to be awfully confused if he isn't aware of any of the Chronicles. Maybe he was never taught. Perhaps they wanted to protect him. These are extremely dangerous times, as you well know. I would probably feel the same myself if it was my child."

"What are you talking about?" insisted Gideon. "Please, do tell me ..." He stopped and looked at Laurel.

Her tiny smile and encouraging nod made his heart jump. Jonathan motioned to him to take his seat, then expertly maneuvered himself around the dim interior, his crutches and braces keeping time as he spoke.

"I don't see where I have any choice but to trust you," he began, making it clear he felt anything but certainty. "Forgive me if I seem overly suspicious, but I've been at this for a long time, and, as you can see, lives are at stake. The bloodtrackers are clever, but I know that the girl you healed was truly near death. Her disease is well documented. The Redemption is arriving and the Sacrament child must be protected."

He noted the blank look on Gideon's face and took a different tack. "The bloodtrackers are trying to wipe out the Guardians in their ruthless service to the Ransom. They want to deny the Sanctuary by destroying the Sacrament child. We Guardians are sworn to find and protect the child until the BloodGuide can bless the sacrament and complete the Redemption. What puzzles me is that none of those people in the farmhouse were Guardians. But there can be no other explanation. The BloodMaster will stop at nothing to prevent the Redemption of the BloodFire. Surely you know of this! You saw for yourself how evil he is!"

"Wait a minute!" Gideon interrupted forcefully. "You're talking absolute nonsense! Sanctuary? Redemption? BloodFire? The bloody ransom or whatever! Are you some kind of religious nuts?"

Jonathan removed his glasses and pinched the bridge of his nose. "We are not religious nuts, and we have precious little time to stay and argue. There are too few of us left, and we are sitting ducks here." He noted Gideon's frown. The tips of the crutches thumped more forcefully with each word. "Unexplained airliner crashes, hit-

and-runs, serial killers—all those have been used against us. The destruction of the Branch Davidians in Waco was meant to be an object lesson aimed directly at us. The bloodtrackers have infiltrated everywhere."

Gideon chuckled at the absurdity of Jonathan's claim. "You're trying to tell me that not only are there secret spy agencies, but there are also secret religions hunted down by the spooks? What are you two, the secret priests? I'm supposed to believe this crap? I suppose you also have proof that there was a conspiracy to assassinate Kennedy, aliens crashed in New Mexico, and the president flew a jet fighter against alien invaders. C'mon, I've read my share of spy novels. Why not send an assassin to shoot you in the back of the head and dump you in the river somewhere if you're so dangerous?"

Gideon looked at Laurel, who was wiping a tear from her eye. "You believe this nonsense?" Gideon asked as he stood up.

"A train crash in Arizona, USAir 427, TWA 800, Oklahoma City. Those people are martyrs." Jonathan's icy tone cut through Gideon's laughter.

"It's true, Gideon. Theirs is just a tiny bit of the history of our struggle for the Sanctuary, but it is written in blood." Laurel spoke barely above a whisper. "The bloodtrackers are desperate. They'll wipe out a whole planeload of people to get one Guardian. The BloodMaster is scared."

"Of what?"

"Of you. And what your appearance means."

"Of me?" Gideon pointed to himself, incredulous. "And what, pray tell, is my appearance supposed to mean?"

"That the healing has begun, of course. The BloodFire Redemption is on the way. Think about what you saw in that house," Jonathan said.

"I saw a little girl butchered like an animal," Gideon replied with bitterness. "A little girl who got lucky and was given a reprieve on life, a second chance to be grow up and be somebody in this dirt hole of a world. But somebody decided she wasn't going to get that chance and cut her throat!"

"You don't have to believe me about the rest. But you know what you saw," Jonathan pushed firmly. "They've been trying to wipe out the Guardians since the beginning."

"*They* being the supposed Ransom's bloodtrackers? And for some reason they've been following me around, or got on to me and my little secret that even *I* didn't know about." Gideon rested his chin on his knees, his pain forgotten as he wondered just how wild of a story they would spin for him. "Why would they want to wipe you out? Why murder so many innocent people to get at one person? Why are they so bloodthirsty?"

Jonathan smacked a crutch against one of his own legs in exasperation. "Twenty-eight years ago, 1971, I was a twenty-year-old sergeant sitting in a bar in Saigon. A kid walks in, couldn't have been more than eight or nine, pulls the pin on a grenade, smiles, and rolls it across the floor. It explodes under my table, and I end up in the hospital, nearly bled out, my legs chewed to shreds."

"You're saying that kid was one of these trackers types?"

"No, he was part of the craziness of Vietnam." Jonathan shrugged. "They patched my legs back together as best they could. But something inside of me was dead. When I got back to the States, I hated the world, I hated these pieces of metal around my legs, I hated the pain, I hated my life. I cursed God, and I waited to die."

"I'm sorry," Gideon said.

Jonathan waved off any sympathy. "One day, when I'm at my lowest and thinking about ending it all, out of nowhere this guy shows up. He knows all about me. Tells me not to give up because he needs me, good legs or not. Sits and listens to me for hours, catching all my bull without batting an eye. Won't let me feel sorry for myself. Tells me I still have a purpose. Goes with me to physical therapy and chews out my butt when I want to quit."

Jonathan stared past Gideon as he spoke, transfixed by his own memories. "Finally, I'm ready to listen to him. He asks me if I'd like a chance to stop the madness that sends little kids into bars with grenades. He tells me I'll be putting my life on the line but not for some politicians sitting in their cozy offices, sending poor slobs like me off to fight their battles. It's a fight to give that boy in the bar a chance to live his life, to give him peace, to have true freedom."

Gideon didn't conceal his bewilderment. "Lots of people fight that battle. What does it have to do with those murders? How does any of that endanger your life? Who was this guy?"

"He called himself Adam. No last name. He told me I could find real hope in becoming one of the Sanctuary Guardians. It gave me something to hang on to when nothing else made sense—not religion, neither psychology nor sociology, certainly not technology. He told me I didn't have to accept it all, simply trust him until I saw for myself. After a while, he recruited me, tutored me about the BloodFire Protocol, trained me, initiated me, and turned me loose."

"Turned you loose to do what?"

Jonathan and Laurel exchanged warm smiles. "Turned him loose to find others, like me," Laurel said.

"And to wait for the arrival of the Healer and the FireGuide and the Sacrament child," Jonathan added.

Gideon made no effort to hide his caustic skepticism. "By all means, you have to protect this noble kingdom that you have here! How many recruits do you have for your little Sanctuary movement?"

Jonathan's smile disappeared. "Laurel is my first. Understand, it takes a certain kind of person. Most just thought I was crazy. Lots of times, I thought they were right. I heard that they tracked down Adam up near Pittsburgh in June of '96—went all out using Special Forces, helicopters, the works. No body was ever found, but most of us faced reality. One crazy old lady swore that he survived, but he's never been heard from again. Anyway, after twenty-eight years of waiting, surviving the savagery of the bloodtrackers, and training Laurel, the signs appeared."

"Don't be so modest," Laurel broke in. "You're the best, Jonathan. You knew this would be the most likely place even before our summons."

"Most likely for what?" Gideon asked.

"Most likely place for the three witnesses to assemble for the BloodFire Redemption. Since you're here, the time must be getting close. I'm simply grateful to be the one to find you."

"But why here? What's so special about this area? What are the three witnesses?"

"Adam said that this land held the seed of the Aleudar."

"Wait a minute," Gideon said, holding out his hands to stop Jonathan. "I just realized something. You mean to tell me that in twenty-eight years of believing this nonsense of a religion, or whatever you call it, you only managed to find one other person who would believe, and she's it?"

"I'm not an it," protested Laurel. "I got into this with my eyes wide open."

"There are very few who believe." Jonathan sounded defensive. "It is not an easy path. The opportunity for Redemption occurs only every thirteen revolutions of the BloodFire star. That is millennia of waiting."

"Millennia?" Gideon said, laughing. "Like in thousands of years? Where did good old Adam get all this stuff? The wall of some pyramid? Stonehenge? The cavemen paintings? No, wait, let me guess. The Psychic Network?"

"In the last twenty-four hours, six people have been murdered because of you and what you stand for—and you mock that?" Laurel shook her head.

Gideon immediately felt shamed. "It keeps coming back to that, doesn't it? I'm sorry. What a waste."

Laurel squeezed his hand by way of acknowledging his apology. Gideon felt a delightful jolt of current shoot up his arm.

"Your arrival signals the liberation of the BloodFire," she said. "You and the FireGuide offer the gift of the Sacrament child. The Chronicles are incomplete, it seems, but we believe that the bloodtrackers want to kill the child so that she can become neither a great prophet nor a tyrant with this gift. Great prophets in the past have given rise to competitive religions. Great tyrants have given rise to competitive empires. Both, historically and inexorably, lead to terrible oppression, wars, and destruction. We have all misused the BloodFire gift for countless generations. Adam, the BloodGuide, said the Thirteenth Redemption would be the last chance for the world."

Jonathan took up the point. "It's not about religion or power or politics. The world doesn't want to understand anything that is not in those terms, however. The Sanctuary is different, too different, for them. And now we are so few. Thankfully, the signs are appearing before we are all wiped off the earth and the Sanctuary Chronicles die with us."

"Why would they die?"

"Because they are not meant to be a written record. They are not a Bible, but the story of the connection we have to the Sanctuary."

It was Gideon's turn to pace the cave, shaking his head as he spoke. "I may not be as educated as I'd like to be, but I'm not stupid either. You're telling me that some nearly extinct secret religious cult is under attack by vicious murderers led by this BloodMaster, and you're the good guys because of the Sanctuary, or whatever, and you believe in healing by blood."

Jonathan's face flushed deep red, the veins in his neck bulging as he pointed one of his crutches at Gideon and shouted, "We are not a cult, you fool! Generations have come and gone, people marrying, having children, working and worrying, all the while waiting—waiting for the one. Waiting for the signs of the beginning of the BloodFire Redemption, the Healer. They have lived and died wondering if it had happened yet, even as we are hunted down like dogs. Was the child born? That question is our hope. We are down to only a handful now at the end of the twentieth century. Without us, the Chronicles are lost. Laurel here is the last generation, willing to stake her life on the Sanctuary and all that it gives to us." Jonathan's voice echoed deep into the darkness of the passage behind the chamber.

Laurel stepped between them and faced Gideon. "If there is no Sacrament child, no Sanctuary, no witnesses, then why are you here, able to heal with your blood? You are the proof that the Redemption is real. Think of it, Gideon. You are part of the next chapter in the Sanctuary Chronicles."

She held up her hand to stop Gideon's protestations. "The blood is the life, and the life is the blood."

Gideon pressed on his eyes with the tips of his fingers. "Why haven't I ever heard about any of this before?" he asked. "If it is so wonderful, why don't more people believe it? Wouldn't these so-called signs be in some world religion or studied by scientists and philosophers? If it can change the world, why not broadcast it to everybody? If I can help someone, okay, I will. But it's no miracle. I'm no sign."

Jonathan stepped close. "What do you think would happen to you if you started healing people left and right?"

Gideon could feel the warmth of the man's breath across his face. "I suppose I could help a lot of people."

"Oh yes, you could help. How many?" Jonathan held up both hands with his fingers splayed. "This many? How much blood does it take? If you healed only one person a day, how long do you think it would be before you would have thousands and then millions standing at your door, demanding that they be next? How much poking and prodding do you think medical scientists will want to do? What will you do when people proclaim that you are the Messiah, or start to worship you, or revile you as some charlatan leading people astray? And when do you get around to honoring the BloodFire Protocol?"

"What if I don't believe any of this mumbo jumbo, hocus-pocus?"

"What if you don't?" Jonathan threw the words back in his face. "Whether you believe or not, those people were still butchered. Somebody else out there *does* believe, and they want to stop it. And make no mistake, they wanted to make damn sure you knew it."

Gideon stepped back, shaken by the import of Jonathan's words. The more he thought about it, the angrier he became. "I've told you, I had nothing to do with those people dying. And come to think of it, how am I supposed to believe a cripple and a rookie 'Guardian' are going to protect me from people who don't hesitate for a second to slit the throat of a little girl and butcher anyone else who gets in their way? All over some demented belief about a Sanctuary and a BloodFire Redemption and some kid being born who might change things but then again might not?"

Laurel laid a cool hand over Gideon's arm. "We didn't know for certain who you were on that mountain, Gideon. If we did, we could have been a little better prepared, and maybe those people would not have died. Don't think that we don't know that."

Gideon tried to gather his thoughts while the anger drained away under her touch. "I'm sorry, I didn't mean that the way it came out. You have to admit, though, that this whole scenario that you two have laid out is way, way beyond belief."

"Give it some time, Gideon. That little girl *did* get well. Let yourself believe that much," she said, not unkindly.

"Being angry with each other won't solve anything," Jonathan admitted. "Forgive me, but there is so much you need to know, apparently, and I've tried to tell it to you all at once. Adam could explain so well, make it all come alive, make me see the wonder and the truth of it all. I can't do what he did. Are you sure your life was not meant for this? Is there anything in your life that foretold, that prepared you for this moment? No signs? No strange happenings?"

"Like today, you mean?"

Jonathan laughed. "Yes, like today. Except maybe not quite as dramatic as being shot at, watching a wild 'cripple' on his souped-up tricycle take on a high-powered rifle and a four-by-four truck, and being told you're in possession of a mysterious and wonderful power?"

Gideon allowed himself a smile. "No, I can't think of anything. Believe me, I would never have come here if they had, except for JP." He took a deep breath, making a decision. "No offense, but I don't want anything to do with it." He couldn't force himself to look Laurel in the eye, as badly as he wanted to do nothing more at that moment. "I appreciate you two saving me, but the rest of this is just so much religious BS. Whoever is out there wants me to go away, stop giving out blood, or whatever is happening. I'm more than happy to oblige. All that you've told me sounds like one more pitiful religion that's making people hate and kill. There's nothing new in that. You can keep your Sanctuary and your BloodFire. Live and let live. Religion didn't stop a car on a foggy road. Faith didn't spare a beautiful woman. No one's prayers saved a child waiting to be born from being ripped …" A spasm of grief gripped his throat in a choking sob.

Their questioning looks spurred him into action. He stood up and began to rummage around, making sure he had everything he needed before making good his escape. He patted his back left pocket to see if his wallet was there. Laurel handed him the keys to his car. Gideon pulled his bloody handkerchief from the front left pocket of his jeans. Something hit the floor of the cave with a metallic clink.

Jonathan picked up a small gold object on a chain and handed it to him.

"What's that?" Laurel asked.

"I don't know." Gideon frowned. Then he remembered. "Oh. That little girl gave it to me. She said that I needed it."

"Do you recognize it?" asked Laurel, stepping closer to look.

Gideon handed it over. "No."

"There's some writing on it. I can't quite make it out though."

Gideon took it back and went over to one of the lanterns, hoping that the others could not tell that his heart was in his throat. He saw Laurel and Jonathan exchange a look he could not decipher. "I'll try out in the natural light," he said in a guarded tone.

They followed him into the sunlight. Gideon studied the charm for a long moment, unable to speak.

"Well," Laurel said impatiently. "What does it say?"

Gideon tried hard to sound calm. Feeling like someone had slugged him in the stomach, he checked one more time, willing it to be different. But it wasn't.

"'E, wait under the willow, near the root. J.'" He blinked repeatedly in the brightness.

Jonathan laid a hand on his shoulder. "Does that mean anything?" he asked gently.

Gideon nodded, tears welling in his eyes, an ache from long ago rekindled.

"Yes," he whispered. "I recognize it. My father gave it to my mother the night before he left. We never saw him again." He hesitated, overcome with the incredulity of the find. "She was wearing it when I buried her."

Chapter 8

The smell. The few times that I've traveled on planes, it has suddenly turned my gut into knots. Or when the beeper I used to wear as a volunteer fireman summoned me on summer nights to some grisly accident, and the suffocating smell of burning gasoline and oil mixed with blood, shattered flesh, and palpable fear hung in the humid air like a cloying, gagging fog. Other times, I would simply be crawling around under the house, chipping away at the earth, or lying on my back, coaxing a few more miles out of the old Chevy, and it would hit me out of the blue—suddenly I'd be a kid again, a terrified little boy.

That unforgettable smell. A devil's brew of jungle rot, kerosene jet fuel, and mothballs. All combined with the scent of Old Spice that my father always wore, even during a sweaty, nail-biting, gut-churning bombing run over some small factory in North Vietnam, juking and jinking his fighter bomber around like a child's toy to evade the surface-to-air missiles that guarded the mission targets over North Vietnam.

He had written home that "jet jockeys" weren't supposed to wear anything other than body odor, not even deodorant, when flying over enemy territory. The odor was too easy for nationals to track if a pilot bailed. But he always bragged that nothing like that would happen to him. So he dumped half a bottle of Old Spice on before each bombing run, daring the rocket-fueled arrows streaking upward from the jungle to try to bring him down. It was personal with him, a combat pilot's worst mistake—the one that finally caught up with him. I shivered with fright and horror every time my twelve-year-old mind imagined him clawing at his oxygen mask while his plane spun apart in flames until the jungle swallowed him beneath its impassive canopy.

His footlocker sat in the middle of our living room at the air force base housing unit for months. And that smell permeated the entire house—clinging to the furniture, the walls, our clothes, until I began to taste it even in my food. My mother absolutely forbade me to touch the corroded chest. I figured it held all of his earthly belongings. He had been away from home more than he lived with us, so nothing around the standard-issue air force housing unit actually felt like his. Or ours, for that matter.

But the footlocker, that was his. I spent hours at night lying in my bed trying to picture what it contained. I imagined a couple of menacing, well-oiled pistols; a bloodstained leather flight jacket; his flight suit and his dress uniform; letters from Mom; some medals and his helmet, covered with rotted jungle vegetation. And, of course, a half-empty bottle of Old Spice.

Eli Marks dropped the dogeared tablet he'd inexplicably brought with him on top of the shoebox that held the despicable gift. He had no idea what the disfigured doll was supposed to mean. He had hustled back to the nurse's station, trying to catch up with the unit clerk to demand more information about the package. When he arrived at the unit, the woman was nowhere to be found. A nurse told him it wasn't her job to keep track of the clerk's breaks but to wait a few minutes, she should be right back.

Eli decided to pass the remaining time reading over his labored efforts to write. He reread the paragraphs about his father's death. As a boy, his world had been irreparably shattered. Writing about it over the past few months forced him to relive the agony over and over again. It was an unfinished piece.

"Write what you know," Jenn said when she proudly presented him with the tablet and new pens. "We'll save up for a computer, but for now, you can use these. Use a piece of coal and the back of a shovel if you have to." She'd grinned, ever optimistic, willing him to find a spark of enthusiasm.

He'd been trying. He caught the writing bug a long time ago, but actually putting thought and feeling to paper proved to be a difficult challenge.

"If you want to be a writer, then write!" Jenn kept telling him.

On the way to McConnell's Mill he'd just about jumped out of his skin, waiting for her to read his fumbling attempts scrawled across the pages, the product of much torturous effort. His wife was crying when she finished. "It's good, Eli. Keep on doing it, okay?"

He nodded as he steered the car into the parking lot at the top of the trail that plunged into the ravine where the old mill waited …

"Mr. Marks? They told me you were here. I've been wanting to talk to you."

Eli ignored the voice. His back and legs throbbed. Every time he replayed the scenes from the mill, his physical pain worsened. *It must be my punishment*, he decided. The acceptance did not lessen the pain, and he groaned.

"Mr. Marks? Are you all right?"

The questioner took a step toward him. Eli involuntarily backed away without looking up.

"Please, I want to help. They told me you were a chaplain too and asked me if I would support you and stand with you." The ingratiating voice was too smooth, the words sounding practiced and automatic, the empathy remote. "I know this must be a terrible decision for you, but I think the choice is clear."

Eli's head came up. "What decision?"

A short, round man, the folds of his chin resting on a soiled Roman collar, leaned toward Eli, the unrelenting glare of the lights reflecting off his shiny dome. The dandruff-dusted shoulders of his tweed sport coat rose in alarm. "Dr. Tournier hasn't spoken to you?"

"About what?"

"Oh my, I thought he'd been here already."

Eli didn't bother to try to hide his distaste for the man's demeanor. "Who's Dr. Tournier? What does he want?"

As if on cue, the elevator chimed, and a slight man with skin the color of milk chocolate stepped out holding a medical chart. He strode purposefully across the hall, his white lab coat billowing behind, and nodded to the chaplain.

"Chaplain Baker, Mr. Marks, I apologize for my tardiness," the doctor said with the soft lilt of a West Indies breeze. "Let's talk in her room." He abruptly spun on his heels and headed for Jenn's glass-walled cubicle.

"The Reverend Doctor Whitimer Baker." The chaplain belatedly introduced himself, reaching across his belly to shake Eli's hand as they tagged along behind the doctor. The cleric's hand was moist with sweat, Eli noted absently.

"What's going on?" he demanded as they gathered around Jenn's bed, the ventilator's wheeze marking time in the stale air. "What's he talking about?" Eli motioned toward the perspiring chaplain, who positioned himself beside the doctor.

"I'm Dr. Tournier. I'm sorry that we did not have the opportunity to speak earlier. The nurse told me that you went home for some rest. That is good. Your wife is being taken care of. I know that you want to be near her, but it is likely that she knows that you are here, and I believe it keeps her from resting as well. Did you bring her some of her things?"

Eli realized that the doctor was looking at the shoebox still clutched in his left hand.

"Sometimes having familiar objects around such as pictures or her favorite hairbrush can help the patient who is in coma to relax."

"Are you saying she's waking up? Has something changed?" He looked down at Jenn. The thick hair fanned out on the pillow around her bruised face shone with fresh-washed luster. He wondered who had been kind enough to minister to her in the busy unit. A maze of wires snaked from under the blanket to blinking and beeping monitors. He put the box down. "How's the baby? Is the baby in trouble?"

"Now, now, Mr. Marks, you mustn't worry about that. The important thing is your wife's potential recovery." Chaplain Baker rubbed his hands together as he spoke.

"Potential recovery? What are you talking about?" Eli looked from one to the other. "What is he doing here, Doctor?"

Dr. Tournier flipped open the chart, ignoring the question. "Mr. Marks, your wife was stable when we brought her upstairs. There is some swelling in the brain, of course, which creates pressure. We are keeping a close watch on these matters, and we should know more in the next twenty-four hours. Your wife is young, strong and a fighter." He finished his litany with a perfunctory nod. "That will help. She is running a fever of 104. We suspect an infection somewhere, but we haven't been able to pinpoint it, probably her lungs. Her blood pressure is erratic, and she is able to breathe on her own, but I feel it is best to keep her on the respirator to help her."

"It's a miracle that she survived," added the chaplain.

Eli gave him a disgusted look before turning his attention back to the doctor. "So you're telling me she's not going make it? That I'm going to lose her and the baby? What did he mean by potential recovery?"

Dr. Tournier closed the chart and stepped to the foot of the bed. Chaplain Baker started to follow. The doctor froze him in his tracks with an icy glare. "I thought that it might be helpful to have someone to talk to," he said, turning to Eli, his eyes quickly changing to display compassion. "This is a very difficult time for you and her mother."

"Her mother? Her mother is dead."

"Perhaps another family member? A friend? I assumed she was spelling you while you were gone."

"I don't know who or what you are talking about!" Eli's eyes widened in alarm. "Was someone here with Jenn? What did she do? Who was she?"

"The nurses assumed she was family," the chastened priest grumbled. "It gets very busy in here. They can't watch everything, you know."

Eli checked the monitors, the ventilator tube, and opened the drawer of the nightstand, before protectively taking Jenn's hand in his. Nothing appeared any different than when he'd left.

Dr. Tournier held out the chart. "She is no different, Mr. Marks. The woman simply stopped in for a short visit."

"What did she look like?" The touch of Jenn's warm flesh on his did little to reassure Eli.

The doctor stepped to the doorway and summoned a nurse. A young woman with big hair, wearing the ICU uniform of a flower print top, peach slacks, and ever-present stethoscope came into the room. She shrugged at the query.

"She was elderly, thinning gray hair, short, hazel eyes." The nurse hesitated.

"What?" Eli pressed her.

"No offense, sir, but she smelled like she could stand a good bath. She was wearing a Steelers sweatshirt and red shorts over long underwear. You know, the thermal kind that you wear in winter." The woman shook her head. "She was something else. Her shoes didn't match. One looked like an old Air Jordan, and the other one was even older. It might have been a Pro Keds, you know, with the little white circle patches over the ankles. That's way before my time, but my father hung onto an old pair for forever. I remember watching her walking down the hallway and thinking, *She must have bad feet.* The toes were cut out of both shoes. My grandmother used to do that with hers because of her corns and bunions."

"What did she want? Did she say anything?" Eli clung to Jenn's hand, wishing he could never leave her alone again.

"She smiled at me, but she didn't say anything. She was carrying a package about the size of a shoebox, maybe, wrapped in brown paper."

"You sound like a shoe detective," joked the chaplain.

Eli considered showing the doll to the doctor but hesitated.

"Is that why you wanted to see me?" he asked Dr. Tournier after the doctor dismissed the nurse with a stern warning to keep closer control over visitor access to the unit.

"No. I apologize for the lax security. I'll be speaking to the head nurse about it. I wanted to review your wife's condition, Mr. Marks." He glanced at the chart once again as if to reinforce his next words. "It is my opinion that it would be best if we take the baby."

"Take the baby? You mean abort it?"

Dr. Tournier nodded. "Your wife's condition is critical. We need to get her blood pressure stable, and her brain waves are a bit erratic. The longer it goes on, the more of a threat it poses."

"Threat? Do you mean the baby or her blood pressure, the brain waves?"

"All of those."

"Will Jenn die if the pregnancy continues?"

The doctor looked away, and the chaplain rocked back and forth on his heels.

"Well?"

"As I said, her condition is critical. To give her the best chance, we need to take the baby."

"Will she wake up then?"

"I don't know. It is not something that we can readily predict."

Eli's mind raced. "If she doesn't wake up and we let the baby go on, will it be possible to keep it?"

"It has been done, but I don't advise it, Mr. Marks. I doubt if your wife could survive."

"But can you tell me if she will wake up? If I let you abort the baby and she never comes back, then I've lost them both." He tried desperately to get a handle on the decision. His tired mind ran around and around in circles. "It's been two days, Doctor. Is the pregnancy a threat to her recovery right now?"

"She is critical."

"Why can't you give me an answer? Can't you just be straight with me? Is my wife dying? If she is, will taking the baby save her? If not, can the baby be saved? Just answer the damn question!"

"There now, Mr. Marks!" The Reverend Doctor Chaplain Baker sprang to life like a windup doll, his face an indignant mask. Dr. Tournier stopped him with a raised hand, and his spring abruptly wound down.

"Her best chance is to take the baby."

Eli held Jenn's hand to his cheek. "Can I have some time? I need to think about it."

"I'll need to know soon. If it goes on like this much longer, things will become difficult."

Eli kept his eyes on the sheet over Jenn's battered form. "We passed difficult a long time ago, Doctor."

To his relief, the chaplain left with the doctor. Eli slid his hand under the sheet and onto her belly. In there. In there was the life they'd made together. "Jenn, I need you. I need your laughter, your sense of adventure. I need your touch. Tell me what to do."

Laying his forehead against her hip, Eli tried not to think about anything, but it was an impossible effort. After a moment, he stood and began pacing the room. He resisted the urge to start pulling out all the tubes and wires that wedded his wife to the ghastly machines. How often he had walked into similar rooms in his role as chaplain, marveling at the technology that held back the despair of fearful family members. He would listen to their recitations of medical dogma and belief in the strength of the struggling spirit of their loved one, then encourage them to see it all as God's hand working. Now, the lights and the muted gasps and mechanical noise mocked his aloneness, his emptiness. Jenn was the one who kept hope alive in him as the greedy pain eroded his own spirit day by day.

His foot struck something under the bed. He knelt to retrieve the box. He lifted the lid for one more look before pitching it into the garbage. Grasping the pen barrel, Eli twisted and pulled at it, determined to erase the image of mock suffering. It slipped from his hold and clattered to the floor. A piece of paper fluttered on a draft. He caught it in midair.

Blue ink in childlike scrawl admonished, "Find the Healr. Sav the baby."

Chapter 9

The damn car wouldn't start. The time with Jenn had not been much of a visit, and Eli took his frustration out on the steering wheel and dashboard, using the doll as his weapon of choice. The head shattered into three pieces, one lodging in the broken tape deck. A leg flew off, scoring a direct hit on his own eye, further enraging him.

Eli slammed the car door and gave it a hard kick. The shock wave traveled through his hip and up his spine faster than a bullet. The baby. He could picture the baby. Not a pink, chubby-cheeked, swaddled cherub but the outrageously oversized head and unblinking eyes of a fetus that was more like a supermarket tabloid rendition of an alien secreted away in the basement of the White House, with webbed fingers and toes, and tiny red threads for veins apparent through translucent skin. It only added to his sense of helplessness.

What kind of a trade was this? He'd killed that poor guy's wife and nearly born son, and now he had to choose which of his own got to die—the fetus in a few days, or possibly Jenn. It sounded like the baby would not make it either way. Why was he hesitating? But what if Jenn never awakened? Maybe the baby could make it before she ... didn't. He wouldn't have the chance to explain to either one what made him choose for or against them.

The cool night air did little to soothe him as he headed for the bus stop. Crumbling nineteenth-century row houses and an adult triple X theater faced a small park where scattered plantings of mums and withered impatiens struggled to maintain a beachhead against the virus of urban despair. A large black man in a green army jacket and navy blue ski cap approached the corner and sat next to Eli on the bench.

"You're being followed," the man said in a low growl.

"Excuse me?" Eli breathed through his mouth, trying to avoid the horrible stench that permeated the three-sided bus stop shelter. Rivulets of sweat ran down the round face that expanded and contracted with the man's labored breathing.

"He doesn't know that I know. It looks like they only sent one." The man stared straight ahead.

"I think you have me mistaken for someone else," Eli said as he stood and took a step away from the bench.

"I know about you eatin' cookies and drinking champagne in your basement with the pretty missus." His lips curled into a tiny smirk.

"What are you talking about?" Eli faced the seated figure, fists clenched. "Who are you?"

The smirk broadened into bemusement. "I'm Paraclete."

Before Eli could respond, a Port Authority bus chugged up the slope from the river. He reluctantly followed the man into the gasping behemoth. The driver rolled his eyes as the odor enveloped him. An old woman nodded off in the front seat.

"Here you go. Sit back here, Godman!" His dark eyes darted around as though searching for a seat. Except for the three of them and the driver, the bus was empty.

"Come on, sit yourself down now." His voice didn't sound angry, just loud.

Eli slipped into a seat halfway back. To his chagrin, his uninvited companion sat beside him.

"Next stop, Brighton Heights!" he called out.

The old lady stirred but didn't open her eyes.

"It's you and me, brother." His breath smelled awful, a mixture of garlic, cheap wine, and vomit. Eli turned away to look at the ugly tenements and sad-looking churches occupying the neighborhoods on the north side of the Allegheny. The bus swung onto Ohio River Boulevard in a cloud of fumes.

"McKees Rocks Bridge! Then Avalon! All out for Avalon!" He chanted like a conductor on a train. He leaned against Eli's shoulder. "They hate it when I call out the stops. People don't want to be reminded of where they goin'."

Eli let out a sigh of disgust. "You forgot Bellevue."

He slapped his knee, cackling through yellowed teeth. "You're right, you're right. They'll just have to pay attention if they want to get off there."

"Why do you call yourself Paraclete?"

The boisterous conductor shouted, "Ben Avon!" to the empty seats before furrowing his brow in concentration. Off to their left, the Ohio River surged northward, glinting dully in the moonlight.

"Watch out for those stars!" Eli's enigmatic companion called to the black shape of an airliner passing over the chemical plants on Neville Island, its navigation lights blinking in a pale imitation of the stars as it made its final approach to Pittsburgh Airport off to the northwest, somewhere beyond the tree-covered hill where USAir Flight 427 slammed into the ground back in '94.

"Universe! Next stop the God almighty universe!"

The bus driver turned in his seat. "Shut up!"

The raucous announcements stopped, but Eli's question remained unanswered. In another few minutes, he recognized the outskirts of Sewickley. Huge houses built by the early steel barons as summer homes stood protected by equally grand trees. The bus pulled off the boulevard to wind through its narrow streets. Small shops crowded a quaint-looking business district.

"Do you know your destination?" the man asked him. He stood. "I have to get off here. They need to know." He leaned closer. "The Sanctuary Guardians will find you, okay?"

"What?" Eli had to crane his neck to look up at the towering shadow.

"Your stop, man. You gotta know where you came from and where you goin'."

"Wait a second. You didn't tell me about Paraclete and who's following me—supposedly."

Dark eyes bored through Eli. "We're all looking for it. We all want sanctuary, man."

The bus stopped, and before he slipped off into the night, he shouted at Eli, "Watch your back, Godman. Watch your goddamned back!"

"I'm going across the bridge, buddy," the driver yelled, looking at him in the big mirror over the windshield after he pulled back onto the boulevard.

"Just drop me by the library in Bridetown." With a start, Eli realized that the old woman was gone. He couldn't remember her getting off. What was her stop? he wondered.

Maplewood Street glowed eerily with golden hues from the streetlights backlighting the gilded maple leaves of the Pennsylvania autumn. The library stood dark and empty on the corner, a pedestrian marble and concrete monument rising to his left, the attempt of yet one more long-ago steel baron to create a legacy befitting the divine right to accumulate wealth on the cheap, backbreaking labor of others.

Beyond the library, the bridge loomed high above the river. The crisscrossed girders and beams of the aging structure formed sharp angles, rising in awkward curves capped by peeling spires, framing a narrow channel of concrete. Eli looked at the bridge, then toward the shadowy canopy of the maple leaves. Neither of the choices felt much like an invitation.

Whether it was fate, or the gods, or the collective hopes of unborn generations, he turned away from the path that would lead him back to the empty house. Instead, he took a few tentative steps toward the bridge, the solid edifice of the library impassively monitoring his journey. His left leg tingled from the injured nerves, starting in his spine and then dancing up and down his leg, wave after wave, growing in intensity as though some insane scientist were experimenting with how much voltage the human body could endure. He ruefully noted how the technological finesse of the morphine pump muted the noise of the pain but did not erase its footprints or the fresh impact of scarring on nerves. It was like an echo being muffled. It was still real noise, only less focused.

Somehow, time had gotten away from him. Without looking at his watch, he knew it was after midnight. The thought that he had been standing on the corner for over an hour frightened him. How could it be more than a few seconds? The wild thought crossed his mind of wishing for the strange Paraclete to appear once more to announce the destination. Maybe then he could get his bearings. Maybe.

Eli kept walking. As many times as he had been near the river, he still expected it to make some grand and mighty noise. His mind conjured up the sound and fury of the raging water at the old mill. A garbage truck roared past, setting off a chain reaction of motion that set the deck to swaying beneath his feet. It felt like the beast was rousing itself. It was bad enough that he hated heights.

A third of the way across, he stopped, gripped the rusted railing, and ventured a look down. The river slid by forty feet below with a mere whisper. Maybe he was too high. Maybe there was too much background noise.

This past year had stayed too long. Every day inched by, weighted down with dread and frustration, his guilt and sense of hopelessness. How could he be driving to work one day, running through the list of those he was to comfort and assure, and in the next moment, the lives of a woman and her unborn child were snuffed out, and his own life shattered? What had become of her husband who lost it all that night? Eli knew that the man worked for the same hospital, but in the struggle to recover from his injuries, he'd not been able to seek out that man … and say what to him?

He didn't know exactly how it happened. No specific thought challenged. No angel spoke, no thunder clapped, no demon threatened. One moment, he had a fragile hold on his faith, his beliefs that had guided him through the years. The next moment, he did not. One moment, he was staring at the swift flow of the current that was always there but never the same. The next moment, he was part of it yet oddly detached, looking at himself standing there gazing over the rail, a worn and beaten-down man fresh out of faith. One moment he was the Reverend Eli Jon Marks, battered and struggling against the drag of his pain and fear and emptiness. The next moment, he was immersed in an overwhelming sense of clarity, looking at the man wearing the skin of Eli Marks, realizing in an instant that meaning was up to him. What door had he just stepped through? He let go of the railing and looked down without feeling dizzy.

Eli shook his head. Ever since he'd stepped onto that bus near the hospital, it felt as though time was speeding up now, suddenly pushing him ahead of itself toward some unseen, unknown destination. Through all the agonizing hours of physical therapy, he'd clung to faith, calling out to the Almighty countless times for strength. Now, the river carried it away, and he let it go, wondering at his lack of remorse.

The hairs on the back of his neck stood on end. Someone was watching him from behind one of the girders. Slowly he swiveled his head and came face-to-face with a bizarre apparition.

Black high-top sneakers, each one with a hole cut out to expose the big toes, were held together with fluorescent pink laces. Bright orange stockings covered spindly legs. Baggy red satin boxing trunks stretched over a small potbelly. A yellow sweatshirt with "Pittsburgh Stillers" printed across the chest completed the ensemble. Eli's eyes rose higher, his heart in his throat.

Outlandish pink rouge formed two perfectly round spots on her cheekbones. Flashy red lipstick and a heavily powdered nose and forehead completed the effect. Eli guessed that she was in her early seventies.

As their eyes met, she pushed hair the same color as the wild stockings away from her cheeks with both hands and tucked it into the collar of the sweatshirt. Something about her eyes threw Eli. They didn't match. In the light from the bridge's streetlamps, he could see that one was darting around as she studied him closely. The other never moved. It was bright blue with an odd blemish running diagonally across the iris.

"I forget things." A quiet, childlike tone made her appearance more unsettling.

"Excuse me?" That strange eye fascinated him.

She took a step closer. "I forget things, but today I remember my name. Pearl. Cracked Pearl." She held out her hand.

"Uh, well ..." Eli shook his head, thinking that perhaps he was too far over the edge now to make any sense out of this specter.

She patiently waited, her hand extended. "Don't stay up here too long."

"Cracked Pearl?" he managed to get out.

She nodded, a frightened expression on her face. "They'll make you move or take you to jail."

"What?"

"I forget things, but don't stay on the bridge. Adam said not to let them see where we live."

He took her hand. It was warm, her grip strong. "Did you say your name is Cracked Pearl?"

She giggled and pointed to her blue eye. "I have a glass eye. It fell out once and cracked. My friends call me Cracked Pearl."

Eli smiled. "Nice to meet you, Pearl. I'm Eli. You're supposed to keep some secret for somebody named Adam?"

She nodded sagely. "You're one of us. They don't like us to stay on the bridge. Think we're going to steal it or something." She let out a hearty laugh at this absurdity.

"Mi casa es su casa. That's Spanish. I used to be a teacher, but I forget things." Her tone became more somber at this revelation.

"You taught Spanish? Where?"

"I don't remember. No, I taught Latin. Latin is …" She wrinkled her brow, then pounded one fist into her palm. "Damn, I forgot. I hate when I forget. Don't tell them I know Latin, okay?"

"Don't tell who?"

"The trackers."

Eli considered the possibility that she might be part of some thief's ruse, but the sincerity of her voice belied that cynical appraisal. "That's okay, Pearl. Where do you live?"

"The tunnels. Adam called them our sanctuary. Do you have a home?"

"No, I don't." Was he letting it slip away along with his faith?

"You can come with me … Eli. That's right, isn't it?"

"That's exactly right," he said, then added, "Cracked Pearl."

She smiled. "You must know me. You called me Cracked Pearl." She picked up a brown bag that sat on the ground behind her. "This is Peter. Do you remember Peter?"

"No, I'm sorry, I don't."

He gasped when Pearl pulled an object out of the bag. It was a doll with a plastic head that matched the one he'd smashed. The cloth body had cotton stuffing poking out of every seam and a serious coating of dirt and grime.

"Peter goes with me everywhere. I have to take care of him. I don't forget him."

"That's good." Eli started back toward the Bridetown end of the bridge. He heard her high-tops slapping against the concrete behind me.

"Wait!"

Eli stopped and turned to face her. Her little potbelly bounced up and down, and her hair flew out in all directions as she hurried toward him, orange toes pointing the way.

"Do you know who I am?" she asked, the corners of her mouth twisting inward.

"Sure," he told her. "You're Cracked Pearl."

She smiled. "You must be a friend. You know my name. Do you know where I left my bike?"

"What bike? I didn't see you with a bike, Pearl."

"Oh dear. That's Peter's bike. Maybe it's in the hole. Are you the Healer?"

Eli stared at her, stunned. "No. Who is the Healer? A doctor?"

"Who are you?" she asked, her agitation increasing. "Are you the one who got the message? I had Angela deliver it."

"Angela? Who's Angela?"

She held out the battered doll. "Peter's friend. Don't you know her?" Her voice rose in a small child's urgent pleading. "She helps me dress."

THE HEALER

Eli suppressed the urge to grab her by the shoulders and shake her while he screamed his demand for an explanation. "Pearl, tell me about the message," he said with as much patience as he could summon.

The confused figure shook her head. "Paraclete rode to the city with me and Angela. I put the pretty necklace on her." She smiled. "Adam gave it to me. I remember that."

Eli racked his brain for some idea of how to make sense out of her words. "Adam gave your friend Angela something? A necklace? Is this it?" He dangled the friendship charm from the fingers of his right hand.

She smiled and clapped her hands. "She did it! Where is she?" Pearl craned her neck, trying to see behind Eli in the gloom.

Eli lowered his eyes, fumbling for words. "She didn't make it, Pearl."

"Did they get her?" she demanded, fear writ large beneath the layers of garish makeup. "Where is my Angela?"

Eli slowly put the fragments of the story together, wishing it could be done with the doll, as well. "Did you take Angela to Pittsburgh for a special reason? Was she supposed to go to the hospital with a message?"

Her brow furrowed. "I don't remember for sure."

"Pearl, remember! It's important."

"That's what Adam said. I remember that. That's good, isn't it?"

Eli sighed. There was no rushing her. "Is there someone else who knows about Angela? Is Adam around here somewhere?"

"Oh no, Adam went away. He's very—" She cut herself off abruptly. Eli held the yarn necklace up to her face.

"Pearl, what about this?"

She roughly pushed his hand away, looking over his shoulder, eyes wide with fright. "No! They mustn't see it."

Eli glanced behind him. Light from the streetlamps reflected dully from the black paint of a police cruiser parked in the shadows near the library. His stomach turned over. What was this all about?

By the time he turned back around, Pearl was already walking away, her ethereal silhouette receding through the patches of gray and pitch made by the girders. Eli tried to follow, hobbled by the effects of the cold concrete on his back and legs.

"Pearl, wait!" he hissed.

She turned, and he could see the tracks of tears through the rouge. "Find Jeremiah on Fourteenth. He knows. He's behind the flower store. Jeremiah liked Angela."

"Pearl, I'll give the necklace to my wife, Jenn."

"Jenn? You know Jenn?" She swiped at her eyes. "What's your name?"

"I'm Eli, remember? Is this for Jenn?" He cradled the necklace in a palm shaking from exertion and a growing, nameless dread. "Why did you give it to her?"

"She said it was time."

"What?"

"Jenn told me to show it to you. She knows it's not for her. It's for you. She said you needed it."

"How do you know my wife? She's in a coma in the hospital, Pearl."

"I know. The water really scared her." Eyes wide open in fear.

Eli held the charm to his chest, where he could feel his heart hammering, as Pearl continued, "The water took her over the dam. She screamed. She doesn't know if the little girl is okay."

"Did you read that in the newspaper?"

"No. I don't read anymore," she said in a voice filled with sadness.

"How do you know what happened, Pearl?"

"She told me. Jenn is very nice. She likes Peter, and she likes you a lot."

"How long have you known Jenn?"

Pearl shrugged. "I don't remember. Jeremiah said to listen to her. Adam wanted us to do it."

Eli leaned against a beam for support. "I don't understand, Pearl."

Pearl giggled. "She knows where the pretty ring is hiding under the hat. She can't wait to get it."

Eli lunged at her, grabbing her by the arm. She tried to pull away, but his grip tightened, his words coming in a menacing growl. "How do you know this? Tell me, old woman! Who are you? How do you know my wife?"

"Stop it! You're hurting me," Pearl cried out in pain.

"Please, tell me," Eli begged, letting her go without apology.

"She told me. She talks to me. She's alone and afraid, and I'm her friend." Pearl pointed to her head. "I hear her, in here. She says the Healer must save the baby. He has the blood gift. Find him before it's too late."

With that, she turned and fled into the night.

Chapter 10

In the heat of the afternoon, a smoky blue haze hovered over the red and gold slopes of the small valley to the west of the magnificent Shenandoah. Gideon sat on an outcropping above and to the north of the cave. Barely visible on the mist-shrouded mountain across the valley, he tried to pick out the spot where, in what seemed an eternity ago to him at this moment, he'd clung to the mountain for his life. Could it be only twenty-four hours?

His finger traced the jagged edge of the broken-heart charm, over and over, as though by sheer repetition he could smooth the sharp peaks. Only something hard and abrasive could do the job, he knew. But the feel of it on his finger brought back the memories of that night when his father scooped him up into his arms, smelling fresh-mown hay and his mother's perfume ... and of fear. A three-year-old couldn't name it, but Gideon knew with a child's certain dread that the edge of sour essence he detected that night betrayed his heroic vision of the father who could never be felled, never fail, never let his family come to harm. His mother's sudden and inexplicable death ten years later pushed him the rest of the way across the treacherous threshold from childhood to manhood.

"Gideon?" Laurel slipped through the stand of scrub pine, Steeler hat reversed over hair that rode the breeze, her denim shirt and tan jeans displaying her desirable contours.

Damn, she gets to me, Gideon noted silently.

Laurel took a seat beside him. "You've been up here for over an hour. We have to make a decision. I know you need some time and space to deal with all that's crashing down on you, but do you want to talk? It might help."

Gideon caught a glimpse of the sunlight highlighting the tiny golden hairs along the curve of her jaw. He tried to resist the longing that rose unbidden, but the effort only served to make him sound angry.

"What should I talk about? A grave robber? A coward of a father who ran away from his responsibility?"

"What does the inscription mean? Maybe it's a sign. Maybe it's showing you what you are to do." Her clear eyes reflected the certainty in her voice. "Maybe it was meant for you too—a message from your father to you."

"How can you have such confidence? I was only three. What would it have meant? Be a man and run out on your family?"

"Because I believe," Laurel answered. "I believe you are a sign."

"From where? God? The force? The Twilight Zone? Bridetown?"

Laurel frowned. Gideon explained, "That's the last place I had a mailing address."

She leaned back on her elbows and waited for him to keep talking.

"I know what you're doing. I'm not stupid." Gideon copied her posture, feeling childish about his determination not to give in to her. He watched a hawk riding the updrafts, first on one side of the narrow vale, then the other. He bit his lip, his sense of her a feeling bordering on pain yet colored with pleasure, anticipation. He could keep silent no longer.

"JP used to say we are circling the well. We can't see the bottom, but we're sure there's water in it. Still we keep circling and circling, dying of thirst. Some say the water is bitter, yet they keep circling. Some say the water is sweet, yet they fear intoxication. Some say there is no rope and no cup, so we never could drink the water anyway. But there has always been a well and always will be."

Laurel slowly blinked. He took that as a sign that she was indeed listening. "JP always said, 'God is a verb with an indirect object.'" Gideon chuckled. "I still haven't figured that one out." He sat up, picked a pebble from the ground, and threw it over the edge toward the patchwork of harvested fields blanketing the earth below. "I don't understand. Why me? Why wasn't I killed? Why didn't they slit my throat?"

Laurel hugged her knees. "I don't know. Why is so much blood being spilled? You *were* waiting under the willow, like on the little charm."

Gideon sighed and turned to face her. "He meant that for my mother, and she did wait." He set his face in a mask of fearlessness. "What was it you believed that made you go with Jonathan? What about your family? What did they think of you running off to be one of these Guardians?" The disdain in his voice betrayed a vain attempt to disguise his own gnawing uncertainties.

A cloud passed before the sun, reflecting dull gray in her eyes. "I know that it sounds like vague, deluded, spiritual speak to you, but the Sanctuary has a real meaning. It is the origin of the BloodFire, the hope of renewal for the human spirit. Community, creativity, compassion—where would we be if we didn't have them? If the BloodFire is extinguished, the human spirit dies. If the spirit dies, we die. Eli, the human spirit is dying. The BloodFire is our last hope."

She sighed. "Those who are dying of thirst are the ones most convinced that there really is such a thing as water, to borrow your grandfather's image. When I was thirteen, my father started selling me to his friends. I ran away at fifteen, but I ended up selling myself out on the streets anyway to survive. The things I did and the crap I saw …" She shuddered, took off the cap, and shook her hair free. "It eats away at your soul. I felt like I was drowning in blackness, like I was taking it in in big gulps until my whole body was filled with it. Nothing but blackness, no light. So, no, my family doesn't enter into the picture anymore."

"Your mother?"

"She's in prison for killing the son of a bitch. If you ask me, it was too little too late. End of story."

Gideon wondered what it meant that he welcomed having her pain touch him, pushing its way into his own. He let this revelation sift through his brain for a while before speaking.

"So, is this Sanctuary a real place or just an idea, another feel-good myth?"

"The Sanctuary is not a place. It just is. Because of the Sanctuary, our world exists, and our spirits are given life and purpose in this huge and silent universe. Now, we are awaiting the birth."

"The birth?"

"Of the Sacrament child. Part of the Redemption is purification and renewal, cleansing—like a forest fire burning off the old, tired deadwood and crowded brush. In its place, new life can grow. If we don't find the child and protect her, then the witnesses will not be united, the BloodFire's journey will end, and the Redemption will be denied. That is the teaching of the Chronicles."

"Wait! I'm lost!" Gideon exclaimed. "What witnesses?"

"Okay, I'm sorry. The Sanctuary is honored by the BloodFire Protocol."

"What protocol?"

"It's about creating trust. The BloodFire Protocol are guidelines for living a life that will revitalize the human spirit."

"You mean something like the Ten Commandments?"

"Well, there's only three. Jonathan's been teaching me about them, but it takes a while. I'm not sure I've got a good handle on them yet. I'll let you decide if they're like the commandments or not. The first guide is *honor the root*, the lifeline of our birth, the Sanctuary. The second is *honor the journey*, the way of those who have gone before us, the way we live our own lives in freedom. And third, *honor the witnesses*."

Gideon held up his hands in surrender. "Whoa! Hold on. That's it? What do they mean? Jonathan sounds like some guru out of the seventies!"

"I've taught you well."

They both spun around at the sound of Jonathan's voice, so engrossed in their conversation that neither had heard his approach.

"The Sanctuary is about honoring the mystery of life." Jonathan gave a nonchalant shrug of the shoulders. "It's about the root of meaning. The BloodFire is what inspires us, or inspirits us, if you will, as a race to believe that there is some meaning to the circle of life, to wanting to drink deeply from the well of life."

"You were eavesdropping?" His pleasure at having Laurel's full attention evaporated at the prospect. "Then, what was all this about a BloodRansom? Why is this philosophy, or religion, or whatever, so frightening to them?"

"Gideon," Jonathan said, speaking his name in a way that sent a chill down Gideon's spine, "you are the proof, the first Witness. Like I tried so ineptly to explain before, your blood is the gift of the

BloodFire. It is present in you in a way like none other. Its essence is expressed in your blood and its power. The Redemption is drawing near. An entire way of life—an entire world of life—will be ending. We don't get any more chances after this one. And many will pay the price, not just us."

Gideon shook his head, still fingering the charm like a cleric with his prayer beads. "How do you know? What way of life?"

"The way of life produced by the civilizations of the last four or five millennia of human history. It is the way of domination, taking without giving back. Worth is measured in productivity. If the Ransom prevails, the journey of the BloodFire will end, and the Sanctuary dishonored, forgotten forever."

"The Sanctuary?" Gideon looked from one to the other and then at the mountains. Only the weight of the tiny talisman from the past kept him from bolting, fleeing back into his self-imposed prison.

"The Healer is the bearer of both the wonder and terror of the BloodFire. Century upon century of searching, building religious systems, creating gods that look and sound like ourselves, and the human race is right back where it started—facing emptiness. We cannot tolerate that for long, but we are frightened of the wonder and terror, the BloodFire that wants to free us and then journey on. We are distrustful of our own yearnings because we have been betrayed time after time by religions and gods that do not bother to disguise their lust for power. The Guardians are saying the Sanctuary cannot tolerate such an existence of dishonoring our root any longer. The Redemption is occurring to cleanse and release the BloodFire so the human race can begin to recreate itself."

Gideon had been watching Laurel watch Jonathan as he spoke. Her lips were slightly parted, fingers trembling, a pink tinge creeping across her cheeks. "But who makes all this happen? Do you follow all this?" he asked her, sounding abrupt and impatient.

"It makes me feel more alive than anything else ever has," she said, stretching her arms out as if to embrace the panorama in front of them.

"The followers of the old blood stories believe that we are encouraging disorder, that the societies of the world will disintegrate if people believe what we are saying. They teach the old, tired notion of a soul as an escape for us after death. But look where that has led us. The bloodtrackers are hell-bent on seeing that the witnesses never accomplish the Redemption."

"I'm still lost on that." Gideon stabbed the air with his finger. "Civilization is going to end if we don't get some new religion right?"

Laurel took hold of his sleeve and turned him to face her. "Listen to me. The Sanctuary Chronicles say that the witnesses are water, fire, and blood. You carry the blood. The FireGuide bears the witness of fire. The Sacrament child bears water. Remember the BloodFire Protocol. When the three witnesses come together in the heart of the Sanctuary, the Redemption will be complete and the BloodFire can come full circle. The cycle can begin anew elsewhere."

"What cycle?"

"Creating faith. When we honor the root, honor the journey, and honor the witnesses, then the human race will be redeemed. We will once again honor the Sanctuary from which we came, the Sanctuary of life."

"Wasn't this a Disney movie?" Gideon's sarcasm fell flat. "So how does that mean the end of the old stuff? What root? What journey? What does the Redemption mean?"

Jonathan lectured him with the satisfaction of a justified prophet. "It could be the end of the world's religions, the end of political systems, the world's economy, the end of our cherished tribal affinities and even nations as we know them. Like I tried to tell you in the cave, the Guardians are down to only a few, and the Chronicles will disappear if we do not keep them alive. But the bloodtrackers are not taking any chances. Survival is the strongest human instinct. Power, way of life, purpose, wealth—it will all be redefined. Can you understand now why we are so secretive and why they will do whatever they must to stop us?"

"You have to find the other witnesses." Gideon found Laurel's urgency unsettling.

"And just how do you propose I do that? Place an ad on the internet? You said yourself you don't know if these witness things mean death and destruction or not. What kind of outfit is this?"

"It is a new day. We will find the way." Laurel breathed the words so softly Gideon wasn't sure if he actually heard her speak or if the breeze was creating illusions in his senses. "Unfortunately, we don't have all of the stories."

"We have seen the gift though," Jonathan said, eyes half-closed.

"You're not saying I'm some kind of god, are you?" Gideon laughed. "We're all in trouble if you are."

"I said mystery, not god." Jonathan sighed, sagging on the crutches.

"Let me ask you something then." Gideon nudged one of the metal supports with the toe of his shoe. "If you believe like you say you do, why haven't you asked me for some blood?"

The other man jerked the crutch away. "Because some of us, believe it or not, are not always thinking about ourselves. Your gift isn't for my personal use to settle problems within the little universe of my life. Don't you understand anything about what we've been saying?" Jonathan waved one crutch in the air as he leaned heavily on the other. Sunlight struck the stainless steel tube, reflecting like a bolt of lightning into the shadows under the surrounding forest cover.

For a confusing second, Gideon tried to figure out how the light could make any sound, let alone the sharp crack of thunder that bounced off the sides of the valley. Laurel screamed and took a step toward Jonathan. He seemed to be struggling to hold his balance against some great wind, though the air was suddenly still. Those fierce, dark eyes held a look of terrible surprise as they strived to focus on the opposite slopes.

Gideon's mind could not make sense of the slow-motion sequence of Laurel's desperate grab at Jonathan's arm as he slowly toppled into the dust, the crutches slipping to the sides in an awkward splaying that mercifully softened the impact of his limp body on the ground. An awful moan escaped Jonathan's lips. Gideon's response caught in his throat at the sight of the dark stain that appeared in an instant on the front of Jonathan's shirt, spreading in an uneven blotch.

"Jonathan!" Laurel knelt beside the fallen man, pressing her hand against the wet scourge. "He's been shot." This last a tense announcement to Gideon. "Get down, you idiot!"

Gideon looked around uncertainly, still puzzled by the chain of events, already replaying the sequence in his mind even as the terrible realization struck like an arrow into his brain. "What?"

"Get down," she hissed, flattening herself across Jonathan's shattered breast, more anger than fear showing in her face.

"What's wrong?" he asked stupidly. "Is he okay?"

She eased off Jonathan, both of them noting his shallow breaths. His features settled into a determined composure, as though he had willfully torn off the mask of pain and terror that stormed his consciousness as he opened his mouth to speak.

"Gideon."

"Don't talk, Jonathan." Laurel tried to shush him while her eyes welled with tears.

Gideon crept to his side. "I'm here. Hang on, Jonathan. We'll get you out of here."

"It's them." Jonathan shook his head against the burbling sound that escaped with each breath.

"I know," whispered Laurel. "They tracked us quickly."

Jonathan raised one hand and feebly waved at shadows they could not see. "Stand fast, Gideon. They want the old rede …" His words dissolved in a frightful fit of coughing. Pink foam coated his lips.

Laurel drew in her breath sharply. Gideon reflexively reached across Jonathan and touched her cheek.

"The gift." Jonathan appeared to be summoning every bit of strength from deep reserves. His eyes shone fiercely, and he clutched Gideon's sleeve. "The gift. The new way … it must be … save the first bor …"

His back arched, and his face contorted in awful pain, but he refused to cry out. He turned from Gideon to look at Laurel after it had passed.

"For the Sanctuary," he murmured with a faint smile.

Before Laurel could reply, he was gone.

Chapter 11

They strained under the weight, dragging the body a few feet and then stopping, panting with fatigue and thirst, neither saying a word, stunned by Jonathan's sudden, violent end. *Would they be next?* Gideon asked himself, allowing the thought to go no further, instead focusing on the gruesome task. When they'd managed to get far enough into the trees, exhaustion overcame them both, and they flopped to the ground.

Jonathan's sightless eyes mirrored the patches of cloudless sky discernible through the canopy of leaves. Gideon sensed more than heard Laurel's quiet sobs as they leaned against an ancient oak. When the sound suddenly stopped, he looked up.

"I have to go back. We forgot his crutches." Her voice sounded jarring in the stillness.

"What? Are you crazy? The last thing he needs now are those awful things."

"He walked more surely than most people ever crawl," she shot back hotly.

Gideon sighed. He'd done it again. Made her mad without even trying. "I just meant it's too dangerous. We don't know if they are still waiting to pick off both of us or sneaking around to cut us off."

Laurel carefully brushed the dust from Jonathan's still face. The gesture touched Gideon.

"We've got to get him out of sight and then get out of here." He reluctantly forced his brain to think ahead.

"I'm supposed to be the one watching out for you." Laurel sighed. "I—I didn't expect this." Her jaw twitched, and the hand that hovered over Jonathan's face trembled slightly. "I'm not ready."

Gideon pushed away from the tree trunk, stifling the cry of pain that rose in his throat as the adrenaline drained away, reawakening the knife-twisting agony of his cracked ribs. His hand covered hers. "We owe him. I believe he knew you could do it. Ready or not, something is happening, and we're in the middle of it."

The trembling stopped. She nodded.

The sun was approaching the western ridgelines by the time they dragged Jonathan's body into a small depression under the roots of a rugged, wind-gnarled, wild sycamore. They covered him with rocks, pine needles, leaves, and dirt.

Laurel knelt beside the pitiful grave and took off her cap.

"We need to say something," Gideon said.

Laurel nodded but remained silent. Gideon looked up through the trees, searching for inspiration in the azure depths above them. "Jonathan was a man of conviction," he began, trying to distill the rapid-fire images of the past two days into a portrait of a man's certitude and character. "I've never met anyone like him before. I don't pretend to understand the source of his convictions, but I respect the man for being willing to die for them and for giving himself to what he felt was a cause bigger than his own needs or wants."

Laurel placed one last stone on the pile. "I'll miss you, Jonathan," she murmured.

After driving the battered ATV into the cave, Gideon pocketed the key and led Laurel to the car.

"Where to?" he asked as they bounced over the rutted track. When he got no answer, he glanced over. Her hands were again trembling violently, bouncing off her thighs as her panic-filled eyes searched the surrounding mountains.

"He's gone."

Gideon stopped the car. He reached out with one hand to capture hers. They pulsed like the heartbeat of a captured animal. "I know. You can make it, though. I know you can."

"Can we just sit here for a while? Please?" She was chewing her lower lip, oblivious to the small trickle of blood at the corner of her mouth.

Gideon looked around uncertainly. Every rock and shadow screamed danger at him. "Yeah, sure." He settled back against the seat.

"No, don't let go," Laurel pleaded, reaching for his hands.

He held her hand again, and for a long time they simply sat—Laurel hunched over as though trying to curl into a ball, and Gideon stretching across the seat, uncomfortable and cramping but holding onto her, determined for the first time in a long time, to his own surprise, to take care of someone else.

"You must be getting sore," she said with a weak smile. "How are your ribs?"

"I'd forgotten all about them, to tell you the truth. Too much adrenaline, I guess."

She knew he was lying for her benefit. "What do we do now?"

Gideon thought of his earlier protests to her and Jonathan about being part of any of this crazy Sanctuary nonsense. Crazy or not, somebody was extremely interested in what he did, to the point of killing those around him for reasons he could not fathom. The images of the bloodshed forced him to reluctantly admit to himself that Laurel was putting her life in danger by staying with him.

"We need to get you to a safe place." He said it without looking at her, torn by conflicting impulses.

"He didn't tell you it all."

The resignation in her voice blanketed them both like a thick fog. Gideon sighed.

"No kidding. What was it, some sort of a test?"

"We had to be sure. Surely, you can see that."

"So, what did he leave out?"

Laurel took in a deep breath, trying to gather herself for the task ahead. The light was returning to her eyes, and her hands no longer shook. "We have to go back."

"What?"

"We have to go back to the farm, your grandfather's house."

"Why? That's insane!"

"Maybe, but we have to try. We need to find some help. I don't know what else to do. Jonathan wasn't kidding when he said the Guardians are few and scattered. Jonathan didn't tell me everything, but he did let me know when we were following you—"

"You were following me? For how long?" Gideon broke in indignantly.

"For a while, okay? We knew you'd be back for the funeral. We can talk about that later. Like I was saying, when we were watching you, Jonathan said that the Chronicles told of the outcome of the Redemption, that it would either be a 'new story of stories' or the 'unleashing of our own plagues.'"

"What's that supposed to mean?"

Laurel twisted in the seat to face him. "That's just it. He had an idea, but he said only the FireGuide would know for sure. When I asked him why"—she rushed on, stopping any protests—"when I asked why, he said, 'The seeds are sown in the old blood story.' I thought he meant something about bloodline."

Gideon shook his head. "Why am I not surprised that it would only get more confusing!"

He shrugged. "If you're counting on me, then you've picked the wrong horse to bet on. My bloodline is my grandfather, who raised me after my mother died, before he withered away from Alzheimer's. Why wasn't there a healer when *he* needed one?"

"What about your father?"

"What about him?" Gideon asked gruffly.

"Did he ever—" She interrupted herself. "The necklace. Your mother's necklace. Maybe it has something to do with her! What did you first think of when you saw it? Did it mean anything? What about the inscription?"

Gideon turned away. "I don't understand how it's still around. It was buried with her. I know that it was. But I'm certain that this is the same one."

Laurel leaned toward him. "Gideon, there was something in your eyes when you read it. I was watching you."

He rested his forehead on the window of the door. "It was nothing. Just a story my mother told me one night."

She waited a moment before asking, "Would you tell it to me?"

He did, reluctantly. When Gideon finished, he already knew what she was going to say.

"We *have* to go back. Something's there that will help us. I know there is."

And he knew she was right.

Five minutes later, they were bouncing and jolting over what could best be called a glorified cow track, which Laurel pointed out to Gideon. "What is this, Bust My Butt Boulevard?"

"I told you, they're probably watching the road. I'm starting to wonder why they know what I'm doing before I do."

"Maybe they're gone," Laurel said. "They will expect us to run like little puppies with our tails between our legs. They think they've proved to us who's in charge. They'll sit back and watch the roads, waiting for us to head out of town and lead them right to what they want." Laurel sighed. "Without Jonathan, they think we'll go into hiding somewhere far away from here. Besides, without the FireGuide, there will be no Redemption anyway."

"Why do you people use such weird names and titles? You're just people, like me. And so are those bloodtrackers out there. Murderers and butchers but human beings nonetheless. Get the police after them, for God's sake."

"This is war, Gideon. This is the final battle. Don't you get it? We are part of the Chronicles. They are as old as the human race—yes, people like you and me who have lived on this planet for millions of years. The Sanctuary is not something some hippie in the sixties pulled out of the drug-hazed air. It comes from our ancestors who figured out marriage and families and community values and morality and—and"—Laurel waved her hand, searching for words—"and why life can be so good long before any written history says humans started to civilize the world ten thousand years ago. These aren't just names someone chose because they might sound cool or mysterious. They are the answers that our generations have lost out of stupidity and pride as well as the ancient cults of the chosen ones."

Gideon looked at her wide-eyed. "I don't pretend do know what that all means. Why didn't you tell me you were a preacher?"

She hit him with the back of her hand across his shoulder. "Don't make fun of me."

He stopped kidding. "If this is a war, when do we get to fight back?"

"I don't know. I don't know what Jonathan saw in me, to tell you the truth."

"It's your passion. You are so passionate about this belief." He glanced away. "Christine was passionate."

Laurel lightly patted his shoulder where she'd struck him. "She was a lucky woman."

"No, I was the lucky one." Gideon nosed the car over the top of a ridgeline.

"What's that?" Laurel pointed to a tower of crisscrossed steel girders with strange objects that looked like huge ant eyes hanging from the top.

"Microwave transmission towers. I don't know if phone companies even use them anymore. We used to walk up here in the evenings, JP and I, to get a 'glory view' of the sunset." He looked up, noticing that the afternoon light was rapidly fading into evening. His stomach growled loudly. "JP always kept some canned peaches and beans in his fruit cellar. Maybe we can finally get something to eat."

Laurel clapped a hand to her mouth. "We left so fast I didn't grab any of our food before we got out of the area."

Gideon waved her off. "Like I said, there might be something."

"But we have to look around, Gideon. We have to find something to help us."

"There's nothing there! No way was JP or my mother mixed up in this crazy cult."

"It looks so peaceful from up here," Laurel said wistfully.

The sun was touching the tops of the opposite peaks, bathing the valley floor in rich, soft tones.

"Damn!"

"What is it?" Laurel asked.

"I must be seeing things," Gideon said, rubbing his eyes. "Did you see that?"

"See what?"

"Down there in the orchard." It felt strange to be looking down on the pastoral scene where he'd fled for his life only that morning.

"I see an old truck, probably abandoned." She pursed her lips. "Wait, that wasn't there this morning!"

"That's JP's '49 Chevy flatbed." As he spoke, smoke belched from the truck's exhaust, and it lurched into gear, heading toward the house.

"Do you think they've come back to get the bodies again?"

He shook his head. "That truck gave up the ghost the year before I left home. JP kept it around for a while for old time's sake, said it was like a member of the family. But he finally got rid of it after I left." He swallowed hard. "We used to ride into town in that thing, my mother with a scarf on to keep her hair from flying all around. JP and I must have made a hundred trips to the mountain …" His voice trailed off.

"How do you know it's the same truck?"

"I just know." The truck stopped by the house, and he sat up straighter, straining to see, a strange feeling tightening his gut. "What's he doing?"

Laurel reached under the seat and rummaged around in something. She triumphantly held up a small pair of German-made binoculars. "Will these help?"

Gideon shot her a questioning look, which she coyly ignored.

"Yeah."

"Can you see anything? Gideon, tell me, what do you see?"

He shushed her, his voice dropping to a hoarse whisper. "It can't be! I know it can't be him."

"Who? Can't be who?"

He shushed her again.

"What? You think he might hear us up here?" she asked with an acerbic laugh.

Gideon turned off the ignition and got out of the car.

"Gideon, what is it?" she demanded.

He studied the sandy-haired man who had gotten out of the truck and stood looking at the house, then silently handed the binoculars to Laurel. "What do you see?" he asked after a moment.

"I see a middle-aged guy with an old truck looking at your grandfather's house. Is he a real estate agent? Is it somebody you know?" She gave him back the binoculars.

Just as Gideon raised them to his eyes, the man stiffened. He looked at the nearest window, then turned and looked directly at the tower. Gideon felt the hair raising on the back of his neck and a strong tingling in his arms as he stared into the man's eyes. His brain realized what had happened, but he was momentarily stunned. Finally he tore his eyes away and thrust the binoculars into Laurel's hands with a terse, "Let's go."

"Why? What happened?"

"He saw us. The sunlight reflected off the lenses and into the windows. He's taking off."

Laurel scrambled back into the car. "What's going on?"

"It's him," Gideon muttered tersely as he slammed the car into gear.

"Who?"

"My father!" Gideon yelled over the roar of the engine as he floored the gas pedal. Stones and gravel shot out from the tires as they fought for traction. A cloud of dust drifted around the base of the tower behind them as the car sped down the mountain, careered around a blind curve, and headed straight toward a boulder in the middle of the road.

"Gideon!" screamed Laurel as he wrenched the wheel sharply to the left.

He didn't answer as he fought to keep the inevitable powerful forces of acceleration, mass, and gravity from seizing control of the car. The rear end fishtailed just as the car cleared the rock slide. Gideon jerked the wheel back to the right, fighting to regain the road, but the rear tires were off the berm and couldn't deliver the surge of power needed to keep control.

The car slid sideways down the slope. They both screamed in helpless terror as the tree line rushed at them in a blur.

Chapter 12

Bridetown's Fourteenth Street ran a few blocks to the north of the bridge, near Olde River Village. The village nestled on a hillock forty feet above the banks of the river, level with the bridge. In the early nineteenth century, a religious group from Europe, expecting the world to end soon, settled along the Ohio River. They lived industrious, prosperous, sex-free lives while they waited for the rapture at the return of Jesus. Now it was a state-owned tourist attraction of sorts, a relic preserved in the midst of a curio of a steel town that no longer produced steel.

Walking down Church Street, Eli fixed his course by the bell tower of the Olde River Village church. As he walked, the bells announced the late hour, a familiar sound. Jenny loved hearing them, especially late at night. Between the bells and the train whistles and the horns of towboats on the river, she said, the nights had their own mystical music. She didn't appreciate his calling it noise.

After two blocks, he reached Fourteenth Street, dark and deserted, no streetlights. The houses were old and world-weary. A wind off the river swayed the high branches, clacking them against wires and gutters. Eli stopped and looked around. Behind him loomed the big house of the village with its green shutters and the original wavy glass in the windows. The leader of the group had lived there in relative luxury, while his disciples accepted the rudiments of life in rows of lookalike simple brick cottages.

A white picket fence encased the ten-acre complex of simple nineteenth-century homes and shops, with flower and herb gardens on two sides. A higher privacy fence protected the sides that were near traffic on the boulevard. Beyond the village lay a sheer drop-off to railroad tracks, then another drop to the river. Eli looked back at the ironworks of the old Bridetown bridge, built with steel produced in the town itself in the first decade of the twentieth century. Up there, his faith had dropped away, not even making a splash in the current.

He turned full circle to face Fourteenth Street again. A movement across the street froze him. Someone dodged in and out of shadows, heading toward the upper end near Merchant and its numerous neighborhood bars and taverns. Eli considered calling out but thought better of it. The flower shop was at the opposite end of the block. He kicked himself for this childish fear of the dark.

He took a few tentative steps, foolishly hoping a porch light would appear as a beacon, wishing that the wild-looking Pearl would materialize again to guide him. An insidious chill invaded his body, setting hands to shaking and the muscles in his abdomen clenching tightly.

"Stop it, you idiot. You're a grown man." The pep talk did little to calm him.

He traveled nearly to the end of the block, and still no lights beckoned. Beyond an early 1900's brick home with rotting wooden columns holding up a bowed porch roof, a cobbled alleyway headed back from the street into pitch blackness. Voices and footsteps drew his eyes upward to the narrow, stilted balcony of a tenement.

"This must be it," he muttered, wondering again why he was there. Cracked Pearl was clearly not all there. Nobody could hear the thoughts of another person, especially not someone in a coma. The doctors couldn't even tell Eli for certain whether Jenn could hear him speaking to her.

An rumbling sound came from above, like someone roller-skating on the balcony. Unfortunately, none of the doorways faced Fourteenth, meaning there had to be a stairway to the apartments somewhere in the alley. Overflowing refuse bins lined the back of the building. Some of the garbage looked like it was moving. Eli stepped closer, only to back away in horror as in the dim light he caught sight of rats scurrying back and forth among the filth. He took another quick step back and slammed into the side of the house with a hard jolt. The charm dropped from his hand. When he bent to retrieve it, his arm brushed against a crate that teetered precariously for a moment on the edge of a barrel before it clattered to the ground. The noises overhead immediately ceased.

Eli froze. Somewhere in the darkness in front of him, a stair creaked, followed by an intense silence.

"Could you help me?" he finally croaked.

Out of the shadows came the voice of a boy. "What do you want?"

"I'm looking for someone." Eli stopped, thinking, *This is crazy. What am I doing here? But what else can I do?* "Pearl sent me. It's about my wife."

Another voice, rich with calm strength, called from above. "Is she Jennifer?"

Eli's eyes couldn't penetrate the black air, but his voice could not disguise his surprise. "Yes."

A light flicked on, and the voice commanded, "Bring him up, Toby."

A small figure stealthily emerged from the end of the alley. "I want you to know I don't believe any of it, Mister."

"Toby!" reproached the voice from above. "Get our visitor up here away from the rats."

Toby motioned for Eli to follow him up the rickety stairs. "Don't touch the railing," he cautioned. "It ain't too strong."

The rumbling sound started up again, growing louder as they approached the top. Eli was startled by the sight of what he first thought was the life-sized bust of a man sitting on an oversized skateboard. His body ended at the bottom of his torso. Eli flinched backward when the bust came to life and moved toward him.

"I'm Jeremiah," he said, extending a heavily calloused hand.

Eli pocketed the necklace before reaching out. Jeremiah's eyes followed the motion, then returned to study Eli's face.

"Eli Marks. I'm sorry to barge in on you in the middle of the night."

Long hair the hue of buckeyes accented gentle green eyes set in a strong-featured face. "That's okay. No apology necessary. We're usually up half the night waiting. Especially now."

Eli swallowed his questions, his weary body feeling twice its normal weight.

Jeremiah leaned to one side, put a hand on the wooden floor of the porch, and neatly pivoted the skateboard to face the opposite direction, propelling himself with his hands. "Let's go in. You look beat, Eli."

Inside the apartment, he tersely instructed Toby, "See if anyone's following him."

The boy nodded and slipped out. This time, Eli did not hear any creaking on the stairs.

"Following me?"

Jeremiah smiled. "You can't be too careful around here. This is my wife, Susan."

A large woman with a broad smile stepped out of the alcove kitchen. Her hand casually touched the comfortably worn furniture as she made her way across the room. A few feet in front of Eli, she stopped and held out a welcoming hand.

"You'll have to excuse me. My diabetes is taking away my sight, so I have to get pretty close to make out your face." Her smile changed to a look of concern. "What's made your eyes so full of pain, Mister …?"

"Eli, Eli Marks. It's a long story."

"Come on in and sit down, Eli. Jeremiah, the man's all done in, and you've left him standing in the middle of the room."

"Woman, we just got through the door!"

Susan stepped closer, took Eli by the elbow, and gently guided him onto the couch. A gasp of pain involuntarily escaped as he sat. The night had been too much for his back.

Jeremiah leveraged himself into a chair. "Back trouble?"

Eli nodded, waiting for the pain to let go a little and trying not to stare at the other man's truncated body. Jeremiah met his gaze with a friendly smile.

"I've never had them, so I don't miss them."

Susan jumped up. "Listen to me. The man is exhausted, and I'm prattling on. Would you like some coffee, Eli? I've got some burnt lemon pie too."

Jeremiah laughed. "Nobody passes up your pie, Suze. Eli, relax for a while. Then we can talk when you're feeling up to it."

The next half hour melded into an oasis of peacefulness and normalcy. The pie consisted of a dark, cakelike layer on top and a creamy lemon filling on the bottom. Susan was getting them third helpings when Toby came back, gliding silently through the doorway, his dark eyes betraying the tough edges of someone aged beyond his years. Jeremiah patiently listened as Eli finished telling about Jenny's rescue of the little girl and the subsequent disaster.

"And you say they have no idea if or when your wife will come out of the coma?" Susan asked with tears in her eyes. "Such a brave woman. And carrying the baby, no less."

"His wife is the one Pearl's been telling us about, Suze."

Her eyes opened wide. "You must be thrilled and blessed!" she said, in awe. "Where is Pearl?"

The reaction puzzled Eli. "She, uh, sent me here. I met her on the bridge. Then we went in opposite directions. She was pretty spooked, saying people were watching us, asking me about Petey's bike."

"She's is such a dear soul." Susan put one hand to her cheek, shaking her head sympathetically.

Eli looked from her to Jeremiah and back, hesitant to voice his questions. "She seemed a bit ..."—he fumbled for words—"well, a bit confused to me."

Jeremiah nodded. "Pearl is all heart, but her mind was damaged twenty years ago. She was a teacher in the Pittsburgh schools. Tried to break up a gang fight, and a stray bullet hit her in the head and lodged in her brain. They said it was too dangerous to try and remove it. Her memory is not good, and her perceptions of the world are childlike."

"Well, what about—I mean—she said some things." Eli didn't want to insult someone his hosts obviously cared about.

Susan closed her eyes for a moment. "Yes," she began slowly, "Pearl has a gift. We don't understand it, but we believe her. Adam told us that incredible gifts—"

"Susan!" Jeremiah abruptly cut her off.

Sparks flashed in her eyes. "Jeremiah, I trust the man." She drew herself up, indignant. "I refuse to believe someone in that much pain would not be welcome in the Sanctuary Guardians!"

Eli stared. "The what? Who are you?"

Jeremiah sighed. "We have to at least be careful, woman. They are always out there."

Eli frowned. "She has a bullet in her head, and that caused her problems? She's out of her mind, but that's a gift?"

"Adam said we were to watch for the sign of the BloodFire Redemption in the birth of the Sacrament child. The child is one of the three witnesses. Otherwise, the BloodFire cannot be liberated." Susan's eyes flashed with deep passion.

Eli rubbed his temples, trying to get the throbbing to abate. "I don't know what you're talking about. Look, all I know is that my wife is near death. The only hope, the doctors say, is to take the baby. But then this doll shows up with somebody's necklace on it. Then some old woman with a bullet in her head and not much else tells me my wife wants me to use the necklace to find somebody that can help the baby! This Pearl said that you could tell me more.

I don't know anything about any BloodFire or whatever you said. I just want to help my wife, but there isn't much time. They're going to take the baby soon." He slumped back into the couch. "I don't know why I didn't just tell them to go ahead right now."

"Because now is the time of the BloodFire. And your child is one of the witnesses." Jeremiah looked him in the eye, holding Eli's gaze for a powerful moment before smiling. "This must be very confusing to you. And coming as it does on your wife's tragedy."

Susan retrieved the coffee pot and refilled their cups. "We have waited for this moment for years. But we didn't know that the child might be born to someone who does not honor the Sanctuary." She perched her large frame on the groaning arm of the couch. "Tell us about your own pain, Eli. What is the story that brought you here?"

"I told you already about my wife."

"There's more." She said it quietly, definitely. Eli looked away.

"Suze, you're prying." Jeremiah's voice was as quiet as hers.

She gave her husband a look of resigned impatience.

"Are you people some sort of cult?" Eli asked, desperate to change the subject from himself.

Jeremiah laughed, shifting in the chair. A strange ripping sound interrupted as he started to reply. "Uh-oh, Suze, I pulled it loose again."

Susan jumped up and lifted a sewing basket down from the top of the refrigerator. "He has to wear those oversized shirts. I shorten the sleeves for him and put Velcro on the bottom. This one's just pinned right now."

Jeremiah put his hands on either armrest and boosted himself into the air, grinning mischievously. "I squirm a lot, thinking about getting my hands on you, woman."

Susan playfully tickled his torso before adjusting the material. When she was finished, Jeremiah let go of his braced position and in one motion wrapped his arms around her waist, pulling her down on the chair beside him. Jeremiah watched with envy as they kissed and looked into each other's eyes in the unspoken language of long-lived trust.

"No, we're not a cult. We're not a church, nor are we a religion. We're not some doomsday anarchists waiting for the end of the world. Just the opposite, in fact. We are Guardians of the Sanctuary. That's why the bloodtrackers of the Ransom are trying to extinguish our light."

He stopped. Eli waited for him to explain, but Jeremiah seemed to think it was self-explanatory.

"You should rest now, Eli," Susan said. "We can talk about this in the morning, Jeremiah."

Jeremiah arched one eyebrow. "I'm not so sure. You're right, we all need some rest. But the situation with the baby is urgent. Paraclete is going to tell us if the trackers try anything."

Eli leaned forward, his heart pounding against his ribs. "Try anything? Is my wife in danger? Why would anybody else care about her and the baby?" He got to his feet. "I've got to go to her. I never should have left the hospital."

"She's okay," Susan said, standing in front of him, so close he could feel her breath on his face. "Paraclete is watching her. We'll hear from him if there's any problem."

"So, you're saying you expect something to happen?" Eli took a step toward the door.

Jeremiah reached out and gripped his arm. "We think they're making a move."

"What kind of move? What happened tonight?"

Jeremiah and Susan exchanged worried glances. "We're not sure, but they're pretty agitated. Perhaps another of the gifts has appeared somewhere. Why were you on the bridge?" Jeremiah asked, still holding Eli in place.

"I just ended up there! I couldn't face going back to the house, and something drew me to the bridge. I needed to think. Things were crazy at the hospital, what with the doll and the message. The doctor said the baby had to be taken, my car broke down, this Paraclete character … How much am I supposed to take? I want Jenn back. Then Pearl shows up and says she talks to Jenn in her head, for God's sake!"

"Maybe he's a plant." Toby stepped into the light. "How do we know who this guy is?"

Jeremiah and Susan exchanged a look that Eli couldn't decipher. "We don't," Jeremiah said.

"I know all I need to know," Susan testified.

"He could betray us." Toby glared at Eli until Eli averted his eyes.

"I don't know what or who I'd could betray." Eli tried to mount a defense, unsure how he could be a threat to anyone.

"The gift of the BloodFire is precious."

Jeremiah sighed at his wife's words. "The promise of the BloodFire must be fulfilled." He swung out of the chair and onto his skateboard. "If we are ever going to fulfill the Protocol, we must protect the child. And this is the child's father. That's all we need to know."

Susan shook her head. "Your wife will be okay." She turned to Jeremiah. "We need to send for help, Jeremiah. Adam said that when the time came, we should send for Jonathan. Jonathan will know what we are to do."

Chapter 13

Eli tried to sleep. Soft light showed under the door to Jeremiah and Susan's bedroom. They had decided it would be best to get some rest before figuring out their next move. "No sense in making bad decisions from lack of sleep," Susan urged her husband. They insisted that Eli stay over, not that he was any too eager to go back out into the night or return to the empty house. As he stared at the ceiling, wondering at all the events of the last day, he could hear gentle murmurings coming from the bedroom. He could not tell if they were the sounds of lovers or of fervent prayers. It could be both.

The smell of brewing coffee awakened him. Susan peeked around the corner, saw that his eyes were open, and brought him a steaming mug. "Did I waken you?" she asked.

Eli's eye twitched at the memory of Jenn asking him that same question on cold mornings. She would be sitting beside him on the bed, pulling her robe tightly around her. He willed the rush of memory to stop and swung his legs off the couch with an involuntary groan.

"I'm sorry we didn't have a bed for you," Susan said, touching him on the shoulder.

He shook his head. "Don't worry. Every morning is like this now." He gingerly stood and stretched complaining limbs and clutching muscles, feeling the angry fire of nerve fibers that were constantly irritated, never silent or soothed.

"How does that thing work, if you don't mind my asking?" Susan pointed to his abdomen, where a small bulge showed on the lower right side of his shirt.

Eli shrugged. "It's about the size of a hockey puck. They put it under the skin and tunnel through my love handle with a catheter around to my spinal cord. The morphine drips into my spinal fluid continuously. Without it, I can't stand up straight, let alone walk or drive. The doctors tell me it delivers a fraction of what I would need orally or in shots. This way there aren't the side effects, and they can refill it every couple of months or so with a nice big needle. I haven't been able to go back to work, though, and they aren't sure if I ever will. My life will never be the same, no matter what."

"That must be difficult for you. I know how much you loved being with the patients in the hospital."

Eli's eyes narrowed. "How do you know what I did? I never said anything to you about my work."

"No, you didn't. But your wife has been quite talkative." She sighed empathically. "The two of you have been through so much. Pearl said that Jenn is very proud of you and what you've done as a chaplain, such a caring and compassionate spirit."

Eli was indignant. "I don't understand that. How can that woman know anything about what's going on in my wife's mind? That's impossible! It's—it's an invasion of privacy, for God's sake!"

Susan smiled. "If I'm not mistaken, it was your wife who started the conversation with Pearl. The BloodFire offerings are only impossible if you don't believe in gifts. I think that's why they are so rarely recognized although they are right there inside each and any of us."

"Do you mean they're some sort of miracles?" They were both perched on stools at the kitchen counter now.

"Miracles? No, miracles are notions from the BloodRansom stories. With them, they can feel like they're on the right side of things, that they are some sort of special chosen ones. That way, they can rationalize their so-called God-given right to dominate the rest of the world." She noted the puzzled expression on Eli's face and spoke again before he could interrupt. "Perhaps I should start at the beginning."

Eli held up his hand. "I need to call the hospital to check on Jenn." He managed a wry smile. "Or I guess I could just ask Pearl."

Susan chuckled. "Good. You still have your sense of humor."

"Not much of it lately, I'm afraid." He made the call, while Susan put out some fresh fruit and bagels. The nurse sounded distracted as she reported that the doctor wanted to talk to him about some test results. When Eli pushed her on it, she finally divulged that it was a test of brain activity, but that's all she would say.

"Something happen?" Susan asked when he hung up.

"I don't know. I need to get there as soon as I can though."

"The express bus stops at the library in another hour. That will give you time to eat something and go home for clean clothes."

Eli couldn't disguise his dismay. "I guess that will work." He looked at the light blue walls with patterned paper borders conveying a sense of warmth in the small apartment. He didn't want to go home. The house wasn't home without Jenn.

Susan pushed a bagel in front of him. "I thought I'd die up on the ladder, trying to get that border straight."

"How long have you been here?"

Susan sighed. "Not long enough. We've moved around a lot. The bloodtrackers are everywhere. Jeremiah has to be careful about what doctors he can trust, who's taking too much of an interest in us, that sort of thing. Half the time, we can't access his benefits for fear of someone tracing them back."

"Why can't you settle down? Did the others—Pearl, Toby, Paraclete—come with you?"

"Only Toby. The others found us after we arrived. That's the way it always is."

"What? That's the way *what* always is?"

"There are always some who are seekers of the Sanctuary, trying still to honor the BloodFire Protocol even if the rest of the population rushes on toward darkness. Guardians are few and far between. If we're all gone, I don't know what would happen if a contact occurs."

"I don't understand any more than before you started explaining." Eli dug into one of the bagels, surprised at not being able to remember the last time he'd eaten a meal other than Susan's pie. "And who's that Jonathan you were talking about last night?"

"He's a primary Guardian, trained by Adam himself. I believe he is the one on watch for the healing gift."

"The healing gift? That's what Pearl was talking about?"

"Yes, the healing gift is to appear to announce the time of the Sacrament child—your child. That will mean that the Redemption is not far off. Pearl said that Jenn knows that the baby is to be saved and that only the Healer can accomplish that."

"Even if it costs her her own life? Is it worth that?"

Susan looked at him steadily. "I can't answer that for you. But I do know that at long last the BloodFire may be able to resume the journey."

Eli banged his mug down hard. "Please, would someone tell me what this damned BloodFire and Healer and Sanctuary nonsense is all about? All I want really want to know is, is there anything you people can do for my Jenn? I'll do anything for her."

Susan didn't appear to be fazed by his outburst of frustration. "Do you like stories, Eli? They play an important role in our lives, whether we admit to it or not. We connect stories to the wonder and imagination of childhood. When we grow older, we discard that wonder and imagination; it's like we just decide to throw it away. We accept the notion everyone else is telling us that the world doesn't work that way. But I believe that sometimes the best way to hear the truth is to listen to the story. Because you must realize that what I am talking about is really something that no words can ever describe. At least not yet. Maybe after the BloodFire is fulfilled, a lot of things will be different in ways we cannot even try to imagine right now. One of the old legends says that the power comes to those who hear the word of the Sanctuary spoken aloud. But I've never heard of that happening."

She picked up an orange and began deftly peeling it. "Funny, isn't it? You with all your studying of theology and philosophy sitting here listening to me tell you a story. But that's the way of the Sanctuary. A lot of people throughout recorded history have felt or believed they had some inkling that things were going terribly wrong. Some decided it was a fatal flaw in human nature and set out to find their own path to personal salvation. People in what to most of modern civilizations would be considered primitive, or indigenous, cultures had even stronger ideas about it all, but their stories are laughed at in today's world. The Ransom says that we of the Sanctuary are trying to steal people's hearts from their blood salvation. What they mean is that it's a threat to their monopoly on power and the dogmas that dominate 99.9 percent of the world's population. It is a very dangerous story."

"Dangerous? Enough to want to hurt my wife over it?"

"Awful things have happened. People have been hurt, many killed, by those who are so frightened by this story that they feel they must eradicate it along with those who tell it."

"Those who tell it?"

"We tell it by the way we live it, Eli. The Sanctuary Chronicles are not a collection of written documents like the Christian Bible, or Koran, or the Torah and Talmud. Our lives are the stories. The stories, the Chronicles, illuminate the BloodFire Protocol. We believe that they mirror the resonance of our own inner rhythms, the rhythms of nature, of the universe itself, of life and all it encompasses, which are, in turn, learned from the Sanctuary."

"You're saying that you all are guardians of some folktales handed down, some oral tradition of stories that explain where you came from? It's just an attempt to sanctify your condition in life—even if it's terrible pain, or loss of loved ones, or no legs? Sorry, I used to buy that, but not anymore! So far, it doesn't sound any different from the emptiness that I used to spout."

"That's why you are here, most likely. The tragedy of your accident, the death of that woman and her child last year, and now your unending pain and fear about your wife have prepared you to take part in the journey of the BloodFire."

"You learned all this from Pearl talking to Jenn? They certainly have been chatting a lot in a couple of days." Eli smiled, but some glimmer of anticipation filled his heart and mind, unbidden yet so urgent that it felt like his body was trembling within as he listened to Susan's simple, sincere words. He knew as they washed over him and penetrated the fog of disbelief and skepticism that he was hearing words that meant there was no going back. It was as though he was standing once again in the house that he and Jenn recreated with such love and labor, familiar with each corner and shadow yet watching someone tear it all down and knowing that it must be so, before it could ever be reconstructed. There was something better, something behind the boards, something beyond the paint and plaster and loving care.

Susan's words cut through the haze of memory, like finding a pitch with a tuning fork, until he was caught up in this picture painted with her words, words that could not be written yet were echoing a new melody of life's power, overwhelming him with a clarity of vision that shimmered like a crystal lake in bright sun. It bespoke an untamed purpose arriving unannounced and unexpected, yet it was as though he'd been waiting for it for a long time and just didn't admit to it before now. He had not allowed himself to believe much in such depth of surrender, yielding to irresistible power within his own being. He felt both frightened and joyful, wondering how that could be possible.

The peaceful current of her voice belied the quivering expectancy enveloping him as she unwrapped one of the Chronicles, ending with, "The Protocol is meant to reestablish the spiritual foundations of the human race. The BloodFire is the promise, the hope and the response to the yearning we humans have to approach the light that's been labeled over the millennia as the divine, the gods, the spiritual, religion—you get the idea. The Sanctuary is the beginning, the present, the future, bringing into existence the universe that we know to be, as well as all other universes. They all exist, *we* all exist, as part of the Sanctuary. It is not a place, it is not male or female, it is not heaven nor hell. It is the Sanctuary. It is what is.

"In the course of the explosive creation of our universe, the world was formed. The space and the matter. The four basic natural forces and the stillness. The laws of physics and the wildness of the psyche. The BloodFire began its journey to complete the earth, to generate and shepherd the gift of life and spirit into an expression of the Sanctuary from which it came. Like a seed, it was sown, cultivated, and harvested to be shared and recycled again in order to release the potential. So earth became the sanctuary of this life seed, this spirit gift, this BloodFire. Life on this world was chosen to be first to be brought into harmony with the Sanctuary by the BloodFire. Think of it as a little shoot from the root of existence, the Sanctuary, generating an expression of itself here in a new world and then moving on."

"Moving on? Moving on where?"

"Why, to other worlds, of course! The BloodFire began its journey in this world, but it cannot be constrained here. It must move on, carrying shoots of the root to other worlds. That is the purpose for its journey." Susan stopped talking for a moment and paced the kitchenette, not needing to reach out to guide herself with her fingers in what was clearly her domain. "This isn't coming out like much of a story, is it? Adam told it so much better. You could experience the power and feel the call of the BloodFire when he spoke of it."

"You're doing just fine, Susan. But I've heard you and Jeremiah say something about redemption too."

"The BloodFire has been restrained, stymied. It was to be like yeast in dough, Aleudar, permeating the mixture until the entire thing is prepared. Then the gift was to move on and plant the seed in other worlds, kind of like Johnny Appleseed, okay? Great, now I'm mixing metaphors."

Eli eased off the stool, walked to the sink, and stared out the window. "You're saying this is about a story of how the world was started and why?"

"Yes, except in this version, the human race has a vital role but not a dominant one. Humans are not intended to rule the earth or to rule each other. Nobody is especially chosen by some distant, judgmental god who demands blood, much as the Ransom declares. The Sanctuary Chronicles are not a God-given book of absolute truths and inerrant dogmas, setting us against each other because some have the one and only truth and the rest do not. We don't claim wealth as our inheritance from this God, or demand wealth from others so that they can ensure their own salvation. Our first task is to help the BloodFire continue the journey to other worlds. They are waiting. They keep sending emissaries to our world, checking to see if the BloodFire is liberated and moving on yet. Those are the contacts."

Eli spun around. "You're not saying …? No, come on. That's ridiculous. UFOs and space aliens? *X-Files* stuff?"

"That's what the world has reduced them to." Jeremiah came around the corner from the bedroom, minus the skateboard, walking on his hands. He positioned himself in front of the stool, wiry muscles showing below the sleeves of his shirt as he hoisted his body straight up two feet, did a neat spin in midair, and landed with a solid thump on the seat.

"Show off!" Susan chided.

Jeremiah flashed her a grin and continued speaking. "Most of that stuff is pure nonsense. There are many more ways to travel and communicate than midnight encounters with flashing lights and bulky spaceships coming to take ET home. It's part of our mentality of"—here he raised his fist and imitated the sonorous tones of a passionate preacher—"'Our way is best. Humans are the top of the evolutionary chain. The world is made for our benefit, and we must subdue it. Progress is power, and power is progress. Manifest destiny forever. Humans rule, dude!'"

He lowered his fist and his voice. "I get so *sick* of it."

"Well, what happened, supposedly?" Eli asked. "Why hasn't the BloodFire moved on? What has kept these 'other worlds' waiting?"

"Greed. Greed for power. Pride. Wanting to make this our world, as though we owned it, brought it into being, could do whatever we wanted without regard to consequences. Tyranny of convictions, both political and religious, especially the conviction that humans are the ultimate in life-forms, the top of the heap in the realm of life. Take that and break it down further into racial and ethnic superiority convictions, and the destructive power unleashed has been devastating."

"You mean the BloodFire screwed up?"

"No, it's more like the Adam and Eve story. The BloodFire brought the desire, but the use of our gifts is a free choice. The option was there, obviously, of mischoosing, misusing. Long, long ago, some Guardians started saying that the gifts were wrong, or that they had disappeared and we are no longer beholden to the Sanctuary. Others said that they were only meant to be symbols, that in reality we humans are hopelessly weak in inner strength, spiritually atrophied. So most Guardians developed their own explanations and explorations, eventually leading to most of the world's religions down through time. In fact, that is where we find humans dividing history from prehistory, as though what came before was inherently inferior, an embarrassment. The Ransom was formed by religious and political leaders to make sure that the true meaning of the BloodFire and our potential was never allowed to flourish. Few of us are left who believe that the gifts are genuine and powerful and that the Redemption will begin at the uniting of the witnesses so that the BloodFire can resume the journey."

"What are the gifts?" Eli asked as a picture of himself on the bridge the night before flashed through his mind. He could see the water clearly, feel the sense of terror and relief as his worn-out faith dropped away.

"The gifts are the signs, or the witnesses, of the Sanctuary. We symbolize them in fire, water, and blood. Their purpose is to keep the world connected to the Sanctuary, our root; to each other in life's journey; and eventually to other worlds through the sacrament of the BloodFire we will universally share."

"I feel like I'm overmatched here in philosophizing. Fire, water, and blood?" Eli could not disguise his skepticism. "Those are the gifts?"

"Yes! Remember: gifts are signs are witnesses. And the things that are happening now are happening to prepare for the deliverance of the BloodFire. The Healer bears the gift of the blood, the gift of life and hope. Your child bears the gift of the water, the sacramental element of serenity that Susan told you about in the story."

"That's two of them. What about the fire?"

"Fire is the gift of renewal and purity." Jeremiah stopped and shot a worried glance at his wife.

Susan nodded. "Tell him all of it, Jeremiah. We must not hedge on the truth, not now especially."

Jeremiah sighed. "Adam told us that the FireGuide is already here as well. The problem is we don't know who he is. No one has seen the signs."

"Or she," Susan prompted. "We don't know who or where *she* is."

"There's already a she," Jeremiah said. "The Sacrament child is a girl." Susan's stern look stopped him. "Oh, I'm sorry," he apologized to Eli. "Didn't you know?"

Eli looked from one to the other, momentarily confused. A look of dawning recognition spread across his face. "A girl? I'm having a girl?"

"Yes!" exclaimed Susan. "You're having a daughter!"

Eli grinned. "A girl. I'm having a daughter."

"If we can get to the Healer." Jeremiah's terse statement brought the others up short.

"We will," Susan said with determination. "If I have to crawl there myself, I'll get to him."

"You know where he is?" Eli's heart began to race. He had not understood most of what he'd heard, but the incarnate sense of hope among them was enough.

"No, but if we can get word to Jonathan, we'll be able to find out. We'll have to do it in a way the bloodtrackers won't catch on."

"There's not a lot of time."

"I know. From what Eli has told us about his wife's condition, we need to have the Healer here within forty-eight hours." Jeremiah pursed his lips in concentration. "I'll go."

"Take Abraham or Toby with you," Susan urged without argument over his voluntary commitment.

"Me too," Eli said.

Jeremiah shook his head emphatically. "No. You stay with your wife." He looked hard at Eli. "And mine."

"But what if you don't find him? What if you don't come back?"

"If I don't come back, you have to fight to keep that baby of yours alive and out of the bloodtrackers' hands."

"But what about the witness of the blood? You said that all three witnesses are needed to bring about the Redemption. You said the future of all the other worlds depend on it. What happens to the BloodFire if the Redemption is stopped or smothered? Did Adam say? Why isn't he here helping you out? How did he know where the witnesses would appear? What happens if the BloodFire never gets to leave?"

Jeremiah climbed down from the stool, reminding Eli of a chimpanzee, the arms grossly out of proportion to the short body. "If the BloodFire never is able to leave, then the other worlds are doomed. If they are doomed, they will act like trapped animals, just like you and I would. They will come here, to an already struggling planet, and conquer us to provide themselves with a new home. Then more would come, other life-forms contending for the only space where the BloodFire exists, and the universes would be in a perpetual state of war. And irony of ironies, they would be fighting over the gift of peace for all of life."

"Or," Susan interjected, "they would simply wither away. And we would never find our own way here on earth. The BloodFire is not a god with omnipotent power. It is the current of the Sanctuary, following its course, making its journey to establish the spiritual foundations for life. Just like you and I are doing," she added with a nod to Jeremiah.

"So, we are holding up, what? The spiritual development of the rest of all that exists?" asked an incredulous Eli. "Because the witnesses have never gotten it together and done their thing? You're putting that on my baby's head? I'd like to talk to this Adam guy!"

"You're not the only one!" Jeremiah's face twisted into dark lines and shadows.

"It's awful," whispered Susan in a choked voice.

"We don't know if he's been killed or captured. Some say he's been forced into helping them."

"I don't understand," Eli said. "Helping who?"

"The bloodtrackers. But Adam sacrificed so much. He would never betray the Sanctuary. It about killed him though when his friend turned on him and became a leader in the BloodRansom. Calls himself the BloodMaster. And now he's the one that's leading the bloodtrackers in exterminating the witnesses."

"I'm afraid to ask," mused Eli.

"Fortunately, he doesn't know all the Guardians we've been able to … uh, replace since he met us," Susan chimed in. "But it makes a body wonder. There may be some of his spies among us."

Eli waited, trying to be patient about catching on to the rhythms of the couple's way of conversing.

"The necklace that Pearl gave you, do you still have it?" Jeremiah asked.

Eli pulled it from his pocket and handed it over. It looked ridiculously small and fragile in Jeremiah's great calloused hands. He reverently caressed the small charm, then handed it back to Eli. "Read the inscription."

"'When the witnesses unite …'"

Chapter 14

Time slowed to a crawl. Gideon and Laurel watched helplessly as the front end of the car, heavy with the engine, began to casually turn around in a slow spin, arcing away from the curving roadway, swinging around until they could see the trees racing toward them head-on.

"Gideon!" A frantic Laurel clutched at the door handle with one hand and dug the fingers of the other deep into the flesh of his forearm.

Gideon sat frozen, helpless to change the laws of physics, not feeling the pain of her grip. The momentum of the skid nudged the front end slightly past the center line to the nearest tree, enough that the car struck it a glancing blow on Laurel's side, jerking it clockwise again. Before either of them could react, the car smacked into a huge oak with a dull whump. Metal crumpled like tissue paper, and the windows shattered, showering them with bits of glass.

The collision sheared off the bolts holding the chair posts to the floor, and they tumbled backward into the rear seat, landing in a jumble of arms and legs. Gideon felt a heavy weight across his chest and carefully opened his eyes. It was Laurel's right thigh. His legs pinned her torso against the side of the car. A nasty bump on her forehead was already turning purple.

He managed to free one arm and carefully lifted her thigh. She didn't stir. He could hear water dripping somewhere underneath him. With a groan, he realized the fuel tank must be leaking. Gideon gasped as he forced himself to clamber over the broken seat.

He switched off the ignition, wondering how he could still be alive. A dreadful fear gripped him, and he quickly turned to check on Laurel. Her hair glittered as though it had been sprinkled with diamonds. He reached over and began to carefully pick the shards out of the soft tresses, willing his own hands to stop shaking, urgently calling her name.

Laurel opened her eyes and immediately put a hand to the goose egg on her forehead. "Next time, I drive."

Gideon smiled. "What, you don't like the way I park it?"

Laurel chuckled, then moaned as she tried to lift her head. "What you men won't do to get a girl into the back seat."

"We've got to get out. The gas tank is leaking." He reached back and took her hand. After a few moments of grunting and tugging, they managed to crawl out the passenger window. With an arm over each other's shoulders, they struggled a few yards away and sat down facing the smashed vehicle.

"It was a great car," Laurel said appreciatively.

Gideon looked at the battered red paint for a long while, trying to feel something about this final link to JP. But he was numb. "This is one unbelievable day," was all he could muster.

Laurel looked up. "It's almost dusk. Do you know where we are?"

Gideon started to giggle. Laurel gave him a strange look, one eyebrow arched.

"I'm sorry," he said. "But you sounded like that old commercial from the seventies. 'It's eleven o'clock. Do you know where you're children are?'"

They both dissolved into hysterical giggles, releasing some of the tension bottled up within, sounding for all the world like two teenagers on their way to a high school football game on a gorgeous fall evening.

Gideon looked again at the car, this time letting himself feel the loss. Tears welled in his eyes. "JP, I'm sorry," he whispered. "I guess we won't catch up to the bastard, whoever he is."

Laurel stopped giggling and sat quietly as the dusk settled around them and night sounds stirred the forest. Gideon took in a deep, shuddering breath. "What is happening?" His despair filled the small clearing.

"I don't know," Laurel said softly, uncertainty written on her face.

Crickets sang descants in the wild evensong, while cicadas responded by filling the air with strident arias. The smell of honeysuckle drifted on a breeze that rustled the leaves like the rhythms of some distant surf on a moonlit beach. And with it came the acrid smell of gasoline.

"The gas tank is shot, and I think the frame is bent," Gideon stated with a hint of resignation.

"Well, if they were watching the roads, they know we didn't come through."

In the dying light, Gideon could see the pain in her eyes below the nasty-looking bump. "I'm guessing they're moving on, expecting us to go somewhere. Except we don't know where that somewhere is."

"We'll find something. I know we will. Those bodies might give us a clue, a message."

"They're a message, all right," Gideon said grimly. "They're telling me that it's personal. They know who I am"—he shrugged—"even if I don't!" He abruptly stood up. "I'd like to know what that guy was doing down there snooping around in the old truck. Come on. Let's get down to the creek and get some cold water on that bump."

Laurel struggled to her feet and headed toward the car. "I've got to get something first."

Despite Gideon's protests, she shook off his helping hand and went over to the car. She leaned in through the window and rummaged around in the gloom. Gideon sighed and crossed to the opposite door. Reaching through the window, he felt for the light knob. Laurel reached under the seat and tugged on an army surplus backpack. Ignoring his questioning glance, she started away from the car at a stumbling trot at the same moment as Gideon finally found the right switch, and with a twist, the dome light illuminated the interior.

"Don't do anything to ignite those gas fumes," she started to yell over her shoulder, but Gideon was already hurrying away, eyes wide with naked fear and recognition of his own stupidity.

For an instant, he thought he'd made a fatal error. Perhaps the coolness and moisture in the evening air lowered the flashpoint, but he made it one more step before the fumes ignited with a roar. The concussion drove him to the ground, landing on his bruised ribs, hot pain searing through his chest.

"I hope you were right about the bloodtrackers sending you a message because you sure are doing your best to send them one," said Laurel, who was hugging the ground right in front of him.

"No, no really, I'm okay," Gideon muttered sarcastically. "Your concern is touching."

"We've got to get away from here. That thing will be like a beacon inviting all the valley to come to a wiener roast."

Gideon sighed. "No sympathy, I can see. What was so important that you had to go back to the car?" His sarcasm had turned to irritation.

In the light of the flickering flames, he saw the familiar flash of anger in Laurel's eyes, and he cursed himself for even caring what he saw there when her appearance in his life had meant nothing but trouble so far. A whippoorwill called in the night.

"Jonathan's things."

Something rustled in the underbrush behind them. Gideon rose gingerly to his knees. "Let's get out of here."

"How close are we?" Laurel rolled over and brushed herself off.

"We're behind the farm near the creek and the willow. It's dark enough now that we can sneak back and hopefully find what we need. Then we can lie low for the rest of the night."

Laurel picked up the old army surplus bag. Gideon reached for the strap, but she forcefully jerked it away from his grasp. "No! I'll carry it."

He shrugged and watched silently as she started trudging downhill. After a few paces, she stopped and turned around. "You coming?"

A smile crinkled the corners of his eyes. "I thought maybe we should go this way," he said, pointing to the northeast, along the side of the mountain. "There's a bear den about one hundred yards in front of you." He paused. "Right before a sixty-foot drop-off." Another pause. "Onto some rocks."

Laurel's eyes shot daggers at him. "All right, already!" Her voice rose with each syllable. "I'm tired. I'm hungry. Jonathan's dead, the car's a total loss, we're out here in the woods with no fo—"

Gideon held up his hand. He motioned to her to follow him, and without a word or a backward glance, he melted into the shadows beyond the small clearing. When he was completely out of her sight, he stopped and looked over his shoulder, smirking.

"Gideon!"

He jumped at the hiss of her whisper to his left. Laurel had quickly navigated through the dark woods to intercept him. His triumphant grin faded.

Laurel stepped close. "I'm not an idiot, you know. I was angry. My mistake."

Gideon opened his mouth, then closed it.

"Neither of us can be Lone Rangers, okay?" She offered a hand.

He nodded and accepted her offer. "Okay."

"Let's go past the farm up here in the trees, then circle back to the creek," he said. "I know where we can rest when we're finished."

The earthy smell of the forest enveloped them as they got farther away from the burnt car. Gideon moved cautiously, aware of Laurel's soft breathing behind him. It had been years since he'd been in the woods at night, following JP as carefully as he could, wanting to please him with his skills, enjoying the quiet companionship. He sighed, wondering where that part of his life had vanished to.

"What's wrong?" Laurel said.

He shook his head. After ten minutes, Gideon turned left and headed down the slope. The winds shifted, bringing with them the smell of rain. JP could smell rain a half day away, feel snow in his back, predict storms by the songs of the birds as he and Gideon worked in the orchard. This would be a cold rain. Gideon hoped the hiding place would still be there after they finished their task.

He heard Laurel slip on some leaves and nearly toppled backward on top of her when she skidded into his legs. For an instant, he resented being in this place and this moment with someone else. Then just as quickly, he realized it was not resentment he felt, rather guilt. Guilt over his actions of the past year. Guilt for his growing unease at being so close to this exasperating and beautiful woman and wanting to help her, defend her, touch her. Guilt at the growing conviction that the surrounding violence and bloodshed really might have something to do with him.

"Do you think anyone knows we're still around?" Laurel whispered.

"Not if I can help it," Gideon muttered cryptically.

"What do you mean?"

He didn't answer. Instead he started off again through the now completely darkened woods, the skills he'd learned as a boy coming back to him with each careful step. Soon he could hear the creek's pacific burble. He stopped at the edge of the trees to survey their surroundings, appreciative of Laurel's skill in quietly negotiating the terrain at his side. Jonathan had taught her well.

He felt her touch his arm. She was pointing across the fields through the low trees of the orchard.

"No police out here investigating," she whispered, not sounding at all surprised.

Gideon shook his head. "I'm beginning to think these bloodtrackers have friends in high places. Either that or everyone this far out has gone over to Sederton for the county fair. Neighbors are few and far between out here."

Gideon could feel her tensing beside him as she said, "The BloodMaster is committed to seeing to it that the Sanctuary believers are never allowed to prepare for the Redemption. He has authority to do whatever it takes: bribe and corrupt officials and politicians, infiltrate police departments, intelligence agencies ... even murder."

"Just your average, everyday good neighbors, eh?"

An owl hooted overhead. They emerged from the shadow of the trees, two dark specters sliding down the steep bank of the creek and gingerly jumping across it. Their journey across the outermost fields and meadows of the farm felt like a dreadful eternity to Gideon. As they reached the orchard, the moon rose over the far end of the valley, casting their shadows behind them as they crept toward the barn.

Gideon held up a hand, signaling Laurel to wait. The door creaked on its rusted hinges, and then the black hole swallowed him up. He felt along the wall, amazed to discover that he remembered the layout so clearly.

The various ropes still hung on the wooden pegs. Next should be the tack for his beloved Brownie. Yes, it was still there. His fingers lingered on the brass nameplate, while he breathed in the faint aroma of oils, liniments, and saddle shine. He let himself indulge in a moment of heartfelt nostalgic longing for the days of riding the auburn quarter horse under the summer sun, over the same fields and slopes he now traversed like a thief in the night. His foot nudged the expected pile of feed bags, right where they'd always been. Grabbing four, he headed for the door.

He latched the door behind him and guided Laurel to the backyard. The smell of smoke hung thick in the air. In the moonlight, he could see the black outline of the hulk of the house against the stars.

Laurel held his arm, taking shallow breaths. "Maybe we shouldn't," she said in a tentative whisper.

Gideon carefully surveyed the shadows around the house before answering. "We don't need the police looking for us along with these heartless killers you call bloodtrackers. Let's deal with one insanity at a time. Maybe we can set some of the terms for once. Or did Jonathan only teach you to be a passive spectator?" He knew he'd done it yet again before the words were out of his mouth.

"Don't you dare!" Laurel hissed, putting her face inches away from his. "I want to find out who's behind this more than you can imagine. It's taking everything I have to focus on the mission and getting your sorry butt out of harm's way. I'd like nothing better than to drop you right here and go find those sick bastards and make them pay for Jonathan's death!"

"Drop me? Go ahead. I don't believe in your sorry mission anyway. I don't need you to protect me. I've been taking care of myself, and I've done just fine!"

"Fine? Who wrecked the car and blew it to kingdom come? Who fell off the mountain and got six people—hey!"

Gideon unceremoniously yanked her down behind the neglected bushes at the side of the house and clapped a hand over her mouth. The lights from a car swept past on the front road. Both involuntarily held their breath. Laurel grabbed his hand and was pushing it away when they heard the screech of brakes and a car backing up.

A car door slammed, and footsteps approached. Laurel and Gideon pressed against the fieldstones of the old foundation.

"They've seen the fire from the car," he said into her ear, adding unnecessarily, "don't move."

"What is that, a plane crash?" asked a voice. "Maybe we should we break into the old Waters' place and call it in."

"I doubt if the phones are still hooked up. Let's go on down to 18 and find a pay phone. From the looks of it, there won't be any survivors. We can meet the cops there and bring them back here to show them where it is."

"Hey, maybe one of those news choppers will fly down to cover it!" exclaimed the first voice, flush with excitement.

"Yeah, we might be on TV! Damn, I wish I had my video camera. We could make some serious cash." Car doors slammed, and they were gone.

"They're all heart," Laurel muttered.

"We don't have much time," Gideon said, pulling her to her feet. "They'll be back in ten or fifteen minutes. We won't be able to turn on any lights."

"How are we going to search this place in that little amount of time?"

"We aren't. I know where JP hid things that he didn't want anybody to find. I don't expect to find anything, but if it will make you less paranoid, I'll show you his spot, and then we can get the hell out of here."

Laurel ground her teeth in frustration. "Paranoid?"

Gideon cut her off. "Shush! We can fight later. Let's go in the back door. My visitors from this morning were rude enough to leave without taking the time to lock it," he added sardonically.

They crept around the back corner of the house. The screen door swung free on its hinges, but the other door was closed fast. "I guess even in a panic I still listened to my mother and closed the door behind me," Gideon said. Somehow it seemed it would be easier to reenter the house without having to actually touch the doorknob.

"I'll do it," Laurel offered without condescension.

"No, I will." Gideon took a deep breath, trying without success to push the images of horror from his mind. The metal felt cold and clammy to the touch, and he cringed. Once through the door, the moonlight glinted off the stainless steel faucet and the knobs on the old stove. "Do you want to wait here?"

"Hell no." She put one hand on his shoulder, ready to follow in his footsteps.

Gideon hesitated. The black air around them quivered as though breathing, alive with the spirits of the butchered souls in the next room. A cold sweat trickled down his spine, making him shiver.

"You okay?" asked Laurel.

"No. I want to run outside and puke, if it's all the same to you."

"Where is this hiding place? Do we have to go past the bodies?"

"Yes. It's in the mantel." He could feel her shivering behind him even as an electric chill ran up and down his own spine.

He nudged the door leading into the hallway. The blackness was nearly complete as the moon traversed the sky and hid behind the mountains. Gideon felt for the stair railing to his right and above. The wood was cool, comforting. The smooth spindles glided across his fingers as he followed them to the newel post, made by JP's own hand over a half century ago. Laurel bumped into him when he abruptly stopped. The doorway was two steps across the hall. Beyond the ebony opening was the dark abyss. Unconsciously, he took Laurel's hand and stepped through.

After two tentative steps, they stopped. Gideon stuck out his toes and felt around on the floor. Nothing. He took another couple of baby steps and repeated the procedure, confusion rising as he met no resistance.

"Something's wrong."

Laurel squeezed his shoulder. "Tell me about it."

"No, I mean nothing is here. There's nothing on the floor," he whispered. "I should have tripped over a body by now."

"Maybe we went around them," Laurel suggested.

A quick rasp of a match being scratched carried with it a flicker of a hope that it was time to awaken from the nightmare. Yellow flame flared in the thick blackness. Gideon looked at his feet. Nothing. The bodies were not there.

A siren sounded in the distance, heading out from town. He held the match toward the mantel, his heart sinking. The carved panel on the far left swung free on hidden hinges. He stepped closer, his throat growing unbearably tight. In the last moment before he dropped the match singing his fingertips, he saw the truth. The small compartment that it had concealed was empty.

"Damn!" The flame burned his fingers. It dropped to the floor, leaving them in utter darkness.

Chapter 15

They were frozen in place, barely daring to breathe.

"Let's get out of here," Laurel whispered as the sound of the sirens grew louder.

"I haven't checked the mantel." Another match flared. Gideon held it out in front of him. "What the …?"

Splintered wood lay scattered on the hearth. Only the two supporting posts protruded from the chimney.

"Somebody hacked it to pieces," Laurel said in a puzzled voice.

"Yeah. Somebody else is looking for a hint from JP." He took a quick glance around the room. Nothing else appeared to be disturbed. "And they knew right where to look. Only four people knew about that spot: JP, my mother, me … and my father."

"Surely he would have told someone else," Laurel argued. "Some of his friends, maybe. You said he's been gone most of your life. He had to tell someone."

Gideon hurriedly searched among the splinters of wood, straining to make out any scintilla of a clue. Nothing. The match fell at his feet.

"Gideon, we have to go."

"Yeah." He silently cursed himself for daring to hope that some sanity might be restored back at what used to be home, some light shed on the crazy and violent spiral that had erupted in his life.

They stumbled through the room and left the same way they entered. With the moon set, the stars were brilliant. A chilly breeze revived Gideon's sagging spirit enough to find the energy to make it to a safe refuge for the night.

"Should we hide in the barn?" Laurel asked. "I'm too tired to take another step."

"No, we need to go back to the creek. Somebody might check in the barn for shovels or firefighting equipment." The sirens echoed off the hillsides, and flashing strobes looked like an approaching swarm of angry lightning bugs. "Let's get into the orchard before they're any closer."

In among the trees. the air was pungent with the smell of apples that had ripened and fallen to the ground, sharp and heady. Gideon took Laurel's hand and led her through the quickest path on an angle away from the yard. He stopped for one more quick look at the canopy of the autumn night sky stretching beyond imagination, drawing him with an almost physical force that made him feel unexpectedly light. He shook his head to chase away the pull.

"You okay?"

He waved her off and picked up the pace, still clutching the feed bags. *If I didn't know better,* he thought, *I might be on some adolescent midnight jaunt to a romantic interlude rich with promise.* At the far side of the orchard, the ground sloped sharply toward the creek. Wild raspberry bushes waved their barbed tentacles in the night winds, grabbing at their clothing with sharp thorns. A quick glance to the right confirmed that the spectacular blaze of the car would be drawing all eyes.

At the bottom of the slope, right above the water level, Gideon stopped to take his bearings, then strode unerringly through a particularly dense stand of underbrush and disappeared.

"Gideon," hissed Laurel.

He reappeared after a moment with a weary smile on his face. "Right this way, ma'am. Your room awaits you."

He ushered her through with a flourish and smiled again at her gasp of delight surprise. "What's this?"

"This is the five-star, exclusive to kings, queens and weary travelers of all ilk, Inn of the House de Spring de la Hacienda de la Gideon, son of Justin, son of JP of the Waters clan …" He ran out of sons of. "*Mi* hideout *es su* hideout."

Laurel laughed in that way that made him feel warm all through. "And pray tell, kind sir, how does a lady of such elegance and standing as I maintain her dignity while crawling through such an unladylike entrance?"

She was pointing to the small hole in the side of the bank, lit by a golden glow from within. "I guess either it got smaller, or I got bigger in the last fifteen years," Gideon confessed with a chuckle. "I managed to get through and light the oil lamp, so if I can make it, you can make it too."

Laurel knelt and crawled into the small cave, dragging Jonathan's worn backpack behind her. Inside, Gideon gave her the grand tour of the approximately six-by-ten-foot space, feeling rejuvenated and warmed by the smile in her weary eyes as he showed her the bunk of his childhood hideout. It consisted of a small shelf of rock lined with decayed and moldy straw. Opposite the bunk were rows of wooden planks resting on cinder blocks. The makeshift shelves held rows of dust-covered Mason jars filled with canned fruits and tomatoes. The floor was covered with rotted plywood. The sight of the results of his mother's labors from a time now lost to him erased the smile from his face and the lilt of pleasure from his voice.

"I should have been here."

Laurel took the feed sacks from his hand and spread them on the straw. "You're here now."

He snorted. "Lot of good that's doing, wouldn't you say!"

"There's a reason for it all, Gideon."

"That's something she would have said. But she's gone. JP needed me here. I knew the Alzheimer's was robbing him of everything. He shouldn't have been alone."

"Why the wooden floor?" She gave the wood a stomp with the heel of her boot. It disintegrated with a squishy thud.

"That's the best part." Gideon lifted off one of the squares. "That's a little eddy pool. The stream has eaten away underneath the bank over the years, so we have our own supply of fresh running water. We won't have to worry about running into anybody out there checking out the wreck."

"Is that food still good?" Laurel asked while eyeing the musty jars.

"I don't know. The fruit will probably have quite a kick to it by now. I know Mother sealed them well. JP turned this into the spring house sometime after the war. He'd been a prisoner of war for two interminable years. He vowed there would always be enough food for his family and any stranger who happened by. This was his not-so-secret reserves. I turned it into my private hideout."

Laurel studied his face for a long moment. "Was it lonely here for you sometimes?"

He ducked his head in embarrassment before rummaging around in the jars of food. "Here's some peaches, best in the county. Pickled watermelon rinds. Green beans. Yellow beans. Tomatoes."

"What! No bread?" Laurel scolded in mock horror. "The service in this fine establishment is abysmal."

Gideon felt quiet gratitude toward her for covering his discomfort so effortlessly. He selected a few samples and then had to struggle to get them opened. Laurel took one, turned it upside down, gave it a good whack on the floor, then casually twisted the lid open.

"Sure, after I get the lid loosened," Gideon said. "I don't suppose you have linens and silverware with you."

"As a matter of fact …" Laurel paused to rummage around in the backpack and extracted two mess kits. She started to close it back up, then spied something buried on the bottom. "My God."

"What is it?"

She slowly pulled out a .9 mm pistol, dull gray, menacing. Holding it with two fingers, she gingerly handed it to Gideon. "I never knew he had this."

"What was all that training you two spoke of then? You mean Guardians are pacifists? Antiviolence? Come on, Laurel. In case you haven't noticed, the other guys are killing people with cars, knives, whatever it takes. I'm glad to see we have a little protection."

"I swear I didn't know that Jonathan had a gun. My training was all about the Sanctuary, learning the Chronicles and how to honor the root, the journey, and the witnesses."

Gideon scoffed at her naivete. "So what else didn't he get around to telling you about this invisible Sanctuary? That it's just around the corner from Mister Roger's Neighborhood, but, oh, don't forget to cover your back before Mister Green Jeans sticks a knife in it."

"Mister Green Jeans was on *Captain Kangaroo*," Laurel managed through gritted teeth.

Gideon ignored the early warning signs and pressed on. "You sure this isn't the Mafia we're dealing with?"

"Excuse me, mister 'please don't bother me with this Healer nonsense.' I realize that just because you have the blood of a little girl on your hands after wasting a year of your life feeling sorry for yourself with every bimbo that came along doesn't mean you have to care about anything or anyone but yourself." Laurel's fury spent, she covered her mouth with her hands, her body wracked with silent sobs as she backed into the farthest corner of the tiny ledge like a small child fearful of yet another blow from her tormentor.

Gideon's anger died in his throat. His chest grew heavy, the gun in his hand a deadweight pulling him down ever deeper into a bottomless hole. When it felt as though he would never take another breath, he sighed and dropped the gun over the edge into the cold water. Laurel blinked in disbelief. Gideon looked her in the eye, holding her gaze, not saying a word.

Finally, Laurel lowered her gaze. "You need to eat something. Your body is trying to recover from that fall."

"To say nothing of my mind," Gideon added, a great weariness enveloping him. He abruptly sat down on the opposite end of the ledge.

Laurel slid off her perch and filled the tin plates with offerings from the jars. Gideon gingerly tasted the beans. He couldn't tell if they were beyond edible or not but shoveled them into his mouth. The fruit made his tongue buzz and tingle with a wicked zing. He ignored it, eating till he was full.

"Did you grow all these here on the farm?"

"Some JP grew in his garden, some he bought from neighbors. You should have tasted his corn. Best corn on the cob I have ever eaten. It was worth walking all day and all night for just one of those ears, dripping with butter and a dab of salt."

"Didn't this stuff freeze in the winter?"

"Nah. We're below the frost line in here. It's probably almost an ideal place for this kind of stuff."

Laurel finished her meal. "Who gets to use the tub first?" She giggled at Gideon's surprised look and indicated the pool of clear water at their feet. "I don't know about you, but I haven't had a chance to bathe in three days."

"That's one cold bathtub," Gideon warned.

"I'll take my chances." She tore off a corner of her shirt and used it as a washcloth, dipping it into the water and wiping her face, arms, and neck. Next she eased off mud-caked boots and slid her feet into the bath, letting out a little shriek in the process. "Do you think anybody can hear me?"

"No, we're safe and sound in here. What's next, a massage?"

She smiled enigmatically and slid her shirt over her head, catching Gideon completely off guard. "Aren't you going to wash up?"

Gideon didn't know where to look, wanting to give her some privacy yet unable to take his eyes off her beautifully formed breasts. The sight of her intoxicated him even as he told himself it was the well-aged fruit that made his head feel so light. She drew water up with one hand and let it trickle down across her shoulders and arms, the chill drawing her nipples into erect, taut buds. More handfuls, and the water caressed the curve of her breasts, down her belly, disappearing into the recesses of her jeans.

"Gideon, did you hear me? I asked for one of those sacks to use to dry off."

"Oh, uh, sorry." He snapped out of his reverie, deep draughts of both desire and guilt washing over him.

While she toweled off, he took his turn, afraid to check to see if she was watching him as intently as had he, not knowing if the prickling sensation on the back of his neck was the heat of self-consciousness or her imagined desire. When he was finished, they divided up the remaining burlap and fashioned a bed, arranged foot to head.

They lay down back to back, the lamp turned low, shadows dancing on the ceiling to the quiet music of the water's steady passage. Gideon replayed the sight of her bathing, committing each detail to memory, fearful that in the long hours till dawn some unknown spirit of the night would snatch away this one touch of joy.

"You asked if I was lonely here." He spoke into the stillness between them. "My mother was always ready to sit and talk with me or take a walk through the fields, picking the wildflowers of the mountains. JP gave me the gift of thinking for myself, self-reliance, and joy in the simple pleasures of this world. But there were times when I would retreat to this place, shutting out the world, wondering why I was here. Why was I sitting on the banks of the stream, enjoying the sky and the mountains, the birds, and the breezes. And this funny feeling would come over me, one that is difficult to describe."

"Like there was a hole in your heart, a yearning to be able to touch those mountains, or hold the sky, or flow on the breezes and talk to the stream." Laurel said the words softly.

Gideon craned his neck, trying to see her face. "Yes! How did you know? Silly, isn't it."

She raised her head and met his gaze. "No. I know."

He sat up, still watching her face. Her eyes never left his. She rolled over and sat up, facing him, her lips parted, a tear wending its way from the corner of one eye, across her cheek. Gideon leaned closer, his heart aching.

An eternity passed. He could feel the steady rhythm of her breath upon his cheek. Slowly, ever so slowly, his hand came up to her neck, molding to its contours, pulling her closer, her hair enveloping his fingers in a soft, scented embrace.

Her lips were on his, firm, yielding, hungry. There could be no sweeter taste of desire.

Chapter 16

Eli stared without seeing as the bus rolled past the busy shipping channels and terraced banks of the Ohio River. Occasionally he roused himself to take stock of the other passengers on the bus. They were the normal assortment of college students, retirees going into the city to shop and feel a part once again of the hustle and bustle that passed for purpose. Unlike the previous evening, there was no brash conductor calling himself the Paraclete. Against all logic, Eli had expected to see him and confront him with the news of the last ten hours.

It was pathetic, he told himself, but he wanted to talk to the guy in light of what had happened. After the accident a year ago, in the beginning, friends stopped by as he struggled to cope with the physical pain and torturous therapy. They made sympathetic noises, but he saw it in their eyes. He had killed someone, an expectant mother. Jenn constantly reminded him that the police said it was an unexplainable accident. But he knew better. Now he was crippled, changed. He was no longer a whole person in the same way that they were comfortable considering themselves. And worse, there was blood on his hands.

The fractured vertebrae needed surgical screws to be repaired. His spinal cord at L4-5 had fierce pressure on it that if left alone would cause paralysis. Because he could not take steroids to relieve the inflammation and because the bones needed to grow back just so, the surgeons tried a new and untested procedure. Jenn had given consent since he was in too much pain to be rational. No one ever said if any consent had been needed from the donor.

Virgin blood, the doctors jokingly referred to it, untainted yet by direct contact with the outside world. With its unique qualities of growth stimulation and even possible regeneration, they'd given him an injection into the affected area of his spine to encourage quick healing. He did in fact heal sooner than usual in terms of the fracture, but in its typically unpredictable manner, the scar tissue grew around the nerve roots. This resulted in intractable, excruciating pain. The constant irritation on the nerves was causing them to degenerate rapidly. The pump was implanted to try to improve his quality of life.

Eli's thoughts began to bounce back and forth between worry about Jenn's condition and the incredible words of the loving but totally off-the-wall couple who had given him their hospitality and, he realized with dread, given him their trust as they sent him into their terribly dangerous world full of conspiracy. A world of violence aimed at preventing a band of misfits armed with a belief in the unknowable from undermining all that the major cultures and civilizations of the world were based upon.

No. He had to stay focused on getting whatever help Jenn needed. The baby had to come second if he was being forced to choose. And according to the doctor, that is exactly what he was being forced to do. He was so sick and tired of doctors. What did Jeremiah and Susan expect of him? What was he supposed to think of their earnest but wild assertions? At the millennium, everybody made crazy predictions and prepared for the end of the world. Not him. He knew it would not come, and it didn't.

When he stood to exit the bus, a nasty spasm grabbed his right hip, squeezing the muscles so tightly that they stretched the nerve at its root. The sensation was akin to having a hot poker thrust into his back and then sending 220 volts of electricity through it. He gasped in pain, frozen in the aisle.

"C'mon, buddy. I gotta schedule to keep," barked the ruddy-faced driver.

"Yeah, I'm coming," Eli managed between gritted teeth. The other passengers looked up at this break in the routine, making him feel like the idiot at a freak show as he hobbled down the aisle. He could sense their irritable impatience as he slowly put one foot on the first step and inched the other down beside it. He repeated the procedure for all three steps. The complete silence unnerved him.

He was relieved when the bus pulled away, leaving him at the edge of the park across from the hospital. Beyond the park, the compact downtown section of the city, dubbed the Golden Triangle, jutted out into the waters of the three rivers like a mighty iron wedge or the bow of an exploring ship. A dozen bridges spanned the waters like so many bow lines keeping the crowded maze of skyscrapers anchored in place. The streets were jammed with commuters stuck in their cars waiting for parking spaces that just weren't there. Better to park across the Allegheny at Three Rivers Stadium. But, of course, that was an anathema to the independent-minded suburbanites who liked to keep their cars handy like a wary gunslinger keeping his pistols within deadly reach.

He was not getting enough rest, he knew, and his body was letting him know it. Tough shit. Eli limped across the street, oblivious this time to the crumbling neighborhood. He made one perfunctory survey of the area, didn't see Paraclete, and went through the revolving doors.

A circular information desk filled the middle of a gloomy rotunda that smelled of ether. A narrow hallway led to the modern addition with its long bank of elevators. People hurried through, ignoring those around them in this clearinghouse of human misery and suffering. The high-pitched barking of the Reverend Doctor Baker floated above the heads of the pedestrian traffic.

"Mr. Marks! Mr. Marks. I've been waiting for you."

Eli groaned and punched the elevator call button with renewed desperation.

"I tried to call you at home. I thought you might need to talk." The man in the rolled Roman collar and sweat-stained shirt folded his hands across his belly and looked over the top of his half glasses with a condescending smile, breathing hard.

Eli felt like a fourth grader caught peeking into the girls' bathroom. He could feel his face flushing as the anger rose in his throat. "Is there something I can do for you?" he asked curtly. "Did I ask for a chaplain to keep nosing around, bothering me? If I need help, I'll get help."

The elevator arrived. The usual throng elbowed their way forward, and Eli let himself be swept into the car. Before the doors closed, he called back to the enigmatic figure, "Pray for my wife. Please."

Jenn's room held a different atmosphere than that of the previous evening. At first, he couldn't place his finger on what had changed, but he knew that he felt a distinct sense of quiet solitude, even tranquility, when he walked through the door. Jenn lay peacefully, the machines still beside the bed but no longer connected to the trach tube. He stepped closer.

She was wearing a nightgown, a light blue cotton top with a flower patterned collar. *Blue was her favorite color*, Eli thought. *Is, not was*, he scolded silently. She wasn't dead yet—and would not die, if he could help it.

Funny, he didn't remember bringing her any nightgowns and did not recall her ever having one that looked like this. An African violet bloomed on the windowsill. Again, not his doing. The purple blooms caught the sunlight and lent the room a touch of graciousness. What was going on?

Eli bent to kiss Jenn's cheek. She smelled of gentle soap, not the harsh antibacterial solutions indigenous to hospitals everywhere. His lips lingered, then moved to hers.

"Mr. Marks."

Eli abruptly straightened, sending a spasm the length of his spine. "Yes." He abruptly exhaled, but it didn't help to soften the jolt.

Dr. Tournier's lips were set in a thin line. "I'm sorry to interrupt, but I must protest these actions on your part." He angrily extended a sheaf of papers toward Eli.

"What are you talking about?" Eli's eyebrows arched in surprise at the intensity in the doctor's voice. "I just arrived. Has something changed?"

Dr. Tournier slapped the papers against his thigh. "This is unconscionable. I cannot allow you to jeopardize my patient in this manner!"

"What the hell are you talking about? Why would I do anything to harm my wife? I haven't signed anything since I was in here last night."

The doctor opened his mouth and then closed it again. It was obviously not the answer he'd expected. "Uh, is this, are these your signatures?"

Eli took the papers. They were various forms giving permission to treat and perform procedures, including disconnecting the respirator and beginning physical therapy. "I never signed these.

Does this mean my wife is doing better"—his heart palpitated—"or that this is ... that she's not ... I mean ... Didn't you order these? Your name is on them along with"—he peered at the unfamiliar name—"a Doctor Gideon Waters."

The slight doctor appeared apoplectic. He fished a different form from his lab coat. "I never signed those. *This* is the one I wanted to present to you. It is consent to perform the abortion. These forged orders are insanity. She's been having inexplicable brain activity that indicates we *must* move with all due haste. I resent you going to another doctor without conferring with me."

"I never met this Doctor Waters. What do you mean by inexplicable brain activity? She looks so peaceful. Someone has obviously been giving her excellent care."

"Her wave patterns keep fluctuating, some of which I've not seen before. She is not awakening by any means."

Eli concealed his surprise at a neurosurgeon admitting fallibility. "Is she getting worse?"

Dr. Tournier wiped his face with one well-manicured hand. "We can't say. My assistant is at the medical library right now trying to match the waves' pattern." He pointed to Jenn. "But this is dangerous. I did not sign these orders. These are a death warrant."

Eli felt torn in both directions. He thought of Joe Martinson saying yesterday how he longed for a word from his wife, a look, a touch. "Is she breathing okay on her own?"

"The nurses tell me that her lungs are holding their own. But her blood pressure keeps climbing. The risk of stroke increases each day, especially in her condition. We have to get that pressure down."

Eli stared at the bright blooms on the African violet, shaking his head at the implausibility of Cracked Pearl's claims of being able to communicate with Jenn. "These brain waves, are they part of anything like dreaming? Or maybe ..." He caught himself before he could add, like in ESP? "Maybe it's her body, or her mind, her psyche, trying to deal with the trauma of drowning."

A condescending smile appeared on Dr. Tournier's face for a fleeting second. "Mr. Marks, I know that you used to be a minister, and I'm sure you were a good one. But right now we must deal with the medical realities. Your wife is my patient, and I must do everything that I can in her best interest. I do not know what these papers are all about, but I will surely get to the bottom of it. I will not let you jeopardize my patient."

"Her best interest?" Eli pushed the papers back at the doctor. "Was it in her best interest to jump into that river to save that girl? No, but she did it, didn't she! Is it in her best interest to have a tube stuck down her throat and god knows where else, to be poked and prodded and stuck in this sterile room while people whisper outside the door or, worse yet, talk in front of her like she was not here? And how dare you imply that I would not have anything but my wife's best interest at heart!" His voice had risen to a shout. Through the glass walls, he saw a redhaired woman look up from the nurse's station and head toward the cubicle.

She limped badly, her feet turning inward in a severe pigeon-toed position. Her hands and arms were bent in awkward angles, spread wide like broken wings, giving her balance. Her progress came in lunges, fits, and starts, her face contorted with the effort and concentration. When she came through the doorway, she greeted them both with a radiant smile. Eli recognized her from the evening before, in the canteen with Joe Martinson.

"Doctor, they need you in surgery," she said, her voice reflecting the same effort and concentration as had her walking. Her lips struggled with some of the sounds, and spittle sprayed the good doctor's immaculate smock.

"My pager did not go off," he countered brusquely. "I am trying to counsel Mr. Marks—" At that moment, the high beep sounded from the page on his hip. He looked at it, surprised. "We will finish this later, Mr. Marks. These orders must be changed." He spun on his heel and strode briskly out of the room.

"I'm Tanya," the woman announced. "Sorry about all the s's," she added with another bright smile and spray.

Eli could not help but smile back at her, feeling his hand enveloped in both of hers as she gently tugged him away from the foot of the bed. She checked the doorway before quietly informing him, "I'm from the Dancer."

Eli caught himself from laughing. "Excuse me? You're a dancer?"

"Not a dancer, Mr. Marks. Don't take me for a fool. I am from the Dancer."

"The Dancer? Who or what is the Dancer?"

In reply, she went to the bedside stand and opened a drawer. When she straightened and turned around, Eli stepped back in alarm. Tanya held out the doll he'd destroyed in his frustration. With trembling hands, he took it and examined the barely visible repairs.

"Where did you get this?"

"It belongs to Pearl. I'm going to return it to her."

"You're one of them?"

"One of them? I don't know what that means, Mr. Marks. I am from the Dancer. The GateKeeper sent me to look out for your wife. He knew of Adam's work in this sector."

Eli's thoughts were spinning so rapidly he felt dizzy. "I don't know anything about any Dancer. Is he like that Healer that Susan and Pearl mentioned?"

Tanya's face flushed a deep pink, and her mouth struggled to form the words. "The Healer? He's here? How do you know this?"

Eli frowned. "You mean you don't know about him? Why are you here caring for my wife? It was you, wasn't it, who brought the flowers and the nightgown and got the machines turned off?"

She nodded. "It made her more comfortable."

"What about the doll? It had a note about the Healer inside."

"I didn't know anything about a note. Paraclete brought me the pieces to the doll. I knew it was Pearl's. He told me he was looking out for your wife and how he was trying to keep the jackals away."

"The jackals?"

"The doctors!" Her spit flew with extra force. "God forbid they should see patients as anything more than consumers of their time and professional skills. Your wife can't speak for herself. I assumed the Dancer wanted me to comfort her, usher her through the portal."

"Usher her through …? You mean help her to die?" Eli grabbed her arm. "Who are you?"

Tanya looked him in the eye. "Don't ever grab me like that again." She spoke firmly and evenly. "I told you I was sent by the Dancer. That's all you need to know. Any more would be dangerous—to you, to your wife, to all of us."

"Is that guy who calls himself Paraclete this Dancer you spoke of?"

She began to laugh, a high-pitched sort of snort and wheeze that went on for a few minutes, making Eli angry. "What's so damn funny?"

"I'm sorry. I'm not laughing at you. Both Paraclete and Dancer would love the comparison. For now, just believe me, please."

"I suppose you're one of these Sanctuary believers? And the others you mentioned as well?"

"Something like that. Listen, Eli. I've looked at your wife's chart, and I've compared her situation to all the old Chronicles that I know of. You are obviously not the Healer, nor is your beautiful wife the FireGuide. Yet something else points to her baby, your baby, being the child of the Sacrament. I don't understand how it could be, but apparently it is."

"That's it? You'll accept some wild belief without proof or documentation? Susan said they are nothing more than stories. There's no Bible, no sacred traditions, no code that lays out the thou shalts and the thou shalt nots? What—it's not a religion, it's a state of mind? Sounds like some license plate slogan."

Tanya sighed. "I doubt that Susan discounts them so casually. I know it's been hard, Eli. You had your nice life with your nice profession, safe dreams, long-term plans, your nice set of beliefs all in a neat row like a shelf full of books. Then it all got turned upside down, like somebody reached in and pulled it all out by the roots. And without the roots, everything began to wither, bit by bit, until all that was left was to throw the dried-up stalks and empty seed hulls into the river."

Her last words struck Eli like a slap across the face. It was as if she'd been there on the bridge with him the night before and read his thoughts as he leaned over the rail. He hadn't told anyone about the unsettling feeling of guilty freedom and scary open horizon that stretched before him. That is, if he got through this first.

Tanya went on. "People have one of two reactions when they encounter the reality of the Sanctuary. They either are overwhelmed with fear—fear of having displeased some ghost of the divine, fear of coming up short, fear of being annihilated and tossed into some black pit. So they react with anger, running away to the blood salvationists, protected by the Ransom. Or they find that they have the power to make a commitment to making the journey together."

"I don't have the faintest idea of what you mean."

"Yes you do. Don't lie to yourself, Eli."

He attempted to change the subject, or so he thought. "What is going to happen to my wife?"

"I'm not a fortune-teller or a seer, Eli. I'm on my own journey, honoring the gift of life as best as I can by serving the Dancer. You need to be strong, particularly if your baby is of the Sacrament. It is not an easy sacrifice."

"Sacrifice? All love is sacrifice."

"There are shadow forces in this place, Eli. Don't let yourself be deceived." She leaned over to stroke Jenn's cheek. "There isn't much time. You must get to the Dancer. Hopefully, there will be word of the Healer. Nothing else will be of help to your wife and child."

"But they say if they take the baby, my wife's chances will be improved."

"Her chances of what? This is a great honor for her, for you. This child bears the hope of the worlds in her heart. Pearl says that your wife is willing to risk her own life. There must be no more drugs, no more machines, no more invasions of her body.

"But I'm not willing to risk her life, don't you see? I want her back. I need her to be with me."

"You do not own her life, Eli. Each one of us builds our lives around discovering our own way to honor the Sanctuary. In that, we also honor the gifts that were given to those around us."

Eli shook his head. "Look, I'm willing to live and let live. Everyone can have their own form of spirituality. Fine with me. At this point, I only want to help Jenn. I have to decide whether to listen to the doctor or listen to a bunch of strangers who profess to know some secret about the child my wife is carrying. If you were in my shoes, what would you do?"

"But I will never be in your shoes, Eli. You must decide how *you* will fill them."

"There she is!" an angry voice shouted outside the room.

"You must remember what I have said," Tanya said, gripping his arm and forcing him to look her in the eye. "Find your place, Eli. Decide about what you have heard here from the Guardians."

Two security officers barged into the room, trailed by Dr. Tournier. They seized the small, bent figure and carried her out.

"Mr. Marks, I will go to the ethics committee, and I will go to court if I have to. That fetus must be terminated." Dr. Tournier folded his arms across his chest and glared at Eli.

"No." The single word hung in the air. Eli took a deep breath and pointed to Jenn. "If you so much as lay a finger on her, I'll come after you, sir. Those orders stand. You go ahead and go to your committee and go to court if that's what you want to do. I'll find another doctor to treat my wife"—he placed a hand on Jenn's abdomen—"and my child."

The doctor's face was grim as he steepled his fingers in front of his chest. "You are playing with fire," he said darkly. "You are asking for trouble."

"Maybe so, but I'm telling you that this is the way it will be."

The two men glared at each other until Dr. Tournier spun on his heels and exited. Eli stumbled to a chair and sat down, trying to stop the trembling in his legs. A movement caught his eye. Jenn's eyes fluttered open, and one hand went to her mouth. Eli crossed the room as fast as he could.

"Jenn! Jenn, can you hear me? It's Eli, babe. Can you talk?"

His heart sank when he looked into her eyes. They stared vacantly, unrecognizing. He'd seen it before on his rounds as a chaplain. Comatose patients with empty eyes. He was silently thankful when Jenn's fluttered shut again.

He made up his mind. He would get back to Jeremiah and Susan to see if they knew of this Dancer. He leaned down and kissed his wife on the lips and on the belly. On the way down in the elevator, he realized that he was still holding the repaired doll. Pearl would be happy to see the precious one. And he knew that he would be glad to place it into her hands. Something was happening in him. He wasn't sure what it was, but it was happening.

He went through the front door and turned toward the bus stop. There was some sort of commotion, people running into the street, pointing excitedly at a car rapidly disappearing down the block. Others were crouched around something on the pavement. A car screeched to a halt in front of him.

"C'mon, Godman, get in!" It was an order.

Eli hesitated, hearing the angry cries of the crowd on the corner and watching someone in hospital scrubs running out with an emergency kit.

"Now!" urged Paraclete. His eyes were round with alarm, his hand gripping the wheel with powerful force. He reached over and thrust open the passenger-side door.

Eli was barely inside when Paraclete stomped on the gas and did a squealing U-turn.

"What's the matter?" asked a bewildered Eli.

The large black man, in the same clothes he'd been in yesterday, nodded his head in the direction they'd just come. "I stole this car to come get you. Somethin's going down."

Eli squirmed in his seat to see out the back window. Before they screeched around the corner, the knot of people parted for a stretcher to be wheeled through. On the ground, he saw a small pile of rags. Arms and legs extended from it at impossible angles. He squinted his eyes and caught a glimpse of a tangle of silver-gray hair. Suddenly he wanted to throw up.

It was Joe Martinson, lying in a spreading pool of blood.

Chapter 17

Paraclete sped east, avoiding North Avenue, instead taking backstreets with worn cobblestone bricks that shook the car until their teeth rattled. He kept checking behind them, muttering under his breath, words Eli could not make out. The blocks of decay gave way to newly gentrified neighborhoods, past a school that had been turned into upper-end condos.

"Why did they do that? All he ever did was talk to me," Eli said after he'd caught his breath and Paraclete deigned to stop at a red light. "He was a lonely old man, worried about taking care of his wife."

"They're scared, brother. They're trying to isolate you. I gotta get you through the Wedding Gate."

"The Wedding Gate? What's that, another one of these stupid Sanctuary names?"

Paraclete's dark look frightened him as much as the scene they were running from. The car skimmed across a short bridge, and Paraclete spun the wheel hard left. They were on an entrance ramp to I-279 heading north. Only when they melded with traffic and he seemed satisfied that no one was following did he answer.

"The Wedding Gate's at the village. I don't know what you mean about that other stuff."

"Sure you do. You know, Sanctuary, BloodFire, Healer, FireGuide, Danc—"

"Do you know what a paraclete is, Godman?"

"It's a Greek word, from the legal system. If I remember right, it means an advocate."

"That's right. I'm an advocate. For the future of the human race. The human race has been around for close to three million years, give or take a few millennia. Ten thousand years ago, we tried to take something that wasn't ours—control of the world. It's time to give it back. It's time to wake up to what we've done. This is the only way." He breathed deeply for a few moments of silence. "Does she know where the Healer might be?"

"She?"

"The Dancer's helper, that redheaded woman with palsy."

"She didn't mention any 'where' yet, uh, I mean, she only said that the Dancer sent her."

"And we've got to get you out of town. The Wedding Gate is just that—a gate in the fence at Olde River Village. It's where the other Guardians go in and out at night. The Wellrock Brigade's got a special access port in there to safety. It's going to be tricky getting you in there in broad daylight, but it's the best way."

"I can't go anywhere! Jenn needs me." He ran a hand over his face. "Especially after what we just saw. Why do I get the feeling that was no accident?"

"Because it wasn't, genius! Godman, you've got to learn to go with your gut now. Your heart and your gut. They're not killin' people for the fun of it. No, by no means. They are scared to death."

Eli only shook his head dumbly. "What about my wife?"

"I got somebody on her, don't worry. If we have to, we'll see about taking somebody in that doctor's family, maybe his wife, holding her until you can get to the Healer."

"You can't be serious!" Eli was shocked, repulsed.

"This is war, Godman. Somebody's got to start fightin' back."

"What would be left in this kind of war? See who can commit the worst horrors to get their religious beliefs to the top?"

"It's been done, believe you me! The Crusades were no Sunday school picnic." Paraclete passed several exits before speaking again. "Okay, we'll stick to your way for now."

"My way? It isn't *my* way. I only meant that, from what I've heard so far, if there is any merit to your people's beliefs in this Sanctuary business, that it meant backing away from the precipice that the human race keeps dangling its toes over. People want a concrete image of the divine, the sacred, the reality beyond all reality. The problem is that there are too many others all too willing to give it to them. And once people have it, they become obsessed with making sure everyone else knows that they have the one true truth and it's about to be forced down everybody else's throats—for their own good, of course."

Eli gave a contrite grin. "Sorry about that. It's been a long time since I preached a sermon. God, listen to me! I sound like some hippie out of the sixties. Watch out!"

A Jeep Cherokee cut in front of them, making a beeline for the exit. Paraclete followed suit, exiting the expressway and getting on Route 19, a sprawl of malls, the latest in trendy chain restaurants, and fast-food joints huddling close to the old highway, trying to catch the runoff of disposable income from the newest suburbs.

Paraclete exhaled loudly. "Look at this! You know who these people are in all these new, overpriced, cheaply built homes? The ones who managed to survive the death of the steel mills. They latched on to this new high-tech service economy and headed out of the old mill river towns as soon as they had the down payments. The population isn't growing here, and neither is the economy. They're simply shuffling the pieces and people around. Meanwhile, those old communities are turning into rat traps, welfare and drug dealer ghost towns. People don't honor the root or the journey, and this is what happens. Endless spinning of the wheels."

Paraclete tapped Eli on the shoulder. "That was my sermon, Godman!" He cackled at this, bright white teeth showing in a blood-red mouth.

"Where are we going?" asked Eli.

"I'm taking the long way back. We'll tell Jeremiah and Susan what's happened." He looked Eli up and down. "Maybe you can clean up, change clothes. You're ripe, Godman."

"I know. I left this morning without cleaning up. I haven't been thinking too clearly lately."

"Your friend's death should clear your mind, I would think. One of the bloodtrackers must have spotted him talking to you. That might mean somebody at the hospital is connected to the Ransom."

After a long series of traffic lights, traffic thinned out a bit. At Wexford, Paraclete turned west, back over the ridge lines toward the Ohio River. Eli watched the tree-covered hills go by, longing for the days of resting comfortably assured in his tightly structured system of beliefs. God was in His heaven, good would triumph over evil, humanity was sin-sick but lovable, and the church was the kingdom of God on earth. What more could he ask for?

"How's your back and legs holdin' up?"

"Okay."

Paraclete looked like he didn't believe him, but he didn't say anything. "I've got to let you out here on the edge of town. You walk on down Merchant Street like you belong there. I can't be seen, or they might tie me and the Guardians here together. This way, if one cell gets wiped out, the other still has a chance."

He pulled over by an electric utility substation, long since shut down along with the factories and the bridge iron works. "Liberation for the BloodFire, Godman!" he called as he sped away, leaving Eli alone.

He had twelve blocks to walk. A year ago, it would have been a welcome invitation on a beautiful autumn day. Now it would be more inviting to climb the stairs to a basilica on his knees, shattered back and all. The picture of Jenn lying so peacefully in her room finally got him to start putting one foot in front of the other. Over a small rise, and the downtown area of Bridetown stretched before him.

People were going about their everyday business. Customers went in and out of the bank. Old men sat in the senior citizen rest area arguing over who could straighten out the problems of the world. Kids from the high school skipping classes attracted attention to themselves with too loud laughter and brash puffing on cigarettes. They weren't thinking about some primal lifeforce called the Sanctuary, he thought. They weren't preparing for what it would mean for the BloodFire to be liberated. Or not. Nobody was calling themselves Healers, or Guardians, or bloodtrackers, Ransom, Dancer. Everything was normal. This was the real world in front of him. What else could it be?

Religious thinking might be an invention, but like all inventions, it served an idea, a vision, a dream. He sighed and began walking.

And like all inventions, there were unintended and unforeseen consequences. Always.

After a half an hour of hard labor, he stood at the head of Fourteenth, looking in the window of the shabby floral shop, choosing not to dwell on the fact that he had avoided going to his own house first. He peered around the corner, amused at how menacing the block had looked the night previous. Around back, it was simply another rickety tenement. The stairs creaked under his feet. The door to the apartment flew open.

"Jeremiah? Is that you?" There was no mistaking the anxious fear in Susan's voice.

"It's me, Susan. Eli."

Her uncertain smile brought a knot of dread to his stomach.

"Oh, Eli. Thank goodness you're back. How is Jenn? Pearl tells me that she had a visitor from the Dancer."

"She's doing as well as can be expected. Where's Jeremiah?"

Susan put out her hands, and Eli stepped to within reach, into her limited field of vision. "Didn't Toby find you? There's a leak somewhere. We've been betrayed. Jeremiah went out to warn the Wellrock people, get some supplies. But he hasn't returned." Her voice cracked.

"Maybe it's taking longer than he expected, Susan. Don't worry."

"I feel it. I can tell in my bones, Eli. Something's wrong."

Eli considered telling her about the hit-and-run in front of the hospital, then thought better of it. He'd go look for Jeremiah himself. Together they could figure out what to do. "Listen—Paraclete told me to get a shower and get to the Wedding Gate. Do you know where that is?"

"That Wedding Gate is pretty." Pearl stood at the door, dressed similarly to last night, only this time the stockings had horizontal stripes of lime green and banana yellow. "It's how I go home."

Susan clenched and unclenched her hands as she struggled to think. "I need to stay here in case Jeremiah calls."

"Susan, you don't know—"

She cut him off. "I know. Pearl, would you go with Eli while he goes home and gets some things and then take him to the Wedding Gate?"

Pearl smiled. "Eli, what a nice name. I met someone by that name a long time ago, I think. His wife is lovely."

Eli realized with a start that he still carried the repaired doll. "I have something for you, Pearl."

She stepped onto the narrow porch. The bright sunlight bathed her face. When she turned to look at him, her glass eyeball caught the light and refracted where it passed through the crack. Instead of a shadow beneath her eye, there was a faint spectrum of colored light, like the bands of a rainbow.

He handed her the doll.

"Angela!" Pearl's cry of delight echoed in the confined alleyway. "I knew she would come back." She hugged the battered doll tightly, a mother welcoming home a lost child.

Eli swallowed his impatience. "Pearl, I saw Jenn this morning."

"Jenn? Jenn's not feeling well. She's frightened, so scared it makes my head hurt."

Eli winced at this revelation. "She has flowers in her room now, Pearl. Maybe that will help."

"Is she dancing? Jenn said she was going dancing. I like dancing. Philip and I would dance under the stars." Pearl's eyes shone brightly.

"Dancing?" Susan asked.

Eli explained. "There was someone with Jenn. She said the Dancer sent her. The Healer might be coming to the dancing ground."

"Oh, at last! I knew he was coming!" Susan put her hands to her cheeks. "Maybe Adam is with him. And Jonathan, maybe Jonathan is there too."

"Where is this Dancer person?"

"By the water," Pearl said. "By the water, where the moonbow meets the three winds."

Susan smiled. "She's right. I don't always know where you are, Pearl. But when you're right, you're right." She turned to Eli. "Up north, beside Lake Erie. That's only a couple of hours away, Eli. Maybe you will know something by tonight!"

Eli looked doubtful. "I'm to get smuggled out of Bridetown to go up to Erie? I'll look for Jeremiah first."

"There's no time," urged Susan. "Go now and get ready."

Eli shook his head. "How am I going to get there? My car is shot."

"The Wellrock Brigade are very resourceful," Susan said. "Pearl, go with Eli over to his house."

"Are we going on a picnic?" asked Pearl, the joy of a child in her voice. "Philip and I love picnics. We'll bring Peter and Angela. Have you met them?"

Eli threw up his hands in surrender. "Yeah, we'll take them to Olde River Village. Let's go."

Pearl chattered nonstop nonsense while they walked the two blocks to Eli's house. He kept checking over his shoulder, eyeing each car that past them. He told himself that he was being paranoid, but the memory of Joe's broken body convinced him otherwise.

As they approached the house, Eli felt a curious sense of reluctance, not because it stood empty but because he wondered if, with Pearl, it was like having Jenn at his side, taking her back for the first time since the accident.

Stop it, you idiot, he chided himself. *They've got me believing all this craziness. She'd get a kick of this version of herself.* He smiled inwardly while surveying the brightly bedecked and confused figure beside him, her arms pumping, legs churning, one hand clutching the paper sack where he presumed Peter and Angela were now reunited, bowed but unbeaten. How did she get here? he wondered. How did a retired Latin teacher with severe dementia end up wandering the streets dressed like a clown, her only family now a ragtag band out to save the world from itself?

"Did you and Philip live in Bridetown?" he asked Pearl.

"I was a bride, yes."

Eli started to correct her but hesitated as they reached the front steps.

"Philip said I was a beautiful bride. He wept on our wedding night." Her eyes smiled with the light of one who sees what no one else can share.

"Philip loved you very much."

"Yes," she said brightly. "Did you know Philip? Did he tell you that? Wasn't that sweet of him to tell his friend about that night!"

"Yes, he was quite delighted to have such a beautiful woman for his bride." Eli remembered his own wedding night. His friends in college used to laugh at his determination to wait for the right girl, at the right time, in the right circumstances. Now he didn't know if he could ever lie with Jenn again and let her know how she completed him as a man, as a human being.

"Come on in, Pearl. I just need to take a quick shower." He unlocked the door and stepped aside to let her in. "Make yourself at home."

The curtains were still drawn, leaving the living room dimly lit. Through the hallway, he could see the kitchen. Something about it struck him as odd, but the open door to the basement blocked most of his view. Eli reached around the doorway to flip on the light and heard Pearl's frightened squeak.

"Oh my God!" Eli cried.

In the faint light, he could see that the room was ransacked. Books and knickknacks littered the floor. The stereo speakers were tipped over, and compact discs were strewn across the room. Eli picked up a piece of yellow canvas. Someone had taken a knife to his baseball cap collection, shredding them beyond repair.

He picked up first one, then another. "Why?"

"Oh, oh," was all Pearl could say.

Eli suddenly remembered and began frantically searching the room. In a frenzy, he tore the rest of the books off the shelves and ran his hands over them. Agitated, he got down on his hands and knees and felt under the couch. "Where is it?" he asked the violated room.

"Can I help?" Pearl asked.

"The ring. I can't find the ring. They must have stolen it."

Pearl covered her mouth, muttering over and over, "No, no, no."

She carefully placed the brown bag on the couch and began to help him look. They went through the furniture, stuffing their hands under the cushions, even turning it over. The dining room fared no better. The china set from Jenn's parents was smashed, the mirror shattered into jagged shards.

"Why didn't they take the stereo or dishes?" Eli wondered aloud.

In the kitchen, pills littered the sink and countertops. Food had been taken from the refrigerator and piled into a stinking heap in the middle of the linoleum. Pearl came to him with his dogeared writing journal.

"Why didn't they rip this up?"

"Maybe they didn't know its value," Pearl answered him, sounding so solemn and sagacious that he almost believed her.

"It's gone," Eli said wearily, a dull throbbing starting at the base of his skull. "I need that ring. It's for Jenn. I have to give it to Jenn."

"I know," said Pearl. She put her arm around him and patted his shoulder. "You'll give it to her someday."

"Pearl, it's gone!" Eli pounded a fist on the counter, making the pills dance. "It's not fair! It's not fair."

A tiny noise came from the basement, a faint creak that made him look over at the door. *Why would they go into the basement?* he thought. *There's nothing down there.*

"Pearl, wait here."

He turned on the light and started down the steps. Halfway down, he heard the sound again. At the same time, he heard sirens, close by, loud. Reaching the bottom of the stairway, he saw the door ajar that led to the root cellar he'd dug in anticipation of a successful career as a gardener. He anxiously rubbed a hand over his face. Tires squealed out in the front of the house, and a car door slammed. He could hear the squawk of police radios.

His hand shook as he reached out and pulled open the door. The source of the noise hung on a large hook, slowly swinging in the cool crypt.

The face stared hideously. Eyes bulged, and the tongue lolled out the side of his mouth. A rope was knotted around the neck and tied to the hook. It couldn't have been a suicide. There was nothing to stand on. And, besides, Jeremiah didn't have legs.

Chapter 18

Gideon drifted off in the damp shelter. Christine came to him again during his sleep. He prayed that she would not, but she did. He wasn't sure why he didn't want her to come. He had nothing to be ashamed of. After their lovemaking, he and Laurel had laid together in silence, watching the shadows dance on the wall.

Gideon lay awake for a long time after Laurel fell asleep, listening to her steady breathing. He had no right to expect the sweetness or the passion to come into his life ever again. Then he drifted off.

"Gideon."

He thought he was still awake, but he was surrounded by light. The voice came from within it—Christine's voice. He figured he had to be dreaming because Christine only came to him in his dreams anymore. She sounded happy, alive, serene.

He tried to reach out to her. If he could touch her one more time, see that she was whole and undiminished, perfect, then maybe the awful images would be banned from his mind. The picture of her torn and broken body, ripped open wide with her blood staining his shoes and his clothing. If only he could know she was complete wherever she was. Then *he* might rest in peace.

"Gideon. I'm all right."

The light surrounded him, enveloping him within a cocoon of gentle radiance. He wanted to see her face. Her voice sounded like it did the time she went to Cleveland to present a paper on Egyptian mythology. Her graduate school professor had been so impressed with it in class that she insisted Christine come along with her to a convention and read it to a room full of other professors.

Christine was so nervous. She practiced it to Gideon time after time, not believing him when he told her she did it perfectly. The night before she left, she threw up five times, her lucky number.

Two days later, he watched as she skipped up the sidewalk, a Cleveland State sweatshirt over her skirt, beaming in triumph. "I did it! I'm all right, Gideon! I couldn't wait to get back here to tell you all about it."

He heard that same tone in her voice now as he lay in the spring house cave. The light dissolved into a scene. He could see her coming across a field, set high on Cradle Mountain, a bunch of wildflowers in her hand. When she came close, she held out the wild bouquet to him with a laugh of delight. He looked at his hand; it held mountain laurel.

Suddenly they were no longer flowers but a small statuette. It was the bronze figure of Isis, the one she kept on the mantel beside the clock with the Westminster chimes. He tried to stop his hand, but his skin came in contact with the cold metal, and a shiver ran up his arm.

"She has the story," Christine said. She took the statue in both hands and thrust it at him. "Isis has the key, Gideon. It's underneath Isis. I can't be the guide. I'm off to dance!"

He called to her, but she was skipping across the field, growing smaller and smaller against the great expanse.

Gideon blinked. He was back in the cave. The songs of the birds filtering in told him it was morning. Laurel stirred beside him.

"Good morning," she whispered. When he didn't answer, she peered over his shoulder. "Cat got your tongue?"

He managed a weak smile but didn't respond.

A shadow flitted across Laurel's face. "Are you sorry?"

"Sorry for what?"

"Don't play dumb. You know what I'm talking about."

"Do I?"

"Gideon! What's wrong? Are you sorry about last night?"

"No. It's nothing. Just a dream." He sat up. "What's for breakfast? Pancakes and sausage with canned beans and tomatoes on the side?"

Laurel sat very still. Her eyes watered, but she tightened her jaw, and no tear escaped. Gideon could not look at her.

"You can't even look at me? Is that all I am to you?"

Gideon found his voice. "A lot happened yesterday. We were tired and on the edge. We let our guard down."

Laurel recoiled as if she'd been struck. "Let down our guard? Yes, we let down our guard, Gideon." Her voice filled with anger and indignation, she raced on. "I knew—I thought that for the first time since forever I could let down my barriers. And there are a lot of them, you know. But no, you got the real thing. It was me. Just as I am."

She reached a hand to touch him. It reminded him of the dream. She saw the look in his eye, and her hand dropped to her lap. Silence jerked a veil across the cave.

Laurel summoned her courage. "Is it me? Is it what I told you about my background? I have to know, Gideon. You mean a lot—I feel …"

"No. There is nothing wrong with you." Gideon wanted to sound emphatic, convincing. Instead, he thought he sounded contrived. "You are beautiful and wonderful, and I feel like a man again. You are more than I deserve."

She stood to face him directly. "Then what?"

Gideon's breathing came faster. His hands went to his head. "She came to me last night."

"Who came? Christine?"

He nodded. "It was a dream. At least I think it was a dream. It was as though—as if I, she …" He forced himself to breathe more slowly. "She was right there in front of me. I could see the flowers and smell the grass. I could look into her eyes. It's like she came to tell me goodbye."

"Goodbye?"

He nodded his head dumbly. "How could she go like that?"

"Gideon, tell me about it. Tell me about her." She looked him in the eye, then away, fearful of his seeing what they mirrored.

"We can't stay here, Laurel. We have to move on."

"I can't go on like nothing has happened, like we don't mean—"

Gideon stopped her with a look. "What's the happiest you've ever been?"

"What?"

"The happiest you've ever been—what was it? When was it?"

"I don't know."

"Come on. You have to know."

Laurel shook her head. "What's that have to do with anything?"

"Just tell me."

"Okay, I will." Without hesitation, Laurel said, "It was last night. I couldn't believe it. On what was probably one of the worst days in my life, with Jonathan being murdered and nearly being killed myself in a wreck and sneaking into that creepy room at the house, and knowing there is probably no one else in the world I can talk to about it all, I realized that …" She hesitated, frowned, and shrugged one shoulder.

"Realized what? C'mon, don't stop."

She let him know her displeasure at being forced into this revelation by giving him an exasperated sigh. "I realized that it didn't matter if there was no one else to tell it to. There was you. I could tell you about it. I've known you for all of two days, and I'm letting you through the walls it's taken me a lifetime to build." She looked at him, daring him to argue, defiant and scared. "I don't let people get to me."

Gideon blinked slowly, trying unsuccessfully to hide the storm of feelings swirling through his mind.

"What about you?" Laurel asked. "What was the happiest you've ever been?"

Gideon turned away from her, staring into the clear pool in the center of the cave. "JP called this his kiva. Do you know what that is?"

"Don't try to change the subject, Gideon. I'm putting myself, my whole heart, on the line here. I'm feeling enough like a fool as it is."

Gideon ignored her protests. "It's from the Indians of the Southwest. The Hohokam and the Anasazi, the ancestors of what most people refer to as the Pueblo Indians. They would make a pit in the middle of their village of dwellings. It had no windows or doors, only a hole in the roof. The men went in and out by way of a ladder. In this kiva, they had sacred ceremonies. They went down into the earth because they knew that they depended on it for their lives. In the middle of the floor of the kiva, there was often a *sipapu*. It was a stone-lined hole that represented the entrance to the cave world, which is where their ancestors emerged."

He stopped for a moment, still studying the water. Laurel made no sound behind him. "JP came home from the Second World War a changed man. He'd been captured, my mother told me. For a while after he got back, he studied the culture of the Indians, traveling across the country to find shaman and medicine men to teach him. I wish I'd known him then."

"You mean he didn't tell you about it while you were growing up?"

"No, not a word. And if I ever asked, he would become distant, shut me out. He said the time wasn't right, I wasn't prepared to receive the story. I couldn't figure out what he meant. But at one time, this was his kiva."

He turned around to face Laurel. "How can I be so stupid as to think that I saw my father yesterday? I was three years old, for God's sake. Did he pop up through the sipapu? What about JP? Why didn't he come to me last night and explain it all? Why didn't he give me some word, some help? Why did Christine come and tell me that it would be okay and then say goodbye and leave me forever?"

He shook his head over and over while continuing. "How can she tell me that it's okay to have another best day, another happiest time in my life? For a year, I've been keeping her alive, holding her close, telling her everything, and she comes and so much as tells me that she's moving on. The happiest time in my life was when she married me. But then last night, after we made love, she comes and tells me goodbye. Did I drive her away?"

"Why would she come to tell you goodbye and to be happy if you had in any way driven her away? If she loved you, why wouldn't she want you to have more happiest days in your life? She'd be selfish otherwise."

"She's not selfish."

"Gideon, I'm no expert by a long shot. But did you keep her up on a pedestal when you married Christine?"

Gideon spun around. "What's that supposed to mean?"

"I'm sorry. I don't mean to upset you," Laurel said. "But it's an awful burden to put on someone to think of them as perfect. It's crippling to a good, strong relationship."

"Oh, here we go. You're such an expert on good, strong relationships, right? You have the nerve to tell me that I wasn't a good husband, that *I* didn't treat Christine right! Who told you about good marriages—your father?"

Laurel recoiled in horror at the maliciousness of his words. She struggled to compose her features so he would not see how deeply she'd been wounded while she pushed past him into the sunlight. The mountainsides shimmered in the new light of the day. She tried taking deep breaths and slowly letting them out as Gideon scrambled out behind her.

"What made you think it was your father that you saw at the farm yesterday? Besides that old truck, was there anything about that man that would make you think after all those years of not seeing him, that it was the same man you knew as your father?"

Gideon scuffed at the ground with the toe of his boot. "Listen, Laurel—"

"No, don't even start, Gideon. Let's just move on." She was all business, her tone crisp and efficient. "It was crazy. I mean, I was crazy to let us get off track. More importantly, it's dangerous."

"Dammit, wait a minute! You didn't *let* us do anything. There were two people in there last night."

"Are you going to stand out here shouting for much longer? Because if you are, I'm going to move away from here before we draw any more attention."

Gideon tugged on his chin in frustration. "Be that way then. Anybody ever tell you that you are the most stubborn woman in the world?"

"Did anyone ever tell you that you're a jerk?"

"Well, I'm trying to apologize, if you'd let me."

"Don't bother. It's nothing. Don't apologize for the truth. I have no business giving you any lectures on love and marriage."

"This past year, there have been times when I wondered if I was losing my sanity. I quit my job and spent all the money from Christine's life insurance. I was too ashamed to come see JP ever, but I told myself it was okay, at least I was providing for him."

"That was a good thing to do."

Gideon shook his head. "I'd told Christine he was dead. She never met him. So, instead of helping him get into a better place where they could take care of him, I spent most of the money on booze and drugs and women. And I even did something more stupid than that."

Laurel waited for him to finish. When he didn't say more, she said, "I don't blame you for doing those things. I don't have any room to judge. Tell me what you did with the rest."

Gideon swallowed hard. "They say little boys are always looking for their daddy. Well, that's what I did. I hired private detectives to look for my father. I didn't even know why I was doing it. I had some stupid fantasy about finding him, beating the crap out of him, forcing him to pay for what he did to us."

"Did they find anything?"

"Nah, just charged me an arm and a leg to tell me the trail was too cold after all these years. One of them ended up getting himself killed, but it had nothing to do with working for me."

Laurel suddenly stepped close, her eyes intense. "What? What happened?"

Gideon backed up a step. "He was in that courthouse that was blown up by one of those whacked-out militias down south. Remember that they caught some redneck who said they were making a statement about violations being committed against the United States Constitution? Well, the guy I hired was in there checking some records, his secretary said. He was in the wrong place at the wrong time."

Laurel put her hand on top of her head, her face a study in concentration. "That's got to be it!"

"What are you talking about?"

"You sent people out looking for your father, asking questions, digging into old records. That detective must have found something, or told somebody who he was looking for. The Ransom is everywhere. The bloodtrackers got real active about nine months ago, Jonathan said. He didn't know why, but something was up. Then came that bomb in the courthouse. I'd bet good money it was aimed at the private eye."

"That's an awfully big leap of logic! You're assuming my father is tied into this Sanctuary stuff."

"There has to be a connection! I can feel it! Maybe they found him and found out who hired him. Then they got rid of him and started watching you! That's got to be it!"

"You're saying there's a chance that I led them back here, back to kill all these people?"

"Gideon, tell me. What made you think that was your father by the farmhouse yesterday?"

Gideon shook his head, half in protest and half in ignorance. "I don't know. I saw my mother's picture of him, of course. But he'd have to look a lot different now. Especially if he's trying so hard not to be found." He looked across the creek, staring blankly into the woods.

"Come on—think, Gideon!"

He pursed his lips. "It was just a fleeting thought. I don't even know why I thought it, where it came from. When I saw the truck in the orchard, I knew it was JP's old one. And for the briefest moment, I thought, *Of course. He's come to see JP's grave*."

"Where's JP buried?"

"On the northern side of the orchard. There's a little rise that looks down over the farm and up the valley toward the river. He's there beside my grandmother."

"Show me."

Gideon could tell by looking at her that she was focusing on the business at hand, that his apology would have to wait. He wanted to kick himself for losing his temper and being such a jackass.

Being with Laurel had been incredible, their fingers slowly tracing patterns in each other's palms until passion overwhelmed them and they made exquisite love, each seeming to sense the other's need and particular pleasure without any words being spoken. Then came the dream about Christine. It had shaken him badly. It wasn't an excuse. There was no excuse for what he'd said, hurting Laurel with such ferocity.

He led the way up the creek bank, carefully checking for any observers, for the first time noticing that he was not nearly as sore as he'd been yesterday morning. He should have felt worse after the accident. His body was going crazy.

He caught a glimpse of the house as they crept through the orchard. Unexpectedly, it brought a lump to his throat. His mother would have loved Laurel. They climbed a gentle slope and stopped dead in their tracks.

The small fenced-in family plot sat in front of them, the sunset maple filling the center. Modest gravestones marked three graves. Freshly turned earth showed dark against the fading grass. But that was not what riveted their gaze.

Beyond the graveyard, a dirt road ran past the poplar trees planted as a windbreak two generations ago. At their base, waiting, sat the old, dark green '49 Chevy flatbed. Empty.

They circled it warily before Gideon peeked inside. On the seat was the morning edition of the local paper, fresh off the presses. He reached in and lifted it out to show Laurel.

The headline jumped off the page. "Young Couple Dies in Tragic Crash." Beneath it was a grainy photo of the burned hulk of Gideon's car.

"Good news," he said. "We're dead."

Chapter 19

"Someone's either taking real good care of us or leading us right into the lion's den," Laurel said.

"Beats walking." Gideon climbed in and patted the familiar seat and steering wheel.

"Where are we going?"

"My house."

"What!"

"You heard me. We're going to my house."

Laurel gave him a wry smile. "Who's going to push this thing, you or me?"

"That's what's so weird. There was only one way to get that old truck started." Gideon felt under the seat, then held up his hand with a flourish, displaying a screwdriver with carbon singe marks along the shaft. "If you weren't parked on a hill, you used the 'modern crank,' as JP called it."

Gideon pulled out the choke, grasped the ignition housing, and jiggled it until it popped free of the dash. He put the screwdriver across the exposed wires, and the engine sputtered to life.

"You sure you remember how to drive this thing?" Laurel asked doubtfully.

"It's like riding a bike. You never forget!"

He ground the gears with a frightful groan, and they lurched down the road, away from the mysteries and tragedies and bruised spirits of the past two days. One valley opened into another as they chugged along the dirt road.

Laurel rolled her eyes. "Feel kinda like I'm on Walton's mountain."

Gideon laughed. "Good night, JimBob."

"Good night, Mary Ellen."

"Good night, Mama and Daddy."

"Good night, John Boy."

"Say good night, Gracie!" They both giggled.

"So, how does it feel to be dead?" asked Laurel, trying to hold the newspaper steady while they bounced and jolted across the ruts. "Says here that you were grieving the loss of your grandfather and were distraught still over the death of your wife. Police speculate that you picked up a local woman and perhaps you were drinking heavily before running off the road."

"Where do they come up with that?"

"Says here that they checked the house and found the mantel destroyed, 'as though in a fit of rage,' but that the bodies were burned beyond recognition." She looked at him sideways. "Did you have a reputation that they tracked down?"

Gideon ignored that. "Maybe they used one of those doctors and one of the nurses. Oh God, isn't there anything these people won't stoop to?"

"I hope they don't find Jonathan's body. No telling what they'd do."

They rode on in silence for a while. Laurel spoke first. "You know these back roads pretty well. I'm lost."

"We're circling behind Cradle Mountain. I'm going to crisscross and double back every so often until I'm convinced we're not being followed. I'm getting pretty paranoid."

"It's not paranoia, it's survival, Gideon."

"So, is this truck fate, or good luck, or someone leading us around by the nose?"

"I've been going over that in my mind," Laurel said. "There are some Sanctuary sympathizers out there. Could be one of them."

"This is plain people country. I have trouble believing they could be helpful when it comes to this."

"Plain people?"

"Yeah, Amish, Old River Order Mennonite, those sorts."

"With the horses and buggies? Them?"

"Them. They have a few districts here in the mountains and all the way on up into Pennsylvania."

"Why did you say they wouldn't be likely to help?"

"Well, because I figure this Sanctuary stuff is anti-Christian in a way, anti all of the big established religions for that matter."

"That answers two questions, mine and yours. You asked before if there wasn't anything the Ransom and the bloodtrackers wouldn't do. The BloodFire Redemption will undercut the power base of the major world religions and all that's tied into them, like economic and political power. People will see what true freedom is all about: reconnecting to our common root as one race, taking different roads but making the same journey, and that in the end, the witnesses act on behalf of us all."

Gideon was scornful. "You have a lot of faith in people."

"But when they see the witnesses in the flesh and blood, it won't be some esoteric philosophy or mental exercise. It will be real."

"Esoteric?"

Laurel smiled. "I've been increasing my word power."

"Tell me something. You're a Guardian. Just what is this Redemption? What exactly is supposed to happen when the Healer, the Sacrament child, and the FireGuide get together? Do we drink blood? Does some big pillar of fire come out of the sky? Are there plagues and earthquakes, or people floating up to heaven?"

Laurel cleared her throat and looked out the window. "I don't know."

Gideon's jaw dropped. "Excuse me? What did you say?"

"I said I don't know."

Gideon did a double take. "You don't know what a Redemption really is? We're going through all this, and we don't know if we're going to unleash some terrible force or plink your little spit of a belief into the world's pot?"

"You need somebody who knows the Chronicles better than me. Jonathan said that the Chronicles are being forfeited because there is no StoryKeeper."

"Well, that's just great." Gideon threw up his hands. "That's just great."

"If you're so skeptical, why are you driving this truck to … wherever it is you're driving it?"

Gideon didn't answer for a long time. They came to a fork in the road. Gideon turned the wheel and headed up a steep slope. The ancient engine strained, and the wheels slowed to a crawl.

"The dream," he admitted quietly. "The dream last night. If she really was saying goodbye, then maybe she knows something about all this and was trying to help."

Laurel squinted at him. "What else did she say?"

"Something about a story in the statue."

"What story? What statue?"

"Christine said the story was in the statue, the one of Isis on our mantel."

"Isis? Do you know who she is?"

"Some Egyptian goddess."

"Didn't your wife tell you? Is that what she studied?"

"Yeah, she told me. But I didn't really listen. I mean I was proud of her and all, but I wasn't really interested in all that ancient mythology stuff."

"What did she think of that? Didn't she want you to be interested?"

Gideon squirmed uncomfortably. "I don't know. I suppose. I know that it made her happy and excited." He shrugged. "Maybe I could have listened better. But I was worried about the baby coming and losing my chance to go to college finally and … and, well—"

"And catch up to her a little bit?"

Gideon pulled a face. "I really don't like you sometimes."

"Among other things, Isis is the goddess of blood and healing."

Gideon stared at her, his eyes wide. "That's a little too spooky if you ask me."

Laurel arched her eyebrows. "This is getting interesting!"

"Too interesting. Let's just pretend for a minute, okay? Pretend that we did see my father in the orchard. Pretend that after all these years, he is sneaking around me, trying to get me to do what he wants." Gideon balled a fist and hit the steering wheel.

"Or pretend," Laurel said, taking up the story, "that it was your father and he can't talk directly to you, for whatever reasons, but he is trying to help you because he knows what you need to do."

"We're back to that!" cried Gideon in frustration. "*I don't know what I need to do, but everybody else does!*"

"It makes as much sense as your scenario."

"Okay, pretend it wasn't my father, and I'm going through some midlife, overstressed, deluded scenario, and any stranger hanging around the farm could look like my father. I don't even want to see the bastard anyway!"

"Yes, you do," Laurel stated matter-of-factly.

"You could get on my nerves, you know that? What do you mean, *yes, I do?*"

"Forget about the murders and violence for just a second. You're getting intrigued by the idea that your life might have something to it. And the possibility that your family is a part of it makes it all the more curious to you. Why else are we going to your house based on a dream?"

"Loyalty?"

"Okay, maybe some loyalty. But I bet you could care less about all the talk of fighting for the heart and soul of the human race and other worlds. Face it. You're a guy, and guys want to know that they're different than all the other guys, that they have something you don't."

"I see. You have us *guys* all figured out." Gideon shifted gears as they crested the peak. "It couldn't have been him."

"Not very likely. But somebody is going to an awful lot of trouble to get us on the road."

"And by the time they make a positive ID on those burned bodies, we'll be long gone."

Laurel snickered. "Not if we don't put our feet through the floor like Fred Flintstone and make this thing go faster."

Gideon hit the gas, and the truck picked up imperceptible speed.

"You remember what happened yesterday when we went downhill! Keep a sharp eye out for anything on the road, Gideon. I don't care if it's no bigger than a pea. There's no back seat this time to catch us."

They rode on for another half hour or so, through the hills and narrow valleys, through the towns of Romney and Piketon. As the morning wore on into noon, they pulled into the small town of Keyser.

"Time to stretch our legs and get something to eat," Gideon announced.

Laurel was more than ready for a break from the noisy, dirty, and hot truck. The small diner on the edge of town had peeling paint and red-and-white-checked oilcloth table covers. On one side of the lot, cows stood along the fence, watching with lazy curiosity. Beyond their pasture was yet another rise of tree-covered hills, while across the road, the ground was flat.

"Lovely odor," Laurel commented, pointing to the bovines.

"You should get a whiff of the town to the west. There's a huge paper mill that stinks constantly of sulfur and worse."

"Why's it so flat over there?"

"That's the flood plain for the North Branch of the Potomac. We came across South Branch near Romney. Terrible flood down there in 1985. JP and I went over to help out. One night, he brought me up here to this diner. He said it had the best chocolate pie, next to my mother's. He was right." Gideon's mouth watered at the memory.

"How long has your family been on that farm? What became of your grandfather?" Laurel asked as they found seats in a booth. "Don't you have any brothers or sisters?"

"What's with all the questions?" Gideon's guard went up, remembering the frayed edges they both revealed when they got up earlier. "We look like something out of the *Grapes of Wrath*," he joked, noting their filthy clothing and the questioning looks from others. He wanted to distract her from the subject.

"They're just questions. Humor me already!"

He marveled at the way her eyes lit up when she was preparing to extract some more personal information from him. He wasn't aware that he'd been noticing it at the time, but he sure noticed it now.

"Quit staring and answer the question."

"Questions, not one, and I'm not staring. I'm sizing up my interlocutor."

"I'm impressed. Somebody else has been spending too many nights with his dictionary!"

Gideon's smile faded.

"Oh damn, tell me I did it again," Laurel said with a sigh of exasperation.

"Did what?"

"You know good and well what. Whatever I did this morning that made you get all quiet and look right through me. I can take a lot but not that. Especially not from … never mind."

"No, I was stupid this morning. I owe you an apology. I didn't mean it, what I said. It's all been so fast, all of it. But there's no time to think about it. Things just keep happening. But that's no excuse for what I said to you, and again, I'm sorry."

"Accepted." Laurel studied her hands. "It's not like we made some sort of commitment to each other, or told each other our deepest darkest secrets, or anything like that."

"Exactly," Gideon replied. "Maybe when this is over and there's time to think about what we're doing."

Laurel gave him a rueful smile. "Yeah, when there's more time. Let's order some chocolate pie or something."

Halfway through their hot meatloaf sandwiches with genuine red gravy on the works, Gideon took a swallow of Coke. "I don't have any."

"Excuse me? Did you need something?" asked a passing waitress.

"No, thank you," Gideon murmured.

"You mean brothers or sisters," Laurel stated.

"How'd you know what I meant?" asked a surprised Gideon.

Laurel shrugged. "I just did. Did you want some?"

"Sometimes. I was really looking forward to having a kid. Christine said she didn't know who was going to be the more difficult child, the baby or me." Laurel smiled at that, and Gideon didn't feel the pain of mentioning Christine's name quite so acutely.

"What about the farm?"

"It's been in my family since after the Revolutionary War. JP told me, though, that since he didn't figure me for a farmer, and neither did I, that if I didn't want the land, it was to be turned into some sort of training place for the disabled, or for something like a school for retarded children, or emotionally wounded kids, something like that."

"How wonderful! I think I'd like to work at a place like that."

"If I ever do it, the job's yours." The thought intrigued Gideon more than he let on. It was something he'd never considered before. JP's request had been made years ago. The events of the past few days had kept him from seeing JP's lawyer and finding out the parameters of the will and the condition of JP's estate. Suddenly, it was very important to him to find out.

They both sensed the drop in the noise level as the door behind them opened. "Damn," muttered Laurel. "The police."

A tall deputy sheriff, his middle-age belly just beginning to develop, walked over and stood beside the booth, one thumb hooked in his holster, the other cradling aviator sunglasses. "How're ya folks doin' today?"

Gideon blinked twice in reply.

"That you're old Chivvy truck parked out there?"

"Yes, it is."

"Where you folks headed?"

"Pennsylvania."

"Back home."

Gideon was puzzled by this clairvoyance.

"We've been visiting family, Officer," Laurel piped up. "Just stopped for some of your delicious chocolate pie and a generous helping of hospitality."

He stared at them from under the brim of his Smokey Bear hat for a long moment. "You've got a broken taillight. Get it fixed when you reach home." He turned and went to the counter.

Gideon and Laurel looked at each other and decided it was time to leave. Back in the truck, they both let out sighs of relief.

"My heart was in my throat," gasped Gideon.

Laurel giggled. "I was trying like crazy to come up with excuses for whatever he was going to say."

"Nothing would be any crazier that what we really are doing." Gideon pointed at the glove box. "See if there's a registration in there."

Laurel dug around as Gideon started the engine and pulled back onto the highway. "Here it is," she reported.

"What's it say?"

"Registered to a Lost Trail Camp, RD 2, North Fairfield, Pennsylvania."

"What? That doesn't make any sense! I don't know anybody up there," Gideon said.

"Where is it?"

"It's up near Erie. One of those rural townships right on the lake."

"That's not where we're going?"

"I'm going to my old house to check out that dream first. If that doesn't give us any help, I guess we know where we'll head next."

"What's a truck from some camp in Pennsylvania doing waiting for us beside the cemetery on your grandfather's farm?"

"I don't have any idea," Gideon said, sounding a bit dazed. "But I get the feeling that whoever left it there is going to be waiting for us when we get north."

"Maybe they're following us now. I think we should get off the highway and hit the back roads again."

Gideon guided the truck onto a little-used road running beside a tributary of the Potomac, heading northwest. Trees grew high overhead, forming a shady cathedral. An abandoned coal tipple, covered with vines, gave silent testimony to the passing years. Before long, they reached the steep climb up Back Bone Mountain.

Halfway up, they ran into the thick Western Maryland fog that the mountain was famous for. The daylight and the side of the road disappeared in a white shroud.

"JP showed me this old road. Sometimes in the winter, there'd be a light drizzle down below, and halfway up, just like somebody drew a straight line, the snow and ice started."

"Does it get clear on top?"

"Usually on top it lifts, but when you start back down the other side—boom! Same as this side."

Sure enough, on top, the road was clear under gray clouds. "I've never seen that before!" cried Laurel. "It's like going up into the heavens."

Gideon laughed. "If you don't know where you're going, it can be more like hell."

Laurel started in her seat. "What was that?"

"What?"

"Over there on the right. I thought I heard children's voices. It was like moaning or crying. I caught a glimpse of something through the trees, but the fog's getting too thick again."

"Probably a deer. Hold on for the descent."

"Wait, Gideon. I want to check it out. You can stop here, and I'll go back to see."

Gideon ground the gears and stopped. "No, I'll go with you. It really gets bad up here. We might as well get lost together on a wild goose chase."

At the back of the truck, Laurel reached for his hand as they retraced their path. At first, they were surrounded by swirling white mist and unearthly silence. Then a sound came from the left. Laurel put a finger to her lips and listened.

It sounded again, and she took off, dragging Gideon behind her. She stepped off the roadway and led him through ferns and grasses soaked with heavy moisture, homing in on the source. After nearly leading him into a tree, she abruptly stopped at the edge of a clearing.

Through the mists, Gideon could make out five small forms on the ground. He stepped into the clearing, and the forms moved.

"Gideon, they're shivering!" cried Laurel.

The faces of five children, three girls and two boys, looked up at him. They all wore the plain dark clothes, starched white bonnets, and black hats of the Amish.

"What are you doing here?" asked Gideon.

"Are you lost?" Laurel asked.

They shook their heads, scattering droplets of dew around the small area.

Gideon pressed ahead. "We thought we heard someone in pain."

"That was us," said the oldest of the five, a girl of about thirteen. "These are my brothers and sisters."

"What are you children doing out here by yourselves in this cold and damp?" Laurel inquired, bending down to wrap her arms around the youngest two. The older boy backed away.

"We're allowed out here. We're not babies!" he protested indignantly.

Gideon half-smiled. "No, you're not babies. Is everything okay?"

"Did God send you?" asked a cherubic four-year-old girl.

"We were prayin' and comfortin'," added the oldest.

"What were you praying about?" asked Laurel.

"Our mama," said the cherub.

"Don't tell our troubles to strangers," warned her big brother.

"We didn't mean to intrude," Gideon reassured.

"She's sick. Our mama's sick unto death," piped up the youngest, a boy of about three.

"We were prayin' to the Almighty to send help." A girl of eleven, all gangly arms and legs said earnestly, adding, "If it be His will."

"We didn't want to disturb Mama," said the oldest. "We didn't mean to cause you any worry."

"Oh, they're not worried," said the cherub in a burst of confidence. "They've come to help Mama. That man is the Healer."

Chapter 20

Eli choked back the bile rushing to his throat. He started to reach for Jeremiah's body, to get the weight off the hook and taut rope, when he heard the police pounding on the door overhead and Pearl's voice trying to explain the exploits of Peter and Angela, her voice strong, clear.

Eli wondered why the police weren't rushing through the house. Pearl must be blocking the door, her freakish appearance slowing the momentum. But why would she be doing that? She didn't know what was down there. Eli began backing across the small basement, away from the body, his mind detached, watching himself act out this strange script to which he was not privy.

At the back of the cellar was a small trapdoor that led to the crawl space under the back porch. His heart pounded, the blood roaring in his ears. His foot kicked something that went rolling across the dirt floor. It stopped just inside the rectangle of light coming from the top of the stairs. The skateboard. Jeremiah's skateboard.

"What's it doing over here?" whispered Eli in the gloom.

He was at the opposite wall now, directly beneath the small opening. The skateboard had been below the hidden exit. He reached up and felt for the latch. The thud of heavy footsteps overhead told him that Pearl's valiant stall was over. His fingers tugged at the rusted clasp. The effort of reaching and working over his head sent his shoulders and neck into spasms.

He bit into the soft material of his denim jacket, desperate to keep from screaming at the pain that raced up the base of his skull and down both arms. With one mighty effort, the clasp gave way. Breathing heavily, Eli pulled on the door. It swung partway open, then stuck. He cursed and began to feel around the bottom of the frame. His fingers closed around something firm and soft. Working it back and forth under the edge of the door, it slid free.

The ring box. Even in the pitch dark, he knew it. His fingers had caressed it so often in anticipation of presenting it to Jenn that he knew every square centimeter by feel. Eli looked back toward Jeremiah's body, wondering.

"Who else is here, lady?" gruff voices demanded to know.

Eli shoved the box into his pocket and with all his strength leveraged himself up and out the small opening. He wriggled underneath the small porch, trying to remain calm, not panic.

After checking both sides of the porch, he lay still, waiting to see if anyone was standing above him. When he heard nothing, he finished crawling from under the boards and into the bushes that stretched along his neighbor's yard back to the alley. He silently thanked the first town planners who drew up so many alleyways in the old retreat of a fringe religious group, then an old mill town. He hoped the police would realize that Pearl was harmless and let her go.

He was easing past the first in line of garages when it happened. The ground beneath his feet trembled. Instantly, he felt a deep rumbling and terrific pressure on his eardrums. Eli turned around just in time to see his house erupt in a ball of flame. Frantic shouts came from the second floor. In slow motion, the walls bulged out, then disintegrated inward, as though taking in a horrific final breath before the floors, windows, shelves, furniture, and baseball caps collapsed into the basement.

A huge cloud of smoke and dust rose into the sky. The nauseating smell of burnt flesh wafted over the apocalyptic scene. Eli covered his face with his hands, horrified. He hesitated, tempted to go back and see if he could do anything to help survivors, when a stealthy footstep sounded behind him.

Eli whirled around and came face-to-face with the enigmatic Toby. The tough visage held eyes of tempered steel.

"Let's go. We gotta get out of here." It was an order.

Eli dumbly nodded and fell in behind him as the skinny boy quietly led the numb and horrified man toward the Olde Village.

After a few minutes, Eli's numbed brain marveled at the skill Toby demonstrated at finding the darkest path through the neighborhood in broad daylight. He glided easily beneath towering sycamores and maples, melting into shadows, choosing a roundabout path that led down narrow pass-throughs between the close-set houses. At one point, he made his way to Merchant Street, stopping at storefronts and seeming to window-shop. After the second or third time, Eli realized that his young guide was checking behind them for anyone paying too much attention or attempting to follow.

"Shouldn't we tell Susan?" Eli whispered as they passed the floral shop at the top of Fourteenth, with the entrance to the village, and presumable safety, at the other end of the block.

Toby shook his head emphatically.

"But she needs to be told," Eli insisted. "She'd want to know how her husband died."

"Does she?" Toby stopped and faced him. "Does she need to know that? Does she need to know that because you are so clumsy and stupid that you stumbled right in on us last night, and that Jeremiah sent me to check out your house?"

"Why?" demanded Eli, his face red with indignation. "What right did you have to break into my house?"

"I couldn't find anything either way," Toby said with disgust. "I couldn't tie you to the Ransom bloodtrackers or to the Sanctuary. Jeremiah insisted that there had to be something and went to check for himself. They were waiting for him. God only knows what they did to him before he died! Damn it, I shoulda gone in with him. I don't even know what he found."

Eli thought of the ring nestled in his pocket. Was Jeremiah bringing it out for him or using it to prove something to the others to allay their suspicions? How did he know of the door? The questions only swam faster and faster in a sucking whirlpool. "The Paraclete. He said something once about seeing us having cookies and champagne."

"Maybe your wife told Pearl about it. Things get a little confusing ... got confusing talking to Pearl."

"I don't get it," Eli mumbled. "Jeremiah was so full of ... of energy and vitality."

"Susan knew that this could happen someday. Well, now it's happened. And we don't know why!" The tough face nearly cracked. "We don't know who you are, mister, but there's some awfully powerful people worried about you." He drew himself up to his full height, his eyes burning with hatred. "If you ask me, there ain't nothin' that you could tell me or show me to convince me it's worth Jeremiah's life."

"And Pearl's," Eli added dully.

Toby's eyes widened slightly at this news, but he kept silent.

"She kept the police busy while I figured out how to get out of there. It seemed like the thing to do at the time. I had no idea that they'd rigged Jeremiah's body to some sort of bomb. You have to believe me. I didn't know."

Toby's chest heaved with a few shuddering breaths, his eyes still burning holes through to the back of Eli's skull, but he said nothing. Eli started back toward the tenement, but Toby grabbed his arm. "We have to get on with it," he said. "The police will be turning this town upside down looking for you. I'll get you to the Wedding Gate. Maybe one of the others will take you on through."

"But Susan—"

"But nothing. Susan knew the risks and the rules. She thinks you're for real. For some reason, she takes Pearl pretty seriously. I'm not some innocent little cherub who says"—here Toby adopted a cherubic smile and childish singsong voice—"'Oh, gee! Oh, golly! We have to believe in Pearl's premonitions. And Santa Claus and the Easter Bunny too! If we all believe together, we'll make the world a better place.' Sorry, buddy, but not me! Now either get your ass in gear and do what I tell you, or I'm leaving you right here and right now."

Eli gaped openmouthed as the intense, age-old man-child added, "And your wife will be your problem and your problem alone."

Eli snapped out of it and angrily grabbed Toby's shirt. "She jumped in the water to save some little girl, then drowned herself. She's pregnant, and if I want her to have a chance to make it, the baby's got to die. If I keep the baby, my wife may be a vegetable. Hell, for all I know, she may be a vegetable either way. But she's the most important thing in all the world to me. Now two people are dead, you crazies are yapping at me to save the baby and saying it's what my wife wants me to do. And yet you've got the gall to threaten me, you little asshole!"

Eli let go and turned to leave. Someone stumbled into his arms, blood-caked hands clutching at his sleeves. He could not have been more shocked.

"Pearl?"

A short while later, they were helping the bleeding, shell-shocked woman up the stairs to Susan's apartment and reluctantly broke the news of her own loss. They tried to tend to Pearl's wounds while coaxing her to not talk. It was impossible.

"I did what I could. I didn't lie. They wanted in, but I keep saying Angela and Peter needed time. They are tired, so tired. Jenn, she knows. She felt the big noise—the earthquake ..." Pearl started to shake violently, tears running from her good eye, which she turned on Eli. "She says go, please go. The Dancer ... through the gate ..."

She descended into nonsensical syllables and moaning, rocking back and forth in Susan's arms, while Susan cried freely, her face twisted into a mask of grief and shock. Eli stood by, feeling stupid and helpless. Barely a year ago, he'd comforted patients and families for a living at the hospital on the hill above town, but now everything had changed. He had no ready words, no patented scriptures, no corner on prayer.

"Jerri?" Pearl used her pet name for the man who was all heart, even with no legs.

Susan pulled the frightened, stricken woman closer, before looking up at Eli with eyes that pleaded with him to not abandon them to the violence of those seeking to destroy the Redemption. Eli tried to see beyond her eyes, searching for a way to express to her the depths of his own fear, his questioning of his own foundations.

His eyes wavered. He could not withstand her searching gaze—until he remembered the ring. Jeremiah had almost eluded his enemies. Apparently having realized the consequence of the ring, he was attempting to return it to Eli. What would compel a man to such sacrifice for a stranger who questioned that same man's commitment to some ethereal force that he believed would reestablish the spiritual foundations of the human race?

It was not for the man's own wife, Eli pondered. It was most meaningful in the situation as a symbol of his own consecrated and joyous love and gratitude for the wonder that was Jenn. Jeremiah and Susan, even Pearl and Toby, knew it to be so. Something tangible radiated from Susan's eyes, from her very soul: a burning, searing heat; light incarnate.

BloodFire. The thought imprinted itself on Eli's mind like a white-hot branding iron. BloodFire. His mind went blank, then empty, and he could sense the difference between the two states. He wanted to ask the question of how that could be, to what end, but the questions never formed.

"Sometimes you can be ready for something that you don't know you are ready for," he remembered a cranky philosophy professor telling the class once upon a time. *Perhaps it is the shock of too much tragedy, too much violence, too much emotional strain, that's getting to me,* Eli thought. *Why am I thinking of BloodFire at a time like this?*

"Eli?" Pearl looked up at him, her overdone rouge riven by a delta of tear tracks, holding another of her paper sacks toward him.

"Yes, Pearl. Do you want me to look after Angela and Peter?"

"No, they are safe with me. I found this in the house before they came, and I tucked it into my big shirt."

Eli accepted the bag gingerly. It was light. He reached in and pulled out the notepad that he'd left on the sofa. "What made you bring this?"

Pearl looked surprised. "Angela wanted to give you a present for getting her all fixed. She told Peter that you were collecting stories."

"Stories?" Susan asked, wiping her nose on a ragged tissue. "Are you a writer, Eli?"

"No, no. Jenn's been bugging me to get on with my life and—look, that's beside the point. Thank you, Pearl. Right now, don't we need to get out of here before the police trace anything back?"

Toby looked relieved at this suggestion. "Someone should take you to the Wedding Gate."

"Where do I go from there?"

Susan stood with a weary sigh. "We'll have to trust that someone will be there. Just do whatever they say."

"Well, what about this Dancer person that"—Eli pinched the bridge of his nose and squeezed his eyes tight—"that, that, oh, I remember! Tanya. That was her name. She said this Dancer might help.

"This is crazy," Eli continued before anyone could respond. "It's only been a couple of hours, but I could barely remember that poor woman's name. What in God's name is going on?"

"I'd better stay here," Susan said, "to make it look like I didn't already know that Jeremiah was in Eli's house. Maybe I'll be able to come wait with the others till you return from the Dancer."

"I smell bad," Pearl piped up. "Is something burning? I smell smoke."

"Pearl!" Toby had reached his limits. "I'm out of here." He turned to Eli. "Do what you want, fool. Just don't get anybody else killed." With that, he was out the door.

Eli started shaking violently. One of the effects of the constant trauma to the nerves in his back was that the slightest of chills or being overstressed could set off uncontrollable shivering. Sometimes he could feel it coming, and other times it came out of the blue. Today's incidents had been more than the slightest of chills or stress, but he'd been too otherwise occupied to notice the episode coming on.

"Eli, are you okay?" asked a worried Susan.

His teeth were chattering too hard to talk, so he nodded. What he desperately wanted were some more of the pain pills, but they were on what was left of his kitchen floor. A handful of Percodan to dull the pain, ease the nerves, and erase the memories of the last few hours sounded like a good idea to him.

What if he just rolled up into a ball right here and now? How much was a person supposed to take? Sure, just a minute ago, the BloodFire stuff almost made sense to him, but die for it? All he wanted was Jenn made well and back in their lovely home, preparing for the arrival of the baby. Now he didn't know if he would even have one out of the three. Those were not good odds.

"Yeah, I'm okay," he mumbled.

"How about another piece of that pie before we do anything else?" Susan started bustling around the kitchen, plates clattering, coffee running through the machine, while she bit her lower lip, losing herself momentarily in familiar, comforting routine.

Eli perched on the stool, same as earlier in the day, wondering where she got her strength. His hand slid into the pocket of his jeans and squeezed the ring. "I'm sorry about Jeremiah, Susan. He was a good and brave man."

Susan nodded. "Yes, he was. He was." She saw that the shakes were diminishing. "Now eat something. You don't know when you'll be able to sit down like this again. Fill up on good, hot coffee." She turned her back, and great sobs shook her entire body. "Why is it so hard?" she asked. "Why is it so hard? I want to see him. I must see my Jeremiah."

At that moment, Pearl came into the kitchen. "Jeremiah? Are we going to see Jeremiah? Someone should tell him about this man's house. Perhaps he could help build a new one. Jeremiah's kind, he who would do just that." She smiled at them both, pleased with her idea.

Susan roused herself with great effort, speaking slowly, firmly. "Pearl, listen to me carefully, all right? I need you to take Eli down to the Wedding Gate. Can you do that for me? After he's finished with his food, get him to the gate. I know it's not dark outside, but this is a special case, Pearl."

Pearl responded in kind. "Would Jeremiah know what to do about this smell? And the ringing in my ears, maybe he could do something about that too."

Eli swallowed hard. He was going to put his and Jenn's lives into the hands of these people. "Susan, I don't mean to pry, but I was wondering if I could ask why you're doing this. You need to mourn Jeremiah, make arrangements for him, look out for yourself, not worry over me."

"I believe." Her eyes locked on his. "Eli, when you get back, I'd like you to do Jeremiah's funeral. I can't think of anything that could give me greater comfort. Would you please?"

Eli stammered, "Su-Susan, I can't."

She stepped closer, her breath smelling sickly sweet, a sign that she was neglecting her insulin routine. Eli could see into the round, dark centers of her eyes. His own eyes looked back at him, haunted, afraid, imploring whatever fire was left within himself to give him light.

"Eli, if not you, then who? He respected you. He told me last night that you showed a great courage in coming to us. He would be honored to have you convene the rite of the winds."

"I don't know what that is," murmured Eli, still watching his own eyes.

"Yes, you do. When you return, you will know. Go in peace, Eli."

Chapter 21

"We're not supposed to do this. This is bad. I don't like to be bad. You don't belong in our home. I don't know you."

Pearl's incessant paranoiac patter got on Eli's nerves. But he didn't want to say anything that might upset her further and make her even more distracted. *No, we couldn't have that now, could we,* he thought sardonically.

"Do you know Jesus?"

Eli looked up, wondering if he'd missed something with his momentary musing. "What?"

"Jesus, do you know him? I think he knew the Sanctuary, but, you know, it might make his father mad."

Before Eli could untangle that one, she continued in a lucid and clear manner, "You know what gets me, Eli? Lazarus. What about Lazarus?"

"You lost me, Pearl." He sighed. "Don't you remember where the gate is?"

"I'm looking, I'm looking. But think about it. Remember what happened with Lazarus. The Gospel of John says that Lazarus and his sisters were good friends of Jesus. He used to stay at their house when he wanted to get away from everything and everyone that wanted a piece of him and just be himself. Can't you picture them talking and drinking and laughing together? That's what good friends do, right? Well, then, answer me this. Lazarus gets sick and dies. Dead and buried. Gone but not forgotten."

"Pearl, is there a point to all this?"

"I'm getting there, Godman." She giggled at his surprised reaction. "Jenn wants to hear that whole story sometime."

Eli clenched his fists in frustration. After quick goodbyes, and after he promised to do Jeremiah's funeral, he and Pearl had set out for the Wedding Gate. Pearl wandered down the block with him close behind. When she reached the fence around the village, she began to follow it around the ragged perimeter, seemingly on an aimless stroll that the longer it went on, the more it drove Eli to distraction. Along with the constant chatter that convinced him that she was completely out of touch with reality.

"Pay attention!" snapped Pearl in a stern teacher's tone of voice. "Like I was saying, Lazarus is dead. He's faced that third and final question."

"Excuse me? Third and final question?"

"Sure. Where do we come from? Why are we given life? Where do we go? The questions that shape our fears and joys and dreams for all of our days. Lazarus has finally found the answers to all three. The fears are gone, right? So what does his good friend do? Makes him come back and start all over again but this time without a birth! Why would he do that? What friend would ask another to reexperience these dark journeys? What? Is he going to have to go through that dying business all over again? Is he going to remember where he went the first time? Will that be the same as wondering where he came from the first time? What do you do for an encore on life and death? Jesus gets raised from the dead, and he books it for heaven. He talked about being born again but nothing about dying again."

She stopped for breath, but Eli had no answers. "The Sanctuary is our womb, Eli. Bear that in mind as Jenn faces this ordeal with you."

"So, what about the BloodFire, Cracked Pearl? What's that about?"

The veil of blinking confusion dropped across Pearl's face as suddenly as it had raised. "You called me Pearl. You must know me. Do you know Angela?"

Eli reached out to her, pleading. "No, come back, Pearl. Tell me." For those few moments, he'd forgotten about the outlandish clothing and makeup that enrobed this gentle, articulate, intelligent seeker, marking her as an outcast, betraying her fragile mind.

Pearl looked at him with curiosity. "Come back? I didn't leave. Who are you?"

"It's me, Eli." He sighed and let his hands drop, wondering if the woman before him knew that her mind went in and out like this. *It must surely be hell on earth*, he told himself. *Knowing that you just keep slipping away from yourself.* "Do you know where the Wedding Gate is?"

Pearl smiled. "Yes. Right here."

They were standing in another narrow alleyway, hemmed in on one side by ramshackle garages and tenements. Across the way, beyond the fence, sat the village. Whitewashed gardening sheds filled the nearest corner, with barns and sheds hugging the fence. Beyond them stretched the herb, flower, and vegetable gardens maintained by the state of Pennsylvania in close to their original state from the 1800s.

Past the gardens rose the granite gazebo surrounded by a lily pond. The settlers' celibacy even within the bonds of marriage meant that the good men and women of the village found other outlets for the fire in their blood, Eli noted wryly. It must have taken a lot of energy to build so many neat, little homes, all in the same boring saltbox style. At one time, vast vineyards and fields of grain and corn had filled the narrow space between the river and the first ridge. His own home stood—had stood—near the south entrance where the vineyards used to be.

The Great House, which had housed the stern, all-powerful leader, stretched for half a block. Beneath it lay the great vault where the group's treasury had been held in the form of gold. Legend had it that some of the gold was hidden elsewhere and had never been found.

Alas, prosperity and celibacy had been the group's downfall. Human nature won out. The richer they got, the less they wanted to work. The group hired outsiders to do the labor, while they chomped at the proverbial bit with the loss of their chief means of sublimation. It was empty now of inhabitants, a curiosity and tourists' one-time stop.

Between two towering oaks, a small gate in a state of ill repair hung by one barely functioning hinge. A hand-lettered sign announced that this was indeed the "Weeding Gate."

"Weeding Gate?" Eli asked with a half-amused smirk. "I thought it was the Wedding Gate."

"You're in trouble," Pearl said in a clear and disconcertingly composed voice.

"Can you show me where to go, Pearl? I need your help."

She looked up and down the narrow pathway, her back to the fence. Convinced it was all clear, she led him through the narrow gate. Immediately they stepped into the shadows between two sheds. A group of middle-aged women strolled past, led by a man dressed in the broadcloth clothes and wide-brimmed hat of one of the many volunteers who dressed in nineteenth-century costume to lead the tours.

The women oohed and aahed over the tremendous amount of sheer physical labor needed to make it through the day in the life of a newlywed woman of 1845. Homemade bread, homemade butter, handsewn clothing, homegrown meat and vegetables, homemade soap, candles. But no homemade children. The women giggled at this last. Eli tried to imagine the life lived here but could not.

The guide paused at a brick wall covered with climbing ivy and called the group's attention to the detail of the wrought iron gate leading to a row of old shops lining a cobblestone street. As he spoke by rote, Eli saw the man's eyes wander over the heads of gray and white hair. They stopped when they came to rest on the space where he and Pearl stood pressed against the clapboards.

An icy chill ran down Eli's spine. No way the man could see them, he reassured himself. But he could swear the man looked directly into his eyes. Eli figured that they could probably talk their way out of being discovered in this part of the park, but something about the man's eyes had made him even more afraid. He told himself that he was imagining things, that events were making him edgy.

The group moved on. Eli checked Pearl, who seemed oblivious to the quick exchange. "They're gone," he whispered.

Pearl stared at the row of horseshoes hung on the opposite wall. "Omegas."

Eli grew exasperated at this identifying the last letter in the Greek alphabet. "Pearl, where do we go from here?"

She stirred and walked back into the sunlight, heading toward the ivy-covered wall and away from the group of tourists. The small, identical brick saltbox houses lined the other side of the wall. One of them shared a common wall with the enclosure, its unusually small door fitting flush.

Pearl grasped the knob and turned. It squealed, and the door swung inward. They stepped through and quietly closed it behind them. The first floor of the home consisted of two rooms, one with spartan parson's benches and a fireplace, the other with a simple wooden frame bed holding a corn husk mattress.

Pearl crossed through the house and peered out a small window at a squat building with huge storm cellar doors. "I remembered it!" she crowed. "I must be getting better, Philip."

"Eli."

"Oh."

"What's 'it'?" asked Eli.

"Follow me. Go fast."

Outside the house, Pearl hurried toward the low structure. Instead of trying to lift the huge doors, she knelt beside one of the ground-level windows, covered with a crude wooden shutter. She pried at one corner, and the whole shutter fell free.

Eli chuckled to himself at the comical sight of the bright stockings wriggling through the opening. He stopped laughing when he had to drag his own complaining legs over the rugged rocks. On the other side, it took a moment for his eyes to adjust to the dim interior.

"Put the shutter back, Philip."

He started to correct her again, thought better of it, and twisted around on the narrow ledge on which he found himself to conceal the opening.

"This way." Her voice echoed in the dry air, thick with a sweet, pungent odor.

As Eli's eyes came into focus, he could make out huge wooden casks lying on their sides in cradles about ten feet below them, lining three walls of the cavernous cellar.

He showed his amazement with a low whistle. "What's all this?"

Pearl pointed down. "Wine. They made their own wine." She scooted along the ledge until she was directly over the cask in the far corner, moving easily. She lightly dropped on top of it and slid down the great rounded sides to the floor.

"This should do wonders for my back!"

"Shh!" Pearl shushed him emphatically with a glare thrown in for good measure.

"Here goes nothing." Pain shot through his left hip as it awkwardly struck the cask. Before he could stop himself, he landed on the floor in a cloud of dust and a yelp.

Pearl leaned over him. "Are you broken?"

"Yeah, I'm broken, Pearl."

"You know my name, Philip. You must be doing better. It's been a while since you remembered my name, darling." A warm smile lit her face, and Eli caught another tantalizing glimpse of the woman behind the garishness and confusion.

Behind the cask, she pulled some lumber aside, got down on her hands and knees, and disappeared.

"If I see a big rabbit, I'm getting the hell out of here," Eli cracked mirthlessly, before following her down the hole. The tunnel was dark and mercifully short. It ended in another, much larger tunnel. Water dripped from the walls, and the stench of aged waste engulfed Eli, causing a sensation of sheer terror.

The trunk. It smelled like the jungle rot that clung to his father's trunk shipped back from Vietnam. He shook his head and looked up. Dim light filtered through the storm sewer gratings overhead, and the sound of traffic caused Eli to lose his bearings.

Then it came to him. The river boulevard curved around one end of the grounds, before passing under the bridge. The river was somewhere beyond the sound. The thought of it gave him a shiver. He turned to the left. Nothing but a black, slimy hole. He figured that was where the tunnel passed under Bridetown.

"Stay close," warned Pearl, and headed for the darkness.

"Are you sure this is the way?"

In reply, she reached over her head, feeling among the old bricks piled there by some twentieth-century road crew. With a grunt of satisfaction, she withdrew a candle and a pack of matches wrapped in plastic. Without waiting for Eli to draw a deep breath, she plunged ahead, holding him firmly by the hand.

The candle's flickering light threw eerie shadows. Eli realized he could no longer hear traffic sounds.

"Down."

Pearl's warning came too late, and Eli smacked his head on some object. He saw red stars and reeled drunkenly. He held on for dear life as Pearl resolutely moved forward.

"Down."

Eli instinctively ducked this time. But Pearl was pulling on his hand while holding the candle over an opening in the floor. The flame illuminated a crude ladder fashioned from scrap lumber. The wispy halo of orange hair shimmered in the soft light as she started her descent. Eli groaned and followed suit, thankful that he couldn't see bottom. He tried counting the rungs but quit after fifteen.

At the bottom, Eli asked, "Where are we?" At that moment, the candle went out. Eli screamed.

"It gets a little drafty in these old tunnels." Pearl's voice came out of the pitch.

Eli clung to the ladder, his legs shaking from the exertion of the climb and out of terror. His back throbbed. This journey to the center of the earth, climbing out the basement trapdoor, the stress and strain of the past few days—everything was too much for the morphine pump to handle.

"Oh, God, we're lost."

A match flared right before his eyes, blinding him. "I'm not lost, Philip. Stay close to me." Instead of relighting the candle, she used the match to search for a flashlight.

"Where are we, Pearl?"

"Oh, Philip, you always did like to tease."

Eli wondered just how close Pearl had been when the bomb at his house had gone off. "Are we under the village?"

"This is the old system. See the bricks." She cast the beam along the walls. There was plenty of room to stand.

Eli did some quick figuring and calculated that they were at least forty feet beneath the surface. That meant they were close to the level of the river, somewhere behind him in the darkness. He immediately wished he hadn't thought of that. The blackness behind him exerted a physical force, dragging him back, pushing down on his shoulders.

"How much farther?"

Pearl led him on and on, their feet slipping on the slime-coated bottom. The revolting smell made Eli more irritated.

"Don't you remember, Philip?"

"Pearl, it's me, Eli. Jenn's husband. Remember?"

"Jenn's not feeling too well. She hasn't said anything since I told her about the house."

Eli's heart jumped to his throat. "Pearl! You didn't tell her about the bomb, did you?"

"She's my friend. I won't lie to a friend. You should know that, Philip."

Before Eli could pursue the matter any further, Pearl led him around a series of sharp turns, then stopped beside a metal plate set in the wall, waist high. She rapped on it sharply and stepped back.

"This is it," she announced, holding her free hand to her forehead. Eli saw the dark circles under her eyes and sweat glistening on her forehead, though the air was cool.

"Pearl, are you feeling all right?"

The plate swung outward with a rasp of metal on brick that set his teeth on edge. "Welcome to Wellrock, Mr. Marks."

Eli's mouth dropped open in disbelief. The voice was unmistakable. A grimy face appeared, followed by an outstretched hand, too smooth for the surroundings. Eli blinked and looked again. There was no mistake. It was the Reverend Doctor Whitimer Baker.

Chapter 22

Gideon checked the rearview mirror for the fourth time in the last minute, his mind flashing back to the girl in the hospital who first called him the Healer. He rubbed his tired eyes and checked yet again. Four small figures huddled together for warmth in the open bed of the truck. The fifth sat between him and Laurel, adroitly guiding them to their farm in a narrow hollow on the northern side of the mountain.

"How did you children get so far from home?" Laurel asked, pulling the little girl closer to her.

"Don't know," Sarah answered. "Reuben and Gilly, that's my biggest brother and biggest sister, kept on walking and talking about Mama and how sick unto death she was, and how Papa's worrying himself to death, and before we know, we was lost in the fog." She turned her innocent eyes on Gideon. "That's when God sent the Healer to help us."

Gideon shook his head. "Why do you call me that?"

She looked at him, puzzled. "You don't know who you are?"

"I'm not real sure at the moment." Gideon's half-serious answer got Sarah riled.

"How are you gonna help my mama if you're not real sure? Don't you have any faith? Ma'am, you're his wife. Why isn't he sure?"

Laurel looked at Gideon over the child's head, her lips pursed and eyes laughing. Gideon frowned back.

"My mama and papa do that," Sarah inserted herself into their silent exchange.

"Do what, honey?" asked Laurel.

"Look at each other and make little sweet faces when they think we're not looking. How many kids do you have? Where are they? Who's watching them while you're out here in the truck?"

"You sure are full of questions," teased Gideon.

"Yes, sir, I am. Like, why is Mama sick unto death? She's been nothing but good. She works hard all day, she takes care of all of us, she has Papa's dinner on the table when he comes in from the fields or from the barn smelling like Sugar—"

"Sugar?"

"That's our buggy horse. Mama named him Sugar. Papa says she's too kindhearted with the dumb animals, but he lets her give Sugar little lumps of sugar anyways. He makes like he's mad, but a body can tell when he's really hoping she'll do it just so's he can act gruff. But then he throws his head back and laughs when Mama thinks he's bein' serious and all."

"Do you always talk so much?" Gideon asked in mock horror. "I thought Amish children were quiet."

"We're Old River Order Mennonite, if you must know. Mama says we're OROs for short, except then she started saying we're Oreos. That's a kind of store-bought cookie, you know. Mama gets us some sometimes when Papa's not looking, but he sneaks them too. Mama knows all about store-bought things, seeing as how she's from New York city and all."

"Your mama's from New York City? I didn't know there were any Amish—I'm sorry, Old River Order Mennonites—in New York."

Gideon looked at Laurel for support in this matter, but her only reply was a huge grin, enjoying the exchange between Gideon and this pint-sized dynamo of a charmer with the soft curls.

"She didn't start out as an Oreo." Sarah giggled at letting the two strangers in on this family secret joke. "She ran away from home to get away from her parents because they didn't treat her right, and she fell in love with Papa, but then he let her go back to New York City to take care of a friend of hers named Matthew who was dying with the AIDS virus, and Papa never doubted that she would come back even though Mama loved Matthew but not the same way that she loves Papa, although Mama stayed away a long time. but somehow Papa knew when she was coming home and met her at the train station like in the movies, which Mama took us to once or twice and told us not to stare at people just because they stare at us 'cause they don't know better, and we do." Sarah got all this out in one big rush of breath before adding, "Turn in here at the lane. This is where we live."

"Now there's a woman I'd like to get to know!" Laurel said in admiration.

Gideon nodded, silently wondering what he should do about the girl's mama as they pulled into the midst of a tidy landscape dotted with whitewashed buildings and fences. The fog was gone, but the afternoon sun had already given its strongest light to the narrow confines of the valley. What was left was a golden glow dappling the autumn colors on the hillsides.

Before the truck was stopped, the children jumped out of the back, running pell-mell across the barnyard toward the neat frame house. A small man with a dark beard and brown derby hat ran to meet them, relief evident on his weathered face. The children chattered all at once, tugging him toward the uncertain Gideon and Laurel.

"You're some kind of doctor?" asked the man, hope written large in his features.

"The Healer, Papa. We were on the mountain praying for Mama, and the fog came like a storm of feathers till we couldn't see—"

The man stopped Sarah's nonstop recital by sweeping her into his arms. "Pardon my manners," he said. "I'm Chester Brechelman. Thank you so much for bringing the children home. I've told them a hundred times if they're on the mountain when that northeast fog billows in to stop where they are and don't move."

"Well, that's what they did, Mr. Brechelman," Laurel said with a smile. "They did exactly what you taught them."

"I'm Gideon Waters, and this is Laurel Rayn." They shook hands while the children danced about impatiently.

"How's Mama?" Sarah asked, her eyes pleading for good news. "Any better?"

It was evident from the sag of his shoulders that Chester Brechelman dreaded having to answer her question. He sent the children on into the house with strict orders not to make too much noise or to disturb their mother.

"My wife, Rachel, is not feeling too well, or she'd be out here herself to greet you proper. We do appreciate you going to all this trouble. Why don't you come in for a moment and have a cup of coffee? Gilly made some cookies yesterday. Take the time to let us thank you proper."

"We don't want to intrude," Gideon protested.

Laurel stopped him with her hand on his arm. "We'd love to come in for a moment, Mr. Brechelman."

"Please, call me Chester."

"Chester, just make sure to tell your wife not to get up on our account. I'm sure that with the children, hospitality will be honored."

Chester looked at her for a long moment as though debating something in his head. "Yes, I agree, Miss. It's a sin to not offer hospitality to a stranger. C'mon in and don't mind the girl's talk about the Healer. I don't know where she got this notion about there being someone coming who has the power to heal with the blood. It's not in any of her books. Maybe she's got one of the Bible stories all turned around in her mind. She means well, but it's devil talk if you ask me. I hope there's no offense."

Gideon swallowed hard. "None taken." He opened his mouth to say more, but nothing came out.

Laurel stepped in. "Chester, what is your wife's condition?"

His long, slow exhalation sounded like the wind sighing around the door on a winter's eve. "Brain cancer. It's ugly, I'll tell you that right now. She knows that her time is about go—" Chester's voice broke. He stood by the door for a moment, trying to regain his composure. "I'm sorry."

"Don't be," Gideon told him. "She means the world to you and your children. We'll help in any way that we can."

Chester blew his nose loudly. "There's nothing that can be done, but thank you." He wiped his boots on the mud scraper mounted by the door and stepped into the house with a loud stomping. At this obvious signal, Reuben and Gilly appeared and offered to get them something to drink. Then they were ushered into the formal parlor. Chester excused himself and went up the narrow stairs.

"What beautiful children," Laurel exclaimed as she sat down on the simple couch. "Look at that!" She pointed to a macramé wall hanging done in teal yarn and appointed with snippets of cloth, tree bark, shells, and colorful pebbles.

Gideon addressed the practical. "What are we going to do?"

"That's Mama's earth blanket." Sarah stood in the doorway, expectation alight in her face. "She says that fire, water, and blood are the foundation and the mystery of life. I love it when she says things like that."

Gideon failed to contain his surprise at her calm recitation of the witnesses. "What did you say?"

Sarah took a step into the room. "Mama's earth blanket. It's something she made when she was taking care of her friend Matthew. She said he died in peace because he'd learned the root of the Cs."

Gideon looked at Laurel, who seemed fascinated by the child's words. "It's true," she whispered. "Others know." Her eyes gleamed when she met Gideon's gaze.

"Sarah, what are the three Cs?"

"Compassion, community, and creativity. Would you like a cookie?" She held out a tray of large star-shaped cookies sparkling with sugar.

Gideon jammed his hands into the pockets of his jeans to hide the trembling. His fingers touched the cool metal of the small charm on the necklace. The little girl in the emergency room must have been about Sarah's age. He didn't want to see anything like what had happened to her ever again. A shudder passed through his entire body.

"Are you cold, Mister?"

Gideon shook his head, willing the terror rising in his belly to stop. "Why did you call me Healer, Sarah? Did someone tell you to say that to me?"

Sarah's eyes grew wide till white showed all the way around the iris. "I don't know how I know. I like to listen to Mama tell stories about her life and about helping her friend who died, and I'll ask her what they talked about. I don't mean to be different or nosy, but I get pictures in my head when I hear her stories. And you, I could see you in my head when she talked about being so angry at the darkness of death. But you would smile. Inside my head, in my pictures, you always are smiling. When Mama got so sick, I started praying and praying and thinking about who you were and where you were. Then today"—Sarah held her arms out wide, astonished at the revelation—"you come walking out of the fog up on the mountain. What's a body to believe? Don't ask for something you can't believe in when it comes. That's what Mama says. So I know. I don't know why I know, but I know I that I know. You are the Healer."

"Sarah!" Chester hollered from the top of the stairs. "Don't be talking such foolishness!"

"But, Papa, it's not foolishness if it's true. Mama says—"

"Daughter!" His voice was filled with anger and frustration born of desperation.

Sarah's mouth settled into a grim line. "Please help Mama," she whispered before running from the room.

Gideon and Laurel looked at each other helplessly. "She really believes," Gideon said softly. Laurel nodded silently.

"Please excuse my daughter's burdening you with her overactive imagination," Chester said apologetically from halfway down the stairs. "My wife says that she would like to meet you. Please excuse her not being able to get up to receive visitors, but she insists on seeing you."

At the foot of the stairs, before they climbed to the second floor, Laurel whispered to Gideon, "That poor man is on his last prayer. Five children, the farm, and his wife so ill. Gideon, you've got to do something."

"What am I supposed to do?" hissed Gideon. "Give her some blood to drink? I'm not a goddamned traveling freak show, Laurel!"

Moments later, they stood in the doorway to the couple's bedroom. Alert, dark eyes set in a pale face looked up at them from an expanse of billowy pillows and quilts.

"Whaddaya doin' in the door? C'mon in, please." A broad smile gathered light from all corners of the room and focused it into a beam of radiance. Her hands waved at them feebly, betraying how much the effort to welcome them cost her. "You'll have to forgive me, but the more this tumor grows, the more I feel like a New Yorker again." Her eyes suddenly snapped shut, and one side of her face drew up into a fearful mask.

"It's sitting on the nerves to her face now," Chester said behind them. "It's growing very quickly. Now it's starting to take away her vision, then her speech, and then her swallowing"—he sighed heavily—"and breathing. She's in and out. She has maybe a week. Maybe more, maybe …"

In the silence that followed, Gideon could hear the ticking of the great grandfather clock he'd passed in the downstairs hallway. The wind moaned in the eaves, and rain spattered against the windows. It rained when he was hanging onto the mountain, begging it for life, he mused. Had he really changed as dramatically as he felt in only a couple days' time? He caught himself actually entertaining the notion that the blood coursing through his veins could defeat the brain cancer that was sapping Rachel's body of life.

No, it must be ego. But who would want such a gift, or curse? No sane man, surely. What journey was he on now? He was being asked to give up every long-held belief and assumption about the way things work in this world, about purpose and meaning, about life and death.

"What are you all staring at?" Rachel's facial spasm ended. Her voice sounded weaker, but she managed to smile at their serious faces. "Somebody cut one? You all look like you just smelled something awful."

"Rachel!" Chester wearily scolded his wife.

"I'm incorrigible, I know. That's why you love me, Chester."

Gideon and Laurel smiled nervously, a bit bewildered. Rachel stopped talking for a while and breathed heavily. Chester rounded up two chairs so they could sit beside the bed.

"You can take the girl out of New York," Rachel resumed her light tone, "but you can't take New York out of the girl. Chester is such a sweetheart for putting up with me."

"You have beautiful children." Laurel leaned over and took Rachel's hand.

"Is this your man?" Rachel asked her.

"Rachel!" Chester tried again to reign in his wife. "You're impossible. You shouldn't talk so much."

"He's been trying to get me to do that for yearshh—yarsh—yea …" Rachel's face twisted into an angry mask as she suddenly struggled to form the words.

Gideon looked at Chester, who nodded solemnly.

"We're here now, Rachel." Laurel spoke in soothing tones while stroking the paper-thin skin on the back of Rachel's hand. "Don't worry. We're here."

Gideon wondered what he was supposed to do. What if he gave her some blood and nothing happened? What if something did happen and she ended up like those back at the farmhouse, Rachel and her whole family? He knew he couldn't live with that on his conscience for the rest of his life. No way.

"Do you know what a Faith Keeper is?" Rachel asked, looking directly at Gideon.

When he shook his head, she continued, "A Faith Keeper is found in the Iroquois culture. His job is to ensure that the stories that define the spirit of the Iroquois are remembered. The stories about Skanientariio, Handsome Lake, who gave a code of conduct describing how to live in a way that considered any action's effects through seven generations on into the future. The stories about how the Peacemaker and Ayonwentha taught the leaders how to trick Tadadaho, an evil one who wanted control."

Sweat dotted Rachel's forehead, and her chest heaved with the effort, but she would not be silenced. "We have lost our Faith Keepers in this world. The stories that tell us who we are have been lost, abandoned, or ignored. Or worse, they have been turned into power cults and religions that bless the desires of one part of the human race to dominate the others."

"How do you know these things?" asked Laurel, who'd been listening intently.

"How do I know that I'm alive? Or that I am questioning, searching, stepping away from the failed stories we've created to ease our guilt, while millions die of hunger and war and misuse of the earth? Where did each one of us and every one of us come from?"

She looked from one face to the other. "Oh, come on. From where? Why, from our mothers of course. Each one and every one came from our mother's womb—" Rachel's body trembled beneath the coverlet as she succumbed to a ghastly seizure.

Chester stepped to the bed, then scratched his beard, hesitating. "This is too much. She is out of her mind with the cancer. That's what's been the hardest on her. She has a wonderful mind that is always questioning, stepping back to get the bigger picture, she tells me." He sat on the edge of the bed to gently hold her shoulders till the seizing eased. His eyes were haunted, bleak, desperately sad.

"I don't know what to believe. Please, if you can do something, help her. She is my life!"

Gideon drew the necklace from his pocket and kissed the small charm. He caught Laurel's look of quiet confidence before closing his eyes. He didn't want to think anymore.

"Chester, could you excuse us for a moment please? We'll stay with Rachel for a while."

He looked only at Rachel's drawn features. He noticed a few freckles scattered across her nose, and for some reason, it made him smile. He could feel Chester looking at him, wondering about that smile, but neither of them said a word. Chester quietly left the room.

Gideon's eyes met Laurel's. "Well," he asked, "what do we do?"

Laurel reached down beside her chair and pulled up Jonathan's pack. "I'm always prepared. I'm a Guardian, you know."

Gideon reached over and took the baseball cap off of her head, freeing her hair to cascade around her shoulders. "Yeah, I know," he whispered.

"Sorry to interrupt," came a weak voice from the bed. "You are the Healer, I know." Her statement of fact carried with it firm conviction.

Laurel asked. "Do you know of the Sanctuary? The Redemption?"

"I've only heard part of the story," Rachel replied, her eyes drooping. "Any open mind can hear them. Stories are our lifeblood. I'll tell you mine someday," she said with a sly grin before she drifted off.

"She's fading quickly," Laurel said. "Ready?"

"What've you got, O lady of the always-surprising treasure pack?" Gideon said with a flourish, then added, "Besides the most beautiful eyes I've ever seen."

"Keep your mind on your work," admonished Laurel with a slight blush in her cheeks.

"This could be fun. You know, playing God."

"If this works, you have a house full of kids who will believe that you *are* God," Laurel reminded him. "Especially Sarah. Then what?"

Gideon sighed. "Good question. One at a time, though. One at a time." He rolled up his sleeve. "What've you got?"

Laurel rummaged around in the pack and extracted a bundle of needles in sterile packaging. "Take your pick."

"I hate needles," Gideon grumbled. "What are you doing with those anyway?"

"Jonathan packed it. He was ready for anything and everything."

"Except one," Gideon said grimly.

Laurel bit her lip hard. "Find a vein."

"Too bad I'm not a drug addict."

"Want me to stick you?"

"No thanks. I've seen them wrap something around their arms up high."

"A tourniquet. It makes the blood vessels pop up."

Gideon took off his belt and wrapped it around his biceps. "Here, pull on it."

While Laurel held the belt, Gideon unwrapped one of the needles and popped the plastic cover off with his thumb. "Here goes nothing."

After several deep breaths, he plunged the needle in blindly. "Ouch! Damn! C'mon, you turkey! Aw, dammit! I can't get anything."

Laurel tried unsuccessfully to smother her giggles. "You do realize, don't you, that the object is to get the needle into a vein and suck out some blood?"

Gideon glared at her. "It's harder than it looks. I saw them do this all the time in the hospital. It didn't look all that difficult."

"Let me help. Here. Pull on this."

Gideon held the belt and grimaced.

"I haven't touched you yet!" cried Laurel.

"I know, but now I know how bad it's going to hurt."

"You big baby. Shut up and hold still."

Laurel felt around with her index finger and found the vein. She quickly pushed the needle through the skin, felt the resistance from the wall of the vessel, and pushed a little harder. She gave a squeal of satisfaction as the dark red liquid shot through the barrel of the needle and into the syringe.

"How much?" she asked, pleased with herself.

"I don't know. That girl couldn't have gotten more than a few drops."

"Give me your handkerchief."

Gideon passed it over. Laurel placed it over the needle and applied pressure after withdrawing from his vein. She held up the results of their efforts. "Success!"

"Not yet," cautioned Gideon. He looked at the still figure in the bed. "Not yet."

Chapter 23

"What kind of man are you? Aren't you afraid of mocking God? Everyone knows that God requires blood to be shed for salvation, but this—what you do, what you are, it is against God!" Chester stood in the doorway, shaking with rage as he watched Gideon plunge the syringe full of blood into the pulsing vein in Rachel's neck.

"Please, wait outside, Chester. You must wait. Then you will see." Laurel went and placed an arm around his shoulders. "I know that it's hard."

While she guided Chester out the door, Gideon finished up. He recapped the needle and threw it into the pack. "Maybe he's right. Maybe I am mocking God." Gideon kept his eyes on the small wound in Rachel's neck. Nothing happened. Nothing changed.

"Are you afraid, Gideon?"

"Yes."

"Nothing ever changes if people are not afraid."

"What if this doesn't work? What if Rachel gets worse and dies?" Gideon's voice rasped in his dry throat.

"I don't know. Everybody has to face themselves every day and ask if they still believe they are who they think they are. This is all part of a much larger story, not just your own, Gideon."

"I'm trying to understand that, but it's difficult. All I know for sure right this moment is that I took some of my blood and put it into hers. Hoping. That's all, hoping."

"Then hope, my love. Hope."

Gideon looked at Laurel through eyes blurred with tears. Her gift to him. He buried his face in the blankets and sobbed. Laurel stroked his hair until his weeping calmed.

He felt a burning sensation in his arm. When he peeked under the handkerchief, he flinched at the sight of the bright stain still spreading and a purple bruise reaching halfway down his forearm.

Laurel's response when he showed it to her was to begin tearing strips of cloth from one of her shirts, fashioning a thick wad and then tying it tightly around the puncture. "I don't know why it's doing that," she said. "I'll keep checking it for the rest of the evening."

They sat with Rachel, neither saying a word for nearly an hour. The whole house felt unnaturally still. The rain stopped, and darkness quickly descended across the small hollow holding the farm. Gideon got up to stretch and walked to the window. A bright spot of light rose over the farthest hill and dipped downward. At first he thought he was seeing a new star, but the motion continued, steadily drawing closer.

Off to his left, he detected motion, and another light appeared, crawling across the dark landscape from the direction of the cornfields he'd noticed behind the large barn.

"Milking time has come and gone," he mused. Laurel came to stand beside him in time to see a pair of lights turn it at the far end of the lane. As the headlights swept over the barnyard, Gideon saw a horse hitched to a boxlike carriage, tied up at the fence around the paddock. A lantern hung suspended from a long pole at one corner of the old-fashioned conveyance.

"Lanterns. Those are lanterns on buggies, or whatever they call them. Laurel, their neighbors are gathering downstairs. I can see them coming from near and far. What are we going to do?"

"What's this 'we' business?" asked a clear, strong voice in the room behind them. "They're my company. I'll feed them, of course."

Gideon and Laurel spun around. Rachel sat up in bed, her cheeks pink, eyes bright, mouth wide in an unabashed grin of joy. All three had tears in their eyes as the import of what they were witnessing sank in. Next they were laughing, holding hands and laughing till their sides hurt.

"The pain is gone!" shouted Rachel, throwing back the covers and springing from the bed. She danced a little jig across the room, which set them all to laughing some more.

"How is this possible?" she asked Gideon when they were calm once again. "What powers do you have?"

"It's the Redemption," Laurel told her. "It's the sign of the new beginning. He is a witness to the truth of the BloodFire."

"I don't know of these things—oh my. Forgive me. I'm so overjoyed I didn't even thank you or ask your names." Rachel stopped and abruptly sat on the bed.

"Are you all right?" asked Gideon.

"Yes. I remembered something. But now it's fading faster than a dream." A frown crossed her face as she went to the window. "Oh, look at the moon. So bright and wild, on her own course yet tied to Mother Earth."

She leaned her head against the pane. "You are the Healer. But how did I know that? How long was I out? It seems that someone spoke to me. A woman, yes. A woman from a long, dark tunnel. She's waiting for someone. I think it is you."

Rachel shook her head in frustration and gnawed at her knuckles. "Something's afoot in the world. But I don't know if it is a terrible evil or a great good. I have so many questions, so much I want to know. Can you teach me?"

Gideon cleared his throat nervously. "We have to get somewhere as quickly as we can."

"We know this is very confusing for you," Laurel explained, "but a lot has happened in a short time, and what's important right now is that you are whole again. You have a special little girl waiting and believing with all of her heart that you were to receive this gift."

"My Sarah," Rachel said with a mother's special understanding.

Gideon clenched and unclenched his fists repeatedly. "Rachel, there is something I feel I must tell you about what has happened here. You could be in a lot of danger."

Rachel studied his face. "Yes, I can see that. Come." She drew them both to the bed where they sat in a small circle. "Tell me what you must and how I can help. My questions can wait."

"You are a special person to be able to approach death's door, receive healing, and hop up ready to ask what you can do for us," Laurel said in tender jest.

Rachel laughed. "I've always said I'm a busybody." She turned serious. "I hate to think, though, that you will both walk out of my life as quickly as you strolled into it. It's lonely thinking the way that I do and having no one around but my Sarah to share it with. My Chester is a good man but not one to tinker with the 'this is the way we've always done it' mind-set, whether it be farming or religion or meeting someone from another world."

"I wish that we could stay, Rachel. I really do." Laurel wiped a tear from her cheek.

Gideon started a quick recap, with Laurel's help, of the mind-boggling revelations he'd received in the previous few days. He also told her point-blank of the terrible bloodshed as well. Rachel grew very still as he recounted the healing and subsequent slaughter of the child in the emergency room.

"Do her parents know what's happened?" she asked.

"We couldn't stay around to find out," Gideon said. "Those responsible for her death and the deaths of the others are very powerful and scared people. The more frightened they are, the more dangerous they become. We can't tell if they're leading us around by the nose, or if someone is trying to help us, or using us as pawns in a deadly game with rules we don't know. I never heard of any of this business about a Healer or the BloodFire or the Sanctuary until Laurel and her friend saved my butt back at my grandfather's farm."

He told her about Jonathan's murder and the strange events since. "I don't know if I'm telling you too much for your own safety or not, Rachel. I feel you have a right to know. I can't explain or prove or justify any of what I've told you. But the sooner we get away from here now, the better for us all."

"I agree," Laurel added. "We need to be horrible guests and sneak out of here. You have a house full of people waiting to rejoice with you and your family. If trouble does come, we don't even know where we will be to tell you to try and get in touch with us."

"This is all so unreal!" Rachel blinked her eyes rapidly. "Yet my heart tells me this is what I've hungered for. And that I'm needed in some small way now to help in whatever way that I can."

She held tight to their hands. "How can I ever thank you?"

"Love those precious children of yours," Laurel said fervently.

"And give us a head start before telling anyone that we've gone," added Gideon.

"I can do that," Rachel promised. "I just know that one day our paths will cross again. They have to."

They exchanged quick hugs. "Take care of each other," Rachel commended them as she put on her simple dark dress cut from broadcloth and tucked stray wisps of hair under her starched white cap. "Maybe I'll see you in New York someday."

She chuckled at Gideon's sour expression. "Come on, New York is good for the soul."

"I'd love to go there someday," said Laurel. "When I was a little girl, I used to dream about going there to get lost in all the crowds."

"Why did you want to get lost?" asked Rachel. "Not that it's any of my business."

"I'll tell you when we meet again!"

"Oh, wait, wait! I have something to take with you." Rachel went to the bureau and opened a hand-carved antique jewelry box. She selected a strange-looking medallion with nine stones of turquoise set around the edge. Its twin stayed in the box. "You must take this. I insist."

"No, we couldn't," protested Laurel. "It's beautiful. It must be very special to you."

"It is. That's why I want you two to have one."

Laurel blushed slightly. "Us? You want us to have it?"

Rachel smiled coyly. "Take it."

"Ladies, I hate to break up your little party, but it's time to go," goaded Gideon, ignoring his own heart's desire to stay and enjoy the company and hospitality of the family. "Rachel, how do we get away from here?"

After quick instructions, they hugged for one last time, and Rachel stepped out of the room. Gideon and Laurel listened as cries of astonishment and glee greeted Rachel as she went down the stairs.

"That's our cue." Gideon started softly humming the theme music for *Mission Impossible* to cover his own nervousness and sadness.

Laurel punched him lightly on the arm. "On to the next adventure," she whispered and crossed to the closet. Gideon turned out the lights and followed.

Laurel felt along the edge of the panel set into the back of the walk-in. Her fingers pressed a hidden spring, and the panel swung out about a foot. "Hard to believe that by plain old random chance we find those kids in the fog and come to a home to help someone whose house just happens to be an old stop on the Underground Railroad," she whispered in Gideon's ear while fumbling in Jonathan's pack for a small flashlight.

"We can debate coincidence and serendipity later," Gideon responded, nudging her through the opening and onto the ladder built into the over thick walls. He pulled the panel closed behind them. "Better safe than sorry," he repeated as much for his own benefit as Laurel's.

They waited until they heard the group below start singing a hymn of thanksgiving, then quickly descended to the basement. Following Rachel's instructions, they found the old tunnel shaft entrance in the root cellar and plunged ahead.

"Seems like we spend an awful lot of time in caves and cellars," Gideon groused. His injured ribs ached terribly, much to his surprise. And the bandage around his arm was soaked through already.

The tunnel smelled of mildew and rotted plant matter. It extended approximately fifty yards, ending well away from the house in a dilapidated shed behind the barn. It took both of them pushing to budge the slimy trapdoor. Gideon carefully opened the door and checked their surroundings.

"Coast is clear," he told Laurel and stepped into the moonlight. He took a deep breath while scanning the stars overhead. "What a night."

Laurel stepped past him without a word and peered around the corner of the barn.

"I said, what a—"

Laurel jammed her fingers into his mouth, choking him. She put her lips to his ear, while he fought back his gag reflex. "There's someone watching the house," she whispered.

Gideon nodded that he understood. Laurel used hand motions to signal her plan. Gideon again nodded and began silently counting to fifty while Laurel slipped away into the night. When he finished, he peeked around the corner. At first, he thought Laurel had nearly caused him to retch for nothing. Then he made out a darker outline in the shadows, someone crouching, listening intently.

Gideon felt his way along the whitewashed boards until he was ten yards from the shape. Crossing his fingers, he spoke forcefully. "What do you want?"

The figure jumped up and spun around. Gideon could tell it was a man of about his own size and build. The initial startled reaction passed in a blink. The figure studied him, warily, without panic.

"I said, who are you? What are you doing sneaking around here?"

"I might ask you the same." The voice was that of someone well trained for tense situations. Gideon's first thought was that he'd scared up a cop.

"Don't bother these people," Gideon commanded.

"Luther."

"Excuse me?"

"I'm Luther Quinn. That's all you need to know."

The man moved, trying to get deeper into the shadows, but Gideon danced to his left, and the man was forced to back away and stepped into the moonlight. He was in his late thirties, Gideon estimated, dressed in dark clothes from head to toe. More alarms sounded in Gideon's brain.

In a flash, a knife materialized too swiftly for Gideon to discern where he'd hidden it. The man stepped closer.

"I'll ask the questions." But he followed with a statement tinged with satisfaction if not glee. "You're the one."

Gideon kept his eye on the blade with the ripping hooks forged into the edge near the hilt. He heard no sound and saw no sign of Laurel.

"How did you get out here?" Luther's voice carried a note of admiration for having been nearly outsmarted. "Never mind. You have no idea, do you." He chuckled at this private joke. White teeth flashed in the silver light as he broke into an evil grin. "Daddy must be so proud," the stranger said in a mocking voice. "Daddy's little boy, all grown up—"

His words ended in a strangled cry. Gideon saw the glint of Laurel's hair as she tried to pull the man down from behind with her body weight on the garrote. But the man was quick and superbly trained. He lunged backward into the force of her grasp, not away. Gideon was a half a heartbeat behind, throwing himself at the man's legs.

Gideon didn't know where he found the strength to hang on, but he fought with ferocity he didn't know he possessed as he struggled to hold onto the kicking limbs. At one point, he felt a stinging pain in his left hip as his own legs flew up around the man's torso while the three of them tumbled around in the mud.

Then, just as swiftly, it was over. Laurel managed to pull the garrote tight long enough for the man to lose consciousness. His body went limp. Gideon still hung on, his shoulders screaming with burning fire.

"Gid-Gideon, he's out cold." Laurel's voice shook as she pulled herself out from under the dead weight and quickly bound his hands.

Gideon rolled over, exhausted.

"Help me drag him back to that shed, and I'll slit his throat, the son of a bitch!" The hatred in Laurel's voice stunned Gideon.

"Why?"

"He's a bloodtracker, that's why. And a mighty important one, from the looks of him. Come on."

Gideon tried to put his weight on his right leg, but the pain in his hip forced him to stop and rest. "Must have twisted my hip funny," he said.

Laurel helped him up and ran her hands over his body. "You're bleeding, bad. He stabbed you in the hip. Almost hit your femoral artery. This guy knows what he's doing all right."

Gideon steadied himself and took deep breaths. "We should go back to the house and get help."

"No, no need to involve them in this," Laurel's tone brooked no argument, and Gideon was too tired to make one.

They each grabbed a leg and dragged the still figure to the shed. Once there, Laurel efficiently hog-tied him, finishing as the man came to. He must have been in agony, Gideon thought, but his eyes showed no pain, no fear.

"What's the matter, bitch? Couldn't do it?"

"What's he talking about?"

Laurel's jaw muscles worked furiously. "Kill him. He's talking about me killing him."

Gideon leaned heavily against the wall, taking the proffered wads of material from Laurel and stuffing them into his pants to try to stop the flow of blood. She kept her eyes trained on Luther Quinn.

"The mighty Healer doesn't look too good," he taunted. "Lover boy looks a little pale, wouldn't you say?"

Laurel reached out and smacked him across the mouth. A trickle of blood ran from his lower lip, but he smiled at her. "I like it rough. How did Jonathan like it, huh? Did he like it when you slapped him?"

Laurel pulled the man's knife from her belt, her eyes wild. "Don't you dare mention his name. You're scum. You're going to die right here and right now." She stepped to his side and jammed the blade against the exposed line of his neck. Luther stared at her, never blinking.

"No." Gideon's strong voice surprised himself. "Don't, Laurel. There's been enough murder, enough blood shed."

Laurel's hand shook violently. Gideon carefully took the knife from her.

"You should have seen the surprise in Jonathan's eyes when I pulled the trigger back on the mountain. It was my greatest shot ever, if I do say so myself." Quinn threw his head back and laughed.

"No!" Laurel screamed. Gideon held tight, keeping her from grabbing the knife and plunging it into the man's chest. He led her to the far wall and made her sit. Limping over to the prostrate man, he took some of the blood-soaked rags from his wound and stuffed them into the bloodtracker's mouth.

"Maybe that will shut you up, you bastard." He pulled open the trapdoor. Without any help, Gideon dragged the repulsive, struggling prisoner over to the opening and pushed him through. With a satisfying thump, the lid fell back into place.

Numbed, shaking, weary, and more afraid than he'd ever been in his life, Gideon set off into the night, leaning on Laurel for support.

Chapter 24

"What are you doing here?"

"My job, Elijah."

Eli stared at the nervous man who kept wiping the sweat from his brow. Several storm lanterns sat on narrow ledges halfway up the crumbling bricks of the tunnel wall.

"C'mon, I'll take you the rest of the way in."

"Where are we going?"

"Farther in and farther on," came the cryptic reply.

"You were expecting me?"

The chaplain stopped and held a lantern up to Eli's face. "Listen—we don't have much time for chitchat. I realize I was probably the last person you expected to see here in this place, but I'm the one who's here."

Eli pushed the blinding light aside, annoyed. "No, you listen, you self-righteous little prick. You're right, I don't have a lot of time. People have died because they were trying to help me and my wife. I'm not sure why this is happening, but I'm not going to let them die for nothing. Pearl, do you know this man?"

Pearl's glass eye glistened in the light. "No—I don't know. Is he from Jenn? No, wait, is he with Jeremiah?"

Eli sighed. No help there.

Whitimer Baker studied him carefully. "Elijah, I want you to take a look at something. Please." He extracted an envelope from his pocket and handed it over.

"What's this?"

"Look at it."

Eli slowly lifted the flap and pulled out an old, creased black-and-white photo.

"I'm from the Witness Team. We, Tanya and I, think that's why you're here. It's the only link that we can find. I'm breaking every rule I know of by letting you see that, but we're in a situation where there are no rules."

"Witness Team? What are you talking about? Link to what?"

"To the Redemption. We had to know if your child was the Sacrament child and, if so, what was the connection to the BloodFire Protocol. The Dancer sent Tanya in to confirm my report, and well …"

"Okay, just hold on a minute. You talk like all this should click somehow in my brain. Well, I just heard about this last night from Susan and Jeremiah, God rest his soul."

"He was a good man. I believe he and Paraclete considered trying to recruit you into the Guardians at one point."

"What? He didn't say anything about that to me!"

"Maybe it had something to do with that." Whitimer indicated the picture with a soft, plump finger. "I really don't know why they never approached you."

Eli held it closer to the lantern. It was grainy, and the faces had shadows on them, some from the harsh sunlight, others reflecting a harshness that came from within. Three men stood in front of an old fighter plane that served as the lawn ornament for a military hospital in the background. Judging from the foliage, Eli assumed it was somewhere in Southeast Asia. One of the men wore tattered combat fatigues and supported himself on crutches. His black legs were heavily bandaged, and the pain showed in his passionate eyes. A sixties-era Afro showed beneath his jungle hat, and his hands looked large and powerful.

He stood to the left of a thin, nondescript man dressed in light clothing appropriate for the tropics. This man's balding head was painfully pale next to the dark-skinned man with the injuries and was bare except for the sunglasses perched on top. He appeared to be older than the other two by a few years and obviously annoyed at having his picture taken, though he seemed to be at ease with his compatriots.

The man to his right had dark, curly hair and a cap pushed back at a jaunty angle. Aviator sunglasses hung loosely from one hand, and his pose suggested a nonchalant cockiness …

Eli sucked in his breath sharply and held the picture closer, his heartbeat thumping loudly in his ears. There they were—pilot's wings. He studied the eyes, the high cheekbones, the obviously clean-shaven jaw. Eli's hand went to his own jawline, then touched the picture.

"It's my father!" There was a lump in his throat. He had to swallow a few times before he could continue. "How did you get this? Who are these others?"

Pearl peeked around his side, trying to see as well. "Oh! Yes. I see. Adam; it's him!" She giggled in her telltale way. "He's so young there. So handsome between those two soldiers."

"Adam? The one Susan and Jeremiah …?"

The other man nodded. "That was taken in the Philippines during the Vietnam War. Adam was there doing what he did best—recruiting for the Guardians. He went after war-weary soldiers during the war, then came home and switched to the world weary, the disabled, the forgotten and discarded."

Eli continued to stare at the photograph, remembering the smell of Old Spice clinging to the furniture, lingering in the house after his father would leave. Eli wore no other brand himself.

"Did my father join him?"

"We don't know, Eli. He may have." Whitimer cleared his throat. "Your father, of course, was killed soon after that was taken."

"Who's the other guy?"

Whitimer cleared his throat again. "One of our very best. His name is Jonathan. Had his legs chewed up in a suicide mission by some Vietnamese kid. Adam recruited him, helped him through rehab and fighting his way back to emotional and spiritual sanity after he came home. Jonathan's the one who's out there watching for the Healer. Thing is he hasn't been heard from for a couple of weeks. Don't know what's going on. Took a rookie out there with him too. Things are so bad he didn't have much choice."

Eli graciously let Pearl hold the picture so she could study her friend's likeness. "Are you saying that there is a connection of some sort from Adam to my father to me that explains why my daughter is supposed to be a part of this struggle of yours."

"It's your struggle now too, Eli, and don't you forget it." The normally slouched posture morphed into an indignant brace. "It's the only connection we can think of. Can you shed any light on it?"

"Nope. I don't remember my father ever saying anything about it in his letters home or my mother mentioning it either. Tell me how you fit in, Whitimer."

The tension melted away quickly. "Call me Whitty, okay? I've always hated the name Whitimer." His half smile acknowledged the incongruity of this name and the persona Eli had witnessed at the hospital. "I specialize at infiltrating or insertion into society at large."

"So, you're one of these Guardians?"

"I'm sort of a jack-of-all-trades. I'm part of the Witness Team at the moment. We're trying to corroborate reports that the witnesses are in place, but it's not adding up. Some things just don't figure. Without knowing what's become of Adam or Jonathan, we all have to muddle through as best we can. The Dancer keeps saying to be patient. Well, we must push on. The others are waiting."

"Others?"

Pearl gave Eli the picture and took up her lantern. "There are some who don't like to come up into the daylight. They leave only at night, if at all, which really is best. There's so much hate and fear. Did you see it? The necklace. In the picture, I saw a chain around Adam's neck. Angela will be so happy to see that picture."

Eli insisted on stopping to reexamine the photo. It looked like a large pendant on a chain. There were stones set around the gilded edges. He assumed they were dog tags similar to what the others wore, though the man wore no uniform. The journey resumed, the three of them plowing through the stagnant air of the tunnel, Eli's mind trying to untangle the jumble of questions and hopes and doubts and disbelief. They went around a few more turns and crawled over ancient pipes until Eli was sure they were forever lost. When Whitty finally stopped, Eli could hear water running nearby.

"That's the sewage from the senior citizens' rest area downtown," Whitty informed him. "The city just lets it drain into these old tunnels. Must have been cheaper than tapping into the modern system." He pointed to a metal plate propped against one side. "In there."

Eli squeezed through the opening into an old catch basin about the size of his now-shattered living room. Pieces of cardboard and lumpy blankets littered the floor. Shelves made of reclaimed wooden skids lined the walls. They held everyday personal items found in most homes: books, pictures, an assortment of dishes, and toiletries. He stepped forward. His foot struck an empty can and sent it skittering across the floor.

Instantly, one of the heaps of blankets came alive. A large man with a gray beard and flattop haircut jumped up, cradling a baseball bat. His cold eyes pinned Eli to the wall.

"It's all right," Pearl assured the apparition. "He has a picture of Adam, so he's okay."

"Easy, Gundy," Whitty said soothingly. "He's with us. Pearl found him on the bridge last night." To Eli he explained, "They go out at night to hunt up what they can, avoid contact with a lot of people, that sort of thing. This is like an aid station, so to speak."

"We don't need another mouth around here," growled the man. He gestured at the other mounds of blankets. "It's bad enough we have to look out for them."

"He won't be staying. We're getting him out of town without being seen. His place just blew up." Whitty paused, sighed, and continued. "With Jeremiah's body in it."

"No! Goddammit!"

Gundy's shout wakened the others under the piles of blankets. Two girls who looked to be in their late teens with empty eyes framed by stringy, dirty blonde hair huddled together, talking animatedly to each other in gibberish. He looked closer and realized that they were identical twins. Farther back in the shadows stood a slender man who nervously chomped on his fingernails, while his brown eyes continually darted back and forth.

"Did this asshole do it?" Gundy took a menacing step forward, the thunk of the bat into his palm getting ominously louder. "Just give me the word, Whitty, and I'll take care of him for you."

"How many times do I have to tell you, Gundy, we don't do things that way," pleaded the chaplain.

Pearl came to Eli's defense. "We went to his house to get his notebook 'cause he writes stories. There was a big mess there. The police came, and then I got out, and it … it made a terrible noise that hurt my ears. Terrible. It was terrible."

"A couple of cops were hurt pretty bad. We think somebody tipped them off, so now they'll be looking for Elijah, here. We've gotta sneak him out when it gets dark in a couple of hours. He's got to get up north to the dancing ground as fast as we can get him there."

"The trackers are making their move." The sallow man in the rear spoke dispassionately.

"Let's give 'em a reason to move on out of here!" Gundy snarled, jamming a Legion Post 198 cap over his salt and pepper crewcut.

Whitty started moving about the room, checking on supplies. "No, we need to stick to what we're here for. Pearl, has Jenn spoken to you lately?"

Pearl nervously chewed on her lower lip after shrugging her reply. Eli eased his aching body onto an upturned crate, figuring there was a lull for a short while and he'd better take advantage of it. He idly studied Gundy, who talked earnestly with Whitty on the other side.

A small American flag was sewn into the shoulder of his jacket. Thermal underwear stuck out from the cuffs of his flannel shirt, and suspenders pulled the waistband of his jeans above his navel. Cheap drugstore magnifying half glasses hung around his neck by a leather string.

Gundy's voice rose to a near shout. "I'm a vet and damned proud of it. I fought in the war nobody talks about—Korea. I get so sick and tired of those whiny, nobody-loves-me Vietnam vet crybabies. I voted not to let them into our post, and I'd do it again. I ain't been warm since I froze my ass off at Inchon Reservoir, but you don't see me applying for no disability benefits. I was proud to serve Uncle Sam. I can't stand the veterans' hospitals nor any other hospitals neither. Nothing but overpriced death traps." With the wind out of his sails, his point made, he concluded, "But I'm one loyal SOB, so I'll do it."

Content that everyone present knew his feelings, Gundy sat down with a paper and pencil and began figuring something. What it was, Eli couldn't tell. Pearl slumped against a Regent Soda crate, humming a tune to her charges. The twins eyed him with alarm, backing as far away as they could, never taking their eyes from him. The thin wisp of a creature curled up again in his blankets.

"So, what do you think of the Wellrock Brigade?" Whitty brought over a cup of water and sat cross-legged on the floor beside Eli.

Eli's eyebrows shot up. "This is the brigade? I heard Paraclete mention it. I thought he was their leader."

"He is, and with Jeremiah gone, he may be the only one I can count on. But he has to keep close to the hospital."

Eli shook his head in disbelief. "Susan and Jeremiah made it sound as though the fate of the human race was at stake. You're telling me that these are our defenders?"

"Susan and Jeremiah were right. We are trying to awaken people to our greatest heritage, the Sanctuary. And our greatest gift, the BloodFire. Over the years, we've been decimated by the bloodtrackers. You take help where you can find it, and this is where Adam found it."

"And somehow my daughter is part of this great hope?"

"As far as we can tell."

"But at the hospital, you seemed to agree with the doctor when he said she should be aborted." Eli's unspoken accusation was like a blast of steam hitting freezing-cold air, his suspicions now finding their voice like the steam's muted roar. Except the roar filled his ears. His head felt light, and the pain in his back and legs intensified by the second. A jumbled picture flashed through his mind. He started to rock back and forth, frustrated that the attack was happening right as he most needed his wits about him.

"Eli, is something wrong? You look ill."

Eli tried to focus. "I'm not sure. The blast might have damaged my pump." Cold sweat broke out on his forehead. "Do you have anything with caffeine in it?"

Whitty rummaged around on the shelves and produced a thermos and slightly used McDonald's cup. Eli greedily gulped down the black liquid, hoping it was merely another of the many similar attacks that had occurred when the pump was first implanted. The adjustment period had wreaked havoc with his digestive tract, sleep patterns, thought processes, and just about every emotional socket in his psyche. With all the emotional and physical stress overload of the past few days, the bigger question was, why hadn't it happened sooner?

"Are you feeling any better?" Whitty's voice sounded like it was coming through a long tunnel. Someone was shaking his shoulder, making him more annoyed by the minute.

Eli opened his eyes. Everyone else in the room was standing around him. He couldn't remember seeing any of them getting up a second ago before he closed his eyes in an attempt to stop the dizziness. "Stop it! Stop shaking me!" His irritation had the odd reaction of bringing smiles to their faces.

"He's back," Pearl reported from somewhere near his head.

"Are you feeling any better?"

"Sometimes we must welcome the blackness, embrace the darkness."

Eli recognized the voice and tried to sit up to see the speaker. "Damn!" The pain in his body teetered on unbearable, and he wanted to vomit.

"Been visiting the land of the shadow spirits, Godman?"

A small smile played across Eli's lips. He would never have expected to feel so glad to hear that voice. He didn't know why, but he started to cry.

"That's okay," Pearl crooned softly. "Jenn says you need to weep."

After a while, he blew his nose and breathed deeply. He felt much better. He shook Paraclete's hand and asked when he'd arrived.

"A couple of hours ago," the big man informed him.

Eli's eyes widened. "Where were you? I didn't see you when I came in here."

Whitty laid a hand on his shoulder. "Eli, you've been out for four hours. It's time for us to move on and get you out of here."

Eli looked from one man to the other. "Four hours? I just closed my eyes for a second!"

He saw Paraclete's frown. "Has something happened?"

"You're not well, Godman. Perhaps this journey is too much for you."

"No! I can do this."

"You're dreams sounded troubled, Eli," Whitty said. "You don't have to go if you really don't want to."

"No. I said I would do it, and I'll do it!"

The others recoiled at the vehemence in his voice. Eli stood and limped to the portal, a flash of memory racing across his mind. Had he been asleep? There was a picture in his mind that had not been there before. With his back still to the others, he studied the pattern of tiny cracks in the bricks lining the walls.

He'd seen a room. It was simply furnished. Through the window, he'd caught sight of a harvest moon rising over the fields. A woman with beautiful hair crouched before a man on a chair. The man's eyes looked nervous, even afraid. On the bed, another woman lay quietly, her face pale, ghostlike.

It was not her face, though, that drew Eli's attention. It was the face of the man. For some reason, it burned itself into his mind. The woman before him was working with something, bending over his arm. With a start, he realized she was holding a needle, and she was trying to insert it beneath his skin.

Eli puzzled over that oddity. No, troubled would be closer to the truth. It was though he was sitting with the man watching the woman manipulate the needle. He'd even felt the sharp jab when it penetrated the skin. He watched with fascination while she wiggled it a little, then plunged it deeper. He'd started to reach out to touch her hair when it happened. The blood, his blood, started to flow into the syringe. He could feel it being drawn out of him, leaving his body. An electric jolt raced through every vessel in his body.

The woman on the bed. They were going to do something with the blood and the sick woman. He didn't know how he knew that, but he was certain of it.

"Eli, time to go." Paraclete clapped him on the back. "Be careful. Whitty and Tanya are going to take you. Gundy agreed to let us use his car."

Eli shook his head, trying to clear away the peculiar image and the deleterious feelings it left stirring around in his head.

"Yeah, I'm ready. Let's go." He turned and gave Pearl a casual wave goodbye. "Thanks for getting me here, Pearl."

Pearl's face was frozen in a mask of fear. She held her dolls close to her chest and did not return his wave.

"Pearl, what's wrong? You look like you saw a ghost."

"I did," she whispered. "Jenn said so. I can hardly hear her anymore. She said somebody named Christine was there and told her it's in the blood." The forlorn and frightened figure began to cry. "I don't understand. I don't understand," she repeated over and over.

"What don't you understand?" asked an impatient Whitty. "You're wasting time. We need to get moving."

Pearl sniffed, obviously saddened and bewildered. "They said they gave the blood to some woman, and now the baby might die. The blood may be losing its power."

The others scoffed and dismissed Pearl's strange message. But Eli's face had blanched white.

Chapter 25

The trip in the old truck took about three hours, most of it spent in silence. Deep and utter silence. There was no discussion of philosophical regeneration of the human spirit, no theological niceties attached to the events of the evening. It had been survival. Raw, visceral, animal instinct. And the satisfaction of being able to strike back, to deliver at least one small blow to the forces threatening to take over his life.

At one point, Gideon turned to Laurel and asked, "Did it really happen?"

"Which?" she countered dully, knowing.

"Both."

Gideon drove on along Route 40, the old national highway, seeing from memory the rolling hills dotted with small farms, the waste pits of abandoned coal mines, and slag heaps of Western Pennsylvania beyond the edges of the asphalt. He didn't know what to expect to find at the house, the home, he'd abandoned a year ago. He'd abandoned JP, JP's farm, his own house, his own life after the accident.

"What was your grandfather like?" Laurel asked at one point. Gideon didn't answer, and Laurel did not pursue the subject.

The moon had disappeared by the time they reached Pittsburgh. Few cars passed them, either on the two lanes around Uniontown, or on the Penn Lincoln Parkway that started in Monroeville at the Pennsylvania Turnpike exit. The eastern suburbs lived or died on which ones attracted the high-tech replacements for steel and basic manufacturing. The chosen few were beholden still to large corporations; only the names and faces changed. The old rules still applied in new ways. The titans of early twenty-first-century information industries would give Andrew Carnegie and the ghosts of the Homestead steelworkers strikes a run for their money.

Gideon exited the parkway at the Point and crossed the Allegheny. Three Rivers Stadium loomed on the left, the city's pride and joy of brightly lit skyscrapers to the right. "I wanted to be a pitcher in the Major League when I was a kid," he said wistfully. "I used to punish the back wall of the barn unmercifully with a rubber baseball until JP made me pay for the busted boards. 'Gotta pay for your dreams, boy,' he told me."

Traveling north along Ohio River Boulevard, Gideon became more and more talkative the closer they came to Bridetown. Then he abruptly shut up again as he turned onto the high end of Eighth Street. He tried to cut down Merchant, but a police roadblock dictated a quick detour through the alleyways and infernal one-way streets. The town shimmered with the strobe flashes of police, fire, and emergency medical vehicles.

"Must be a big fire somewhere," mused Laurel.

Gideon was gripping the wheel tightly, concentrating on breathing as he shifted gears and climbed the steep grade to Highland Avenue. After he parked the truck a block shy of the house, newly educated in the art of being overly cautious, he and Laurel melted into the shadows. Laurel insisted that he use his key.

No sense breaking into someplace where they could just stroll in. Gideon objected, unsure why.

Gideon's hand shook as he attempted to fit the key into the lock. He tried to steady it with the other hand but to no avail. It wasn't like he was breaking in, he reassured himself. *After all, this is my own house.*

He had to make a conscious effort not to hyperventilate as the key turned in the lock and he stepped across the threshold. The clock over the kitchen sink softly clicked away the seconds. The curtains were Christine originals, and he could still see her coming to him with a proud smile of accomplishment at her newly discovered domestic side, her belly just beginning to show a roundedness that he found incredibly sexy. The sheer material swayed in the night breezes that scampered in through the screens that remained in the door from when he left for what he swore was the last time.

Gideon paused in the doorway, looking past the china closet into the living room. A streetlight cast an orange sodium vapor glow through the windows, highlighting the bronze in the statuette on the mantel. It was a rendition of the Egyptian goddess, the *tat* at her breastbone. The figure pulled at Gideon, drawing him into her space.

"Is it hollow?" asked Laurel.

"I never really paid all that much attention to it," confessed Gideon. Next to the figurine sat a small framed print of the Great Mother of Sernobi, a goddess representation from around 5000 BCE. "She got interested in prehistorical religious expression around the time we learned she was pregnant," Gideon explained. "I generally tuned her out. I was more concerned with how we were going to afford a baby."

"You check for anything in that statue. I'm going to take a quick look around the house and make sure no one else has been here looking into your previous life."

Gideon stopped dead in his tracks. "My previous life? You make it sound so final, like some sort of death and rebirth."

"Isn't it?" Laurel asked pointedly. "Do you actually believe you can ever come back to this?" She swept her arm around to indicate the house and all that it represented.

Gideon didn't want to think. "Go on." He sighed and picked up the statue. The weight felt good and solid, reassuring. While Laurel took out a small penlight and drifted away through the other rooms, he went to the window to try to catch a better light.

Why would Christine hide something? he asked himself. They had been completely open, uninhibited, holding no secrets. Or so he thought. He gripped the cold metal in frustration. How do you fight with a dead woman? He needed to look into her eyes while she answered his questions, faced his concerns, shared his frightful experiences of the past two days, of the past year since she'd been ripped away from him.

The room felt stuffy, close, closing in around him, so he opened the window a crack. He shook the statue, but nothing rattled. He turned it over, held it close to his face, looking for anything out of place. He fished a key from his pocket and scratched at the surface, prying for wax or fillers of any sort. Nothing.

Laurel returned empty-handed. "Maybe she had another statue."

Gideon shook his head. "No. This was her reward to herself for making a presentation to some academics. She was proud of herself, as much as I was. This represented her conquering a challenge, taking a new direction in her life. It was to be my turn next, but then she got pregnant."

"With a little help from you, I trust."

"What? Oh, yeah, of course."

"Your life has taken on a whole new direction now, wouldn't you agree?"

Gideon nodded absently, an unnamed thought haunting the back of his brain. He climbed the narrow stairs to the second floor, stopping outside their former bedroom. The air smelled stale. The next door was the nursery. He peeked inside, swallowing hard, fighting back tears. A bassinet and crib still waited, filled with stuffed animals now saturated with dust. He cursed himself for torturing himself and went back to the master bedroom. On the dresser right inside the door lay a single compact disc. He didn't know how he'd remembered where it would be, but that didn't matter at the moment.

Back downstairs, Laurel followed him into the kitchen. On the counter sat a small boom box. "She took this everywhere," Gideon commented, the lump in his throat burning fiercely. He inserted the disc, a small smile of satisfaction on his lips as he punched in number five.

Stars were falling deep in the darkness
as prayers rose softly, petals at dawn
And as I listened, your voice seemed so clear
so calmly you were calling your god.

The sound of harp, bass, and esraj built the foundation for Loreena McKennitt's clear and heart-strong voice. He bit his lip, the tears now flowing freely.

Somewhere the sun rose, o'er dunes in the desert
such was the stillness, I ne'er felt before

Was this the question, pulling, pulling, pulling you in your heart, in your soul, did you find rest there?

Gideon swiped at the tears. "I didn't want to do this anymore. I told myself I wouldn't mourn for her now."

Laurel put her hands on his shoulders from behind, resting her forehead against his back, between his shoulder blades. He leaned into her, eyes closed in memories as the final stanza melted away. When the last strains faded, he shut off the machine and headed for the back door.

"Where are you going?" asked Laurel in alarm.

He motioned for her to follow and stepped into the backyard. A cedar fence enclosed the small plot, bordered in long-neglected flowerbeds. The sunset maple they'd planted together to celebrate their new home showed off its prepubescent glory in silvery moonlight.

"Christine liked to come back here to read and meditate," Gideon whispered, cognizant of the prying eyes and ears of neighbors if they made any untoward noises. "She would bring her statue of Isis out here and set her on the crosspiece of this little wishing well we found out in Ligonier. Said the goddess would watch over her flowers and our marriage, keeping us safe." He could barely say this last phrase.

"Then she would put the disc in the player, close her eyes, and be lost. She told me she was praying—emptying and focusing her mind. She said once that silence, music, and story are the languages of the spirit." He paused, seeing through the argentine light. "She invited me to join with her, but I never did."

The mournful call of a tow boat horn drifted up the hillside on the evening breeze. The neglected garden moaned, alive with the rattle of dried plants in the wind and the creak of the rope in the wooden well. Gideon crossed the brick walk and stood beside the waist-high object. "Under the Isis," he murmured, lost in thought.

"What?"

Gideon looked at her and smiled. "Under the Isis. She did say something to me." He knelt on the hard ground and began running his fingers over the bricks around the base of the well.

"What are you looking for, Gideon?"

"Help me move this thing." Together they wrestled it to one side. Gideon took the statue and began lightly rapping on each brick. Each in turn let out a dull ping as he worked his way toward the middle. Finally, one rap produced a thump. Laurel knelt beside him to help dig around the false brick with her fingertips. In only a few minutes, they'd worked it free.

"That wasn't too difficult," Gideon noted. "I know it couldn't have been here when we placed the well." He knocked the wooden block against the edge of the well.

"Wait," cautioned Laurel. "Let's take it inside, away from other ears and eyes."

Gideon examined it thoughtfully as he spoke. "If it's all the same to you, I don't want to spend a lot of time in there. Let's put this well back in place and get the hell out of here."

They worked together efficiently, putting the yard back the way it'd been when they arrived. "Want to take it down into the basement?" Laurel asked.

"No." Gideon started to feel agitated, like his skin was crawling with ants. "Shut the door again and let's get back to the truck. Besides, the basement is just a hole I dug out. There's no tools or anything down there. Let's go see what's in your magic bag from the mountain."

Laurel lingered a moment at the door to the kitchen, wondering what sights and sounds might have filled it in a different day, a different time. It was not for her to know, she chided herself. She had her own destiny to fulfill at the moment, whatever it took. She caught up to Gideon and led him back to the truck, taking a long, circling route to check for any unwanted attention.

"Coast it down the hill and start it when we're away," she directed him.

Gideon popped the clutch below Lenz Avenue, and the engine sputtered to life. Police cars still raced through the downtown and Olde Village sections of town. "I'm going to cut across the bridge and head north. There's a coffee shop up the road where we can look at this."

His mind turned over endless possibilities as he steered the old truck along Constitution Boulevard. Across the water, the lights of Bridetown sought to offer comfort and reassurance, but he would not be fooled. Laurel held the box, restraining her urge to force it to reveal its secrets. Gideon pulled into the parking lot of King's Country Shop.

"This is the best coffee around, bar none."

Laurel let out an exasperated sigh. "Enough already!"

Gideon reached for the box but instead touched her arm. "Whatever it is, it was put there by Christine. And I only know about it because of a dream."

"I know." Laurel conveyed compassion without pity. "I don't pretend to understand it all either, Gideon. But we're on our own with this, and we need all the help we can get."

He ran his finger around the near invisible seam where the two halves met. It was too tight for a fingernail. Laurel's metal nail file failed also. After various attempts, it sat on the seat between them still intact.

"I guess we could try something like a screwdriver," said Gideon.

"The key we tried didn't even gouge the wood," Laurel replied. "Didn't even make a scratch."

Gideon shrugged. "It's not like it's a special heirloom. I never saw it before in any of her things."

"Maybe she had secrets."

Gideon squirmed uncomfortably. "I'm having enough trouble with following guidance from dreams. One surprise at a time."

"She was right, though, wasn't she?"

"You mean about finding something under Isis? Yeah, but that could be my mind playing with old information I've forgotten. Who's to say I didn't see her with it once and thought it was a shoebox or something else at the time. Or I was sleeping in that old cave, and I unconsciously made the association—"

Laurel smiled and shook her head. "I need some coffee."

Gideon tried to lodge a protest. "It's possible!"

"Or, maybe, it all is what it appears to be, or will be revealed to be, or is what Jonathan and I reminded you it is."

"Reminded?" Gideon opened the door and jumped down from the cab. Laurel did the same. "Why don't you believe me that I never heard of any of this stuff before?"

"Wait!" Laurel pointed to the box still lying on the seat. "We'd better keep this with us."

They reached across the front seat simultaneously, their hands arriving at the same moment. The top slid easily into Gideon's hand. He gaped, stunned. Laurel's mouth hung open, too, as she stared at the other section in her hand.

"It's beautiful! Gideon, look at this."

Gideon studied the lid. "This is hand-carved from some kind of wood I've never seen before. The grain is like a star pattern, rather than rings of growth. Where did she get this?"

Laurel came around the front and held out her half. "It's gorgeous, whatever it is. I wonder why we couldn't open it until we both touched it just then."

"Probably was swollen with moisture from the ground and dried out from the truck's heater."

"We didn't have the heater on," Laurel pointedly reminded him.

Gideon ignored this provocation. "Well?"

Laurel held out a small bundle of papers to him.

"What do they say?"

"I think you should be the one to read it, Gideon. She put them in there for a reason, and I doubt if she was thinking about me at the time. There might be some personal things in there."

Gideon reluctantly accepted the proffered items. "Nothing else?"

"Nope."

"Let's get that coffee first."

"Gideon! I'll go get us some takeout. Now read!"

He watched her walk across the parking lot. He tugged on his earlobes and ran his fingers through his hair. The papers felt heavy in his hand. It wasn't clear to him why he was reluctant to delve into them. He walked over to a garbage dumpster by the back door, stepping into a faded pool of light.

Finally, he could delay it no longer. The first small bundle was a folded envelope, plain white, no writing on the back. He turned it over and blinked a few times, curious but not wary. The addressee was Christine. The handwriting JP's.

The second bundle consisted of several pages torn from a notebook. His heart jumped in recognition of Christine's own neat hand. He leafed through them, noting the various dates carefully recorded in the top right-hand corner of each page. She liked to be concise, no more than one page per day. He smiled at the memory and the countless times he teased her about rambling on, while she teased right back about his doctor's style handwriting. He never let on that it stung him, that he continued to nurse his discontent at being a lowly patient aide with no education beyond high school.

He held the envelope up to the light. His brow furrowed in disbelief. The postmark was only eighteen months old. JP couldn't have been sending any letters then. The Alzheimer's put him into the nursing home three years before he died. Even then, his handwriting, let alone his thought processes, had deteriorated into indecipherable ramblings.

The pangs of guilt assaulted Gideon anew. Both of them possessed stubborn streaks a mile wide and a mile deep, his mother had reminded them constantly. Stubbornness was cold comfort to him now.

He took out the letter, his body sagging against the dumpster as he read:

My Dear Christine,

As the time of the Dance approaches, I fear I will be gone without seeing my Giddy. It was his father's place to tell him all, but we didn't know what became of him. I always believed he'd make it. It was so hard to let him go, harder yet to see Giddy wondering and wandering all those years. Don't know if it was right thing sometimes. This damn disease is taking away everything. It was bad enough to be here with my mind intact. I dread the thought of what lies in store for me now, but that day is fast approaching.

As you said, the time is coming. I don't know how dangerous it is to write even this much. I know that I forget more and more. My mind is being embezzled by nature. You take care of yourself and my boy. Don't worry about me.

Love, JP

Gideon turned the paper over, hoping for more, but it was blank. He folded it and returned it to the envelope. He tried to focus on the pages of Christine's journal, but his mind stayed on JP. He longed to see him, to sit on the porch, singing and teasing each other until darkness enveloped.

The words on the pages of the journal were not making any sense. She seemed to be retelling a story that had been told to her. He casually leafed through the rest of it, deciding Laurel could read it to him while they drove. He glanced at the last page and froze.

It was dated the day before Christine died. He read and reread it, aware that the writing was hasty, scrawled, unlike her usual style. But it was not the handwriting that made his hand tremble or his stomach rise in his throat.

He finally returned. He showed me a necklace, small, like a child's friendship charm. It is a broken heart. He did not tell me where the other half was. He only said, "When you see these joined, it will be the Redemption drawing near. It will be the time for you to assume your role as the FireGuide." The BloodFire lives.

Chapter 26

"What is the greatest fear of the human race?" Tanya asked as the trio headed north. The hum of tires and enforced intimacy of a car ride at night seemed to calm her spasms.

Whitty took the bait. "Death, of course."

"No, I don't think so."

"Like hell it isn't. Then what?"

"That there is a god but that he or she is impersonal."

"Impersonal? You mean not real?"

"No, I mean not of the person persuasion."

"I don't get it."

"Not a god you can talk to. Doesn't take an interest in human affairs. *Can't* take an interest in our lives, our hopes, our fears."

"You mean we can't pray to him? What kind of god would that be?"

Tanya paused to give directions. "Turn there, yeah. We'll go through Beaver Falls and hit Route 18. That kind would be an impersonal god. Sits there in heaven and watches us running around like idiots down here."

"That's a load of crap to most. They say, 'Of course he's personal. I pray to him every night.' You know, we should have gone across the river so we could stop and pick up some coffee at King's."

"Too late now. Drive through McDonald's and get some. Just don't spill it on yourself, or we might have to sue. Your enemies pray to him as well as your friends. And so do the Jews, and the Muslims, the guy that runs the bank and the guy who is going bankrupt, the woman who's praying for her straying husband and the woman who's hoping that the husband will really leave that wife like he's been promising, and on and on."

Eli sat in the back seat of the '79 Impala listening to Tanya and Whitty's apparently familiar lines of attack. *How many rides do they go on like this?* he wondered.

The car was one Gundy rescued from a junkyard and got running through some magic only he knew, he'd proudly proclaimed. He decorated it with American flags "because American workers making American cars with American steel is the only thing that's gonna save this back-assward country."

Eli laid his head on the weathered upholstery and asked, "Why is Gundy living in those stinking sewers if he has this car?"

"I wouldn't ask him if I were you," cautioned Tanya.

"He uses his disability check to buy the twins' and Abraham's medicines," explained Whitty. "They don't trust the system. Some psychiatrist writes the script, but they neither one can much stand going to the surface anymore. Too much's been done to them by people, so they trust nobody but Gundy." Whitty added, "And Jeremiah. They trusted Jeremiah. Nobody knows for sure what happened to the twins. That's their own private language they speak to each other. And Abraham's is a sad, sad story. When he was fifteen, his father committed suicide. Right in front of his own kid! Can you believe that? He wanted Abraham to join him, said if he really loved his old man he'd do it." Whitty squirmed around to face Eli. "Like I said, a sad one. Paraclete you've met, I presume, and that's the rest of the Wellrock Brigade. So, how's your back feeling?"

"Like a gigantic gorilla is jumping up and down on it." He shoved his hands into his pockets and felt the small heart charm. "What exactly is this place where we're going?"

Whitty cleared his throat, and his eyes darted back and forth as he wiped the sweat from his brow. Eli got the impression that what he'd seen of the obsequious chaplain at the hospital was not all an act. He wished he could speak to Susan about it. He trusted her implicitly and admired the way she and Jeremiah worked in such an easy and natural partnership. Why did they have to kill him?

"It's an old church camp, built in the late forties, early fifties, up beside Lake Erie, right near the Pennsylvania-Ohio border. Beautiful little spot. The Dancer lives there with a caretaker and his wife, who run it now as a camp for disabled children, emotionally damaged children, even some who are terminally ill. They are essential to performing the dance."

"What is the dance?"

Tanya's face took on a wistful look. "It's a way of expressing what cannot be expressed any other way. I'm sure there's lots of big fancy words you learned in seminary that might describe it. All I know is that it's like waking up and finding that your best dream is still there."

"Why is it called the dancing ground?"

Tanya and Whitty exchanged a look. "Because it's where the dancing occurs."

"The dancing?"

Tanya twisted around, his eyes narrowing. "Why don't you know this?"

"I don't know why I don't know," Eli replied bluntly. "You tell me. This whole thing has been a shock to me. I keep expecting to wake up at any moment, lying in the grass beside Slippery Rock Creek, listening to the water crash around the old mill, with Jenn napping beside me. No screams, no drowning, no impossible hopes."

Whitty said with a trace of regret, "Believe me, you're not dreamin'."

"So, if this dancer does his little dance, will all of this killing and running and hiding stop?"

Tanya shrugged. "Nobody knows what will happen. All we know is that we are dedicated to the BloodFire Redemption. It's not about revenge, you know. It's about ending the domination obsession that we humans have—the domination of sexes, the domination by all the competing 'chosen peoples' of the world. Whoa, I can't imagine that ending without a fight! That is why the Sanctuary is seen as being so dangerous to the Ransom. They see it not only as taking away a way of life but life itself. To them, there is no other way. There is one right way to think and believe in faith, and all others must be brought into compliance or submit to being dominated. But, like I said, I really don't know."

"When is this dance? Is that what we are going to see?"

"No, the Sacrament dance won't be until the child is ready. We want to know if those at the dancing ground know anything of the Healer." Whitty thought for a moment. "Let me put it to you this way, Eli. You're a minister, you've studied the theologians, the great philosophers and thinkers and historians. How does the human spirit communicate?"

"The human spirit?" Eli made no attempt to disguise his skepticism. "I give up. Words? The way we live our lives?"

"Those are ways we express our response to the spirit. But how does the spirit inherent to making us human communicate what is transcendent? How do we communicate what is beyond the limits? How do we tell of the beyondness of experience and knowledge, the BloodFire that makes us want to know who we are? Are you with me?"

Eli nodded uncertainly. "I think so."

He expected Whitty to continue, but the other man turned around and looked out the windshield. Tanya glanced over, but she also said nothing.

"I said I think so," Eli repeated.

The only noise was the hum of tires on pavement. Eli gave up in disgust and slumped back in his seat. The silence stretched on and on until even the tire noise receded far into the background and all he heard was his own breathing, then his own blood rushing through his head.

"Do you see?" asked Whitty, without turning around.

"See what?"

"Silence. The language of the spirit is first and foremost silence. Then dance and music and story can enter the heart that's been prepared by silence. We as a race are terrified of that silence, so we fill it with gods made in our own image. We swear up and down that they are not like us, but they all are. On the other hand, a few of us still remember that in the silence is the Sanctuary, the womb of life, the root of all that is. The desire to know that, to see ourselves as being part of the Sanctuary and thus know ourselves, is the BloodFire. That BloodFire has been within us from the beginning, but we have tried to own it, to dominate it. When we do that, fear rules, and fear leads to the BloodRansom way of thinking and the BloodRansom way of living. But Redemption isn't about blood, about making the Sanctuary be like us somehow or to want us. It is about accepting that silence as the root of life. Only then will the BloodFire be free to journey on to others' worlds and enable them to know themselves as they are. Then they will be able to create their own version of community that best fits them. Freedom, community, compassion—that's what it's all about."

Whitty sat back, breathing heavily, apparently exhausted. "I'm just piling words on top of words. The Dancer dances the story of all this, making it accessible to all, real. We have been without a StoryKeeper for too many generations, and people are forgetting the power of the dance." He waved his hand feebly over his shoulder. "It is said only fools will believe. Look around you, Eli. You are surrounded by fools!"

Silence descended on them once again. Eli turned the broken heart over and over in his hand, lost in thoughts that had no words. After another half hour, they stopped in Mercer, a rural county seat just north of I-80. Eli's legs didn't want to function when he crawled from the back seat. He leaned against the car, hands on his knees, willing the pain to subside. Whitty returned from the convenience store with a cup of coffee for him.

"Where's Tanya?"

Eli accepted the steaming drink. "I don't know. She did have the map spread out on the hood, but now I think she's making a phone call."

Whitty frowned. "We should all stick together." He surveyed the parking lot and the street. "Damn. Paraclete warned me to be careful. Be ready for anything, Eli."

"What are you talking about?" asked a bewildered Eli.

At that precise moment, Tanya rounded the corner of the building, smiling beatifically, wiping her hands on her pants. "No towels," she explained, somewhat sheepishly.

Whitty spun on his heels. "C'mon, we gotta keep moving. We'll be there in less than an hour."

"What's the matter with him?" Tanya asked.

"Nothing, just a little paranoia. Probably not a bad idea, though," Eli said.

He volunteered to take a turn behind the wheel while Tanya stretched out in the back seat. The narrow roads wound their way through the pitch black of a farm country night. Going through a series of curves, the headlights picked up something on the road.

"Watch out!" yelled Whitty as they rolled over a mat of spikes.

The steering wheel started to shake violently, forcing Eli to slow the car and pull to the side of the road.

Whitty got out and squatted beside the front tire on the driver's side. He scratched his head as he stood up and went around to the other side. Eli took the keys from the ignition and opened the trunk. The jack had gotten wedged in the spare tire well, so he picked up the tire iron and gave it a good whack. "This jack is stuck," he called out. When he received no answer, he poked his head around the side. And froze.

A man in a long, dark coat stood over Whitty, who still crouched beside the second flat tire. What terrified Eli was the gun in the stranger's hand, which he pointed at Whitty's head. "Where's the necklace? Give me the damn necklace!" It was a commanding snarl.

"I need that recognition code!" He jammed the barrel into Whitty's left ear. "Do you want to know what a bullet sounds like going through your brain?"

"Wh-what's going on?" Eli managed to get out.

"He's a lying, thieving Metamelonian! They're trying to take the benefits of the BloodFire from the earth by force!" Whitty spat the words with murderous vehemence. "A nightcrosser."

The nightcrosser straightened and looked over his shoulder at Eli with a grim smile. Then he wheeled suddenly and viciously kicked Whitty in the kidneys. The portly chaplain screamed and toppled over, writhing in agony.

"The name's Grutt." After this announcement, the nightcrosser calmly pointed the pistol at one of Whitty's knees and pulled the trigger. Blood and bone fragments splattered the tire. The injured man's screams rent the stillness.

"Now, once again. Where is the necklace?"

"I don't know what the hell you're talking about," the wounded man gasped through gritted teeth. He turned his head and vomited.

Eli stayed rooted to the spot, his knuckles white on the cold iron of the jack handle.

"I'm getting a little impatient," said Grutt, raising the gun and aiming it between Whitty's eyes. "Let's try this one more time so you'll quit playing hero."

Eli reacted without thinking. His arm came up, cocked and ready. He flung the heavy metal hard and true. The snap of iron breaking bone sounded simultaneously with the sharp crack of the gun. Both men collapsed, Grutt writhing in paroxysms of pain. Eli scrambled across the few yards of gravel and snatched up the gun.

He pointed it with wavering grip at the nightcrosser. Grutt clutched his shattered wrist, panting, his features twisted in pain. "I seek only the truth, just like yourself."

Tanya scrambled from the back seat, her face drained of all blood. "Don't listen to him. Never trust a nightcrosser. They don't belong here."

"What's a nightcrosser?" asked Eli, the gun heavy in his hand. His legs shook so badly he thought at any moment he'd collapse in a heap.

"What makes her any more believable than me?" Grutt asked, using one hand to scoot over to lean against the car.

"Don't, please don't listen to him, Eli. Nightcrossers come through the Gateway to try and influence the disposition of the BloodFire. They're sent to try and manipulate matters on earth so that whatever group is in power in their world can get the best contract out of it. We know that the bloodtrackers have offered a deal."

Eli looked from one to the other. "A deal. What kind of a deal?"

"The trackers have told the Metamelonians that they will see that the BloodFire gets to continue the journey on to their world and they can do what they want. But in return, the nightcrossers help the trackers—"

"Help them what?" scoffed Grutt. "Keep the status quo here on this miserable little planet? You think people here really want to change? Do you have any idea of the magnitude of the changes that would occur if the Sacrament child survives? This will be the best deal this miserable race will ever get."

Eli's head was spinning. The gun wavered as he tried to stop the dizziness by holding his head with the other hand. What were these two saying? "You're saying if my daughter lives, that will mean at the least things will stay the same and we'll be safe? This nightmare will be over for us?"

Grutt nodded. Tanya struggled to keep Eli focused. "It's a deal with the devil. The Ransom said that if the nightcrossers help them get to the BloodFire, then they can have it."

"You don't need the BloodFire here. You have well developed civilizations, high technology, arts and thinkers, religions for any and all. We have none of that, and we are dying. Look, I gain nothing personally from this. Once a nightcrosser comes over, we have no guarantees that we can ever go back. We may be stranded here, sacrificed to help our world." Grutt looked into Eli's eyes. "Go ahead, ask Tanya if I'm lying or telling the truth. Go on."

Tanya's glum look confirmed the veracity of the other's words.

"How would they stop the BloodFire from being effective here?" Eli asked.

"The child would be sent on before the sacrament of the Redemption."

None of it was making sense to Eli. "Who knows about this? I can't believe Pearl is capable of scheming to—wait a minute! Sent on? What do you mean the child will be sent on?"

Grutt's eyebrows arched in surprise. "You don't know? Yes, the daughter will be sent to my world in order to save it, to give it a soul, if you'll pardon the expression."

"Yeah, and the Healer, FireGuide, and all those who are Guardians of the Sanctuary will be exterminated so that there will be no chance of a recurrence of the BloodFire Redemption ever again," Tanya spat out with angry despair.

"You mean if we don't find this Healer, my wife and our baby die? But if they live, then the nightcrossers get my child but not the bloodtrackers, and other worlds can grow while earth will go on as it is?"

"He's a quick learner," Grutt said with grim appreciation. He turned to Tanya. "Tell that to your precious little Dancer, you cripple!"

"Shut up!" barked Eli, desperate to make his head stop its incessant throbbing. He could feel something, sense a powerful presence nearby. He began pacing, the stars whirling overhead like they'd gone crazy.

"What are you going to do?" stammered Tanya.

"Do the right thing," said Grutt. "What's best for you."

Eli stumbled over a rock. He fought to maintain his balance, the gun waving wildly as his arms flailed. Out of the corner of his eye, he saw Grutt scramble to his feet and start running across a field. Tanya was bathed in harsh light, and beyond her, Whitty's body. Eli couldn't understand where the light came from.

He landed on his knees with a jarring crash. He lost his grip on the gun, and it skittered over the gravel toward the ditch along the side of the road. Eli looked up into a set of bright headlights bearing down on him. He heard the squeal of brakes and squinted his eyes against the glare. A door slammed, and he pulled himself upright on shaky legs, stepping to the side to get a better look. It was an old flatbed truck, a Chevy, probably late forties.

Another door slammed. A man and a woman appeared in the pool of light. The woman had her blonde hair tucked into a Steelers cap and stood beside a man who looked vaguely familiar to Eli. Before he could say anything, however, everything went black, and he fell.

Chapter 27

In the lot of the coffee shop an hour earlier, Gideon accepted the cup from Laurel, his hand still shaking. He handed her the letter and diary pages with an abrupt, "Let's go." He wanted to get away from this place now. He wanted to get in and keep on driving until they reached somewhere far away from the bizarre, away from the cycle of death and violence, secrets and betrayal, power and domination.

"Nothing like a cup of good coffee," Laurel murmured appreciatively, sipping the cream-laced brew. Gideon drove the ancient Chevy truck in silence. Laurel tried not to look over too often, lest he snap at her again for "fretting over me like I was a horse that needed to be put down." She knew after a cursory glance through the papers that they held pieces of the puzzle, answers that Gideon longed for and feared, answers that led to more questions. She hesitated to read them to him.

"Nobody asked to be born." Gideon broke the tense silence, stalling for time to think. "Don't you get it? Nobody asked to be born. Forget about who you have for parents, what country or what race. Forget about eyes and hair color, fat or skinny, beautiful or homely. Nobody asked to be here. Period."

"I know."

"Not the Aborigine in Australia, not the Tutsi woman in Africa, not the slave trader or the Tibetan monk, not the Aztec priest or the Spanish conquistador, not the queen of Hawaii or the Celtic storyteller, not the Iroquois warrior or the first woman to fly the Atlantic. None of them asked to be born." Gideon slapped the dashboard with one hand. "Well, guess what? Neither did I."

"Are you saying life isn't fair?"

"Don't insult me, Laurel. We've slept together, but that doesn't mean you can call me stupid." He saw the look of hurt in her eyes but told himself he didn't care.

"I'm just trying to understand."

"Well, so am I!"

"What did you do after your wife died?"

"She didn't die; she was killed. She didn't ask to be born either, and she certainly didn't ask to die impaled on the shaft of a gearshift." Gideon stared at the broken white line racing past in a blur, each fragment in the light for a barely discernable moment. "Why did she have this secret? If we were going to have such little time together, why did she have a secret? I've mourned her day and night since she was killed—but the dreams, what about the dreams? Have I been inventing them out of my imagination?"

"Dreams? There's been more than one?"

Gideon cursed himself for letting his secret slip. It was every night, every time he lay his head down to sleep. "Just a few," he said, shrugging, trying too hard to sound casual.

Laurel let his lie go unchallenged. "How much of this did you read?"

"Enough to know that either someone was forging JP's handwriting a year and a half ago, or that Christine was hiding something from me. According to those papers, she knew about this FireGuide business and the BloodFire. Am I leaving anything out? What does it say, that she discovered this pseudo-cult in some women's magazine and started sending some New Age shyster money and thought about running away to a commune?" Gideon's voice grew more and more bitter.

"Stop feeling so damned sorry for yourself! I'm getting tired of saying it, but too much blood has been spilled already for you to indulge yourself in your little pity party."

Gideon glanced into her fiery eyes, his heart aching to reach over and touch her on the cheek. "What does she say?" he asked, barely contrite.

"She tells the story of how your grandfather saved the Guardians from extinction."

Gideon nearly swerved off the road as he gawked at her, too stunned to say anything.

"I thought that might get your attention." Laurel pushed a few strands of hair away from her cheek. "Did you know that your grandfather was a prisoner of war in World War Two?"

"Yeah. What's that have to do with anything?"

"Your wife talks about JP writing to her of his experiences in the camps."

Gideon shook his head. "He never would tell me anything about what he went through. Why would he tell her? And why wouldn't she tell me?"

Laurel held up the sheaf of papers. "I haven't seen anything yet that explains that. They must have had their reasons. Come on, Gideon. Both of these people loved you more than anything. They had to have good reasons. You have to trust them."

Gideon snorted. "Trust? Where has trust taken me? This is completely insane."

"Stop shouting, please, and I'll read some of this." Laurel shuffled the pages around. "Here it is."

JP wrote to me of his experience during the war. He went into France to help the Resistance. One night their cell was betrayed by a collaborator. He was sent to a secret camp near the Alps. In his barrack was a young man who worked in the camp infirmary. JP didn't know if he'd been a doctor before the war or simply had experience of some sort in a hospital.

JP struck up a friendship with this young man, who called himself Aleudar. He told JP he had no permanent home, but JP got the impression that he had some American Indian blood in his background. JP helped Aleudar care for those prisoners who were dying, trying to sneak them extra bread, a tiny fraction more gruel.

The winter of 19–4–45 was fierce and unrelenting. Many were dying just as liberation and victory was within reach. The German guards were under orders to liquidate all of the weakest prisoners. One day they came to clean out the infirmary. Aleudar tried to stop them from taking one patient, a young boy who'd been brought in with his father and brothers. He was the last of his line.

Aleudar offered to take the boy's place, even though he'd told JP earlier that the commandant had already guaranteed him safety till the Allies came. For some reason, the guards agreed to Aleudar's sacrifice. Before they dragged him away, he managed to whisper to JP and told him to look in a particular spot in the camp. That what he found there would be his now in appreciation of his friendship and trust.

When JP went to the secret cache, he dug up a mysterious box, the likes of which he'd never seen before. The strange thing was he could not open the box. Try as he might, it would not open. He assumed that the box itself must have been of special significance to Aleudar, perhaps a family heirloom. So JP kept it and brought it back to the farm when the war was over.

He put it on the mantel as a reminder of his friend's sacrifice. One day when his wife was cleaning, it accidentally fell off. They both reached down to retrieve it, and when they both touched it, it fell open. Inside, undiscovered all those years, was the gift from Aleudar.

Laurel stopped reading. Gideon let his breath out slowly and looked at the box between them on the seat. When he looked up, his eyes met Laurel's. "Well? Are you going to tell me what was inside?"

Laurel slowly nodded. "This is incredible. Look, my hands are shaking."

"Read it already!"

She cleared her throat and finished the journal entry.

JP said that inside was a packet of papers in Aleudar's handwriting. It was a journal that he called the Sanctuary Chronicles. Also inside was a small gold charm, the kind of trinket young girls who are best friends might give to each other; a small broken heart. The papers told of what was to be done with it.

The note from Aleudar said that whoever had them was charged with continuing the Chronicles. One day a Healer would be born, and the Healer needed to find the FireGuide. Their child would be the Sacrament …

"Why'd you stop?"

"There's some pages missing. It looks like she ripped these pages out of a notebook and stopped after this page, then went to a different section to rip out some more."

"It stops there?" His fist pounded on the steering wheel. "Why didn't he ever tell *me* any of this?"

"It sure sheds light on what's going on though, Gideon," Laurel pointed out.

"Oh, yeah, it's as clear as mud. What are the rest of the papers?"

"It looks like she skipped ahead and took out some entries from the last year of her life." Laurel rapidly skimmed through, then looked up with a worried expression.

"Aren't you going to read them to me?"

Laurel sighed. "She talks about you in some of them."

Gideon studied the scrolling pavement. "Let's hear it," he said softly.

> Adam has been such a dear friend to me. At first I didn't want to believe him when he told me who he was. Said it would be too dangerous, that anybody known to associate with him was a target for the Ransom. It must be terrible lonely for him, all these years with no one to lean on.
>
> He told me that JP's ruse appears to have been successful. After he went into the nursing home, he was taken off the watch list by the bloodtrackers. Adam told me about setting out to find the Witness Council all those years ago and giving his life to reestablishing the Guardians. He has recruited around the world, but very, very few have ears to hear the message and know the truth.

Adam is worried. He fears that the Alzheimer symptoms that were mild are progressing rapidly in JP. He laughed when he described how JP faked them worse than they really were to get into the home, but now the real thing is catching up to him. I'm going to tell Gideon tomorrow about what Adam says is to be his role is in the Sanctuary. Perhaps then Gideon will stop being so stupidly stubborn and go see his grandfather. He has to. He's the only one who can help him.

Adam seemed preoccupied—

"Stop! Stop reading. My wife was the FireGuide, and JP was in on it? Does that mean this Adam is my father?"

Laurel nodded. "Apparently, he left part of the necklace with your mother and took the other part to give to the FireGuide whenever he found her."

"I'm lost. My baby was to be the Sacrament child? That bastard that killed my wife also killed the Sacrament child?" Gideon pulled the truck to the side of the road and killed the engine. "My father left to go take care of keeping the Sanctuary Guardians alive? But he couldn't come back when my mother died?"

"It was probably too dangerous. Don't forget your mother gave her blessing on it too."

"But why didn't they ever tell me?" Gideon climbed out of the truck so he could pace. His agitation increased the more he thought about the rush of revelations in Christine's journal. "I sure hope whoever the hell is at this camp can give me some answers. It feels like my head is going to split open and my brains are going to explode all over this damn truck."

He leaned against the rear, breathing hard. He noticed that the crude bandage around his thigh was soaked through with blood again, but he ignored it. Laurel came around to him and cupped his chin with her hand to lift his face to her. She gave him a tender kiss. "It seems like an eternity since we made love last night, Gideon. I want you to know that I believe in you. I don't understand all of this either. Maybe no one has all the pieces. But I believe in you. I trust you. The only other person I ever trusted was Jonathan."

Gideon sucked in his breath sharply. "You certainly know how to get me to shut up and calm down."

She smiled, and he gave her a sad smile in return.

"Let me take a look at your leg," she insisted.

He perched on the back of the truck bed. When Laurel peeked beneath the bandage, she let out a small gasp. "I don't understand why you can heal others but it doesn't seem to work on yourself."

Gideon stroked her hair. "I'm tired of all my questions, Laurel. So, so tired. Yet that's all I have at the moment. How can all this have been going on around me, and I didn't see it or suspect anything, discover some aspect of … of the truth?"

"We better keep going," she reminded him, tearing off the bottom of her shirt and packing it around the bandage.

Back on the road, he asked her to read some more of the journal to him. He wanted to face the truth without turning away now. It was time to face his life, he decided.

> I feel that something is wrong. Adam promised to return by last month, but he never came, and I have not heard from him. JP's mind and body are at war. I grieve for him. And for Gideon. He wanted to not go back till he could show his grandfather that he could make it, that his choices had been right. But now he is too embarrassed by his job and lack of education. I think he wants to be able to sit with JP like the old days that he tells me so much about. I don't know if he

truly is happy about the baby or not. I know he had his heart set on enrolling in college ... he is so unhappy with himself, I believe.

Adam said that he had something of great importance for me, then Gideon could be told. I am excited at the prospect and also frightened. What if Adam is in trouble? I have left the box open until he returns. I feel this cloud coming over me. I almost told Gideon about the people I keep seeing wherever I go, like they were following me. Today I saw a man with no legs ...

"That's where it stops."

"How did she get this stuff into the box?" Gideon rubbed his eyes, tired of thinking.

"I don't know. Maybe she never closed it till the end." Laurel's own eyes were red with fatigue. "Do you want me to drive?"

"No, I think I'll get off this road and cut across country though. The shorter the better."

"I was thinking. Christine says that half of the necklace was left with your mother, which you said was buried with her. And the other half was for the FireGuide. According to this, that would be herself, but there was no other half of the charm with this stuff."

"The deeper we get into this, the more questions than answers we find. That old man in the parking lot, was he one of Adam's recruits or just a messenger?"

"Look! There's something up ahead."

Gideon saw an older model Chevrolet sedan pulled off to the side of the road, its lights on. Two figures were on the ground, and a third stood over them, holding what looked to be a gun.

"It looks like there's been some injuries." As he steered the truck to the berm, the man with the gun took a step, stumbled, and fell to his knees, the gun sliding away somewhere underneath the car. To Gideon's surprise, one of the those on the ground scrambled to his feet. He glanced at the oncoming lights of the truck. He was small, wiry, with Asian features. They watched in amazement as he fled into the night before the truck completely stopped.

Opting for caution, Gideon pushed the box under the front seat before climbing down to offer help. The man tried to regain his feet, but something appeared to be wrong with him. He looked at Laurel and Gideon, then collapsed in a dead faint. A picture stirred in the back of Gideon's mind.

Before they could reach him, the back door of the car swung open. A woman with an unruly mass of red hair laboriously climbed out. "Help us please. Whitty's been shot."

The other man on the ground came around slowly. Laurel wiped his head with an alcohol swab from her supplies, while Gideon checked out Whitty's body by the front wheel.

"Who was this guy?" he asked Tanya, noting her watching him intently. "Who shot him and why?"

"He's a hospital chaplain," Eli managed weakly as he sat up. "He saved our lives."

Gideon's brow furrowed at his words, the unclear memory continuing to slip in and out of the shadows of his mind. What was a hospital chaplain doing out here in the middle of nowhere? But that was not what stirred his memories.

"The nightcrosser wanted to force us to take him to the Dancer. Seems everybody's been waiting for the Healer." Tanya talked while she limped around, helping Gideon drape an old moving pad from the trunk over Whitty. "Don't act like you don't know what I'm talking about," she said to Gideon with a smile. "I'd recognize you anywhere."

"Me? Why? I've never seen you before."

"Maybe not, but I know who you are. You're the Healer. Your father must be so proud of you. Is he with you?"

Chapter 28

All eyes turned to Gideon. He shrugged dismissively.

"Sounds like we need to compare stories," Laurel said. "Let's get the body into the truck and then decide who goes first. I don't think your nightcrosser friend will be back here tonight."

They wrestled Whitty's body onto the bed and covered him with a blanket. "You both look completely exhausted," Tanya said. "Have you been on the road long?"

Laurel winked at Gideon with a tired glint in her eyes. "Since forever."

Gideon struggled with Tanya's words about his father. The more the bizarre events of the past few days unfolded, the more his father popped up. He looked to Laurel for some clue as to whether she trusted this ragtag band or not. He was all for trusting no one at this point, but Laurel seemed to be accepting them at face value.

"Okay, I give up." He sighed. "What did you mean by that crack about my father? Just who the hell are you?"

"Gideon—" Laurel tried to calm him, but he held up his hand.

"No, I want to know. Who are you? There have been too many coincidences these past few days for me to just say, 'Oh, okay, here's my story, and I think we're all on the same side here.' Uh-uh. You called me the Healer. It's your turn. I see one dead man in the back of the truck, and another man ran away as we pulled up. Who knows how many more you've killed."

"Wait just a damn minute," Eli protested as vehemently as his pounding head and screaming back would allow. "Whitty was murdered, but it wasn't by us. These people are trying to help me find healing for my wife, and it's already cost two other people besides him their lives. It's all because some crazy lady thinks she can hear my wife talking, even though she's in a coma. Pearl went through this elaborate scheme to get some child's trinket to her as a recognition code."

"Trinket?"

Eli pulled the necklace from his pocket. "I haven't seen one like it since I was in grade school."

Laurel leaned close. Her hand came up slowly, stopping within an inch of touching it. "It matches."

Gideon snatched it away from Eli. "Where did you get this?" He grabbed Eli by the front of the shirt and pulled him up till he was screaming into the man's face. "Who gave this to you? This does not belong to you. You have no right to this—"

"It's not mine!" Eli gasped as pain seared the nerve endings across his lower back. "Pearl said Adam gave it to her, and she gave it to my wife. It says something about the three witnesses on the back. I never heard of any of this until Jenn was nearly drowned."

Gideon let him go and shoved the two halves of the necklace charm into his pocket. Eli crumbled in agony.

"You're in a lot of pain?" Laurel asked.

"Yeah. Automobile accident last year. I'm way beyond my pain medication with all that's been happening in Bridetown the past two days."

Gideon gave a start, the nagging thought now a vivid image—a blood-soaked picture. This was the man! He forced himself to slow his breathing to remain calm. After all that had happened in his life since that fateful night when he'd been summoned to the emergency room, here was the man responsible standing right in front of him!

Laurel noticed the change in him, and she squeezed his hand in a silent question. When Gideon ignored her, she whispered, "Is your leg bleeding again?"

Tanya overheard and frowned. "Are you hurt?" She shone a flashlight over him, stopping at the leg of his jeans now soaked through with blood. "My God, this looks like we're setting up a MASH unit. You've lost a lot of valuable blood, Gideon."

"Your concern is touching." Gideon's sarcasm bit hard. "Don't tell me. You were wanting it for yourself?"

Tanya shuffled closer, tapping his chest with her finger. "If time wasn't so short, I'd take your head off for that. I'm here because the Dancer asked me to be here." She turned to Laurel. "Where'd you guys find him? I can imagine what Jonathan thought when this guy turned out to be the Healer. Is he coming later?"

Laurel shook her head. "Jonathan's not coming. He's … Jonathan is dead."

Tanya was stunned. "Oh no. Not Jonathan too."

Laurel frowned. "Who else?"

"Jeremiah."

Laurel felt numb. It was too much to comprehend at the moment. "It's just us?"

Tanya nodded. "Along with Susan and Paraclete."

The two women were silent as the realization sunk in of the enormity of what was happening. Gideon took Eli by the arm and led him aside.

"I know who you are," he whispered in a growl.

"I don't know what you mean."

"You're from Bridetown? Me too. About a year ago, I was working at the Riverside County Medical Center one night when my wife was brought in. They told me that there was so much blood in the ambulance that they had to hose it out. My wife and baby died that night. Ring any bells, Reverend Elijah Marks? What happened that night, Mr. Marks? Funny, I don't remember seeing you ever again, not that I really wanted to. But you couldn't face me, could you? You could not even say 'I'm sorry.' Was it really an accident, man? Was it?"

The blood drained from Eli's face. Before he could respond, Tanya came over. "What's wrong, Eli? What did he say to you?"

"The truth. I asked him about the truth." Gideon spun on his heels and stepped away from the light cast by the truck's headlamps. His body trembled with pent-up rage and hatred, grief and pain cascading over him anew. He stumbled into the field and looked up at the stars, countless and constant, frail bits of light in the satin sky.

The cry welled up from deep inside of him, pulling at the roots that wend their way through even the marrow of his bones: His pain from the gaping wound of losing Christine, the life of his child snatched away before it began. His hatred, nurtured and harbored, taken out over the months to be furtively fed, immersing himself in it till it became a part of his soul. The wrenching realization that Christine kept secrets from him, not trusting him with shrouded mysteries that pertained to who he was, who she was, who they were together. The guilt over abandoning JP, his mentor and best friend.

The feeling of opportunity lost whenever he tried to better his station in life, his inferiority, his fear of abandoning himself to acceptance, and of being abandoned once again. And finally, the role of Healer being thrust upon him, too great a mystery to comprehend, beyond faith, beyond rationality, yet pulling him in deeper and deeper into the needs of not only himself but also those of the strange community of the Sanctuary.

Unbidden, it came. He could see it all, crystal clear as the night sky. And he clenched his fists and cried out with furious pain. And frustration. Emptiness. He screamed until he could cry out no more.

A kairotic silence descended around him, and on him, till its very weight embraced him. An intense itching started in his leg, breaking the spell. He impatiently tugged at the bandages around his thigh.

Then he became aware of Eli standing beside him. Slowly, ever so slowly, Eli knelt before him and carefully peeled away the layers of blood-soaked bandages. The bleeding had stopped. Perhaps a healing had begun.

Gideon lowered his eyes and placed his hand on Eli's head. "No. Don't kneel there. Get up. I'm just a man."

"You don't understand. I didn't understand it myself until just now," Eli began, but Gideon again shook his head.

"I do understand."

Eli's hands trembled. Gideon watched the muscles of his jaw twitching, his Adam's apple bobbing up and down. His face wet with tears, Eli tried to explain. "I didn't have to go back in that night. I–I was wanting … I was thinking about something, someone. She wasn't my wife. Oh, God, I'm so sorry. You have to believe me. I was writing a note to her about where to meet me in the hospital, and I dropped the pen. My hand slipped, and I dropped my pen. I don't know why I tried to pick it up while I was driving, but I took my eyes off the road. Just for a moment, but when I looked up, the light of the train beside the road blinded me. That's all I remember. The next thing I knew I was waking up in the hospital."

Eli stayed on his knees, his body wracked with great shudders as he confessed. "I was wrong, but I never told anyone, not even my wife. I couldn't bear to hurt her. My pain is my punishment. I spent all I had this year to buy my wife a diamond, a sign of starting a new life. She's giving us a child. Do you understand? I've lost everything … I want the baby to live, and I want my wife to live. She is good. She is …" He couldn't go on. His words sounded selfish in his own ears. *What kind of man am I?* he wondered.

Gideon pulled him to his feet. "I don't know what I'm supposed to do, Elijah. Who am I to give life or death? They tell me that your child is the Sacrament child. Right now, I don't know what that means, but if I can help it, she must live. And your wife as well." Gideon exhaled in a long, slow release, his breath silver in the moonlight for a moment, then gone.

The two men stood there together, peering into the sky, wondering what lay beyond the moment. In the silence between them, they struggled with their own questions, their own desires. The moon began its descent.

Eli spotted a shooting star streaking across the horizon. "I guess that's why they call them nightcrossers. Across all of that vast emptiness," he said, sweeping his hand before him.

"I'm having trouble enough right here." Gideon sighed. "I'll worry about nightcrossers later."

Laurel called to him. "Gideon, I think it's time we move on now."

He looked Eli in the eye. "Yes, I think it is."

Tanya insisted on riding in the back with Whitty's body, keeping vigil, maintaining that even the smallest gesture of respect would honor the sacrifice of those who had lost their lives seeking to keep the awareness of the Sanctuary alive and moving forward as time grew short. Eli wanted to join her out of respect for Jeremiah, but the others persuaded him that riding in the front would be torture enough for his back.

"What brought you to seek the Dancer?" Laurel asked Eli as they followed the ridgeline of the gentle hills to the west of Meadville.

He recounted the horrible incident at McConnell's Mill and the events that had followed in such rapid fire sequence that when he finished telling the tale, he could scarcely believe it himself that so little time had passed. Day and night ran together in his memory into a nightmare of dull grays and bright reds.

"So, your father may have decided to follow the call of the Sanctuary?" Laurel asked him when he'd finished.

"It's possible. He never said anything about it in his letters to us. But Whitty showed me the picture, and I wasn't sure what to think."

"As far as you know, your wife didn't know of any of these matters before you did?" Gideon yielded to the temptation of self-pity about Christine's secrets.

Eli studied him and didn't answer. Instead, he took out the photo and showed it to Laurel. Her cry of anguish brought Gideon back to the moment.

"Jonathan! Gideon, look! It's Jonathan!"

"That's my father." Eli pointed to the cocky pilot.

Gideon's eyes were fixed on the figure in the middle "What year was this taken?"

Eli did some quick figuring. "It must have been around 1969 or '70. Why?"

"Laurel, imagine some years on that guy. Who do you see?"

Laurel studied the figure intently for a moment. "He looks familiar, but I can't quite place him."

"Pearl said it was Adam." Eli's eyes widened at the reaction his statement caused in the other two.

"Then it's true!" Laurel threw her arms around Gideon. "Now you know. It's him, it's really him."

Gideon remained stony faced, his heart strangely unmoved and his thoughts uneasy.

"Gideon, what's the matter? Your father is Adam. Adam, the guy who's been trying to recruit others to help preserve the Sanctuary Chronicles all these years. Adam is your father!"

"Doesn't it bother you that we just happen to run across these people out in the middle of nowhere, who just happen to also be part of the Sanctuary business, who just happen to have a picture that appears to show that my father and this Adam character are one and the same?"

"He always look gift horses in the mouth?" Eli asked Laurel.

"He's big on throwing cold water over the simplest pleasures," Laurel confirmed his assessment. She turned back to Gideon. "Has *any* of this seemed very probable to you? Three days ago, would anyone in this world have been able to convince you that in the next seventy-two hours you would heal terminally ill people with the blood from your own body?"

"But what if . . ." Gideon struggled to put his thoughts to words. "What about the blood, my blood? What if there is some other explanation, some other reason those people got well?" He rubbed his eyes, avoiding looking at Laurel as he admitted reluctantly to his own doubt. "What if it's not me, not a gift? What if I'm not any different, or it's just some fluke of nature?"

"Gideon, what is your heart telling you? Forget about coincidences and mysterious dreams and strange mysteries that disturb you. Look within yourself, Gideon. What is the heart of the matter for you?"

Laurel's soft, earnest challenge, said with eyes that he knew held great love for him, warmed him. "You," he said quietly.

Laurel laid her head against his shoulder. "You make me feel like I'm the first person in the world to discover love, Gideon."

"What do I do?" he asked.

"Follow where it leads," Eli offered his contribution to the matter. "I'm only learning that now myself. Think about it a minute. We've both been given new chances in life by a small group of people, bound together in a community of those trying to faithfully honor this BloodFire Protocol for the Sanctuary. Maybe, just maybe, their actions and willingness to lay down their lives for the world acts as a manner of concentrating compassion and goodness into a very real power that can act beyond their personal and individual capabilities."

"You mean like prayer?" Laurel piped up in a spontaneous burst of insight.

"Yeah, maybe so," Eli said, trying to pin down what his own heart was saying. "It's not coincidence or a miracle or some sort of paranormal nonsense that is beyond science or reason. Maybe what we are experiencing and witnessing is the inexpressible spirit of the Sanctuary."

"The BloodFire. Maybe this Redemption isn't about blood at all but about accepting life and letting go of the desire to control the BloodFire." Gideon pinched the bridge of his nose. "All this thinking is wearing me out. You make a lot of sense, Eli. I think you'd make a much better Healer than me."

"No. It is as it is." Eli's words sounded a benediction as they neared journey's end.

But there were many more miles to go before the story came full circle.

Chapter 29

"Do we have to know where evil comes from? Isn't it enough that it's always around?"

"Oh, no! Don't try to sucker me into one of those discussions of yours."

"I get this way when I'm nervous," Tanya protested as the small band stood looking at the open gateway across the narrow lane.

"Are you sure this is the place?" asked Gideon.

Laurel punched him lightly on the arm. "Sorry, I get like *this* when I'm nervous," she said with a wicked grin, rebuking him for his lack of confidence in Tanya's knowing her own way home.

"Will Whitty be okay?" Eli nervously rocked back and forth on the balls of his feet, his one hip higher than the other from the spasms in his lower back.

The truck sat beside a one-lane paved road in the flatlands of the southwestern shore of Lake Erie. They'd passed few houses in the rural, undeveloped townships near the Ohio-Pennsylvania border. Pussy willows grew on the banks of the small stream that wound its way through a quiet meadow beyond the whitewashed fence that stretched on either side of the gateway. Overhead, the simple sign announced, "Lost Trail," and underneath proclaimed, "A Seed Community."

"What does that mean?" wondered Gideon, but no one answered. They crossed underneath the arching wrought iron and followed the dirt track parallel to the stream. After a hundred yards, they reached the edge of a wood. A rustic barn sat back from the roadway with various mowers, a rust-spotted pickup, and an ancient tractor scattered around it like weary sentinels.

Tanya spoke in a hushed voice. "That's for maintenance. The cabins are on through these trees."

A night breeze stirred the leaves overhead, bringing the scent of water and the faint rush of waves on the beach. Beneath the dense canopy, the side of the track disappeared into impenetrable darkness. The group instinctively reached for one another and held hands as Tanya led the way, her awkward gait sending a unbalancing ripple through them all.

The track curved right then left, the rhythmic hiss of the surf growing louder as they cleared the wood. They suddenly stopped, mouths open in wonder-filled delight. The road widened and continued on, following the edge of a great natural depression that formed a large bowl in the middle of the camp. At the end, nearest to where they stood, sat a chapel built of pine logs. At the far end, the side of the bowl sloped gradually to the top of a bluff overlooking the restless waters of the lake. Along the top of the oblong basin, simple cabins lined the road, sheltered by more of the large trees.

What had drawn the gasps of delight from the travelers were the hundreds of luminaria, their candles still flickering, filling the long expanse of thick grass that carpeted the bottom of the bowl. The golden glow of the scores and scores of flames formed huge, luminous circles that overlapped dozens of times until the entire basin was alive with spiraling halos and dancing wraiths of shivery beams.

"It's the dance of the night sky!" called a voice from the center of the field of stars.

Gideon shielded his eyes, trying to make out the source of the voice amidst the myriad reflections and refractions. A dark shape moved, walking toward them across the carpet of light. Gideon made out a man of medium height and soft build. As he drew closer, Gideon could see his balding head, thick glasses, and trimmed beard. His belly lapped over the top of his jeans. A friendly smile creased his face.

"Welcome! We've been expecting you."

Gideon stepped forward, resigned to accepting this news at face value. "Thank you. The lights are beautiful."

"She danced the story of the night sky this evening. I was just making sure the field didn't go up in flames like a huge birthday cake." He chuckled and surveyed the weary group. "Pardon my manners. I'm Daniel, Daniel Morrison. Guardian of Lost Trail. Let's get you someplace where you can rest." They made their introductions.

"You said *she* danced. The Dancer is a woman?" Gideon could not hide his surprise at this revelation.

"What's wrong with that?" an indignant Laurel asserted.

"I didn't say anything was wrong with it. I just assumed—"

Daniel jumped in before the two of them could get into a full-blown "screechy fit" as he called it. "Let's head down this way. Gideon, let me ask you this: Imagine you are among the first humans on this planet to arrive at the state of consciousness, to know that you are aware of yourself and your ability to think in a way that no other creature on the planet shares. And you finally get around to wondering, *Now, where did I come from?*" He stopped and looked at Gideon with raised eyebrows.

The rest of the group looked at Gideon as well, who met their expectant gazes with a nonchalant shrug. "You mean, who made the world? You mean like God, or something like that?"

"Nothing so technical or esoteric. Remember—you are a human on the earth, oh, let's say, a hundred thousand years ago. You know nothing of modern science or philosophy. But what do you know? Think, Gideon. Where did you come from?"

Gideon screwed his face up into a mask of exasperation. "I don't know! My mother?"

"Brilliant. The man's brilliant." Laurel clapped softly, aware of the wooden walkways linking the silent, dark cabins they were passing. Sturdy railings and ramps attested to the main population type that it served.

Gideon pulled a face at her in the darkness, and she replied by entwining her fingers through his.

Eli slapped his forehead. "Susan said it! She said the Sanctuary is the womb of life. If I was an early human, I would see that life came from the womb of the woman. I would marvel at my own awakening yearning to create, to dream, to see life in everything around me. And I would see that new life always issued from the woman."

"Speaking of life," Tanya interrupted, sounding a sobering note, "don't forget about poor Whitty."

They explained briefly to Daniel how Whitty had died, and he promised to send two workers immediately to tend to the body. Gideon silently wondered at how readily they seemed able to accept death as the consequences of their convictions, yet no one had said anything about an awaiting paradise or heaven, purgatory, or hell.

"Okay, okay, I surrender. I'm no longer surprised that the Dancer is a woman." Gideon sought to extract his foot from his mouth. Daniel ducked into an office and summoned two workers from their sleep to retrieve Whitty's body.

"Well, actually, she's a child," he said when he returned. "She is a ten-year-old, part Aboriginal, part African American, part hybrid mix of other assorted races as far as we can tell, all wrapped up in a precocious little girl who is deaf, dumb, and blind. Tanya, you didn't tell them?"

"It never came up," she replied coyly, enjoying the reactions of the rest. They were seated around a fire ring situated on the lip of the bluff, in front of a low building used as a recreation center for the camp.

"How can a child, let alone one with such—so many—problems be the Dancer?" Eli demanded to know. "Why entrust enormous responsibility to someone who is so … so … vulnerable?"

"Why not?" was all Daniel would say in response. "Why do you assume I had any say in the matter? And why do you think in terms of enormity?"

Tanya added, "Who better to remind us of the need to develop our spiritual senses—the eyes, ears, and voices that we use to discover the guideposts on the BloodFire journey."

Gideon sat lost in thought. "I guess none of this should surprise me. What was it Rachel said, Laurel?"

She knew exactly what he meant. "She said that community, compassion, and creativity were the gifts given to the human race, symbolized by blood, water, and fire. With these we can fulfill the BloodFire. They don't elevate us to the position of dominating either nature or each other, as the Ransom would have us believe, but rather help us to take our place in the community of life."

"So this is what other worlds and other communities in places even our imaginations cannot go are waiting for?" Eli blinked at the reflections of the first rays of dawn on the water below them. "No wonder they've been knocking on the door of this world asking when we are going to get it done so they can have their turn."

"Badly enough to send nightcrossers." Tanya reminded them anew of the power of righteous desire denied. "Is she up to doing the BloodFire Sacrament dance?" she asked Daniel.

He nodded. "Have any of you learned how the displacement was accomplished?"

The puzzled looks on their faces gave him his answer. "Adam said that it seemed the order had been altered."

"The order? What order?" Gideon asked.

"The Healer and the FireGuide are joined and create the Sacrament child. It's as ancient as the Sanctuary Chronicles, older in fact."

Gideon and Laurel exchanged a knowing look of sadness. "The FireGuide is dead," Gideon quietly offered. "My wife was killed in an accident a year ago, and our child perished with her."

"Yet everyone seems so certain the Sacrament child is being borne by Jenn," Eli continued the thread. "I was the one who killed his wife and baby."

The streaks of dawn disappeared behind a gray cloud bank and, angry whitecaps appeared on the lake.

"Remember—it's about freedom," Daniel said. "Freedom is the hallmark of the Sanctuary. It is what we are to cherish and nurture with the power of the BloodFire. Apparently, a way has been made for the Sacrament child to complete her journey. It may not be what we would have predicted, but it is real nonetheless."

Tanya leaned forward, the tiredness from the long night causing her limbs and muscles to jerk viscously. "I'm sorry, I forgot you weren't here, Daniel, when the word came and I was sent by Adam to Pittsburgh. He'd had Guardians watching the Healer and the FireGuide since before they married. After the accid—"

Gideon practically lifted her out of her seat with his incredulous shout, "What? He'd been spying on me?" He looked wildly at Laurel and the others. "He knew about the accident and didn't come to me?"

Laurel reached for him, but he brushed away her hands. "Did you know about this?"

"I swear to you I didn't know. I've been with Jonathan going through all sorts of training in the mountains. We didn't have contact with anyone else."

Gideon spun on Eli. "What about you? Was all that last night an act to get me to feel sorry for you?"

"Gideon!" Laurel protested.

"It's okay," Eli said. "No, I knew nothing about any of this until the necklace showed up and Paraclete soon after that."

"My wife and child are killed, my father is nearby and knows about it, yet he can't be bothered to come?" Gideon shouted. "And now I'm supposed to believe he is some white knight in shining armor out there doing good for the world?" For a tense moment, he was silent. Then he started to laugh, a giggle at first, growing to a full-throated, head-thrown-back roar.

"Gideon," Laurel said firmly, desperately, her face inches from his. "You're forgetting all the blood that has been spilled."

Daniel's voice broke in. "It tore him apart to see what happened to you, Gideon. But he had to do it for your own protection. He could not reveal himself to you and put you in danger. His life's work was about to perish. The bloodtrackers were hard on his heels."

Gideon's gales of laughter died, his eyes empty of joy or hope. "Every time I think I've just about got it, the meaning of this thing slips away from me again. I'm so, so tired."

A woman approached, ambling down the path between the cabins on the near side of the bowl, with a young girl in tow. The woman smiled and waved to Daniel, who's face lit up when he saw her and waved back. The girl let go of the woman's hand and ran toward the group on the porch, her dark hair fanning out behind her.

"I'd like you to meet my wife, Coll," said Daniel. "And this bundle of energy is Serena, the Dancer."

Eli's mouth dropped open. "But I thought …"

Daniel laughed. "She knows her way around this place so well that when my wife waved to me, Serena knew why and zeroed right in, as you saw. She's amazing, isn't she?" He beamed proudly.

Coll slipped an arm around his waist. "We adopted her a little over a year ago. Her life was filled with horror before then, but that's a long story. You all look so tired. Daniel, have you given our guests food and a place to rest?"

He grinned sheepishly through Serena's splayed fingers. She kept them on his face, seeing and hearing through her sense of touch. "We got to talking, and the next thing we knew it was dawn."

Coll offered to take them to the dining hall and on to waiting beds. Daniel asked Gideon to wait a moment.

"Your daughter is beautiful," Gideon said.

Daniel took her hands and placed them on Gideon's face. Her features immediately became animated, her fingers tracing his hair, nose, eyebrows, cheeks, and lips over and over. Then she took Daniel's hand and spelled out a short sentence in his palm, using her fingers.

Daniel's face twisted into a quizzical expression, and Serena again spelled out her sentence, this time more forcefully. "Okay," Daniel said, communicating this acceptance to her with a pat on the head. "She wants to know if you have something for her. I'm not sure what she means, but she's definitely worked up about something."

Gideon shrugged. "Does she mean a gift? I don't have much with me." He dug into his pockets and pulled out the two halves of the broken heart charm necklace. "Do you mind if I give her these?"

With Daniel's permission, he placed the trinkets into her hand. She caressed them, fingering the small link chain and the worn yarn. At one point, she even tasted the cool metal. Then she nodded her head vigorously at Gideon and skipped off with her new treasure.

"I don't know what that's all about," Daniel said. "It's not like her to demand gifts."

"No problem," Gideon reassured him. "What did you want to talk to me about?"

Daniel led him to the top of the bluff. The clouds scuttled by quickly, hanging low over the water. "Gideon, your father came here some years ago when Coll and I were first married. He needed a place to heal, a place to have his spirit regenerated and refreshed. Why that was and how Coll and I came to be here is a long, long story that I won't bore you with. But I did want to tell you some of your father's story before things go any further."

Gideon silently studied the angry waves crashing below on a rocky beach. Off to the west, in the distance, an old lighthouse sat on a finger of land that extended far into the lake.

Daniel went on: "He told me about your grandfather's experience in World War Two and of coming home with the mysterious box. Your father was a young man before JP ever told him anything about it. They accepted the awesome responsibility of becoming keepers of the Sanctuary Chronicles. The story contained within them is the most powerful story that humanity can ever hear. They tell of the incarnation of the voice of the Sanctuary itself; the living power of the BloodFire.

"That story is what enabled the human race to survive and thrive for hundreds of millennia. About ten thousand years ago, something went wrong. The civilizations that arose, as have the ones that inhabit the world today, ended up spiritually empty, meaningless, without redemptive purpose. The power of the BloodFire was stilled, the story forgotten, the voice silent. Only the Chronicles, placed into the vessel of the Aleudar, were left. The first Guardians prepared the way for the story's power to be preserved and passed along until the day a Healer would arise to be joined to FireGuide. Only then the BloodFire could be released and sent on its journey to other worlds.

"We have no idea where the young man who gave the gift to your grandfather came from or how he came to have the Chronicles. You must remember that the voice of the Sanctuary cannot be heard speaking the story, lest its holy power be released and consume the world and us with it. It is the BloodFire that plants the seed of that story within each of us, filling us with its heat without consuming.

"After many months, your grandfather and father decided what they would do. With his heart full of sorrow, your father decided to dedicate his life to reviving the Guardians of the Sanctuary. When he was ready, then he said that he would let you read the story and accept its power to become the Healer. Apparently you know the story, because here you are."

"No, I don't know the story," Gideon said indignantly. "I have no idea about any of this."

"Yet you are the Healer," Daniel confirmed.

"It sure looks that way," Gideon said with a groan. "So, what are you saying? Don't be angry with my father? Well, things are pretty screwed up right now, magic box or magic story or whatever. If he has any way to get things right, now would be the time to show himself."

"Believe me, it broke his heart to leave your mother and his young son. But he knew of the danger that his work would place you both in. He took on a new identity and called himself Adam, hoping to keep the bloodtrackers away. Now none of us know where he is or what's become of him."

"Well, I can't help you there, that's for sure. All that was in the box when Laurel and I opened it was some journal entries from my late wife. She told some of the recent events, which was all a surprise to me. But I've never heard any of this mysterious story you've been referring to."

"Surprises? Did I hear someone mention surprises? I love surprises."

The voice speaking behind him made the hair on the back of Gideon's neck stand on end. He slowly turned to face the intruder. His eyes narrowed into slits, and his hands gripped the fence. The figure in torn and muddy clothing stepped closer.

"Did I miss anything?" Luther Quinn bared his teeth in what might have been a smile. "We can't start the festivities without the BloodMaster, now can we?"

Chapter 30

"Is this any way to welcome a man back from the dead?" the bloodtracker asked in mocking indignation. "What's the matter? Weren't you expecting me, Gideon?" He laughed and took a step closer. "Did you have any trouble finding the place? I figured this would be the best opportunity to talk some sense into you, Gideon, my boy. Leaving the old truck for you at the farm, now that was a nice touch, wouldn't you agree? And you were so gallant, helping that poor Amish woman. But then you couldn't finish me off when you had the chance, could you, Gideon? No balls." Quinn tsk-tsked. "Now, me, I have balls. You have to in order to survive in this game." He chuckled and dangled something shiny from his hand.

Gideon recoiled in horror. It was Rachel's turquoise-studded brooch. With a shout of rage, he lunged at the taunting figure. His fingers locked around Quinn's throat, choking the life from his body. He could feel Daniel pulling at him, yelling something insensible. He gritted his teeth and strained harder, glaring with murderous rage into the bulging eyes of his tormentor.

With supreme effort, Daniel dislodged him and forced Gideon back to the fence. "This is neutral ground, Gideon. You can't touch him here. Everyone abides by the rule, bloodtrackers from the Ransom, Sanctuary Guardians, and nightcrossers. The dancing ground is neutral."

Gideon's chest heaved as he watched the BloodMaster take in great gulps of air. "Where's it say anything in that precious story of yours that you can try to murder me?" Quinn managed to gasp between desperate breaths. "I can show mercy. I merely went back through the tunnel and stole this to prove that I could have killed them all if I wanted to."

"Doesn't stop you any, does it!" Gideon shot back. "How much blood do you have on your hands now, you murdering bastard?"

Quinn drew himself up to his full height, shaking off the effects of Gideon's attack. "I'm protecting what's right, you misguided fool! I am the BloodMaster! If it wasn't for people like me, the world would drown in its own shit. Before the BloodGuide came along with his quixotic mission, we could swat you Guardians down like flies. That fool Adam thought he could spread his nonsense, but we have stamped it out! And soon we will stamp him out too." His voice growled out these last words with dreadful finality.

"Adam? You know him?"

Quinn smirked. "Why don't you ask me instead how I managed to get here? Aren't you the least bit curious? I was near death, you know, when you threw me into that odious pit."

Gideon stared hard, curious indeed but not wanting to give the satisfaction of asking.

"*You* did it, fool! You confirmed for us that you are exactly who we were looking for. You stuffed a rag soaked in your blood into my mouth, remember? It worked like a charm. I was fit and well in no time." Quinn slapped his knee at this, laughing while Gideon seethed.

Daniel tugged on Gideon's arm, pulling him away from further confrontation. "C'mon, you need to cool down and get some rest."

"What did he mean about Adam? What's happened?"

"I don't know, Gideon. You are not going to be any good to anyone though until you are refreshed."

Still seething, Gideon allowed himself to be led toward a cabin set back from the others. Inside, Coll insisted he have something to eat before she showed him to his bed. The room was obviously Serena's. "Whatever you said or gave to her, she's been a little whirlwind ever since," Coll reported.

"Where is she now?"

"Where she goes every time before a dance. The Wind Altar, back in the woods. She'll be there for hours, sitting quietly, thinking her thoughts and waiting for the spirit of the dance to inspire her."

"This is all so strange," Gideon said as he wearily flopped on the bed.

"Let me take a look at that leg," Coll said. "I promised Laurel that I would. She's such a dear soul, Gideon. You have yourself a good woman."

Gideon mulled that over, while Coll took off the bandages and checked. "It closed up, but it's all blue, like the tissues are not getting enough oxygen. How do you feel?"

"Like I've been run over by a train, caught in a whirlpool, and had my brain turned inside out. Other than that, I'm fine."

Coll smiled and tugged off his pants. "I'll get these washed up. Have you been living in these or what?"

With a start, Gideon realized that that was exactly what he'd been doing, living in his clothes. Ever since he'd changed into them after the funeral for the climb up the mountain. After Coll left, he stared at the ceiling. "JP, I'm sorry. I need your help now. I need your wisdom, your strength."

Gideon drifted, not fully asleep but lolling in that state between consciousness and slumber. The morning wind off the lake came in through the open window, setting the curtains to dancing. His body felt heavy and more weary than he'd ever felt before in his life. He wished Laurel were with him, holding him, whispering comfort.

At first, he thought that she had come into the room. He heard a voice, soft and sweet, calling to him from a great distance. He looked around, but he was no longer in the small bedroom. He was back on the mountain.

Gideon felt something hard and unyielding under his fingers. It was the rockface. The storm burst overhead, the lightning and thunder more fierce than ever. He desperately pondered his options, same as it had happened that day. He made the same choice—letting go, feeling the sickening drop, the rockface rushing past in a wet blur. The scrape of his cheek across sharp, jagged edges bringing stinging pain. The hard landing, the blow to his head.

And the voice. That brief moment of hearing the voice. His mother's voice. Coming across a great chasm, speaking to him clearly, earnestly. What was she saying? Gideon strained to hear in the blackness, concentrating, the sense of urgency building. Just as he began to make out the words, he felt the painful tug, and the voice faded away. He cried out, calling to her to speak clearly, he wanted to hear, but someone was pulling him out of the blackness.

Gideon's eyes sprang open. Instead of Laurel ministering to him in the raging rain, the empty eyes of Serena floated above him. Her hands flitted across his face, checking to see that he was awake. From each wrist dangled half of a broken heart.

Gideon took her hands and held them to his cheeks, startled to discover that they were wet with his tears. He hadn't known that he was crying, but he knew it had more to do with the words his mother was speaking to him on the mountain than with anything else in his life.

Serena broke free of his grasp and began to dance about the room. Gideon enjoyed her fluid beauty, the motions of her hands, head, and feet creating an intricate language of movement.

"She's giving you the dance of the gifts," said Coll from the doorway. "The Healer is the blood, and the blood is the Healer. The blood is the life, and the life is the blood. It is her thanks to you for the gift of the broken hearts." Coll's face took on a curious expression. "Something about a baby. I'm not sure, though."

Gideon waited for her to say more, but Serena abruptly stopped and left the room. "What does that mean?"

Coll thrust her hands into the back pockets of her jeans. "That's only an approximation. Any gift she gives must ultimately be understood by the one who receives it, Gideon. Do you have any children?"

Gideon lowered his eyes. "Uh, no. Do you have children of your own?"

"I'm not able to have kids," Coll told him without reserve. "It's a long story, something that goes back to the first summer that Daniel and I met as teenagers. Your father was here. Daniel's written it down if you'd like to read it someday."

Gideon shrugged. "Sure. Right now, I'd better round up the others and compare notes, figure out our next move."

"They're down at the barn with Daniel. It's getting to be dinnertime. Serena will be dancing after it gets dark. Daniel said to ask if you would like to be one of the drummers this evening. It's quite an honor. The children fight over who gets to have a turn. It's amazing how tuned in they are to the rhythms of the world."

"Well, I'm not so sure I'll be able to do it justice. But I would like to do it for Serena's sake"—he paused for a beat—"and for my own child who didn't get the chance to dance."

After retrieving his clean clothes, Gideon wandered out of the cabin and surveyed the scene spread out before him. Children of all ages and a multitude of disabilities played on modified volleyball and basketball courts, gathered in animated groups to talk about the subjects universal to childhood, or were pushed, pulled, or simply accompanied on excursions around the beautiful campus by college-aged and older adults, many of whom had disabilities as well.

The luminaria were gone from the grand basin that formed the heart of the retreat with its sylvan slopes and grassy plain that stretched nearly one hundred and fifty yards from the bluff above the lakeshore to the chapel nestling in the edge of the wood. Oak, elm, and pine trees towered over the low cabins around the rim.

He headed back along the track, drinking deeply of the fragrance of water, wind, and sun-drenched meadow. At the barn, he found the others gathered around the ancient truck, watching while Daniel disassembled part of the front end.

"What are you doing to my beautiful truck?" Gideon cried.

Laurel greeted him with a kiss and a searching look deep into his eyes. "Another dream?" she asked.

"How do you know that?" Gideon responded, amazed at how effortlessly she connected to him. "I'll tell you about it later. What's going on here?"

"Daniel had an idea about how to help Eli," Tanya reported.

Daniel slid out from under the truck and motioned for them to close the doors.

"I'm fashioning a centrifuge from the fan on the old truck engine."

"A centrifuge?" Gideon noticed them all watching him intently.

"Yes," Eli explained excitedly. "We're going to empty my morphine pump and replace the drug with blood serum."

"Why?"

"We're hoping it will preserve the power of the blood gift long enough for Eli to get back to Pittsburgh and inject it into Jenn." Tanya gesticulated wildly, smiling broadly, spraying them with abandon.

"If he's stopped by the nightcrossers, it will be next to impossible for the blood to be discovered. Daniel used this digital cell phone to arrange for Susan to call in about an hour and summon Eli back with an urgent message." Laurel punctuated her part of the recitation with a squeeze of Gideon's hand and by pulling two hypodermic needles from the pack.

"How will you do without morphine, Eli?" Gideon asked. "What about when it's time to be filled once again and they discover it's empty?"

"I don't know how I'll do for sure. I'll have to worry about that later. Besides, after all that's happened these past few days, I expect we'll have to get away from Bridetown and hide out for a while. Maybe we can even find a doctor from the Sanctuary who will be able to take care of the pump."

Eli swallowed hard when he'd finished. The prospect of not having the pump putting painkiller into his spine was frightening. He didn't know if he'd be able to stand up straight, let alone walk.

"Let's get started," he said with a clap of his hands, trying to inject an air of confidence in the plan.

Laurel first took some blood from Gideon and handed it to Daniel. He picked up the glass tube from a baster that had been corked in one end and emptied the syringe into it. Laurel repeated the process four more times, much to Gideon's chagrin, until she and Daniel were satisfied that they had enough. Then Daniel stoppered the tapered nozzle end and duct-taped the tube to a fan blade.

The engine turned over, caught, and let out a steady roar as Daniel coaxed maximum rpm. While the makeshift centrifuge whirled, Laurel turned her attention to Eli, stretched out on some old horse blankets laid across bales of hay. She poked and stabbed him repeatedly, trying to find the port in the pump beneath his skin. A thin film of sweat appeared on his brow.

"Sorry," she said.

"That's okay. You know, I think there might be enough medication left in the catheter to get me through the trip back. It's about thirty-six inches long, and as long as the serum doesn't mess up the mechanism, I should be okay." He kept talking to keep the anxieties at bay. "It's running at maximum speed, but we can't get to the timing chip without a computer and wand. It will start pumping serum into the catheter where we can't get to it. Fill it up so we can get enough back out to do some good."

Daniel switched off the engine and held up the results. A thin layer of cloudy yellowish liquid lay atop the dark red cell matter. A tiny cheer went up from the group, and they quickly finished the process. The serum was transferred to a syringe and injected into Eli's pump.

"I hope they don't check your abdomen," Laurel said, indicating the copious angry purple bruises around the pinpricks, marking her attempts to gain access to the pump.

"When are you leaving?" Gideon asked, feeling the weakness and dizziness returning. Tanya was right; he had lost a lot of valuable blood. What was he to do with it now that the Sacrament child had a reasonable chance to be spared? He found the question disquieting.

"Right away." Daniel sounded grim, tense.

"I thought of something while Laurel practiced using me as a pincushion," Eli said. "Tanya, how did you know that my child was the Sacrament child?"

"She had the marker. Adam directed me to get some blood, make a smear, and send it to a post office box in Toronto. He sent word that the marker was there, but I don't know what kind of marker he was meaning."

"I've got it!" Eli snapped his fingers. "They used cord blood on me the night of the accident. It was to help my spine heal. Somehow it kept the swelling down so that my spinal cord wouldn't be damaged."

"Cord blood?" Laurel shook her head, confused.

"Umbilical cord. They've experimented with it on multiple sclerosis patients. That night, the doctors asked Jenn for permission to try a new technique using the cord blood on me. Don't you get it? They must have used blood from Gideon and Christine's child."

Eli and Gideon faced each other in silence.

"We are in each other's debt," Eli said after a long while.

"No, there are no debts between us," Gideon responded, his head clear, his resolve strong.

"The fruit of your and your wife's love is now the life of Eli and Jenn's child, the fruit of their love. Such is as it should be," Daniel said in quiet benediction.

"I've hated you since the accident," Gideon said with difficulty.

"And I have hated myself. But now healing is taking place, and I am grateful to you forever." Eli extended his hand.

Gideon took it in both of his. "May your journey be swift and your family restored to you once again."

Coll arrived with a large tureen of steaming stew. The rich broth was crowded with chunks of fresh vegetables and beef and topped with buttermilk biscuits. They all ate their fill, mostly in silence as they realized that this could be the last time they fellowshipped.

It was time to go. The others wished Eli well before they left the barn. Evening was upon them once again. The moon rose above the trees, giving them silver light for the walk back toward the dancing ground. Laurel and Gideon hung back while he told her about the dream.

"There was something in my mother's voice, something about her words that filled me with such peace, such intense feelings that wavered between pain, yet joy, that—I don't know, it was like I didn't want it to end."

Laurel stopped. "Maybe it was no dream."

"But I woke up."

"No, I mean, back on the mountain. You said you thought you heard her voice right before you lost consciousness. Gideon, what if it was real? What if she was speaking a word from the Sanctuary story to you in that moment? What if she was telling you the story of the BloodFire, preparing you for your mission?"

"And that's what gave my blood this power, this gift? Simply hearing her speak the words gave me this unearthly power?"

"Who's to say it's unearthly? We need to find more of Christine's journal. I think we should go look for your father too."

"The womb of life. The exclamation of the Sanctuary. BloodFire!"

"What?"

Gideon put his arm around her shoulder. "Nothing. The future looks a lot better with you in it."

They stopped and sought each other's lips for a lingering, tender kiss. Laurel pressed her head into his chest. "What's that do to your blood?"

Gideon held her close, his fingers lightly caressing her sweet spot. "I'll show you after the dance. I'm to be a drummer, you know."

"Girls go crazy for drummers."

They laughed. Gideon would come to cherish the memory of it in the days that lay ahead.

"Let's meet at the chapel," Gideon whispered in her ear. "After the dancing, we'll find our spot under the trees and make love until the stars sing."

They resumed their journey, guided by the sound of the drums calling on the night breezes.

Chapter 31

It came to pass, that I am alive.
I have life … and then I don't.
There's no me … I have life … then I'm gone
Is life about anything other than me?
I live my life with joy, following wonder.
We belong to life.
We belong to the world.
We are needed here.
Isn't that enough?
A wonder.
Joy.

Gideon felt the urgent pulse of the drums traveling through the ground and up his legs as he also tried to listen to the interpretation Daniel was speaking to him and Eli as Serena danced in the pale light of the moon and stars. The drums were large, hollow logs, carved as totems, along with various other percussion instruments, all attached to stakes driven into the ground. The Dancer heard the music through the vibrations sent into the earth. A pyramid of branches and old lumber waited in the middle of the meadow. This bonfire would be lit for the second part of the dancing. Gideon would join the drummers while Eli slipped away.

Daniel's words came slowly, distinctly, as he watched Serena's uninhibited leaps and turns, her graceful sweep of her hands, and the dazzling footwork. "Eli tells me he is hoping to become a writer. There are so many stories to add to the Chronicles: Serena's, Coll's, your own and that of your family. The Chronicles are the voice of the BloodFire."

Gideon nodded absently, caught up in the power emanating from the small, fragile figure whose sense of music and motion unearthed the mysteries of the universe. The children and staff of the camp clapped, whistled, and kept time to the drums, adding their own voices in exclamation of the completeness of the Sanctuary.

"Life is about hearing that exclamation," Eli whispered, his tone that of awe. Gideon glanced at him, surprised that they had been sharing the same thought.

Laurel sat across the way, abiding by the segregation by sex that was required during the Dance of the Evening. Gideon could only see the outline of her head as she knelt among the various wheelchairs listening to two of the children. One reached out to touch her hair as though it were the robe of an angel. Gideon turned to say something to Eli, but he was gone, already off to resume his journey. He hoped for another opportunity to sit down and visit with the pain-crippled man with the heart that agonized over making up for the death of Christine. Maybe someday.

Serena's dance ended to wild applause. She flitted away to rest briefly while the bonfire was lit. Gideon felt someone sitting down beside him. He turned and frowned at the discovery of Luther Quinn settling in. "Find somewhere else to sit, you bloodsucking bastard."

"Now, now, really!" the BloodMaster chortled. "Can't a man come and watch his own daughter perform?"

Gideon twisted around violently, his eyes narrowed in angry disbelief. "What? You're lying!"

"Am I? Ask your friend Daniel. Serena is the product of a brief love affair. Her mother was a most exotic woman but one who could not stay away from the lure of cocaine and heroin. I found out about the child only after she was born. By that time, the state had placed her here, and I found no reason to remove her. It's what keeps this as neutral ground, so don't give me your self-righteous act."

He stretched his legs out on the grass. "See, Gideon, I'm not an unreasonable bloodsucking demon as you seem bent on believing."

A shout of glee rose from the crowd as the pile erupted with a roar of flame and light. "When are you going to stop this silly little game you're playing of making believe you are the Healer?"

Luther's words struck Gideon hard. He realized that Luther had taken control of the conversation with some purpose in mind. He hated the feeling of being jerked around, waiting for Luther to tell him the next subject they would be pursuing in the contest between them. He kept his mind focused on the fact that it was a contest with deadly consequences and kept his mouth shut.

"What's the matter, Gideon? Afraid to speak for yourself? Okay, have it your way then. Tell me, Giddy, haven't you been wondering why your mother and father, good old JP, and even your dearly departed wife kept all this a secret from you? Now, what on earth could they have been thinking? Didn't they trust you with the enormity of their misguided and misplaced belief in this perverse story? Were you the weak link in the chain perhaps?"

Serena returned, stepping into the light of the burning pyre to begin the dance of the BloodFire. "Would you die for her?" Gideon asked, breaking his silence. "You kill at will trying to stop those who hold this misplaced belief, as you put it, but what would *you* die for, Quinn? Would you die for your daughter?"

Luther asked, obviously irritated at Gideon's seizing this opening, "How can these imperfect creatures appreciate such beauty of movement?" He gestured at the campers. "She should be on tour, displaying her gift to the world for all to see and appreciate, not dancing here for people who can't even dress themselves or wipe their own asses."

Gideon pictured Rachel's daughter, Sarah, telling him of the three Cs: community, compassion, creativity. Here they were, on display right in front of him. *But how to explain the evil next to me?* he wondered. What did the Sanctuary Chronicles have to say about that? In the back of his mind, a tiny spark flared briefly, a picture that he could not quite retrieve. Something to do with his dream earlier in the afternoon, he knew that much. But what?

"But hey, I'm a good guy," Luther was saying. "I'll even let Serena live here. And if there's anybody still interested by the time this supposed Sacrament child is born, I'll be the first one here for the Dance of the Redemption." He leaned close. "But I don't think there will be anyone who really gives a damn."

"So you're saying you'll leave the Sacrament child alone?"

"You really are in the dark here, aren't you, Giddy?"

"Stop calling me that."

"Sorry, force of habit. I'll let you in on a little secret, *Gideon*. Your father believed in you. He believed that one day you would learn the story and become a new creature. I don't mean turn you into a new man, like a drunk who finds religion. He and your mother and grandmother and JP all believed that because of Aleudar's gift, one day you would receive the gift of hearing the Sanctuary word spoken, and it would change you. Me? I don't know what happened to you, but something has changed. You can heal people with your blood." He started to laugh as the drums came up, filling the bowl with primal reverberations of the pulse of life. He laughed till tears rolled down his cheeks. "I'm the proof in the pudding, wouldn't you say?"

The pounding of the drums grew in fierce intensity. Daniel and Laurel had moved to the section off to the right where the drummers sat, motioning to Gideon to come take his place of honor. He shook his head at them, unwilling to break off this conversation, one-sided as it was, so far.

"She's a beautiful and troubled woman," the BloodMaster said in a distracted voice. "Always a dangerous combination."

"You touch her, and I'll rip you apart with my bare hands," Gideon hissed, his fists clenched.

"I believe you," Luther replied carefully.

Gideon had a sick feeling in his stomach that he'd blundered in some way with his passionate outburst, but he did not regret it in the least.

"As I was saying, there *is* something different about you. We tested the blood of that girl back in Frenchville. It had traces of an unusual and, up until now, never-before-seen telomerase marker. I strongly suspect we'd find the same with the Amish woman from last night. So you see, there is a scientific explanation for what's been happening, and these people are trying to exploit that fact about you."

"What is a telomerase marker?"

The BloodMaster leaned close to Gideon, speaking directly into his ear. Even at that, Gideon had to concentrate fully to hear.

"Telomerase is a protein, the immortality chemical of the human body. Ordinarily it disappears after a fetus finishes its development in the womb. If it comes back, it means trouble, cancer to be exact. In adults, only cancer cells routinely make telomerase. Rather interesting, wouldn't you say."

Gideon didn't bother to give the man a look of disgust. He was having enough trouble sitting still while his skin crawled from the proximity of this butcher.

"This story of the Sanctuary that Aleudar supposedly carried in him is reported to have the power to give the blood gift. That so-called blood gift we believe to be actually a mutation of the telomerase chain. That's the marker that showed up in the fetus of Eli and his lovely wife."

Gideon spoke without moving. "Wait a minute. You're telling me that I have some mutated chemical or gene or whatever that can give people immortality?"

"No, no. It simply acts to reverse the aging process and the disease process. We won't know now, will we, what effects it has beyond that. Seems like everyone who gets some of your blood meets with a most untimely and unfortunate death."

Gideon spun around. "You said you didn't harm Rachel."

"Now, now, don't get all hot and bothered. You don't want to cause a scene in front of all these smiling children, now do you, Giddy? I didn't think so. Rachel is alive and well. As long as she never tells another soul about what happened, she'll stay that way.

"As I was saying, we don't know a lot about it. Like what really causes it. Your grandfather and your father believed that Aleudar was right, that hearing the words of the, now what did they call it? Oh right, the womb of life."

The BloodMaster was enjoying his own performance immensely. "Hearing some mysterious pronouncement caused this gift to be loosed on the world signaling the beginning of the redemption of the BloodFire.

"Now, we're not stupid. JP got Alzheimer's and died with drool running out of his mouth and that empty look in his eyes that said he didn't have a clue as to who he was in his oversized diapers. We weren't able to get some of his blood to test. Seems Adam beat us to it. And what about dear old Dad? Named Justin, after his father, but leaves home, wife, and son and changes his name to Adam. We don't know if his blood carries this marker either. We've tried. Believe me, we've tried."

A cry went up as a shower of sparks arced into the black sky. Gideon tried to digest all that he was hearing. Was it really his father back at the farm after all? Had he been the one looking for something of JP's? How did he keep the bloodtrackers from JP's body? The questions swirled around and around in his head. He would have to run all this past Laurel later this evening. He could count on her to get a handle on it.

Gideon tried to make out the spot where she was sitting, but he couldn't see very far into the shadows among all the wheelchairs. Luther tugged on his shoulder, eager to take up the tale again.

"But lo and behold, there it is, plain as day, in the blood of that little girl! She was a real sweetheart, that one. And the same marker showed up in the Marks' baby. And we both know that it really should have been your baby, don't we, Gideon? The Sacrament child is to be the child of the Healer and the FireGuide. We don't know if Christine is, I'm sorry, was the FireGuide, but we assume she was because Adam would have found her and gotten her together with you."

"What?"

"Surprised, Giddy? Didn't know that Daddy set you up with your beloved Christine? He's been a busy little beaver. He actually got some other crazies to believe that this Sanctuary nonsense and BloodFire Protocol blather and long-awaited Healer horse manure was really sugar. Of course, look at the caliber of people he recruited. Well, you've met them. Real salt of the earth types, wouldn't you say, Giddy?

"I digress. We both know where this is headed. No reasonable person can believe that hearing some mystical voice speak some secret word can give a person the power of healing with his blood."

"Show me the reasonable person, and we'll discuss it," Gideon hissed over his shoulder.

"You sound just like your father."

This time, Gideon could not resist the urge to laugh. "Are you telling me that you know my father, not as some prey you're hunting down but man to man?"

"That's what I'm saying. Gideon, I almost fell into the same trap. Your father and I trained together. JP recruited me, taught me all the tricks of the trade, drummed into my head all of the Sanctuary Chronicles, the promise of reclaiming the spiritual foundation for the human race, the whole nine yards. It was a class of two, me and your father."

"What happened?"

"Too long to tell you here, but let's just say I saw the real light. It's why your dad left. Did you know that? Left his beautiful wife and little son who adored him, needed him, and set off to keep me from winning. Tell me, Giddy, what's the score? Who would you say is winning?"

Gideon's fist shot out, but Luther met it in midair. "You may have surprised me once but never again." Luther's voice was hard, cold, filled with barely restrained rage. "Your father has cost me plenty, though. We should have wrapped this up a long time ago. When I catch up to him, and mark my words, I will, I'm going to tell him that right before I kill him."

Gideon stared into the dark, joyless eyes of the BloodMaster. "It's meant to be," Luther said. "It's the natural order. Man is to be on top. Humans are the superior species, and the world is ours to subdue. We are superior creatures, and I don't care what nightcrosser comes from what godforsaken other world, man will always be the leader, the ruler. It has to be. We have God on our side."

"But what about the Sacrament child. Why is she still alive? You can't tell me that the bloodtrackers arranged for Eli's wife's drowning."

"No, we're not that good. But we aren't stupid either. I know that Eli is going to make it out of here with some of your blood. I know that you are not a fool. I hope he can fool the nightcrossers though. They're getting mighty impatient. And if he does, we'll deal with that in good time."

"Wait a minute! What about the nightcrossers from these other worlds? How do you explain that to this world?"

The BloodMaster chuckled. "Explain what? We just have to keep feeding them little dribbles of supposedly leaked, highly classified documents about UFOs, or extraterrestrials, space invaders, and on and on. People eat it up or dismiss it all as kooky. Which is just fine with us. Nightcrossers don't come from outer space. That's not the darkness they traverse. It's the best-kept secret the world's ever had because people want to believe the *Star Trek* stuff."

Gideon spread his arms. "What are you talking about?"

"Think about it, Giddy. What other worlds are there? If we can't get to the edges of the universe for a few centuries at best, if ever, and if there is no higher intelligence than the intelligence found here on earth, which by the way we do know now to be a fact, then where are they coming from and how are they getting here? You'll figure it out. Your father always said what a bright boy you were."

His smugness and obfuscation infuriated Gideon. "Who the hell are you?"

Luther Quinn got to his feet and pulled Gideon up after him. "Don't disappoint me, Gideon. I'm a patient man, but I've got my limits. You know who I am. You just don't know that you know—yet."

Gideon forcefully removed the other man's hands from his arms. "What's that supposed to mean?"

"Look around."

Gideon became aware of the silence in the small hollow. The fire burned low, and Serena held her father's hand as they walked across the grassy floor. The attendants were busy helping campers toward their cabins. Laurel was nowhere in sight.

"She's not here."

Those three words spoken quietly by the BloodMaster struck fear into Gideon's heart, fear like he'd never known before. He took a few steps toward the retreating figure of Daniel and Serena, ready to shout to them with his desperate query.

"Don't bother."

Gideon felt his blood turn to ice in his veins. He hated this man more than he loved his own life. He'd been so stupid. The long conversation was not about sounding him out. It was a distraction while Laurel was taken away.

Gideon took a deep, shuddering breath, using every ounce of strength that he possessed to keep himself from attacking and killing this evil incarnation standing before him. He spoke carefully, his jaw tight. "Where is she?"

Luther had the audacity to smile. "I'm a generous man, Gideon. Be on the beach at dawn. You can say goodbye to her then. She'll be going with me and will stay with me—until you bring me your father."

He held out one finger, stopping Gideon's protestations. "There is no bargaining. She is safe and will remain safe as long as you are carrying out your mission. If you try to take her from me tomorrow, I will kill you both then and there."

"No, you can't do this. Don't take Laurel. Take me instead. I'm the one you want. I'm the one who has the bloodgift. Maybe you could figure out how to replicate it. Think about it, Luther. Think of the power you would have—"

Luther cut him off again. "I don't want you. I want your father."

Gideon tried to play for time. "I don't know where my father is. I don't even know if he's still alive."

"Yes, you do. He's alive, and he's mine. Why do you suppose we've let you live, Giddy? We needed some leverage, and we need to know all that he knows about this cancer of the Guardians of the Sanctuary so that we can end this madness once and for all."

"Madness?" Gideon screamed. "These last few days have been the madness. Why not live and let live? What are these people going to do to you, let alone the rest of the world?"

The BloodMaster patted him on the cheek, further infuriating Gideon. "If you are so concerned about them, come with us, Gideon. Maybe we *could* learn how to replicate that telomerase. Think of all the good you could do. You hold the key to stopping all this terribly messy killing that's been necessary."

Gideon swallowed hard. The memory of Jonathan's bravery and passionate words back in the mountains of Virginia replayed themselves in his mind. Freedom. What about freedom? No, it wasn't about him being a Messiah for the masses. He had to decide. He had only the story, the word. And the blood, to guide him. "No." He spoke slowly, clearly, with a new deepfelt conviction. "I choose freedom. I choose to serve the community of life. There are those here and beyond who deserve to have the same choice."

"You're a fool!" The BloodMaster bared his teeth in an evil smirk. "You are blinded by your lust for that woman."

"If I'm blind, Luther, I'm blind to my own disbelief and arrogance. Life will go on if I fail to do what I'm to do. But the human race is needed. Not to possess or dominate all that is. But to take our place and to be who we are *among* all that is. And to pass on the gift of the BloodFire."

Luther's eyes flashed, and spit flew from his mouth as he ranted: "Man was made for the earth and the earth for man. Be fruitful and multiply and subdue the earth. Ye shall have dominion over every *beast*. That's what they are, beasts. We will always be on top. It is our destiny, and no one will be allowed to stop it!"

Just as quickly as it had come, the madness left his eyes, and his next words frightened Gideon more than those that had come before. "What's the matter, Giddy? Do I frighten you? Good. Remember that. Now, have a good night. You can say goodbye to your lover at dawn."

Chapter 32

Eli paused before driving through the Lost Trail gate and heading back toward Bridetown. Daniel had loaned him his own tracker for the journey, making him promise to return it when he could bring a revived and rested Jenn with him. Eli looked back over his shoulder at the old barn and then carefully patted his sore abdomen.

At the last minute, Tanya had appeared at the secluded spot where the car was waiting and warmly wished him well. She reminded him that in no more than six hours, the serum would be worthless. She apologized for not being able to return with him to look after Jenn, wished him Godspeed, and headed back toward the dancing ground for the beginning of the BloodFire dance.

Now as he drove out the gate of Lost Trail, he wondered anew at the terrible cost in lives for wanting what any man who's ever loved a woman would want, for his Jenn to be healed. Jeremiah, Joe Martinson, and Whitty, too much bloodshed. How could he ever make it up to the others who continued on in their quest for the BloodFire Redemption and the protocol reestablished as the spiritual foundation for the human race?

Eli decided to go due east and pick up Interstate 79 south near Erie and head straight for Pittsburgh. He'd be there in a little less than three hours, leaving plenty of time to get the life-giving serum into Jenn. What would he say to her about the events of the past few days? Of course, according to Pearl, Jenn might be able to shed far more light than he on the matter, what with all of their conversations. He smiled as the interstate signs hove into view, and he switched on the radio. As he accelerated up the on-ramp, he noticed a bedraggled young woman with pleasant features and no luggage standing beside the pavement.

The closer he got to the spot where she stood, arm outstretched, thumb hooked in the direction he was traveling, the more concerned he became. "What's a kid doing out here?" he asked himself. She looked to be about sixteen years of age, dressed in tight clothing that showed off sublime curves.

He'd made the decision to pass her by and continue with his own mission, when he thought of Pearl and the others. With a weary sigh, he pulled over. She came running up, a sweet, all-American look about her, polite to a fault.

"Hi! I really appreciate you stopping for me." She pulled open the door and stuck out her hand. "I'm Terralessa."

"That's an unusual name. Where are you headed?"

"Pittsburgh. I ran away from home about a month ago, but now I'm heading back. I can't wait to see the expression on my parents' faces." She bubbled over with adolescent energy and naiveté.

Eli figured he could use the company and do a good deed for someone else in apparent need of forgiveness and understanding. What the hell, he knew what that was like. Out on the deserted highway, he set the cruise control for seventy and looked over at his young companion. "Isn't it risky hitchhiking, especially in the dead of night?"

She shrugged. "Are you planning on raping me or killing me?"

"Nope."

"Then I guess it wasn't so risky, was it? Can you pull into this rest stop? I've gotta go."

"But we just barely got started!"

"I'm sorry, but I didn't want to go in the bushes back there. I'm deathly afraid of snakes. They give me the willies!"

Eli laughed. "Okay, I give up. My wife is the same way. And cockroaches—you can just forget about it!" He pulled into the empty parking lot and left the motor running. "I'll wait here."

Terralessa hopped out and ran to the restroom. Eli punched the seek button on the radio, hoping to catch the results of the Pirates last game of the season. They needed to win two out of three to avoid a one hundred loss record for the baseball season. He'd forgotten to ask Laurel if her Steelers cap meant she was a fan.

A sharp rapping on the window interrupted his thoughts. Thinking Terralessa had forgotten something, he rolled down the window. "They out of toilet pap—"

"Shut up and get out of the car. Now!"

The menacing orders came from a dark-clothed man holding a peculiar-looking cane. Eli fumbled with the latch and eased out of the car, his knees shaking and teeth-grinding pain shooting down his left leg. "What do you want?" He stole a furtive glance in the direction of the restrooms. Terralessa was striding confidently toward them, too late to shout a warning.

"Etanleo, don't hurt him!" she called.

"Quiet, girl! I know my business," the man hissed in return.

"What's this all about?" Eli stammered. "You set me up?" he asked Terralessa.

"Time is short," the girl explained, "and we are the last hope."

The man raised the heavy-looking staff to stop her words. "The man has problems of his own." He stepped closer so that Eli could see his face. Eli's mind told him that he should recognize the features, but he could not place him.

"I am Etanleo of Metamelonia. A nightcrosser."

Eli's chest tightened. "Back there? You killed Whitty."

"No. As in your world, however, we have enemies who are desperate to subvert the BloodFire. They adopt the standards that they've seen here, violence and taking what they want, the ultimate sign of weakness." He waved a hand dismissively. "We will take care of Grutt. My daughter and I are here to stop that rogue and return with what our world so desperately needs."

"Your daughter? Terralessa is your daughter?" Eli looked from one to the other. "I know, the Olde Village! You're a guide there."

Etanleo nodded. "It teaches me more about your history while permitting me to investigate the confinement of the BloodFire. My wife remains in our own world, fighting to stave off the revolutionaries who demand we take what we want. We are exposing ourselves to terrible risk by being here and revealing our identities to you."

Eli rubbed his eyes, struggling to make sense out of yet one more out-of-the-blue kick in the pants to his understanding of reality. "Why the little charade?" he asked Terralessa.

"We don't trust many humans. Adam has been teaching us as best he can, but the situation deteriorated back home, and I decided to come find my father. I knew that neither he nor my mother would approve, so I did in fact run away. It was my idea to get to you all alone out here and offer our services. I guess I wanted to show my father that I could be a trusted ally in this battle."

Eli looked from daughter to father. Etanleo had a universally recognized mixture of exasperation and pride written on his face, the mark of the parent of a teenager. "Adam is in your world? Does anyone else know that?"

Etanleo shook his head. "Who would we tell?"

"What is that in your hand?" Eli asked, trying to buy time to think.

Terralessa answered. "That is the mark of his calling, the Telling Staff. It lets everyone know that he is the keeper of the sacred stories, the Chronicles of the Sanctuary. However, our people are forgetting, turning away, scoffing at the ideas in the protocol. They mock his badge of honor."

Etanleo's eyes brimmed with tears of pride and sorrow. "My wife gave it to me at my initiation as a keeper. I have it with me always to keep her close while I serve as a nightcrosser."

"The others didn't care much for nightcrossers," Eli stated honestly.

"As in many things, there are more sides than what is generally known, or believed to be known. Our worlds are not that different. After all, we come from the same womb," Etanleo responded gravely.

"Well, let's get this show on the road then," Eli said, opening the door and motioning to the others to join him. They piled in, amid apologies from Terralessa and many questions asked all at once between the three of them.

After they'd been on the road for a half an hour, it dawned on Eli that neither one had asked him where he was going or why he was out on the road in the middle of the night. He decided to feel them out.

"I was wondering why you picked me to contact. Is it because I used to be a sort of 'keeper of the sacred stories' or just my devastatingly handsome looks and dry wit?"

"Yeah, right," Terralessa sarcastically replied.

"Don't be rude, child," Etanleo admonished her.

"I'm not a child! I am grown and capable of helping our people," she shot back in a fit of another apparently universal parent-child friction over identity.

Eli tried to defuse the tension. "So, this is what my wife and I are getting into?"

"Jeremiah said that your child could be the one," Etanleo said.

"You knew Jeremiah?"

"Yes, Adam sent me to him as my first contact. I assume you have found help for your wife and child?"

Eli hesitated. *How much to reveal?* he worried. *Maybe this is part of honoring the journey*, he told himself. He was beginning to see why the Chronicles were vital to maintaining a link with the root of life. "I have, but it may be better and safer for you at the moment if I don't reveal more to you. I don't mean to offend you, only to protect all concerned."

Etanleo nodded sagely. "We will honor your wishes. Trust is slowly built and quickly lost."

They made good time the rest of the way and arrived outside Three Rivers Metro Hospital well before dawn. The nightcrossers stayed behind, while Eli went in. He decided the best approach was to walk right in as though he belonged and had every right to be there. On the elevator, he dug into the inner pocket of his jacket, reassuring himself that the hypodermic needles were still secure.

He passed the room where he'd heard Joe Martinson making the lame joke to his stroke-felled wife. Pausing for a moment, he peeked in. A middle-aged man snored loudly. Eli hoped that there was someone to mourn both Joe and his wife.

He breathed a sigh of relief when he rounded the corner and saw that the nurses' station was empty. He'd probably get only a few moments. Best to hurry. He crossed to the room.

Jenn's cubicle was darkened. He slid open the glass door and froze. The bed was empty.

Chapter 33

No dawn could be more dreaded or more craved. And that was the madness of it, of course. Daniel had been expertly distracted, as well, and could offer no clue as to Laurel's disappearance. Coll gave Gideon a sympathetic hug and set about making them all some tea.

"I can't just let him walk out of here with her." He turned on Daniel. "I thought you said this was neutral ground?"

"It is. But this is the first time ever we have been so close to the Redemption. She may have had reason to walk out on her own. We have to consider the possibility."

"She wouldn't leave without letting me know. Well, let's break some rules of our own then." Gideon's fist crashed down on the table, rattling the teacups and sending a spoon to the floor.

Coll sat down opposite him. "Tell me, which rules should we break? The BloodFire is about honoring the Sanctuary. Should we dishonor it in order to bring about our own desires?"

"I thought you would understand!" Gideon brooded. "Didn't you say something about enduring great pain for your love?"

Daniel patiently but firmly took him to task. "Gideon, all of us must constantly choose what our lives are about. You can't keep looking to the events of the past and saying that they entrap you. That's dishonest. Screw up if you have to, but do it honestly, with your own emotional capital. In the same way, you cannot abdicate your responsibility altogether and say my life will simply drift along on the currents of my desires, my moods, my emptiness."

His words stung Gideon, but he could not escape their truthfulness. He longed for Laurel's presence next to him, giving him strength and resolve to take the gift of his life into his hands and set out on the journey, whatever it was, wherever it led. "There are so many questions, yet all I can think about is what that monster is doing to Laurel!" he cried. "How can I possibly find this Adam when no one knows where he is?"

"Maybe your father is ready to be found," Coll offered, "now that you are claiming your heritage in the Sanctuary."

"Is that what I'm doing?" Gideon picked up an orange and began to peel it. "Laurel said she believed that when I fell on the mountain, I heard my mother's voice telling me the word of the story of the Sanctuary and that its power entered into me and gave me the bloodgift. Luther Quinn said that the bloodgift is a genetic mutation of the blood chemistry, a potentially valuable resource for the world if it could be replicated and harnessed."

Daniel spread his hands. "Again, you alone can choose. Science and story do not have to contend with each other. As a matter of fact, they can enrich each other when done honestly. But completely discounting the power of the word and the reality of the BloodFire seems the most dangerous of errors."

"Sift through the stories of your life, Gideon," Coll gently urged. "Not only the events since you fell on the mountain but the entirety of your life. Much wisdom is written there, much love given and received, a root of light that stretches back through your family, your ancestors, back to the womb of life itself."

"Like a taproot," Gideon said softly. "That's what this is about? Laurel and Jonathan tried to teach me about honoring the root, the journey, and the witnesses. I accused them of being from a crazy sect or a being some cult of religious fanatics. But it's simply about life the way it really is, a journey that fills me to overflowing when I am seeking the good of the community, not only for myself. And the witnesses are what? Visual aids maybe? At the simplest, a man and a woman joining in love and producing a child. And the root of it all?"

Daniel and Coll listened intently, encouraging him with their eyes as he sought to find his way. "The Sanctuary is our root," Daniel said. "It is not a hiding place, but rather it is protection from our misguided thoughts that we must be more than we are and settling instead for less. You're right; it is like a taproot, and life is the tree which it nourishes. Thinking that this world is ours to dominate and subdue threatens to cut us off from the nourishment of the Sanctuary and the light of the BloodFire and thus cut ourselves off from what makes us human."

"But there is a price, make no mistake," Coll mused. "It is signified by the Sacrament child being offered to the next waiting world, bringing the BloodFire to them. It is not ours to deny." She sighed.

"We sound like armchair philosophers, as JP would call it." Gideon laughed. "I will admit though that it only becomes a clearer as I go out there and try to honor the Sanctuary and all that it stands for. I guess there really is no choice."

"Do you think you're ready to find Adam now?" Coll asked him.

He smiled. "Is he ready for me to find him? It's going to be one hell of a reunion, I can tell you that much!"

They laughed with him, then left him alone to rest and gather his courage to face the morning's farewells. Gideon knew that sleep would still be elusive and quietly slipped out into the night. He noticed the head of a pathway leading into the wood and decided to follow it.

As he walked, he thought about JP. His grandfather had never pretended to have ready answers to all of life's mysteries, but that had not stopped him from accepting responsibility when the mystery of Aleudar landed in his lap. Gideon marveled at what it must have taken to know that his own fate and that of his family would be forever and irrevocably changed, as long as there were generations of Waters alive on the earth. The thought made him acutely aware of his own renewed desire to perpetuate that family history.

He wanted Laurel to be the one to accompany him on that journey. There had to be a way to gain her release. Unable to formulate any reasonable plan, Gideon wandered through the wood aimlessly until he stumbled into a small clearing atop a small hill overlooking the lake. A pile of rocks sat in the middle. Her back to him, the small figure of Serena stood perfectly still, arms outstretched, as though she were listening to the wind, whose fierce breath sent her hair streaming behind her like a bride's veil.

Gideon stayed where he was, poised to withdraw yet enticed into the clearing by the sheer dynamism of the small Dancer who in the stillness focused the yearnings of fire, water, and blood into kinetic power barely held in check by her lithe form.

Gideon knew that he'd stumbled onto sacred ground and lowered himself to the earth, kneeling, tears coursing through the stubble of several days. His hollow eyes watched in wonder as finally Serena slowly lowered her arms and removed the bracelets she'd fashioned from the broken heart charms. Her nimble fingers braided the two strands into one strong chain.

Suddenly an intense, searing pain started in his belly and shot to the base of his throat, threatening to tear him in two. Gideon cried out as every fiber of his being burned with the fire of all the hopes and fears, frustrations and dreams he'd kept entombed inside. When he felt he could bear it no longer, a sensation like that of a mighty wave broke over him, washing through, suffusing him with an icy stream of purity he'd never imagined.

From his knees, he watched helplessly as the Dancer began to sway to and fro, gently at first, then faster and faster until she bent nearly double, her hair sweeping the ground around her. Gideon thought he heard distant music. He strained to hear it, astonished when he recognized the sweetness of "Dance in a High Meadow," his own composition, which Christine had loved so. The music dissolved into the sound of drums, pounding a steady beat of the rhythm of her dance. Slowly, he realized it was the sound of his own heart, pulsing to the staccato syncopation of the dance of life.

Serena swung the braided charm necklace over her head, then around the pile of stones, the Altar of the Wind. Faster and faster it whirled, catching the light of the stars and sending it back toward the heavens. The wind blew harder until it howled in his ears with the throats of a thousand wolves.

A faint cry sounded in the distance, carried away on the wind. It went on and on until, in a heartbeat, it was replaced by a sound like that of delicate crystal wind chimes, tinkling in a playful breeze. The sound coalesced into a song, never losing its fragility though, until it filled Gideon's brain. He closed his eyes, lost in the delight of the melody now storming his soul.

When he opened his eyes, Serena stood directly before him, smiling shyly, her hands clasped at her breast. Gideon reached out and touched her cheek as a sign of his gratitude. Serena opened her hands and extended them to him.

Gideon stared, overcome by amazement and awe. It was the most beautiful thing he'd ever seen. The yarn and small link chain were still entwined. But dangling from their circle combined was a new creation.

It was a magnificent diamond, spherical, wondrously fashioned by a thousand facets radiating the fiercely joyful light of its fire. Encased within the diamond were the two halves of the broken heart, now refused into one whole.

Gideon accepted the gift, hanging it around his neck and tucking it carefully inside of his shirt. He swept the young girl into his arms and twirled her about the clearing until, exhausted, they collapsed to the ground. Gideon pressed his hand to his heart, feeling the new gem next to his skin.

"It is enough," he said as he faced the east and the coming dawn. "It is enough."

Chapter 34

Eli ran down the hospital stairs, ignoring the pain knifing through his back, terrified of what might be happening and not wanting to wait for the elevator. He made it to the bottom, but before he could reach for the exit door, he doubled over in excruciating pain. Wave after wave of nausea swept through him until he felt too weak to lift his head.

The sounds of an argument filtered through the closed door. Cautiously, Eli crab-walked the remaining few steps and gingerly pushed on the panic bar. Dr. Tournier and a couple of nurses and administrative types rushed past, caught up in a heated argument.

"What do you mean she's gone? Has anyone seen her husband?" Dr. Tournier made no effort to disguise his feelings about the situation. In response to something said by one of the suits that Eli couldn't make out, he ranted, "Of course I should have taken the baby, but the woman was nearly brain-dead. The fetus would have died with her, you moron! It was only a couple of months along."

Eli's heart was in his throat. Was she already dead? Was all of the effort and spilled blood an exercise in futility? Should he have even bothered?

"Now I've got all of these spooks and government types putting on the pressure. Something about the blood chemistry of the baby. How the hell do I know the baby's blood chemistry? How do they know about it?" Tournier waved his arms, his lab coat flapping behind him as he swept past Eli's hiding place.

Eli slowly exhaled and counted to ten. Hearing no further noises, he opened the door and headed back outside. Etanleo and Terralessa stepped from behind one of the ornate columns of the hospital's entrance portico. Their faces appeared pale, and they stared straight through Eli, ignoring his greeting.

"What's the matter? You two look like you've seen a ghost," he said, bewildered.

At that moment, a shadowy figure materialized a pace behind the father and daughter, clothed in an ankle-length black leather coat and matching hat. "Where's the blood?"

Eli froze. He knew that voice. Grutt rammed the barrel of a pistol into Terralessa's back and shoved her hard. "You heard me. Where's the blood?"

"I—I don't know—"

"Don't try to deceive me, Mr. Marks. I came to your wife's room to wait for you. I know where you went and why. The Healer's blood will bring great power to those waging the revolution back in my homeland."

"Ha!" Etanleo turned, ignoring his own safety. "Revolution? You want to exploit what the Sanctuary has given to us and use it to dominate and destroy. That is not a revolution; it is suicide!"

Grutt swung the gun, striking a savage blow to Etanleo's cheek, sending him to the ground in a limp heap. Terralessa screamed and lunged at the nightcrosser. He easily caught her and spun her around into the crook of his elbow, the revolver pressed into her temple.

"We bleed and die like anyone in this world, Marks, so don't be a hero. Hand over the blood or your new friends will die right here."

Eli searched the surroundings with his eyes, but the landscape shrubbery shielded the portico from the street, and the nurses and staff coming on duty used a different entrance. "I can't," he managed to choke out.

The nightcrosser became more enraged. "You can and you will!" he shouted, pushing the gun with such force into Terralessa's head that she gasped. Grutt took a step toward Eli, dragging her with him. With one hand, he frisked Eli's body, thoroughly investigating every pocket and crevice. The longer he searched, the more agitated he became. "The blood! Where is it, Marks?"

In Grutt's single-minded focus on Eli, or out of brazen arrogance, he ignored Etanleo, who carefully and surreptitiously began to uncurl his body and renew his grip on the staff. In one motion, he rolled to his knees, swinging the staff upward with all his might, directly between Grutt's legs. The rock-hard staff connected, and the nightcrosser screamed in agony. He let go of Terralessa and, too late, tried to protect his vulnerability.

"Run!" commanded Etanleo. "Run now!"

"No," cried Terralessa, stopping to grab his hand and pull him to his feet. Eli grabbed his other hand and tried to persuade his own pain-sick legs to move faster. Etanleo quickly regained his mobility and noticed Eli's struggles.

"Go on," he yelled to the two of them. "I'll watch your backs. Get back to the car."

Eli started to protest, but Etanleo cut him off with a shove. As he started down the steps, Eli saw a bus roaring down the avenue, belching great clouds of black diesel smoke behind it. It sped through a red light and nearly collided with a car, heading in a straight line to the fleeing figures. It screeched to a stop, and the doors swung open.

"Get in, Godman!" roared the smiling Paraclete. "I got me a bus! They rigged your car. Get that girl in here and let's step on it!"

"Wait!" Terralessa cried. "My father!"

Paraclete looked at Eli, the question in his eyes.

"It's a long story," Eli cried over the noise of the engine. "He should be right behind us."

They all looked at the same moment. Etanleo cleared the shrubbery and started down the steps. He saw them and waved his arms, motioning to them to board the bus. "Go!" he yelled "He's coming!"

Eli pushed Terralessa up the stairs and scrambled up right behind her. Paraclete gunned the engine until it screamed for mercy. "Let's go, man!" he called.

Etanleo put his foot on the sidewalk when the shot rang out, a sharp crack. His eyes widened in surprise. His knees buckled. Eli heard Terralessa scream, and he turned back to the door. Etanleo was on his knees, his chest an explosion of red. With one motion, he put his arm back and flung the staff, straight and true, to Eli in the doorway of the bus.

Grutt appeared at the top of the stairs and took careful aim at the bus. "Go!" Etanleo screamed. "Get out of here!"

Eli looked at the staff in his trembling hand, losing his balance as Paraclete stomped on the gas. The bus lumbered away from the scene as the nightcrosser ran into the middle of the street firing wildly.

"Daddy! Go back!" Terralessa screamed, struggling to get past Eli, who had landed on the top step.

"Get down, girl!" Paraclete ordered and pushed her roughly into the first seat.

Eli managed to pull himself up beside her and pulled her close, looking over his shoulder in disbelief. Paraclete took a series of sharp turns as the suspension groaned and protested with hysterical shrieks. The last he saw of the evil Grutt was him climbing into Daniel's car. In another second, the sturdy tracker exploded in a ball of flame.

Terralessa stared helplessly at the scene of carnage.

"Where's Jenn?" Eli beseeched Paraclete as the bus stormed up the boulevard.

"We got her out last night. We figured something was up. She's in bad shape, though, Godman. I hope we're in time!" He put a beefy hand out, first patting Terralessa on the knee and then grasping Eli's hand for a quick squeeze.

In Bridetown, Paraclete passed startled commuters with a cheery wave. He passed the library and slowed down to make the turn down Church Street. The grinding of the gears reminded Eli in a quick flash of the old mill a few long, difficult days ago. "Hang on, Jenn," he whispered. "Hang on."

Paraclete slammed to a stop at the head of Fourteenth. "She's up there, Eli. Godspeed. I've got to dump the bus after I get it as far away as possible."

The pair climbed down and dumbly headed for Susan's apartment. Terralessa had not said a word since her father's murder. The door flew open, and there stood Susan. She stepped close and gave Eli a huge hug. Then she looked into Terralessa's eyes and wordlessly embraced her, holding her close while the girl broke down and sobbed.

Gundy appeared in the living room and motioned to Eli. Eli followed him down the small hallway and into the bedroom. Jenn lay there, her chest rising sharply as she labored to breathe. Her skin was starkly white, and her mouth gaped with the gray cast of death.

"My God," Eli murmured involuntarily. "Jenn, I'm here."

"Do you have it?" Gundy asked. "Daniel got in touch with us so we'd be ready."

Eli tugged at his shirt, exposing the angry bruises. "C'mon. There's not much time."

Gundy went to the bureau and returned with a sterile wrap syringe. "Will this do it?"

Eli took it from him. "It's too short!" he yelled. "This needle is too short to get through my skin and into the port. There's only a little serum in there." He balled his fists and hit his thighs. "No, no, this can't be! The damn needle is too short."

Susan came to the doorway. "What's the matter?"

Eli wordlessly held up the needle and pointed to his abdomen.

"Isn't there another way?" she asked.

"We need to find the port right away and get this stuff transferred," Eli cried, frantic with his frustration.

"Okay, okay," Susan counseled. "Be calm. There has to be a way."

Terralessa stepped into the room, her eyes red. "Can we take it out?" she asked, sniffling. "My father taught me some techniques in case either of us was injured in the crossing."

Gundy and Susan looked at her with open curiosity but not hostility.

Eli took a deep breath. "There is a way. Susan, get me something sharp. Gundy, get me something to bite on. No wait, I have these pills." He dug the bottle of painkillers out. "I'll take a few of these, but don't wait."

Susan returned with a scalpel and a bottle of alcohol. "I use this on my bunions, and Jeremiah used it on the callouses on his hands. Are you sure, Eli?"

Eli nodded. Gundy said, "Well, I saw worse in Korea. I reckon this little girl and me can get you through this."

Eli lay down on the floor. In seconds, he could feel Terralessa washing his belly with the cool alcohol. She cleansed the blade and paused. "Ready?"

Eli shut his eyes and nodded. Gundy held his legs, while Susan held his arms so he wouldn't bump Terralessa in a spasm of pain. He felt the blade bite into his skin.

"Not much bleeding," Terralessa calmly reported. "Another cut," she warned.

This one was deeper, and the pain made his back arch. The two holding him struggled to keep him still. Eli felt a tugging in the area of the pump. "It's stuck!" Gundy cried.

"It just sits in a little pocket of fat, but it's in a little mesh sack," Terralessa said. "Must be so the adhesions will hold it in place."

She tugged again, and Eli screamed. "I think I can get to it," the young nightcrosser mercifully reported.

The adults relaxed their grip, and Eli opened his eyes. Terralessa opened the packaging of the syringe and inserted the needle into the port. "Not much is coming out," she said, worried.

"Get all you can," Eli gasped.

After several attempts, they reached a quick consensus, and Terralessa went to the bed. "In the neck," Eli managed between gritted teeth. "The Healer said to put it into her neck."

Terralessa gently probed Jenn's neck with her fingers. She isolated the carotid artery, expertly inserted the needle, and sent the pitifully tiny volume of viscous serum into Jenn's bloodstream.

Chapter 35

Daniel and Coll accompanied Gideon to the top of the path that led to the beach. The first rays of dawn's light stabbed at a cloud bank gathering to the northwest over the water.

"It'll be too cold here soon, and the children need to go back to their homes and schools," Daniel fretted.

"Why are there no prophets anymore?" Coll asked. "Do they no longer exist or do they lack the requisite courage?"

Gideon was brought up short by her questions. "I'm a little short on answers at the moment. I was thinking about JP. He went into the nursing home to throw the bloodtrackers off. I wonder if he believed in me, that I would come back and take up the cause one day. He just kept doing what he had to do, and now it's my turn." He gave them each a quick hug and started down the path.

Halfway down, he paused, standing on a curve in the path. Looking to the top, he could just see the upraised hands of Daniel and Coll. Below and in front lay the rocky beach and the calm sea. He studied the horizon a moment, watching the clouds lying close in. A tiny black dot appeared in the distance.

"Must be a gull. Hurry, friend. Fly before the storm!" he called to it.

At the bottom, the beach was deserted. To either side of him, as far as the eye could see, every hundred yards or so, bulky concrete breaker jetties stretched into the water, the remnants of long-abandoned attempts to thwart the storms of winter in their yearly calls to collect a ransom by erasing the sand from the beaches. The rocks were flat and worn smooth.

A sound behind him made him spin around. Luther Quinn approached, pulling Laurel by the arm. Her Steelers cap was gone, her clothes and hair disheveled, and dark circles ringed her eyes. She never looked better in Gideon's eyes.

He told himself to remain calm, to resist the temptation to rip this bloodsucking monster's heart out and feed it to him. "Are you all right?" he asked Laurel.

She nodded as she attempted to stand straight and tall. But the effort pained her, and she grimaced as she slumped again.

"You animal! What have you done to her?" Gideon shouted, white-hot anger igniting in his belly.

"Relax, you cretin. She slept on damp concrete last night." The BloodMaster smiled and brushed some stray sand from his pants. "So, what do you say, Giddy? Did you have a good night?"

"I want to talk to her."

"Hold on, Healer man. We talk, then you can say your sweet goodbyes."

Gideon glared, desperate to find a weakness, an opening. The last thing he wanted to do was make a mistake and bring harm to Laurel.

"I've been waiting for this, Gideon." Luther spoke in low tones, silvery smooth, hypnotic. "I've been biding my time, watching and planning, figuring all the angles, all the odds. And it's every bit as sweet as I imagined it would be." He laughed till tears ran. "What's the matter, Giddy? Aren't you having any fun here? Feeling like maybe you're in over your head?" He laughed again.

"Yes, I do," Gideon said, breaking his silence. "In the past three days, I've seen more pure evil than I ever dreamed could exist. Yet I've seen more commitment and trust in goodness as well."

The BloodMaster dismissed the sentiments with a wave of his hand. "Don't start preaching to me, Giddy. Next you'll be saying those Guardians are filled with faith. Am I right? But you probably couldn't tell me what they placed that faith in, could you?"

Gideon shrugged. "If you say so."

"What happens," Luther said, taking out a cigar and lighting it up, "if we lose control? Did you ever think of that? What happens if people all around the world, the only world we humans have, mind you, decided that there was one uniting factor of faith, not in their gods but in your Sanctuary? What if they all decided that the guiding force in life was to be honoring this root and believed that we all came from the same place? And what if they made a big deal about honoring this journey we all share for the time of our lives and pass along to others when we die just like the BloodFire leaves its mark and journeys on? And what if they honor the witnesses—meaning they see some spiritual sensibility in the natural course of life, men and women getting together to create love and more little humans, families—families that come in all shapes and sizes?"

"I say you're making my case for me," Gideon replied warily. "Why don't you tell me something, Luther? Why should we be punished or rewarded for being alive? None of us asked to be here, and none of us has a say in what lies beyond death. There is only freedom. That's what the Sanctuary is about. That is the power of the story. It reminds us that we are free!"

Laurel smiled at him through the weariness of her heart.

"It's a fool's story!" yelled the BloodMaster, triumphant in his self-assurance. "Don't forget, I know it well." He adopted a mocking tone. "Did you know, Gideon—or make that Healer—that giving away your blood diminishes you? You haven't really solved anything with your precious blood tricks. It keeps all the pain alive, all the disease, all the hurt, it's all still alive. You didn't conquer it, you fool. You only chased it into yourself. One hell of a side effect, wouldn't you agree?"

He sounded a conciliatory note. "Let me help you, Gideon. Why, I'll even throw in the lovely Miss Laurel. Come with me and let us play around with your gift. We can master it, splice it into genetic codes, heal millions upon millions around the world. You'll be the biggest hero the world's ever known, Gideon! We might even stop hunting down your daddy."

"Well, now, you see, there's the rub," Gideon stated, resting his chin on one hand. "You are so consumed with finding my father. I've got to ask myself, why is that? What does he have that you want so badly? Does he have some masterful world-class organization? You've seen the Guardians, so we know that's not it. Does he know something about you that would embarrass you, some indiscretion perhaps? Somehow you don't strike me as a man who frets over indiscretions. Do you straight-out hate him? Of course you do. But not enough to jeopardize your position as the BloodMaster by pulling this little stunt." Gideon nodded toward Laurel, who watched impassively, her eyes dull. Gideon became alarmed at how she was deteriorating before his eyes and stopped talking.

Laurel doubled over, retching.

"What have you done to her?" Gideon cried, grabbing Luther by the lapels of his jacket.

"Just a little reminder that I hold the power of life and death over her," Luther replied smugly, prying Gideon's fingers away from his clothing. "I cover all the angles."

"Except one," a deep voice said from behind one of the concrete jetties.

They all turned to look at the intruder. He stood on the stone breaker, framed by the storm clouds, his hair and clothes whipped by the rising wind. He was tall, firm as a rock, his face browned by constant exposure to the elements. The creases around his eyes bore witness to many a tale of danger, danger faced and attacked head-on. His eyes were the slate gray of the clouds. Behind him, a small craft bobbed on the waves.

"Well, well, as I live and breathe!" Luther bowed low.

The man stepped down and splashed through the surf to the beach. He stopped momentarily in front of Luther, smiled slyly, then stepped to Laurel and Gideon. "It's been a long time," he began, but his voice broke. "It's—I've missed you! Believe me how I've missed you."

Gideon stared, not comprehending. Laurel reached up and laid a hand on the stranger's cheek. He took it in his own and kissed it. "It's enough," he whispered, looking her in the eye, then turning to Gideon. "It is enough."

The words echoed in Gideon's mind, the very words he'd spoken last night with the Dancer. "Dad? Is it you?"

The man enfolded Gideon in his arms and drew him close. They hugged and cried and hugged some more.

"You've got your mother's eyes!" Adam exclaimed.

"You've got JP's sense of timing!" an overwhelmed Healer cried.

"Knock it off!" Luther's shrill, hatred-filled voice cut in. "What are you doing here, Waters?"

The sound of his own surname being used to address his father struck pride into Gideon's heart. And a sense of recognition. Justin Waters was here. The man who'd left when he was three was no monster, uncaring and untouched by the consequences of his decision.

"Or should I call you Adam?" Luther smirked. "Must be my lucky day. Looks like I've hit the trifecta!"

Adam reluctantly released Gideon and turned to Luther. Without a word, he took the BloodMaster by the arm and walked him down the beach. Gideon gingerly placed an arm around Laurel, and she rested her head on his shoulder. The two men talked with intensity, their heads close together, their faces animated. After a lengthy debate, they returned.

"This is how it is," announced Luther. "He goes with me, and she stays."

"What?" Gideon cried. "My father—Dad, you're going? You just came. This is insane!"

"I'm not afraid … son," Adam said calmly.

"His life for hers," Luther announced again, with what seemed to be a touch of admiration, if not respect. "After some long and fruitful conversations, of course. Now, get out of here before I change my mind."

"But you can't," Gideon pleaded, feeling his heart being torn in half as he regained one love only to watch another leave.

"I can, and I am." Adam put a hand on each of Gideon's shoulders. "It's my choice. It is my gift—to the two of you."

He embraced them both in one hug, pressing the diamond sphere into Gideon's chest with his own. "There are those who need you," he said, looking first at Laurel, then at Gideon. In a quiet breath, he added, "For the BloodFire."

"What should I do?" Gideon begged him for an answer with his eyes.

"Tell the truth, honor the Sanctuary, live free." There was a glint in his eye as he added, "Follow the root, son. I'll be there." With that, he turned and began walking down the rock-strewn beach, head held high, not waiting for the BloodMaster and not looking back.

As quickly as he'd come, he was gone.

Chapter 36

Eli took a moment to study the small group gathered at the graveside. Standing to his left, Gundy was decked out in his best flannel shirt, a bright red and black checkered pattern. On the right, Paraclete towered over Pearl and the heartbroken Susan. Directly across from him, completing the circle, Terralessa was adorned in a simple tunic of white cloth. Around her neck hung a beautiful necklace with a turquoise pendant, and on both wrists were bracelets of every kind. Each finger bore a beautiful ring, and elegant anklets completed the curious accessorizing.

When the others saw her before the long walk up the hill to the potter's field, she explained that in her culture, mourners wore their finest adornments to demonstrate how their own lives had been enriched by having known the deceased. That announcement had sent Gundy scurrying for his finest shirt, and Pearl her loudest outfit. Susan smiled and assured them all that Jeremiah would be pleased to have the first mixed-worlds funeral.

The newspapers and television news were full of the case of the disappearing patient. Some postulated that it was evidence of how burdensome the lack of a coherent national health plan was for those of little means. Others guessed someone in the hospital screwed up and simply lost a patient, or gave her the wrong identity bracelet, and that eventually the red-faced hospital would declare she'd been found in another of their excellent units.

There were those who accused the hospital of dumping her on another hospital, a practice not openly discussed but widely practiced. And still others swore that they had seen a large unidentified flying medical ship from another world and that Mrs. Marks was at this moment being miraculously healed by extraterrestrials of superior intelligence and that she would probably rather not return to earth. No mention was made of a murder in front of the hospital early in the morning of the disappearance, nor the car bomb. The far reach of the bloodtrackers, Paraclete assured them. That fact struck fear into the minds of the small group but not into their hearts.

Eli himself was stumped. Gideon and Laurel told him that the blood worked almost immediately. Twelve hours had passed with no sign of change in Jenn's condition. Except one. Her heart was racing. None of them knew what that might mean for her or the baby.

Eli was scared. Deathly afraid. So afraid that the awful pain in his back and legs was almost a comfort. At least it remained, never failing, never disappointing. Susan had tried to convince him to put off Jeremiah's burial, but Eli insisted. He'd promised. It was the very least that he could do, although he had no words to say. Only the willingness to honor a courageous man.

Eli gingerly held his abdomen where the pump used to be. There was no sense putting it back in. It was empty, and he didn't know how he could get it filled again. It wasn't like he could walk into a hospital and explain what had happened. Terralessa's expert stitching sealed him up again, but the angry fire in every nerve fiber from the waist down scared him badly.

He hadn't asked the others yet how they had managed to get Jenn out of the hospital. The story could wait. Maybe after they saw what was going to happen with Jenn. Maybe.

He took a deep breath, more like a sigh, and leaned heavily on Etanleo's Telling Staff. The beautifully intricate carvings were alive with the promise of many stories to be told. Etanleo should have been there, telling them. The others were watching him, waiting, gathered around a half-sized grave for a larger-than-life man, Jeremiah. They were honoring Etanleo as well, wherever his body lay at the moment. And Whitty, along with those who'd sacrificed their lives as the Healer began his mission in the last four days.

It was time to begin. "Every religion says they have a story. It is a story about how the world began, how life began, how humans received that life, and how we've corrupted that life. The stories sound remarkably similar, as though we were all trying to answer the same questions. And we say that our stories are the truth, the absolute truth. We say our stories are the truth, and yours are not, and we keep on saying it so often and so loudly that soon the stories are nothing but breaths of air, their meaning long forgotten, empty of power.

"But what if there is a story, a story so full of meaning that a single word of it has enough power to give each living heart the courage to be free. And that word makes us sing and dance and laugh and love and worship … and tell stories. Suppose it teaches us to be still. To welcome the silence of the womb where that story began. The Sanctuary.

"The only way we can truly honor that story is to free it, to let it continue its journey so that all life in all worlds can join in enjoying that freedom. I do not know how that will come about ultimately. All I know is that the BloodFire lives. It lives within each one of us. And I do know that I will dedicate the rest of my life to living that story as my way of saying it must be so. The BloodFire must be awakened in all of us and released, for only then will our world be redeemed.

"Jeremiah walked in the way of the BloodFire. And yes I do mean to say *walk*. He was free, and he wanted all of us to be free.

He lost his life defending that freedom. Now his life is part of the Sanctuary, and we are its Guardians. Farewell, Jeremiah. Your journey has ended."

One by one, the group stepped to the edge of the grave and dropped a token of their love onto the casket, signifying that Jeremiah's, and Etanleo's, and the others' lives meant more to them than their possessions. It was done without show, and no one knew what anyone else placed into the grave. After Gundy's turn, he stepped close to Eli.

"I found this." He held out a framed diploma, granted by the Pittsburgh School of Theology. Tucked into one corner, behind the glass, was a scrap of paper.

Eli cradled it gingerly. "Where?"

Gundy smiled sheepishly. "I went back to where your house blew up. I snuck under that yellow police tape and rummaged around. You never know what useful stuff you might find. No harm meant."

"None taken," Eli replied. "I wonder how this survived the explosion."

Gundy shrugged and walked off. Eli worked at the cardboard backing, finally managing to slide it back. He discarded the frame and diploma and carefully studied the small piece of paper.

It was a signature, an autograph. The letters slanted, some indecipherable. But he knew. Roberto Clemente. Right fielder for the Pittsburgh Pirates. One of the best at throwing out runners. He also became deeply involved in the community, helping poor children have a place to play baseball back in his native Puerto Rico. A hero who died flying relief supplies to Nicaragua after a devastating earthquake. As a boy, Eli had cried all day after hearing the news, vowing he would never have a hero again.

Now he lightly ran his fingers over the yellowing, fading signature. On a sunny summer afternoon, his father had patiently waited to get the superstar's autograph. His mother found it in the old, rotting trunk with a note explaining how his father wanted to give it to his son after his tour of duty. It was Eli's pride and joy, next to the diamond ring for Jenn.

Eli stepped forward and let it slip from his fingers. It fluttered on a tiny breeze before settling into the earth on the grave of a new hero.

Susan and Paraclete walked on either side of Eli, lending moral support as he struggled back down the long slope. "We have something to show you, Eli," Susan said, her hand resting lightly on his arm for guidance. "The others and I all agree."

"Agree about what?"

"You're the man," Paraclete remarked, repeating for emphasis in a booming voice, "you are the man, Godman!"

Eli frowned in bewilderment. "What on earth are you talking about?"

"Terralessa agrees too." Susan confirmed the mysterious ballot was unanimous.

"Please, somebody, tell me!"

Everyone stopped. "There is much to be done," Gundy said, struggling to contain his enthusiasm.

"Father would have agreed," Terralessa added.

"I spoke with Gideon and Daniel late this morning, and they agreed," Paraclete said. "Those digital cell phones are a marvel—and secure too."

Susan looked into Eli's eyes. "We want you to be the next StoryKeeper, Eli. You will be the keeper of the Sanctuary Chronicles, the one who collects and tells the tales. The time is ripe with possibilities. A Sacrament child is appearing in the near future. Someone must care for the story, keep it fresh on our minds. Please, will you?"

Eli looked at each of them in turn. When he reached Terralessa, she smiled and said, "The staff is yours now. Lean on it, for it is strong. Father gave it to you back at the hospital for good reason."

Eli slowly nodded his acceptance of the honor.

At the gate of the run-down cemetery, Eli started to turn right, back toward Susan's apartment, his temporary home. But she tugged him left, refusing to answer his questions. They proceeded to Eighth Street, stopping before a neat cottage with a fenced garden in the rear. Across the arbor gate hung a hand-lettered sign, The Bride's Gate.

"This was Gideon's home. When I spoke to him, he said that he wished to make a present of it to you and Jenn. He is moving on to 'another life,' as he called it." Paraclete handed Eli the keys with a solemn handshake.

"Come," said Susan. "Someone is waiting." She led him to the front door and opened it for him.

Eli stepped through. He admired the mantel with its statues of Isis and other artifacts that instantly excited his curiosity. Someone stirred in the kitchen. Abraham stepped into the room and silently motioned him up the stairs.

Eli used the staff to make the climb. *Terralessa's right*, he mused. *It is easier with this.* At the top, he saw soft lights flickering in the master bedroom. He limped to the doorway and stopped.

The room was filled with candles. They sat on the dresser, the vanity, the windowsills, bathing the bed with a golden glow. Eli's breath caught in his throat. Jenn lay in the bed, deathly still, her hair fanned out on the pillow. On either side of her sat the twins, too shy to look up as they kept faithful watch.

When Eli stepped into the room, they silently left, leaving him alone with his wife. He carefully knelt beside the bed where he could watch Jenn breathe. He reached out and stroked her hair, whispering her name. After a long while, he stood and began removing his clothing. Something fell out of the pocket of his jacket. He bent over to retrieve it, wondering how he could have forgotten it.

He smiled. He had been a little preoccupied these past couple of days. Eli gently eased into bed beside Jenn, hardly daring to breathe. He began to run his hands over her body. His fingers traced tiny swirls along her arms, across her neck, her cheeks. Her breasts and belly were warm, her hips cool.

He rolled onto his back and captured her left hand in his. Bit by bit, he slid the diamond ring over her finger, finishing it off with a kiss. Music filled the room. He didn't know if it came from a player somewhere in the house or if it came from his own heart. While he listened, his mind drifted.

Then he felt it. At first he thought he must be imagining things, that his own fatigue and weary muscles were playing a trick on him. It happened again. He felt it for sure.

Bit by bit, Jenn's fingers closed around his own until she could gently squeeze his hand. Tears stung the corners of Eli's eyes. He turned back on his side and watched her peaceful face. Ever so slowly, she opened her eyes. Eli reached up, cradling her cheek in his hand.

She smiled …

Chapter 37

Gideon stood in the middle of the dancing ground, alone. Laurel slept in Daniel and Coll's living room on the couch, too exhausted from the night to make it as far as the bed. The warm sun of Indian summer beat down on his head as he watched the buses loaded with the children heading back to the Pittsburgh and Cleveland areas. He wondered if JP had known about this place, even sent his son here, away from his family, his roots, off on a journey that had no end, a journey to find Guardians for the witnesses.

Gideon took off his jacket as the heat became uncomfortable. After a while, he removed his shirt, then his shoes and socks. He lay down on the grass, wondering what it was he was trying to strip away. Closing his eyes, he listened to the silence, immersing himself in it as a bath, a cleansing unction.

What had brought his father back and from where? Had the dance he'd witnessed at the Wind Altar been a summons? Where was his father now? The questions rose to consciousness, then faded away without answer, till he simply accepted the silence once again without expectation or agenda.

Enrobed in the blanket of light, he slept without dreaming.

Something tickled his nose. He lazily brushed at it and went back to sleep. The tickling continued, and he erupted in a ferocious sneeze.

"Bless you." Laurel giggled.

Gideon's eyes popped open. She was propped on one elbow, using a long blade of grass to torture him. He reached for her and began tickling her in the ribs. She shrieked, and for a few minutes, they tumbled and rolled in the field, two children of the Sanctuary enjoying the true purpose of life. Soon they fell back exhausted, panting, watching the sky together.

"I didn't know that clothing was optional," Laurel teased.

"Sure. Don't you feel overdressed now?"

She reached over and examined the diamond sphere dangling around his neck. "Where did you get this? It's beautiful."

Gideon told her about the mysteries of the night before, ending with "I knew then that I could bear anything as long as I could tell you this morning that I love you."

"Do you believe that our thoughts have power of any kind?" Laurel asked, seemingly reluctant to acknowledge his confession.

Gideon felt a blast of cold air sweep through his heart. He'd overstepped and decided to follow her lead, partly to cover his own embarrassment. "I don't know, maybe. Why do you ask?"

"Well, I was thinking about how you were sure that you saw your father back at the farm and how finding the truck seemed to confirm it."

"Yeah, but it turns out that the BloodMaster trained with my father but for some reason decided to oppose the Sanctuary. So he must have been close at one time to Justin and learned all about the farm and the truck, about me and the Aleudar gift."

"Right, but do you think that maybe, just maybe, your being willing to believe that your father was still out there, doing good, trying to help you, made some sort of connection with his own—oh, I don't know, maybe his spirit—and brought him to you in our hour of need."

Gideon was silent for a moment. "I don't know, Laurel. He found me just in time to be taken away again."

Laurel took his cheeks into her palms. "Last night, all I could think about was how much I wanted to have one more opportunity to tell you how much I love you. And now here I am; I'm with you. Gideon, I will go anywhere, do anything for you to help you find happiness."

Gideon at first thought he'd not been paying attention. But her eyes confirmed his deepest desire. She loved him too. A smile slowly spread across both their faces. "You sure took a long way around to tell me that!"

She grew serious. "I want to go with you."

"Where?"

"Don't play dumb. After the BloodMaster and your father, of course."

"Of course. Silly me. Let's just dial 911."

"Gideon, I'm serious. Don't you at least want to try?"

"You are amazing. Yes, I want to give it a try. Where do we start?"

"I don't know. That's your part. I've done mine."

He grabbed her and resumed tickling her again, giddy with the prospect of enjoying her love, now and always.

The sun was setting as the group gathered at the Wind Altar. Daniel and Coll, Serena, Tanya, Gideon and Laurel. All that remained of the Witness Council. They did not know how many Guardians of the Sanctuary were out there yet, faithfully preparing for the Redemption.

"The Sanctuary is free to light the way," Daniel had proclaimed when news reached them about Jenn's healing.

They were gathered at the moment to perform the celebration dance of the Together circle. "You've got it all." Coll laughed. "Gideon Waters, the Healer, bearer of the bloodgift is taking as his wife the woman of fire, Laurel Rayn. Blood, fire, and water. The witnesses."

"What are your plans?" asked Tanya.

"We want to go after Gideon's father. We owe him everything."

Daniel sounded a solemn note. "Do you think that is wise?"

"I don't know, and I don't care," replied Gideon, jamming his hands into the pocket of his jeans. His fingers closed around a small piece of paper. He pulled it out and opened it. They watched his expression grow puzzled.

"What's that?" Coll wanted to know, speaking for the others.

"My father must have slipped this in when he hugged me on the beach."

"You really must learn to check your pockets more often," Laurel chided him. "Maybe I should do it for you at least once a day!"

Gideon made a face at her, and she mussed his hair. "It says, 'We have the same teachers: JP and your mother. The next one should be Melody. In Metamelonia.'"

Nobody said anything. Finally, Laurel broke the tension. "Sounds like a good place to honeymoon! How do we get there?"

"Remember what Paraclete said on the phone earlier? About the nightcrossers that helped Eli? You'll need to ask Etanleo's daughter how to make the crossing." Daniel sounded concerned.

"I wonder if we'll need passports." Gideon winked at Laurel. "Well, I never said it wouldn't be an adventure."

"Your father had to know what Luther wanted with him. Let's see where it leads, my love." Laurel winked back and grabbed his hand and Serena's. "For now, let's dance!"

Serena lead the happy couple around the altar, dipping and swaying, humming a melody softly, repeating it over and over until the others joined in. "After we dance, we feast!" cried Daniel. "Long live the BloodFire!"

"Love and courage to the Healer," Coll said, taking up the cry, "and the FireGuide, partners in the journey that is rooted in love."

She leaned over to Daniel and whispered, "I wonder if they know that Serena is leading them in the fertility dance."

Daniel shrugged. "They will soon enough!"

The setting sun became a fiery orange and red ball sinking slowly into the water, filling the sky with a riotous palette of colors and hope for the journey yet to come.

About the Book

GIDEON WATERS faces mortal danger when he discovers his blood can cure disease. A ragtag group of Guardians are trying to convince him he holds the key to the future of the human race ... and beyond, to other races in other worlds. But anyone who helps him is brutally murdered.

Gideon races to find the woman pregnant with the last hope of humanity, who lies dying in Pittsburgh. Pursued from the Shenandoah Valley to the shores of Lake Erie by those defending the centers of power and faith in this world, Gideon becomes a reluctant warrior in the bloody conflict, as well as the hesitant harbinger of the hopes of all peoples of this world and those beyond.

In a fast moving journey with unexpected twists and revelations, heartbreaking confrontations and losses, Gideon rediscovers love with one of those sworn to give up her life to protect him and confronts the man who caused his deepest pain.

Bertram deH. Atwood says, "John Thomas Tuft is a worthy successor to Frederick Buechner in his characters and style of storytelling."

Also by John Thomas Tuft

* * *

Even the Darkness

Milton Keynes UK
Ingram Content Group UK Ltd.
UKHW040709050124
435493UK00001B/349